CAPTIVATED

She watched the iron muscles ripple on his back when she tried to move her arms and he stayed her. Brenna admired strength and courage; she always had. But this man's strength was unbelievable. He held her with such ease when she tried her mightiest to move him. Though such a powerful body was magnificent to behold, that she lay at the mercy of its strength was unbearable.

CONSUMED

"Garrick—Garrick." He looked up at her, puzzlement in his eyes. " 'Tis the first time you have used my name. I like the sound of it on your lips."

CONQUERED

"Garrick, release me." Her tone of voice was the closest she could come to pleading. He smiled softly, his eyes afire with passion. "Nay, my beauty, 'tis too late for that."

Other Avon Books by
Johanna Lindsey

CAPTIVE BRIDE
A PIRATE'S LOVE

Fires of Winter

Johanna Lindsey

 AVON
PUBLISHERS OF BARD, CAMELOT AND DISCUS BOOKS

FIRES OF WINTER is an original publication of Avon Books. This work has never before appeared in book form.

AVON BOOKS
A division of
The Hearst Corporation
959 Eighth Avenue
New York, New York 10019

First Avon Printing, September, 1980

AVON TRADEMARK REG. U.S. PAT. OFF. AND IN
OTHER COUNTRIES, MARCA REGISTRADA,
HECHO EN U.S.A.

Printed in the U.S.A.

To my husband, Ralph,
and my sons, Alfred, Joseph and Garret.

Chapter 1

A FEW miles inland from the west coast of Wales, and to the left of Anglesey Island, a small village was nestled in a tiny clearing. On a steep hill overlooking the village stood an imposing manor. The gray stone building looked down on the village, almost like a mother guarding her children with a watchful eye.

The village basked in the luxurious warmth of the midsummer sun. Not so the manor on the hill, which remained cold and forbidding, even with the sun touching its harsh gray walls. Travelers passing through the countryside often had the same impression of coldness. Today was no different.

A stranger slowly found his way to the heart of the village, keeping a wary eye on the manor. But soon the activity around him took the tall newcomer's attention away from the protecting mother on the hill. His unease gradually left him, and was replaced by a feeling that he was about to have some long overdue good fortune. More than once he turned in a complete circle, his hard eyes feasting on the peaceful tranquility, the dozen or so closely-spaced cottages, the children dashing here and there, playing their innocent games, and the women—ah, the women!

1

He quickly spotted five or six who were to his liking. They didn't even notice him, as they went about their everyday chores.

The stranger, his trousers gartered but deplorably threadbare, with a filthy wolfskin serving as his mantle, could hardly believe his eyes. There was not a man in sight, not a single one. And the women, so many, and of all ages! Could he have stumbled on some ancient Amazon village? But no, there were children, boys and girls alike. The men must be working in the fields somewhere to the east, for he had seen none on his way.

"Can I be of help, good sir?"

Startled, the stranger jumped, then swung around quickly to face a girl with a bright, curious smile, whom he judged to have seen no less than sixteen winters. She suited his tastes perfectly, with her neatly braided flaxen hair and wide green eyes set in a cherubic, innocent face. His eyes traveled downward, but only for a second, so the girl would have no hint of his intentions, but in that instant her overripe breasts, pressed hard against her brown shift, and her wide, sturdy hips caused an ache in his groin.

When the stranger did not reply, the girl spoke again, cheerfully. "It has been many months since a traveler has come our way—not since the last of those from Anglesey Island passed through on their search for new homes. Do you come from Anglesey also?"

"Yea, 'tis not the same anymore," he finally answered. Oh, he could tell her of his woes if he was of a mind, but she would have her own soon enough, if he had his way, and it was not a sympathetic ear that he was in need of. "Where are the men of your village? I do not even spy an old man whittling away his time."

The girl smiled sadly for just a moment. "As it happens, the old ones took the fever two winters past, and are no more. Many young and old died that year." Then her smile brightened. "A wild boar was spotted this morn, and the men who remain have given chase. There will be a feast tonight, and you are welcome to join."

His curiosity prompted the man to ask, "But are there no fields to tend? Or is a wild boar more important?"

The girl giggled unabashed. "You must surely be a man from the sea, or you would know that the crops are planted

2

in the spring and harvested in the fall, with little to do 'atween."

A frown creased his haggard brow. "Then you expect the men to return shortly?"

"Oh, nay, not if they can help it," she laughed. "They will linger over the chase, to enjoy it more. 'Tis not often a boar comes this close."

The man's features relaxed somewhat, and his thin lips curled in a grin. "What is your name, girl?"

"Enid," she replied easily.

"And have you a husband, Enid?"

She blushed prettily, her eyes lowered. "Nay, sir, I live with my father still."

"And he is with the others?"

Her green eyes gleamed with laughter again. "He would not miss the chase!"

This is too good to be true, the man thought gleefully before he spoke again. "I have traveled far and the morning sun is so warming, Enid. Might I rest a while in your home?"

For the first time she looked nervous. "I—I don't—"

"Only for a few minutes, Enid," he added quickly.

She thought for a moment. "I am sure my father would not mind," she replied, and turned to lead the way.

The dwelling she entered was small indeed: only a single room, with a makeshift wall separating two sleeping mats placed in a corner of the dirt floor. A blackened stone hearth occupied one wall; two crude chairs and a table were placed before it. Two exquisitely crafted chalices inlaid with semiprecious stones were on the table. They caught and held the man's eye. They were easily worth a small fortune; he could not understand how they might have found their way into this humble cottage.

Enid watched the man curiously as he eyed the gifts she had received from the lord of the manor for her services gladly rendered. The tall stranger was not handsome, but neither was he repulsive. And although he obviously owned little of worth, he had a strong back and could provide well for her as a husband. She had little chance of finding a husband among her own people, for all those who were eligible had already tried her charms, and though they did

3

not find her lacking, neither would they take her to wife, knowing their friends had also tasted of her.

Enid smiled to herself as she developed the scheme. She would speak with her father on his return and lay her plan before him. He was sympathetic to her plight, and longed for a son-in-law to help him in the fields. Together they would coax the stranger to stay for a time. Then Enid would use her wiles to bring forth the man's proposal. This time, yea, this time she would have the marriage first and the play after. She would not add another mistake to her long list.

"Would you have some ale for your thirst, good sir?" she asked sweetly, drawing the man's attention to her once more.

"Yea, 'twould be most welcome," he replied, and waited patiently for her to set the cup in his hands.

The man eyed the open portal nervously, and seeing the thatched door beside it unhinged against the wall, he finished the ale quickly. Without a word, he moved to the door and set it in place, blocking out the morning sun. The door was not made for protection, he could tell, but merely to keep out the cold or the heat and, to suit his purpose, prying eyes.

"The morning grows hot," he offered in explanation, and the girl accepted this, not in the least frightened.

"Would you have food, sir? 'Twill not take long to prepare for you."

"Yea, you are kind," he answered, his thin lips turning up in a grateful smile. But to himself he admitted the food could wait; his loins could not.

The girl turned her back on him and went to the hearth. In that moment he pulled a knife from beneath his tunic and slipped stealthily up behind her. Enid's short frame stiffened when the knife touched her throat and the man's chest pressed into her back. She did not fear for her body, as most girls her age might, but for her life.

"Do not scream, Enid, or I will have to hurt you," the man said slowly, one hand cupping her rounded breast. "And anyone else who would come to your aid. 'Tis a tumble I want, no more."

Enid choked back a sob, seeing her newly formed plans

4

dissolve with his words. Such a short-lived dream—to have a husband at long last.

A little to the south of the village, a lone figure hobbled along through the trees, mumbling every step of the way. The horse that had long since thrown its rider was nowhere to be seen, but still the youth turned and, raising a small fist, cursed loudly.

" 'Twill be a cold day before I take you back, you pampered nag!"

Pride was more bruised than the rear end on which the rider had landed, and with a hand pressed firmly against the offended area, the youth continued on to the village. Anticipating a place to rest, the youth raised a proud head and endured the curious stares of the villagers.

One woman approached, and without voicing the obvious question—what had happened to the youth's horse—she said instead, "We have a visitor, Bren. Enid has given him welcome."

Cool gray eyes turned toward Enid's cottage and then back to the woman. "Why did they wish privacy?"

The woman smiled knowingly. "You know Enid."

"Yea, but she does not give her favors to strangers."

Without another word the youth, sword in hand, crossed the short distance to Enid's cottage and moved the closed door aside. It took a few moments for the silver-gray eyes to adjust to the darkened cottage, but then they lighted on the couple in the corner, unaware of the intrusion. The stranger was mounted atop Enid, thrusting his slim hips like a rutting boar.

At first the gray eyes were fascinated, watching the mating of the two creatures, the deep plunging of the male between the spread thighs of the female, listening to the grunts and groans that drifted from the corner. But then the flash of silver caught the gray eyes, and like clouds warning of an approaching storm, the youth's eyes darkened, drawn to the knife in the stranger's hand.

Without a second thought, the youth crossed the room with purposeful strides and raised sword, then skillfully cut into the stranger's behind. A shocked scream echoed through the cottage, and the man jumped up off the cowering Enid and scrambled away from his attacker.

5

Enid gasped when she saw the reason that the stranger had jumped up. "Bren, what are you doing here?"

The youth stood with legs astride and answered without emotion, " 'Tis fortunate, I suppose, that the nag I call Willow threw me, or I would not have come in time to see justice done. He forced you, did he not?"

"Yea," Enid answered and could not stop the sobs of relief that shook her body.

"The girl was not a virgin!" the stranger blurted out angrily, cupping both hands over his bleeding backside.

This was not the girl's father, the man easily surmised, but just a boy, and a very young boy by the sound of his high-pitched voice. The boy was clearly not of the village, for the youth's wealth was apparent from the richly embroidered mantle covering the silver cloth tunic which matched the angry eyes of the wearer. The sword that had so accosted the stranger was like none he had ever seen: a broadsword surely, but exceptionally thin and lightweight, with sparkling blue and red jewels encrusted on the hilt.

"That she was no virgin did not give you leave to take her. Yea, 'tis known that Enid is generous with her favors," the youth said, then added in a lower voice, "but only to those of her choosing. She bid you welcome, and you repaid her in this unspeakable manner. What shall be the punishment, Enid? Shall I sever his head and lay it at your feet, or perhaps that shriveled organ that stood so proud but a moment ago?"

The man sputtered with outrage. "I'll cut out your heart for that, boy!"

Giggles came from a bevy of females who had gathered in the doorway upon hearing the scream. The naked man's face turned livid with rage. To add further to his humiliation, the youth's own tinkling laughter joined the others.

Then, to everyone's surprise, Enid spoke indignantly. "Bren, you should not make fun of him."

The laughter stopped, and the youth shot her a contemptuous look. "Why, Enid? The stranger obviously thinks he is a match for me. I, who speared my first wild boar when I was but nine, and killed five worthless scavengers with my father when they would do harm to your village. I, who have held a sword in my hand since I could first walk, who have been trained diligently for the seriousness of warfare. This ravager of women thinks he can cut out my heart with that toy in his hand. Look at him! Tall though he may be, he is but a sniveling coward."

This last insult brought a roar of outrage from the man, and he jumped forward, knife in hand, arm raised, fully intending to carry out his earlier threat. But the youth had not boasted falsely and stepped aside with lithe grace. A slight twist of the arm drew a long streak of blood across the man's chest. This was followed by a booted foot to his already crimson behind.

"Mayhaps not a coward, but certainly a bungling oaf," the youth taunted as the man slammed into the opposite wall. "Have you had enough, rapist?"

The knife fell from the man's hand when he hit the wall, but he quickly grabbed it and charged again. This time the youth's long blade cut skillfully from the left, and the man looked angrily at the perfectly formed X on his upper chest. The wounds were not deep, but sufficed to cover his chest and lower torso in his own sticky blood.

"You inflict but scratches, boy," the man growled. "My blade, though 'tis small, will still find a deadly mark!"

Since the opponents were now only a foot apart, the man saw his chance, and swiftly went for the slim white throat of his antagonist. But the other stepped aside with the ease of a matador moving out of the path of a charging bull. The man's knife slashed through open space, and a second later it was struck from his hand with a vicious blow and clattered across the room, out of reach.

The stranger was left facing Enid, who glared at him without pity. "You fool! Bren was but toying with you."

He saw the truth of her words and paled visibly. And though it nettled him sorely to be bested by a mere boy, he now feared for his life. He faced the boy and prayed that the death blow would be swift.

There was no mercy in the cold gray eyes that regarded him, and the laugh that came from the soft, sensuous lips chilled his blood.

"By what name are you called?"

"Donald—Donald Gillie," he answered quickly.

"And from where have you traveled?"

"Anglesey."

At the mention of the name, the gray eyes narrowed.

"And were you there last year, when the cursed Vikings struck Holyhead Island?"

"Aye, 'twas a horror to see such slaughter and—"

"Cease! I did not ask for an account of what the bastards did. Know you this, Donald Gillie! Your life rests in the maid's hands." The youth turned to Enid. "What shall it be? Shall I end his ravishing days here and now?"

"Nay!" Enid gasped.

"Then shall I maim him for what he has done to you? Sever an arm? A leg?"

"Nay! Nay, Bren!"

"Justice shall be done here, Enid!" The youth snapped impatiently. "My justice is more lenient than my father's. Were it Lord Angus who had found him rutting 'atween your legs, he would have skewed him on a pole and left him for the wolves. I have toyed with him, yea, but his crime I have seen with my own eyes and he will pay for it."

Enid looked on with wide, fearful eyes. Donald Gillie stood with his shoulders slumped, awaiting his fate. The youth's smooth forehead creased in thought, then the gray eyes lit up with a solution.

"I have it, then. Would you take the man for a husband, Enid?"

The barely audible whisper was not long in coming. "Yea."

"Will you agree to this, Donald Gillie?" Gray eyes pierced him sharply.

The man's head snapped up. "Yea, I will!" the words gushed forth.

"So be it, then; you shall be wedded," the youth spoke with finality. " 'Tis a good bargain you've made, Donald Gillie. But know you this. You cannot say yea today, then nay on the morrow. Do not make me regret that I have let you off so easily. If the girl comes to harm, or if you have in mind to desert her, there will not be a hole deep enough for you to hide in, for I will find you and right the wrong with your life."

The man could not contain his joy at having such a light punishment. "I will not harm the girl."

"Good," the youth replied curtly, then turned toward the door and yelled, "You women, off with you now. You have had your entertainment for this day. Leave these two to get acquainted." He turned back and said, "Enid, wash him quickly before your father returns. You will have much to explain to that good man."

"Your own father has truly raised a merciful son, my lord," Donald Gillie replied.

The youth laughed heartily. "My father has no son."

Donald Gillie looked after the departing figure, then appealed to Enid for explanation. "What did he mean?"

" 'Twas no he." She laughed at his confusion. " 'Twas the Lady Brenna who spared your life."

Chapter 2

BRENNA swung open the heavy, solid-oak door, letting the midday sun spill into the darkened hall of the manor. The hallway was empty, but voices drifted out through the double doors of the large receiving chamber to the right. Brenna could hear her stepsister Cordella and the cook discussing the fare for the evening meal.

Cordella was the last person Brenna cared to see now—or at any time, for that matter. Especially not now, though, when she was so tender from her fall—damn Willow, anyway—and not at her best.

Accustomed to dashing through the hall on her merry way, Brenna was sorely put out to have to amble along at a snail's pace. She felt as if every muscle in her lower region ached, and the short bout with the stranger Donald Gillie had not helped any. She had been hard pressed to keep from flinching everytime she moved about in Enid's cottage, but a strong will had kept the pain from showing on her delicate features.

Ha! The stranger had thought she was a boy. This had done much for her ego. Wasn't it the impression she wanted to give? For those few minutes she was truly her father's son, not just the young-hearted boy in this cumbersome woman's body. Angus would have been as proud as she was herself.

She climbed the few steps at the bottom of the wide stairs, then turned abruptly to climb the remaining ones that led to the maze of halls on the second floor. A stranger to the manor would surely get lost in those halls, for it was as if two separate builders had begun the manor, each on the opposite side, and tried to meet in the middle, without success. Angus's father had built the house in this fashion because it suited him to confound his guests. Angus was already a young man when the manor was completed, for it had taken a score of years to build such a conglomeration of mazes.

The first floor of the manor was like that of any other such building, but the second floor had nine separate chambers, each one with its own private hallway. Brenna turned right at the first hall and passed the single door that led to her father's room. He would be there now, in bed, for he had become ill a week past, and had yet to improve. She considered going in to tell him of her sport with the stranger. But perhaps later; she needed a bath first.

Brenna turned at the end of her father's short hall and entered that of Cordella and her husband. To the left were her own chambers at the front of the house. Hers was a corner room, giving her ample light from two windows in the outer walls. Having seen only seventeen winters, she did not mind the long trek to her chamber except on a day like this one, when every step was an effort.

Brenna felt like screaming in relief when she finally opened her door, pausing only to call for Alane, her servant. She closed the door slowly and hobbled to the bed, taking off the mantle which hid her glorious long hair as she walked. Her long hair. It was the only thing that did not conform to the image she liked to affect. Her father forbade her to cut it, so she kept it hidden. She hated this very obvious symbol of her womanhood.

Before Brenna's head touched the pillow, Alane rushed into the room from her own chamber around the corner. Alane was past her prime, but it did not show overly much. Her red hair bespoke her Scots forebears. It had been carrot-colored at one time, but now was a dull yellow-orange. Still, her dark blue eyes twinkled youthfully. She was not as sprightly as she used to be, however, and was given to frequent, long illnesses during the winter months, when Brenna became the servant and waited on Alane.

"Oh, Brenna, my girl!" Alane said breathlessly, holding a slim hand to her chest. " 'Tis glad I am to see you back in time. You know your father would have his fits if you missed your lesson with Wyndham. So 'tis through dressing like the son for now; time to dress like the daughter you are. I did fear, when Boyd came with news of the boar, that you would not return in time."

"Curse Wyndham and his kinsmen!" Brenna snapped tiredly. "And curse that bloody boar too!"

"My, but we're in a fine mood this day," Alane clucked.

"We're not—I am!"

"What brought on this bit of temper?"

Brenna moved to sit up, winced, and lay down again. "Willow, that pregnant cow! As well as I've trained that nag, she had the effrontery to be spooked by a rabbit. A rabbit! I will never forgive her for that."

Alane chuckled. "I take it you lost your perch on that spirited filly, and your pride is a wee bit bruised."

"Oh, hush up, woman! I don't need your prattling. I need a bath—a hot one to soak these sore bones."

" 'Twill have to be a quick one, my dear," Alane replied, unoffended. She was quite used to her lady's blustering ways. "Wyndham is expecting you soon."

"Wyndham can wait!"

The large receiving chamber on the lower floor was where Brenna met Wyndham every afternoon. It had been thus for almost a year now, since the bloodthirsty heathens came from the north and raided Holyhead Island in A.D., 850. Brenna endured the hated lessons because she had no choice. She learned what she was taught, but for her own purpose, not because Angus ordered it.

Wyndham stood up when she entered the room, a dark scowl across his fair features. "You are late, Lady Brenna."

Gowned in sea-green silk, which went well with the raven black hair that flowed freely down her trim back, Brenna smiled sweetly. "You must forgive me, Wyndham. It grieves me that I have kept you waiting, when I am sure you have more important things to do."

The tall Norseman's features softened and his eyes darted about the room, looking everywhere except at Brenna. "Nonsense. There is naught more important than preparing you for your new life and home."

"Then we must begin immediately, to make up for the time we have lost."

To give credit where credit was due, Brenna could be a lady when the situation warranted it. Her Aunt Linnet had seen to that. She could be gracious, charming, and use her wiles to suit her purpose. It was not often that she called on these female ploys, but when she did, all men were lost to her.

The bath had helped, but not enough to allow her easy movement. Brenna crossed slowly to one of the four thronelike chairs that faced the huge fireplace and joined Wyndham. He started the lesson where they had left off the day before, with Norse mythology. He spoke in Norwegian now, which Brenna clearly understood, for that language was the first thing Wyndham had taught her.

Was it really less than a year since they received the news of Holyhead Island? It seemed like so much longer. The story had been a shock and put the fear of death into them all. It was two days later that Augus sent for Brenna and told her of the solution to their predicament. Brenna had not even been aware that they were in one.

She saw the meeting clearly in her mind. It was a scene that haunted many of her dreams. Her father, sitting across from her in this very room, was appropriately wearing black. Black, the color of doom. A black tunic as dark as his shoulder-length hair and as somber as his blue eyes. Angus Carmarham's eyes were generally sparkling and clear, unusually bright for a man of two score and ten. That day the blue eyes were clouded with the eyes of an old man.

Brenna had just come in from a morning ride on Willow, her silver-gray mare, when she was given the summons. She was dressed in her boy's finery, a dove-gray tunic and short mantle threaded with silver; fine, gartered trousers of soft deerskin; and boots of the best Spanish leather. Her sword swung from her hip, but she removed it before she sat down in the high-backed velvet seat across from her father.

"You shall be wed to a Norse chieftain, daughter," were Lord Angus's first words.

"And I shall breed twenty fine sons to come and raid our coasts," Brenna answered.

Angus did not laugh at her jest, and the very soberness of his expression turned her blood cold. She gripped the arms of her chair, waiting tensely for him to deny his statement.

He sighed tiredly, as if all his years and more had just caught up with him. "Mayhaps they will raid our coast, but not us."

Brenna could not keep the apprehension from her voice. "What have you done, father?"

"The arranger was sent on his way yesterday. He will travel to Norway and make a pact with the Vikings—"

Brenna jumped to her feet. "The Vikings who struck Holyhead Island?"

"Nay, not necessarily the same. The man will seek out a chieftain who will take you to wife. A man with power."

"You would barter me from door to door?" Brenna accused, looking down on her father with wide gray eyes, feeling for the first time in her life as if she did not know this man who sired her.

"You will not be bartered, Brenna!" Lord Angus said with conviction, feeling by all that was holy that he had acted correctly, no matter how much it pained him. "The man will use discretion. I sent Fergus. He is a diplomatic man. He will make inquiries. He will find a man of power who does not already have a wife and make the offer to him. You will not be bartered. Fergus was told to ask only once. If he has no luck, he will return and that will be the end of it. But heaven help us if he returns without the name of your future husband."

Brenna saw red, blood red before her eyes. "How could you do this to me?"

" 'Tis the only way, Brenna."

"Nay, 'tis not!" she stormed. "We are miles from the coast. We have naught to fear!"

"The Vikings grow bolder each year," Angus tried to explain. "The first news of their daring came before I was born. The land across from us is lost to them. To the north our brothers serve them, on the east of Brittany where they have settled. And now they have finally reached our shores. 'Twill only be a matter of time before they raid inland— mayhaps next year. Would you see our village laid to waste at their feet? Our men killed, the women taken as slaves?"

" 'Twould not have been so!" she cried. "You are a knight skilled in warfare. You have trained me in the same arts. We can fight them, father—you and I!"

"Ah, Brenna, my Brenna," he sighed. "I am too old to fight. You could kill many, but not enough. The Norsemen are a race of giants. There are none like them. They are fierce and without mercy. I would see you live, not die. I would protect my people."

"By sacrificing me!" she hissed, beside herself with rage. "To an old chieftain, who by your own words will be ferocious and without mercy!"

"I have no fear for you on that score. I know you can hold your own."

"I will not have to!" Brenna stormed. "I will not agree to the marriage!"

Angus's brow darkened threateningly. "You will! Fergus carries my word of honor with him."

"Why did you not tell me of this yesterday? You knew I would stop Fergus, didn't you?"

"Yea, I did indeed, daughter. But what is done cannot now be undone. And 'tis partly your own doing. You are available. Cordella is not, and your aunt, though lovely still, is too old. The Viking will expect a young bride."

"Do not put this blame on me, father! 'Tis wholly your doing."

"I have put scores of men before you, men of wealth, title and handsome appearance, but you would have none of them!" Lord Angus reminded her gruffly. "You could have been married long since, but then, unfortunately, we would have been doomed."

"You showed me naught but boorish braggarts and handsome fops. You expected me to choose from that handful of fools?"

"I know you, Brenna. You would not have chosen no matter who I brought before you. The very idea of marriage rankles you, though I know not why."

"You are right there, milord," she returned dryly.

"So I have choosen for you. You will wed the man Fergus finds. The deed is done."

Brenna whirled around and faced the fire. Her mind revolted at the thought, but she felt utterly helpless. She, who had been trained to fight, could find no way to combat this. She grasped at straws before finally conceding.

"Another can take my place," she said flatly. "No one would be the wiser."

"You would pass a servant off as a lady?" Angus asked incredulously. " 'Twould bring the Vikings here for revenge of the worst kind if you did such a thing. Fergus will extoll your virtues, Brenna. *Yours!* What servant here or anywhere, has your beauty, your manners or your courage? 'Twould take years to teach a maid your qualities. You are of noble birth, and a lady in all respects, thanks to your aunt's gentle teachings. I thank the day Linnet came and took you in hand, else you would not be fit for marriage to anyone, let alone a Norseman."

"Well, I curse that day for what it has brought me to!" she shouted.

"Brenna!"

At once she regretted her words. She loved her aunt dearly. Motherless since birth, Brenna had attached herself to the lovely Linnet when she first came, four years earlier, after the death of her husband. Linnet was Angus's younger sister; she acted and looked only half of her two score years. She had taken Brenna in hand, even though it was too late to curb her boyish ways completely. She had been a second mother to Brenna, whereas her stepmother, a thorn in everyone's side, spoke to her stepdaughter only to upbraid her. Even Angus sorely regretted marrying her. But at least her presence did not have to be endured for more than three winters, for she died the year after Linnet came. However, she left her daughter Cordella behind, who carried on her shrewish ways.

"I'm sorry, father," Brenna said softly, her silver-gray eyes downcast, her shoulders slumped forward in defeat. " 'Tis only that I so abhor this decision you have made."

"I knew you would be upset, Brenna, but not this much," Angus replied, and stood to wrap his arm around his daughter's shoulder. "Take heart, girl. You admire courage and strength, and no people have as much as the Norsemen. You may thank me one day for this match I have made."

Brenna smiled tiredly, for she had lost the will to argue. A fortnight later she was introduced to Wyndham, a merchant Norseman who had settled on the Emerald Isle and whom Angus had found in Anglesey. He was handsomely rewarded for tutoring Brenna in the Norwegian language and customs, so that she would not "walk blindly into the lion's den," as her father put it.

At harvest time, Fergus returned with the name of her betrothed, sealing her fate once and for all. Brenna's future husband was not the head of his clan, as Angus had hoped, for no such men, still unmarried, were to be found. He was a merchant prince, the son of a powerful chieftain —a young man who had already served his years at war and was now making his own way in the world. Garrick Haardrad was the man's name.

Nay, Fergus had not seen him personally, for the merchant was trading in the east. Yea, Garrick would return by the following summer and come for his bride before the fall. The terms were agreed upon. It was all set. Set, set, set, with no escape!

Brenna counted the days after that with a melancholy dread, until her youthful energies drove her to wipe the unpleasant future from her mind. Only her daily lessons served as a constant reminder of it. As time passed, however, she resolved to make the best of her situation. She would meet the enemy on his ground; she would not be dominated. She would exert her will over that of her husband, and would be free to do as she pleased. A new land, yea, but not a new Brenna.

Brenna's attention returned to Wyndham, who was preparing to summarize this day's lesson.

"And so Odin, Lord of Heaven, is chief of all the gods, a culture god; god of all knowledge, aware of the future. He is also the god of war. Odin, with his army of dead warriors gathered around him by the Valkyries, rides through the clouds on his tireless eight-legged steed, Sleipnir. The dream of every Viking is to join Odin in Valhalla, the eternal banquet hall where one fights all day and feasts all night on sacred boar served by the Valkyries, Odin's adopted daughters.

"Odin's blood brother is Loki. Comparable to the Christian Lucifer, he is sly and treacherous, and plots the downfall of the gods. Red-bearded Thor, on the other hand, is greatly loved—a cheerful god free from malice, but easily angered. He is the god of thunder, the storm god whose mighty hammer pounds out thunderbolts. A replica of Thor's flying hammer can be found in every Norse household.

"Tyr, also a god of war and tamer of the gigantic Fenrir wolf, and sober Hel, daughter of Loki and goddess of the underworld, are only minor figures, as is Frey, god of fertility. You shall learn more of these minor gods on the morrow, Brenna."

"Oh, Wyndham," Brenna sighed. "When will these lessons come to an end?"

"Do you grow tired of me?" he asked gently, surprisingly so for such a large man.

"Of course not," she replied quickly. "I am quite fond of you. If all of your kinsmen were like you, I would have naught to fear."

He smiled, almost sadly. "I wish it could be so, Brenna. But in truth, I can no longer be called a Viking. A score of years have passed since I have seen my homeland. You Christians have tamed me.

"You are an adept learner, my dear. You know now as much of my people as you do your own Celtic ancestors. From now until your betrothed comes, we will only review what you have already learned."

"Can you not tell me more of this clan I will wed into?" she asked.

"Not much more than I have already told you. I only knew your betrothed's grandfather, Ulric the Sly. He was a man of great courage. Ulric ruled with an iron hand, and fought with Loki by his side. But he was a strange man. Rather than come to blows with his son, Ulric left his family, turning over the bulk of his lands to his son, Anselm the Eager. Anselm was true to his name. He was overanxious to be chief of the clan.

"He did not go far, mind you, only a few miles up the fjord to a piece of his land that was not in use. There, with horses, twenty head of cattle and a handful of servants, he constructed a house like no other in Norway. It was built on the cliffs of the Horten Fjord with stone bought from the Frisians. It is a large place, though not as big as your manor here, and with a fireplace in every room."

"But that is no different from here, Wyndham," Brenna pointed out.

"Except that the wooden houses in Norway do not have fireplaces as you know them, only large fires in the center of the room, with no place for smoke to escape except through an open door."

"How awful!"

"Aye, and very hard on the eyes and nose."

"Will I have to live in a wooden house such as you have described?"

"Most likely. But 'tis a condition you'll get used to soon enough."

Chapter 3

THE large hall was the brightest room in the manor at the dinner hour. Nine flickering flames danced in an ornate candelabra in the center of the long table, and lamp bowls on every wall added to the abundant light in the room.

Smoke-darkened tapestries hung from the walls, including a half-finished landscape worked by Brenna's mother, who had died in childbirth before she could complete it. A tapestry woven by Linnet depicted a castle by the sea; Cordella's war scene hung beside it. The last tapestry in the room was of incomparable beauty; it came from the Far East, and was a gift from the duke of a neighboring kingdom.

It was not surprising that no tapestry made by Brenna graced the wall, for she did not have the patience required for that gentle art. In truth, she could not abide any skill which was solely a woman's.

Her youngest, most impressionable years had left their mark on her, for during this time her father treated her like the son he had hoped for. She was a son to him until her body developed curves that bespoke the lie. The year her figure changed was a nightmare for Brenna, for her increasingly feminine body warred with her male mind. The mind won out. Brenna ignored her changed body unless she was reminded of its significance. Cordella took the most delight in causing Brenna to remember her sex.

Cordella, with her flaming red hair, river-green eyes and shapely figure, which she took pains to flaunt in daringly cut gowns, was Brenna's constant antagonist. She was a comely wench as long as she was silent. Brenna understood the reasons for her shrewishness and tried hard not to lose patience with her.

She knew that Cordella was unhappy. A woman of only twenty years, she had married Dunstan at a young age, of her own free will. She loved Dunstan at the start, and was a different woman in those days. But for a reason that no one except perhaps Dunstan knew, Cordella now hated him. It was this hatred that made her the venomous creature she had become.

Cordella entered the hall and joined Brenna at the long table. Servants brought the meal of thick rabbit stew only moments later. Cordella, arrayed in yellow velvet that set off her hair and made it appear even brighter than it was, waited until they were alone before she spoke.

"Where is your aunt this eventide?"

"Linnet decided she would feed father this night," Brenna answered as she dipped a ladle in the large pot of stew and filled her plate.

"You should be doing that, not your aunt," Cordella returned.

Brenna shrugged. " 'Twas Linnet's choice."

"How is my stepfather?"

"If you took the time to see for yourself, you would know that he is not improved."

"He will," Cordella said dryly. "That old man wil¹ outlive us all. But I did not expect you here for the meal. I understand a boar was killed today and there is a feast in the village. I thought surely you would be down there with your peasant friends, as are Wyndham and Fergus."

"I see Dunstan finds the village more to his liking also," Brenna said coldly, reminded of her fall in pursuit of the boar. "I want no part of that bloody boar's carcass."

"My, but you are touchy this night," Cordella replied, a mischievous smile on her full lips. She purposely ignored

Brenna's mention of Dunstan. "Could it be perchance that Willow returned to the stable today long after you? Or mayhaps because the time grows shorter before your betrothed comes?"

"Be careful, Della," Brenna said, her eyes darkening. "I have not the patience for your wagging tongue this night."

Cordella stared at Brenna with wide-eyed innocence and let the subject pass for now. She was sorely jealous of her younger sister; she admitted it to herself freely. It had not always been so. When Cordella and her mother had first come to live in this fine manor eight winters past, Brenna was only a scrawny nine-year-old. In truth, it was a month before Cordella learned she had a sister, not a brother, as she assumed.

Of course, they had not liked each other from the start, for there was resentment on both sides, and to make the gap even wider, they had absolutely nothing in common. With her boyish ways, Brenna was leery of Cordella, who even at twelve was wholly female. Cordella thought Brenna was a fool to prefer swords to sewing, or caring for horses to running a household. Yet the two lived together without an eruption of hostility, and the years passed.

Then Cordella met Dunstan, a big, brawny male who set her heart aflutter. They were wed, and for once Cordella was truly happy. But their joy lasted only a year. It ended when Linnet insisted Brenna begin wearing female clothes on occasion, and Dunstan saw what a beauty she really was. Brenna, damn her, was not even aware that Dunstan lusted for her. Nor was Dunstan aware that his wife knew. He only knew that her love for him died that year.

Cordella's jealousy was mixed with hatred—for Dunstan and for Brenna. She could not openly attack Brenna, though many was the time she wished she could claw her eyes out. Brenna was a skilled fighter, thanks to her father, and when riled, she turned Cordella's blood cold. She had killed men without batting an eye. She had proved herself well, to Angus's pride.

Since Cordella could not fight Brenna, she could give her stepsister cause to fear the one thing Brenna had yet to experience—being with a man. Cordella took great pleasure in expounding on the horrors, and not the pleasures, of knowing a man. She taunted Brenna at every available opportunity, feeling joy at the terror that leaped into those gray eyes. It was the only revenge Cordella had. Now if only she could pay Dunstan in turn . . .

Brenna would be leaving soon, a prospect Cordella knew the young woman dreaded. Then there would be no one for miles to compare with her own loveliness, and Dunstan would be brought to heel.

Cordella pushed her plate away and eyed Brenna speculatively. "You know, sister, the ship from the north could come any day now. 'Tis well into summer already. Are you ready to meet your future husband?"

"I will never be ready," Brenna replied dismally, and pushed her own plate aside.

"Yea, the princess thrown to the lions. 'Tis unfortunate that you had no say in the matter. I would not have expected your father to do this to you. After all, *I* had a choice."

"You know why 'twas done!" Brenna snapped.

"Yea, of course. To save us all," Cordella replied, her voice heavy with sarcasm. "At least you know what to expect. If I had known what it would be like, I would have been like you, wishing never to marry. Lord, how I dread each night, knowing the pain I must bear!"

Brenna glared at her icily. "Della, I saw an act of coupling in the village today."

"Really? How was this?"

"Never mind how. What I saw was not as horrifying as you would have me believe."

"You will not know until you experience it yourself," Cordella returned sharply. "You will learn that you must bear your pain in silence, else the man will beat you. 'Tis a wonder more women do not cut their throats rather than submit to such agony every night."

"Enough, Della! I do not wish to hear anymore."

"Be thankful you know. At least *you* will not go unsuspecting to your wedding bed." Cordella finished and left the table, her lips curving in a smile as soon as she was out of Brenna's sight.

Chapter 4

BULGAR, on the eastern bend of the Volga River, was a large reshipment port where West met East. Here Viking longships traded with caravans from the steppes of Central Asia and Arab freighters from Eastern provinces. Leading eastward from Bulgar was the legendary Silk Road to China.

A cornucopia of humanity abounded in Bulgar, from thieves and murderers to merchants and kings. At the start of summer, Garrick Haardrad anchored his splendid longship here and set out to add to the fortune he had accumulated on his travels. A wondrous business, trading.

Having unexpectedly spent the winter with a tribe of Slavic nomads, Garrick was not inclined to tarry long at Bulgar. He was anxious to be homeward bound. He still had to stop at Hedeby to dispose of the twenty slaves given to him by Aleksandr Stasov so he could make the journey home with greater speed. His first trip to the East had been full of surprises, but very satisfying.

After leaving Norway the previous year with a cargo of furs and the slaves he had chosen to sell, Garrick and his crew of nine sailed to Hedeby, the great market town on the Schlei River, where he traded half of his slaves for an assortment of merchandise made by the craftsmen there. He took combs, pins, dice and gaming stones, all made of bone, as well as beads and pendants crafted from amber brought in from the Baltic lands.

From Hedeby they sailed to Birka, an island trade center in Lake Malar, situated in the heart of Sweden opposite the Slav town Jumne. Birka was a well known Vic, or trading market; in its harbor could be found ships owned by Danish, Slavic, Norwegian and Scythian peoples. Here Garrick bartered for Rhinish glass, Frisian cloth, which was so valued for its fine texture, jeweled stirrups and Rhine wine, much of which he kept for himself.

Thence Garrick and his crew sailed to Uppland, went on to the Gulf of Finland and then, by way of the Neva, passed the marches and continued on to Lake Ladogo. Old Ladogo, the trading center, was located at the mouth of the Volkhor, and here they stopped for provisions. By then it was midsummer, and they still had a long way to go. They sailed eastward into the land of the Western Slavs, over the Svir to Lake Onega, and on several smaller rivers and lakes to Lake Beloya, until finally they reached the northern bend of the great Volga River.

Halfway between there and Bulgar, their destination, they came upon a ship under attack by a group of Slavs who lived along the river bank. The screams of both men and women rent the still air. Garrick manned the oars and reached the ship before the bloody attack was finished. He and his men boarded the small sailless vessel and killed off those marauders who did not flee quickly enough when they saw his great Viking ship.

Only a young woman and her baby were left alive, and that because they had hidden away inside a large, empty barrel. Haakorn, one of Garrick's men and a seasoned traveler, spoke the woman's Slavic tongue. He discovered that she was the daughter of a powerful chieftain of a Slavic tribe. Her husband had been killed, and she lay weeping by his mutilated body as she told of the massacre. The assailants were members of an enemy tribe intent upon killing her and the baby to revenge actions of her father's. This attack had not been their first.

Garrick held an immediate council with his men to decide what to do with the woman. It was Perrin, Garrick's closest friend, and as near to him as a blood brother, whose sound advice won out. Since they had already made enemies of those who had fled, they did not need to make more enemies by returning the girl to her tribe for ransom. They would be traveling this route in the future; it could only be to their advantage to have friends in the area.

Thus they returned the girl and her babe to her father without asking for a reward. Feasts were given in their honor, one after another, and days turned into weeks. The rains came, giving them another excuse to linger, for Aleksandr Stasov was an excellent host and they wanted for nothing. Finally it was too late to reach Bulgar and return home before the cold, so they stayed the winter.

In the spring, the grateful chieftain sent them on their way with twenty slaves and a bag of silver for each of the crew. All in all, the time lost to them was worth their while.

In Bulgar the last of the cargo was sold. The furs alone brought an enormous sum, especially the white fur of the polar bear, of which Garrick had four. Each man sold his own goods, for this was a joint venture, among friends, even though it was Garrick's ship that had brought them.

And so, being young men on their first voyage east (for only Haakorn had traveled this far before), they lingered long, reveling in the new and unusual. Garrick purchased many gifts for his family. Some he would distribute on his return; others he would save for special occasions and ceremonies. He had necklaces and armbands made for his mother from precious jewels he bought cheaply from the Arabs, and he also obtained Chinese silk. For his father he found a splendid sword like his own, with its prized Rhenish blade, and the handle richly engraved and inlaid with silver and gold. For his brother Hugh he purchased a helmet of gold, a symbol of leadership.

He bought gifts for his friends and trinkets for Yarmille, the woman who ran his household and commanded the slaves in his absence. For himself he purchased extravagantly—Byzantine silks and brocades to make fine robes, tapestries from the Orient for his home, and a barrel of iron utensils that would delight his slaves. Each day they stayed in Bulgar, Garrick found something new to add to his collection. Finally his friends began to make wagers on how much silver he would part with before the day ended.

This day in midsummer, with the cloudless sky almost white in its intensity, Garrick entered the house of the engraver, Bolsky, his friend Perrin at his side.

The little man looked up from his work table in the center of the room and fixed his squinting eyes on the two young Norsemen dressed in short, sleeveless tunics with tight-fitting long leggings. They were both of towering height with broad chests; corded muscles rippled on their bare arms. They had taut, powerful bodies without an ounce of excess flesh. One had auburn hair and a trim beard; the other was blond and clean-shaven. The blond had eyes that were cold and skeptical for one so young. They were the color of aqua, like shallow waters on a bright day. The other had laughing eyes like glowing emeralds.

Bolsky was expecting the blond Viking, for he had requested the engraver to make him a fine, silver medallion with the picture of a beautiful girl engraved on the underside. He had given Bolsky a sketch of this girl, and the engraver was proud of the finished work. On the front was a proud Viking ship with nine oars, and above the ship was a hammer with crisscrossed wings and a broadsword. On the back of the medallion was the girl, worked in minute detail, the very image of the sketch. A sweetheart, perhaps, or a wife?

"Is it finished?" Garrick asked.

Bolsky smiled, and opening a fur-lined bag, produced the medallion with its long silver chain. "It is done."

Garrick tossed a pouch of silver on the table and took the medallion, slipping it over his head without even inspecting it. But Perrin, his curiosity pricked, lifted the heavy silver disk from Garrick's chest and examined it closely. He admired the symbols of wealth, power and strength, but when he turned the medallion over, his brows drew together in a disapproving frown.

"Why?"

Garrick shrugged and started for the door, but Perrin was close on his heels and drew him to a halt. "Why torture yourself this way?" Perrin asked. "She is not worth it."

Garrick raised an eyebrow in surprise. *"You* would say this?"

Perrin grimaced. "Yea, I would. She is my sister, but I cannot condone what she has done."

"Well, do not fret, my friend. What I felt for Morna is dead—long since."

"Then why that?" Perrin asked, gesturing at the medallion.

"A reminder," Garrick answered, his voice hard. "A reminder that no woman can be trusted."

"I fear my sister has left her mark on you, Garrick. You have not been the same since she married that fat merchant."

A shadow came over the younger man's blue-green eyes, but a cynical smile twisted his lips. "I am simply wiser. I will never fall prey to a woman's charms again. I laid my heart open once, and will not do so a second time. I know them for what they are now."

"All women are not the same, Garrick. Your mother is different. I have never known a kinder or more giving woman."

Garrick's features softened. "My mother is the only exception. But come, enough of this. Today, our last night, I intend to drink a barrel of ale—and you, my friend, will have to carry me back to the ship when I am through."

Chapter 5

BRENNA sat in the center of her large bed polishing her sword with the care given a prized possession, which indeed her sword was. Finely crafted and honed just for her, the weapon was lightweight but razor sharp. It was a gift from her father on the day she celebrated her tenth year. Her name was inscribed on the silver handle, surrounded by rubies and bright sapphires the size of plump peas. Brenna cherished this sword more than any of her possessions, if for no other reason than because it was a symbol of her father's pride in her achievements.

She held it up now against her forehead, her thoughts gloomy. Would her female body imprison her in her husband's land? Would she ever be able to wield this sword again, to fight for what was her own as any man would? Or would she be expected to act the wife in every way, never to use her skills again, to be a woman and do only what a woman should?

Curse men and their set ways! She would not be treated thus. To be undermined and ruled, nay! She would not be acquiescent. She was Brenna Carmarham, not some simpering, cowering maid!

Fuming indignantly, Brenna did not hear her aunt enter

her chamber and quietly close the door. Linnet stared at her niece with tired, heartsick eyes.

She had nursed her own husband through months of suffering, each day sapping more of her strength. When he died, a part of her did too, for she loved him dearly. Now she had been doing the same for her brother Angus. Lord in Heaven, please: no more death.

Brenna gave a start when she perceived the haggard figure out of the corner of her eye. She turned to Linnet, hardly recognizing her. Her hair was unkempt and her gown soiled, but it was actually her face which was so disturbingly different. It was powder white, her lips were taut, and there were dark circles under her red-rimmed eyes.

Brenna got off the bed and led her aunt to the long gold couch beneath the window. "Linnet, you have been crying. 'Tis not like you," she said worriedly. "What is wrong?"

"Oh, Brenna, lass. Your life is changing so much. 'Tis not right to have it all happen at one time."

Brenna smiled weakly. "You have been crying for me, Aunt? You need not."

"Nay, love, not for you, though I will surely. 'Tis your father, Brenna. Angus is dead."

Brenna drew back, her face a sickly white. "How could you jest about this?" she accused harshly. " 'Tis not so!"

"Brenna," Linnet sighed, and reached out to caress her niece's cheek. "I would not lie to you. Angus died but an hour past."

Brenna shook her head slowly, denying the words. "He was not so ill. He cannot die!"

"Angus had the same illness as my husband, but at least he did not suffer overmuch."

Brenna's eyes were the size of saucers, and filled with horror. "You knew he would die?"

"Yea, I did."

"In God's name, why did you not tell me? Why did you let me go on believing he would be well again?"

" 'Twas his wish, Brenna. He forbade me to tell anyone, especially you. He did not want to see you weeping by his side. Angus never could tolerate tears, and 'twas enough that he put up with mine."

Tears now sprang to Brenna's eyes. They were altogether unknown to her, for she had never shed them before. "But I should have been the one to nurse him. Instead, I went on my way as if naught was amiss."

"He did not want you grieving overmuch, Brenna. And you would have if you had known. This way you will mourn for a while, then you will put it behind you. Your forthcoming marriage will help you."

"Nay! There will be no wedding now!"

"Your father's word has been given, Brenna." Linnet spoke a bit impatiently. "You must honor it, even though he is dead."

Brenna could hold back the heartbreaking sobs no longer. "Why did he have to die, Aunt? Why?

Lord Angus Carmarham was laid to rest on a clear blue morning. Birds had only just begun to greet the day, and the fragrance of wild flowers drifted through the chill morning air.

Brenna, her eyes dry now, was dressed in black from head to foot. She wore a tunic and trousers gartered with leather trousers, topped by a short, flowing mantle trimmed with silver thread. Her long raven tresses were braided and as usual tucked securely beneath the mantle. The only outstanding colors were the white of her face and the shining silver of her sword.

Her aunt had expressed disapproval at her apparel, but Brenna remained adamant. Her father had treated her and raised her as a son, and she would dress like that son for their final farewell.

The people of the village were present, and many wept loudly. Linnet stood on Brenna's right, her comforting arm wrapped around the girl's shoulders. Cordella and Dunstan were on her left. Dunstan spoke words of praise and past glory, but Brenna did not hear them. In those few moments she was reliving memories: a young child sitting on her father's knee; a proud man yelling encouragement when his daughter rode her first horse. She recalled the tender, cherished moments.

Brenna felt lost without him, and a terrible feeling of emptiness washed over her. But she stood proud for her people to see. Only her eyes, lackluster and deadened, told of her heartache.

The moment when Dunstan spoke no more was silent and solemn. It was with much surprise that those in attendance saw a rider burst through the trees and descend upon the large gathering. He jumped from his horse and made his way quickly through the throng to Brenna's side.

"Your betrothed has come." The young man spoke breathlessly. "I was returning from Anglesey and passed the party on the way."

"How do you know 'twas my betrothed?" Brenna asked apprehensively. She was not prepared for this news, not with her father just laid in his grave.

"Who else could it be?" the man replied. " 'Twas a large group of huge, fair-haired men. They are Vikings to be sure."

Alarmed voices broke out in the crowd, but Brenna could only think of her own predicament. "Lord in Heaven, why now?" she cried.

This the young man could not answer. Linnet drew her close, saying, "Never mind why, my dear. 'Tis done." Then she spoke to the messenger. "How close are they?"

"On the other side of those trees." He pointed northwest. "About a mile."

"Very well," Linnet replied. "We must receive them at the manor. You people return to your village. You have naught to fear from these Vikings. They come in peace."

Back in the manor, Brenna paced restlessly in the large receiving room. Fergus sat anxiously with the rest of the family. He was responsible for the Vikings being here, and was eager to make them welcome. He had spent a good deal of time in a hostile land finding the Haardrad clan. The head of the clan himself had received Fergus and made the bargain for his son, giving his solemn word that all would be as agreed upon. With the death of Lord Angus, the bride was worth a great fortune, for his lands and manor were now hers, and thus her husband's. The Vikings would be pleased indeed.

"Brenna, love, 'twould be more seemly if you would change to a gown," Linnet suggested.

"Nay."

"Brenna, you cannot receive your future husband this way. What will he think?"

"I said nay!" Brenna snapped, and continued her nervous pacing.

Cordella eyed her stepsister smugly. She was amused, for she guessed why Brenna was fretting. The young woman was worrying if her betrothed would want to marry her before they sailed. The wedding could be this very night or on the morrow. And then came the wedding night —and the terror. Cordella almost laughed aloud. There would be pain that first night, and Brenna would think it would always be thus, thanks to her. What sweet revenge. If only she could be there to see it.

Brenna was thinking exactly that. She was not ready for marriage, and never would be. She was not geared to suffer pain without retaliation. She would fight! Lord in Heaven, what if she killed her husband for claiming his rights? It would be her own death sentence.

These wild thoughts were tumbling through her mind when the first large boulder struck the manor door. Startled exclamations came from one and all. Questioning glances met confused looks, but when a choked cry came from the yard, followed by yet another boulder against the door, Brenna dashed to the window to take in the scene with disbelieving eyes.

"Holy God, they are attacking!"

A servant lay decapitated by the path from the stables, and the yard was crawling with Vikings, their swords, axes and spears drawn and ready. A small, crudely constructed catapult was worked by two men. A third boulder hit the door. From down the hill, dark curls of smoke drifted skyward—the village was afire.

Brenna turned to the group behind her. Wyndham was among them, and her eyes met his accusingly. "Is this the way your kinsmen come for a bride?"

Wyndham had no answer, but Fergus spoke with uncertainty. "These Vikings cannot be the ones I sought out."

"Look, then, and see if you know them!" she ordered harshly.

"Brenna, calm yourself," Linnet said, though her own voice betrayed her anxiety.

Fergus went to the window, and it took only a second for him to recognize the tall chieftain of the Haardrad clan. Anselm the Eager stood before his men shouting orders.

" 'Tis not possible!" Fergus cried, facing the small, terrified group in the room. "He gave his word!"

Another boulder against the door prompted Brenna to action. "Wyndham, are you with us or with your treacherous kinsmen? I would know before I turn my back on you."

He looked sorely affronted. "With you, my lady. I do not claim kinship with these Norsemen who do not honor their word."

"So be it," she replied. "Those fools have given us time to prepare by bombarding an unlocked door. Dunstan, go bolt it now before more damage is done."

Dunstan drew back from her, his eyes filled with horror. "Brenna, they are thirty or more to our three!"

"Four, curse you!" she snapped. "Do you think *I* will sit back and watch?"

"Brenna, be reasonable. We have no chance!"

"Do you suggest we surrender? Fool, have you forgotten Holyhead Island? Those who did not fight, as well as those who did, all met the bloody axe. Now bolt the door! Fergus, gather the servants and arm them. Wyndham, secure the rear of the manor, then meet me in the hall. We will be ready for the bloody bastards when the door finally gives way."

All left to do her bidding without further question. Cordella sat huddled in the corner, weeping hysterically. Linnet was also near tears when she grabbed Brenna's arm to stay her.

"You cannot fight them, Brenna! They will kill you the same as a man!"

"They would kill me anyway, Aunt. My father trained me for this. I will die fighting with honor, rather than weeping in self-pity as Della is wont to do!"

"They would not kill you, Brenna, if you do not resist them," Linnet persisted. "They take women—"

"Never!" Brenna cut her short. "I would rather die than be a Viking captive!"

With that, Brenna stalked from the room, leaving Linnet and Cordella to their prayers. But before all the servants were roused and armed, the barrier was broken and a blood-curdling war cry sounded from the yard. A moment later, a dozen men lusting for blood burst through the demolished door and stormed into the hall.

Brenna stood by the foot of the stairs, legs astride, sword drawn. An axe missed her by inches. Halfway between her and the enemy, Dunstan was the first to fall. The Vikings divided their party. Three went to the back of the hall and three into the receiving room, closing the door soundly after them. Wyndham came from the rear and took on two of his kinsmen. He fought valiantly, but he was old and tired quickly. He felled one, however, before the other's sword entered his body and ended his life.

Five men came at Brenna. Four passed her and mounted the stairs, only to lose themselves in the maze on the second floor. She met the remaining man without fear. His broadsword was heavier than hers, and each blow she countered was backed by enormous strength. Her arm and back ached with the effort, but the screams coming from behind the closed door of the receiving room added to her determination. With strength she had not realized she possessed, she knocked the man's sword aside and pierced him smoothly with her own. She kicked him away, but another, older man quickly took his place. Her stamina failing, Brenna continued to fight until, with a powerful downward stroke, the man's sword split hers in two.

Brenna stared stupidly at the broken weapon in her hand. She did not see the death blow coming her way, or hear Fergus's anguished cry. "Cease! 'Tis the Lady Brenna!"

Then Fergus was between her and the glittering sword, pushing her back. The mighty double-edged blade severed his arm, which dropped to the floor with a sickening thud. Fergus, his life slowly slipping away, fell at Brenna's feet.

Anselm the Eager looked at the girl curiously. To think he had fought her and almost killed her. A fine honor that would have been to take home. He would never have lived it down. So this was the girl they would wed to his son. A stunning maid, to be sure, now that he saw her for what she was. And such spirit and courage as he had never seen in a woman before. She had even succeeded in wounding one of his men. That one would go home in shame. Bested by a woman—ha!

It was too bad she was the enemy. This black-haired beauty would have made a fine daughter-in-law. She would have bred sons with strength and courage to match no other. In truth, it was a pity.

The servants, late in arriving, fell all around Brenna. Blood flowed everywhere. The screams from the receiving room had ceased. Two of the Vikings came out of there, laughing and clapping each other on the back before they joined the others to ransack the manor. Linnet and Cordella, were they dead too? wondered Brenna.

From the top of the stairs came another garbled cry, and Brenna turned mutely to see its source. Alane was there, a short dagger in her hand. It slipped from her fingers as Brenna watched, horrified. Then her old servant, face gray and eyes bulging, tumbled down the stairs to land in a pool of her own blood. An axe was grotesquely embedded in her back, which gushed crimson.

It was the final horror, the last act of madness which pushed Brenna beyond her endurance. Something snapped in her mind and blackness engulfed her, yet did not blot out everything, for she could still hear voices, and she was still standing erect. Someone else was screaming and screaming. It sounded so close, she knew that if she reached out she could touch whoever was making that agonizing noise. But she could not move her arms. No matter how much she willed them to move, they would not budge.

"Anselm, can you not stop the wench from screaming? Her madness is beginning to spook the men. They would sooner give her to Hel than listen to that."

"There is only one way I know of," Anselm the Eager replied tiredly.

Brenna did not feel the blow, but at last the blackness was complete. She no longer heard the terrible screaming of one demented.

Chapter 6

THE march to the coast was slow. It took two hours more to return than it had to come. The horses, cattle, pigs and carts loaded with plunder slowed their progress. Still, they reached the ship before nightfall.

The Viking longship was a horror to the prisoners, all of whom were women. It was a sleek sixty-foot-long vessel, at least fifteen wide in the middle. On the prow was an intricately carved, hideous monster from Hell. This ship would take them from their land and sever all ties with the world they knew.

The proud Viking ship was beached in a little cove, hidden by tall trees. Two men had been left behind to guard it. They had been instructed to put it out to sea in case of trouble. But there had been no trouble, and the two men greeted the returning warriors with whoops and bellows.

Usually the Vikings spent the night on land, but because of the number of enemy who had escaped into the woods during the attack (possibly to run for help), and because of the wide trail the Vikings had left behind in transporting the livestock, Anselm the Eager hoisted the square purple sail that night.

A handful of men made the sacrifice to Thor to insure a safe journey while the others loaded the cargo. The women were put in the stern, where a crude tent was erected for them. Other than that, they were left alone. The men had satisfied their blood lust and their carnal lust, and would not need to do so again until the ship reached land once more.

All of the women had been raped, some many times, save for Brenna, who remained unconscious from the blow Anselm dealt her until after the ship sailed. There were seven prisoners in all; Linnet and Cordella, along with Enid and three other young girls from the village. Most of the men had been killed, except for those who managed to flee into the woods or those left gravely wounded who were not expected to last the night.

Brenna knew this, and it was an additional torture to her. She had failed to protect her people and she had failed to protect herself. Her defeat at the hands of the Viking chieftain, a man past his youthful prime, was the shameful blow she could not bear. Her hate for this one man surpassed all reason. *He* had rendered her helpless; *he* had struck her down. He had shown one and all that she was just a woman after all. He would pay for that, and for everything else.

The ship glided over the waves like a sleek monster, leaving Wales behind. The women were fed twice a day on dry codfish, ham or pickled meats, flat bread and butter. It was cold, dry food, which many could not keep down. Cordella frequently dashed to the side of the ship to empty her stomach. The men found this amusing, and their laughter added to the women's shame.

Brenna ate only to sustain her strength for the goal she had set for herself: to kill Anselm the Eager. She would not speak to her companions or listen to their fearful wailings. Linnet tried to comfort her, but she could not tolerate any kindness and would not even speak to her. Her shame was too great, her bitterness too new. Wisely, Linnet gave up for the time being.

Anselm the Eager came occasionally to look at Brenna. He was a huge man with the girth of a bear. His hair was tawny-colored, as was the beard that covered his face, and he had piercing blue eyes. He was a man to strike fear into the hearts of his enemies—but not into Brenna's. When he looked at her curiously—almost admiringly, it seemed— she would meet his look with a venomous one, such open hostility and hatred in her eyes that he would walk away disgruntled.

Anselm almost regretted what he had done, but he would never admit it aloud. He had given his word of honor to the enemy. Yet there was no dishonor in breaking his word to his enemy—to a friend, yea, but not to the enemy.

He who had arranged the marriage had promised much wealth would accompany the bride, and, unsuspecting, had told where it was to be found. There would be no bride for Anselm's son, but the gold was there for the taking. The chieftain was returning home a wealthier man, and his men had their share and were happy.

When Anselm looked at the young beauty, he was amused by her show of defiance. Her pride was equal to his own, but he wondered how long it would last. The thought of such a spirit being broken left a sour taste in his mouth.

He remembered watching her fight the man she had wounded. He had thought her a slim young man, and was amazed at the skill with which she fought against such brute strength. It was a pleasure to watch such courage, which was prized among his people. He had been reluctant to kill her even when he thought her a male, but he could not lose any more of his men to her. And then to discover she was the young girl offered to his son in marriage, and such a magnificent female at that . . .

After her valiant effort and remarkable display of courage, Anselm was disappointed to see her crumble. When she saw the old woman with the red hair die, she went berserk, screaming and screaming, her small fists pressed against her temples. Had she seen her father fall? Could the woman have been her mother? But no, the black-haired older woman who stayed near her now bore more resemblance. If only they could speak the same language, then he would have the answers he sought. But he would have to wait until they reached home, where Heloise could talk to them.

For now, he could only wonder about this Celtic beauty.

She was a prize indeed, and he resolved to keep his men away from her. Her virginity made her an even better acquisition. Surely she would please his son Garrick.

They sailed on through the Irish Sea, stopping at the Isle of Man to spend the night and have a cooked meal. Those of the men who were so inclined, raped the women again, but still they did not approach Brenna with her look of wild hatred. Some thought she was mad. Soon they were in the North Channel, sailing past the Scottish coast, where they spent another of the nights the women so dreaded. Then they made a stop on Hebrides Island, where many of their kinsmen had settled. There they stayed two days. Thence they sailed past the Orkneys. Their final night on land was on the Shetland Islands.

After this they entered the strange, deep sea, where no land was in easy reach and where monsters and dragons of unbelievable size could at any moment surface and swallow them all alive—or such were the constant complaints of the women. They would rather face anything than the unknown. An unexpected, violent storm did not help to calm their fears. Huge waves lashed out at them, and the ocean opened its arms. There, serpents with fiery tongues were waiting. Even Cordella, whose mockery of Brenna's silent withdrawal and whose condescending attitude toward her stepsister was at its peak, was reduced to weeping pitifully for her life until the storm abated.

Linnet had great difficulty trying to calm the women when her own nerves were raw. She pleaded with Brenna to help, but received no response. She understood some of what Brenna was going through, why she brooded silently, but thought this was no time for her to abdicate her leadership. A few brave words from Brenna would lessen the others' fear. Cordella was no help either, crying and screaming that the world was ending.

If Linnet had not been so worried herself, she might almost have felt pleasure in seeing the state Cordella was reduced to. It was appalling that the young woman had not shed a single tear for the loss of her husband. Only hours earlier the fiery-headed Della had been boasting that she was not afraid of what the future held, so sure was she that every man aboard the ship, including the chieftain, desired her above all the others—especially since they left

Brenna alone. Cordella was sure that she would find a comfortable place for herself in the new land.

Perhaps Cordella did not boast falsely. More of the men did go to her when they spent a night on land. And she did not fight them anymore, as she had that first time. Even the leader sought Della out.

Linnet cringed, remembering her own ravishment by two of those brutes who had burst into the receiving room that fateful day. She had been bothered only once since then, by none other than the leader himself, who at least was not as rough with her as the younger men. It was actually a tender interlude, for she had lost the will to fight, and he was gentle in his way. She had been a widow for so long, and had not had a man in as many years. Still Linnet prayed it would not happen again. There was nothing she could hope for from Anselm Haardrad of Norway. He was already married, by Fergus's words. There was nothing Linnet could look forward to at all.

The storm did not last overly long, but left everyone limp and exhausted. A day later, miraculously, land was sighted. Norway's long coastline extended as far as the eye could see. They did not stop again for provisions but, eager to be home, sailed night and day, further and further north, until finally they altered course and turned inland to the Horten Fjord.

It was midsummer, and the bright green of the trees and grass was welcome to the eye. The sky was deep blue, and dotted with puffy white clouds. Ahead, one fluffy mass stood alone in the sky, in the shape of a mighty mallet— Thor's flying hammer.

The women saw the cloud, but thought nothing of it. The men, however, gave a deafening cheer. It was a good sign, for it meant that Thor gave them his blessings.

Rocky cliffs rose on both sides of the ship like steep walls. When the banks were level again, the ship rowed to shore. The journey was over.

Chapter 7

THE settlement was crude, to say the least. Set back only a quarter mile from the fjord stood a large windowless house made of wood, flanked by many smaller houses and livestock sheds. In the fields behind the settlement were other crude houses spaced far apart.

A few women and children accompanied by many dogs ran down to the landing to greet the men; others waited by the main house. Brenna and the other women were tied at the wrists before they were unloaded, just like cargo, and two men escorted them to one of the smaller houses.

All eyes followed the trim figure in black who walked with a proud gait and fearless air. The other captives moved along slowly. They were shoved inside the little house, and the door was slammed behind them. They were surrounded by darkness.

"What now?" Enid cried.

"If I knew, I would not be so frightened," another girl answered. " 'Tis not knowing that is so terrible."

"We will know soon enough, to be sure," Cordella snapped impatiently. "This darkness is insufferable! Did you see that none of these houses have windows? Are these brave Vikings afraid of light?"

45

"We are far north, Della," Linnet replied. "I would imagine it gets colder here than any winter you've ever known. Windows, no matter how well covered, would let the cold in."

"You have an answer for everything," Cordella hissed sarcastically. "What is our fate then, Linnet? What is to become of us?"

Linnet sighed wearily. She stood in the center of the room next to Brenna, but could see nothing in the black gloom. She could not say what she feared, that they were all slaves now, and nothing more. There was no reason to further frighten the younger girls, for her suspicion was not yet a certainty.

"As you said, Della, we will know soon enough," Linnet finally answered.

Brenna remained silent, unable to offer reassurance. She too guessed what their fate was, but her mind retreated from the possibility. Her frustration over her inability to protect them when they needed her most kept her mouth closed in a tight line. What could she do without a weapon and with her wrists bound? They had been raped and brutalized, but she had been unable to prevent it.

The fact that she had not been violated herself gave her little comfort. She could only reason that she was being saved for the arranged marriage. That would never happen now, for she would rather die than be a Viking bride. She only wanted revenge, and she would have it somehow.

The ship was unloaded, the plunder locked in the treasure house and the livestock put out to pasture. A feast was underway at the main house. A large boar was being turned on a spit in the center of the room. Slaves or *thralls* were busy in the cooking area preparing flat bread and fish dishes.

The men crowded at long tables in the main room wasted no time in dipping their cups into a large vat of mead. Some were involved in drinking contests; others took sides and placed wagers. The large thronelike chair at the head of one table was empty, but Anselm's company was not missed as yet.

In the bathhouse, cauldrons of water boiled over a fire.

Smoke and steam combined to sting the eyes. A giant tub, large enough to accommodate four or five comfortably, sat in the middle of the room. A cup of mead in his hand, Anselm relaxed in the tub, water up to his waist. A pretty slave girl leaned over the side and scrubbed his back. His first-born son, Hugh, sat on a bench pushed against the wall.

"Sure you won't join me?" Anselm asked gruffly, then continued, "Damned bother, this ritual bath your mother insists on. I would not mind at any other time, but she knows I am eager to join the feast, and still she makes me come here first."

"You are not alone, father," Hugh replied with a grin. "She does the same to me and Garrick, when we return from raiding. She must think the blood of our enemies still clings to our skin and must be cleansed posthaste."

"Whatever the reason," Anselm grumbled, "Loki smiles at my displeasure. I don't know why I put up with it."

Hugh laughed heartily, his sharp blue eyes sparkling. "You have said more than once that your wife rules the home, and you the sea."

"True, except that woman takes advantage of the power I give her. But enough. Has Garrick returned yet?"

"Nay."

Anselm frowned. The last time his second son did not return for the winter, he had been taken prisoner by the Christians. But he was raiding then. The spring before last, Garrick had sailed to try his luck at trading, so Anselm would not worry yet, not till the cold set in again.

"And my bastard, Fairfax? Where is he?"

"Whaling off the coast," Hugh answered curtly.

"When?"

"A week past."

"So he will return soon."

Hugh stood up stiffly. A powerfully built man of thirty years, he was the image of his father. He resented his half-brother and any attention his father gave him.

"Why do you concern yourself with him? Granted, his mother is a freewoman, but he is still a bastard, no different than those you sired from the slaves."

Anselm's blue eyes narrowed. "The others are daughters. I have only two legitimate sons and Fairfax. Do not begrudge me my concern for him."

"Loki take him! He is no Viking. He is weak!"

"My blood, though little of it, is in his veins. I will not speak of it again. Now, tell me how it went while I was gone. Was there trouble with the Borgsen clan?"

Hugh shrugged his large shoulders and sat down again. "Two cows were found dead near the fields, but there was no proof that pointed to the Borgsens. It could have been the work of a malcontent slave."

"But you doubt this, son?"

"Yea. More likely 'twas done by Gervais or Cedric, or one of their cousins. They are asking us, nay, begging us, to retaliate! When will you give us leave to attack?"

"This feud will be fought fairly," Anslem returned with annoyance. "We were the last to openly attack."

"So it is their turn?" Hugh continued, his voice filled with sarcasm. "Thor! Just because you and Latham Borgsen were once friends is no reason to conduct this battle with honor. Years have passed without bloodshed."

"You are too used to fighting our foreign enemies, Hugh. You have never fought our own before. 'Twill be done with honor. Latham was not to blame for what happened, but he had to stand by his sons and take their side."

"Are you forgetting you lost your only legitimate daughter because of his sons?" Hugh hissed.

"I am not forgetting. As Odin is my witness, the others will pay one day as Edgar did. But there will be no sneak attacks, no foul play. 'Twill be done with honor." Anselm rose from the tub and was quickly wrapped in a woolen robe by the pretty slave girl. "I trust two of their cows were also found dead?"

Hugh grinned and relaxed. "They were."

"Good," Anselm replied. "So 'tis again their move. And now that Heloise can find no fault with me, I will dress and meet you at the hall."

"I was told you returned with captives."

"I did. Seven in all."

"I am curious," Hugh continued. "They say one was a small man with very long black hair. You have enough male slaves. Why bring this one?"

Anselm chuckled, the corners of his eyes crinkling. "The

one you speak of is also a woman. In truth, she is the one they would have wed to your brother."

"Eh? The Lady Brenna? I am eager to see that one."

"She had courage like I have never seen in a woman. She fought us with sword in hand, and wounded Thorne. Her spirit was magnificent to watch."

"I want her."

"What?"

"I said I want her," Hugh replied. "Garrick hates women, and you have Heloise. My wife is timid, as are my slaves. I want a woman with spirit."

"You have not even seen her yet, Hugh," Anselm remarked, his lips turning slightly upward. "This little beauty has more spirit than you would want. She is viciously hostile, filled with bitter hatred."

"Her spirit can be broken," Hugh said, his eyes lighting in anticipation. "I still want her."

"Her spirit need not be broken," Anselm said harshly. "It is my wish to give her to Garrick. She is what he needs to end his own bitterness." He did not add that she was still a virgin, for then Hugh would surely want her, and as first born he had the right. "There is a flame-haired wench with spirit who would be more to your liking. She is better curved, as you like them, and more pliable."

"And if I choose the Lady Brenna?"

" 'Twould please me if you did not, Hugh," Anselm warned.

"We shall see," Hugh replied noncommittally as they left the bathhouse.

The door flew open. Dust swirled, then floated gently in the shaft of sunlight that fell on the dirt floor of the small house. When the prisoners were led out into the yard, all of them shielded their eyes from the glaring sun. They were escorted to the main house, pushed through the open door that allowed the smoke from the fires to escape, and left to stand in the center of the crowded room.

Linnet recognized the men seated at two long tables and on benches against the walls. They were from the ship. Many were gathered at the end of one table, where a board game was being played. A large man she had not seen before was examining a fine gray horse that had been brought into the room with the women. She gasped when she saw that it was Brenna's horse, Willow. If Brenna saw that, there was no telling what she would do. Luckily, she did not. She was staring with undisguised loathing at Anselm the Eager, and did not even glance at the horses when they were led from the room.

Anselm sat at the head of one table. He was served by young girls dressed in rough, undyed wool—slaves, no doubt. Beside him was a woman not much older than Linnet, regally gowned in yellow silk. Next to her was another woman. young and plump, with the same blond hair that most of the people here had.

The tall man who looked Willow over now came to where the prisoners stood. Pushing Linnet aside, he stopped in front of Brenna. He lifted Brenna's face to examine it, just as he had done moments earlier to the horse, but she knocked his hand away with her bound wrists, the fury in her eyes defying him to touch her again.

Brenna smelled the maleness of him, the smell of sweat and horses. He so resembled Anselm the Eager that if she had a knife, she would gladly have cut his throat, and to hell with the consequences. Greedily she eyed the dagger in his wide belt, but his deep laugh drew her eyes back to his.

"By Thor, she is a beauty!"

" 'Tis as I said, Hugh," Anselm replied from his place at the table.

Hugh smirked, and moved from left to right to view her from different angles. Her eyes reflected no fear, even though she knew she was helpless with her wrists bound in front of her—unless she had a knife to clutch in both hands. Brenna was so intent on this thought that she did not notice Hugh had moved closer.

Standing near her so that no one who understood his tongue could hear his words, he whispered in her ear, "I will wipe that bloodthirsty look from your eyes, my lady. I will break the spirit my father so admired."

He could not know that she understood his every word. She felt only contempt for his boast until one arm yanked her to him and his demanding lips crushed hers. His other hand covered her breasts and cruelly squeezed them as he taunted her with his strength. Her arms were useless, trapped between her body and his, but her teeth came down on the probing tongue violating her mouth. He pulled back just in time, and shoved her away from him, so that she fell against the other women.

"Daughter of Hel!" Hugh cursed loudly and came forward to strike her, but was checked by Anselm, who bellowed his name. Hugh lowered his arm and turned on his father accusingly. "She would spill my blood without the sense to know she would die for it!"

"I warned you she is full of hate," Anselm replied.

"Hatred that she would die for. Bah! She is mad, I think. Give her to my brother Garrick, then, as was your wish. He hates women and will take pleasure in abusing this one. Let him use her body as a release for his hate, and see if they do not kill each other. I will take the fiery-haired wench."

"Enough of this talk, Hugh," scolded the woman dressed in yellow silk. "Do you forget your mother and your wife are present?"

"Your pardon, mistress," replied the unabashed Hugh. "I did forget, indeed. I am finished here. You may do my father's bidding now, and question the captives."

"I was not aware I needed my son's permission to do so," the woman retaliated, her tone coldly authoritative.

Loud guffaws came from those listening to the exchange, and Hugh bristled. A warning look from his father stilled his caustic retort. Hugh spread his arms wide. "Your pardon again, mistress. I know better than to duel verbally with you."

Brenna seethed inwardly. She had heard clearly what the bastard Hugh had said about her, just as everyone else who understood him had heard. Give her to Garrick? Let him abuse her with his hatred of women? Well, they would learn soon enough that she would take no abuse. The man she thought she would marry would die if he dared to touch her. God, how she hated them all!

Linnet was watchful, apprehensive. She forced herself not to interfere when the Viking mauled Brenna, hoping that his crude treatment would at least snap Brenna out of her bitter silence. But it did not. She wished to high heavens she could understand what they were saying. If only she had joined Brenna's lessons with Wyndham. Ah, how little did they guess the future then. How could they communicate with their captors and even discover their true circumstances, unless Brenna was willing to speak for them? Only she knew their language.

Linnet's anxieties were dispelled a moment later when the Viking dame in flowing yellow silk left the table and came to stand before them. She was a small, graceful woman with chestnut hair and dark brown, almond-shaped eyes.

"I am Heloise Haardrad. My husband is Anselm the Eager, chief of our clan and the man who brought you here."

Linnet quickly introduced herself and the others, then she asked, "How is it you speak our tongue?"

"Like you, I was brought to this land many years ago, though not under the same circumstances. I was betrothed to Anselm and we married. I am a Christian, as I assume you are."

"Yea, of course!"

Heloise smiled. "But I also worship my husband's gods, to please him. I will help you all I can, but understand that my loyalty is here."

Linnet braced herself to ask the question that was uppermost in all their minds. "What is to become of us?"

"At present, you are my husband's prisoners. 'Tis up to him to decide what to do with you."

"Are we slaves, then?" Cordella asked in a haughty tone, although she had little to be arrogant about.

Heloise raised a brow in Cordella's direction. "You lost your rights when you were captured. I am surprised you need to ask the question. Did you think you would be brought here and set free, given homes and property of your own? Nay, *you* are the property. You will belong to my husband, or whoever he chooses to give you to. I do not particularly like the term slave. I prefer "servant," no different than what you must have had in your own land."

"Our servants were free!" Cordella snapped.

"You may have called them free, but in truth, they were not. And you, my girl, had best learn your place quickly, or 'twill not go well for you."

"She is right, Cordella," Linnet said quietly. "Hold your tongue for once."

Cordella turned in a huff and ignored them. Heloise laughed softly. "I think you and I can become friends, Linnet."

"I would like that," she replied sincerely. At this moment she needed a friend more than anything.

" 'Tis unfortunate that you are here," Heloise continued sympathetically. "But I hope you will all adjust quickly. I do not condone my husband's raiding and returning with prisoners, but I have little say about this part of his life. I realize that you and your family were deceived into thinking there would be an alliance, and I am sorry for this."

"Your husband gave his word!" Cordella interrupted again. "Does a Viking have no honor?"

"Della!"

"I do not blame her for feeling wronged. Yea, my husband has honor, but not for those he considers his enemies. He gave his word falsely to your arranger, the man you sent here. You see, my youngest son, Garrick, was taken prisoner by your people once, and treated inhumanly. My husband has hated you Celts ever since. He had no intention of keeping his word when he gave it. He would never allow our son to marry a Celt."

"Was that man Garrick?" Linnet asked curiously, nodding to the tall Viking. "The one who looked my niece over?"

"Nay, that was my first born, Hugh. Garrick is not here, though 'twould make no difference if he were. There can be no wedding, you understand."

"Yea."

"Garrick knows naught of this. He sailed in the spring, before you sent your man here. I am truly sorry for what has happened, and especially for the deception. If I could change your lot, I would."

"Should you let them hear you say this?"

Heloise laughed. "They cannot understand us. I did not teach my husband my language; I learned his. My husband knows how I feel about taking captives, that I disapprove. As you can see by the servants here, all of whom were taken at one time or another, I cannot stop him. This is just another part of Viking life."

"What will become of my niece?" Linnet asked with deep concern.

"She will be made to serve, like the rest of you," Heloise answered and turned to Brenna. "Do you understand, child?"

Brenna said nothing and Linnet sighed. "She is stubborn and resentful. She will not accept what has happened."

"She will have to," Heloise said gravely. "I will not lie to you. If she proves troublesome, she could be sold at one of the markets far from here, or she could be put to death."

"Nay!" Linnet gasped.

Brenna showed her contempt by glaring hostilely at Heloise before she turned stiffly and walked to the back of the group.

"Do not worry on it yet," Heloise said. "The girl will be given time to adjust. My husband admired her courage; he will not wish to see her come to harm."

Linnet looked worriedly in Brenna's direction. "I fear she will bring harm to herself."

"Take her own life?"

"Nay, seek vengeance. I have never seen such hatred. She has brooded silently ever since we were taken. She will not even speak to me."

"Her bitterness is understandable, but it will only be tolerated for so long."

"You do not understand why she is filled with more hatred than the rest of us," Linnet said quickly. "Her father died the day before the attack, and she has yet to recover from this. She was never in accord with the marriage to your son, but her father gave his word and she would have honored it. So she was prepared to receive her betrothed, not your husband, who attacked us without warning. She saw so much death that day. Her brother-in-law, her servants, cut down before her. She could hear the screams of Cordella and my own when—when . . ."

"I understand. Go on."

"And then Brenna was bested. To understand what this did to her, you have to know that she had never been defeated before. She was her father's only child, raised without her mother, who died giving birth to her. To Angus, her father, she was the son he never had. He knew naught of a girl child. He taught her everything he would have taught a son. That day, when she was defeated, I suppose

54

she felt as if she had failed her father. And then her personal servant, a woman who was like a mother to her, was brutally killed. Brenna screamed hysterically then for the first time in her life. She must feel shame now not only for that, but for being unable to help her people. She has brooded silently ever since."

" 'Tis a shame," Heloise agreed, her dark brown eyes thoughtful. "But she is an intelligent girl, is she not? She will realize that she has no choice but to accept what has befallen her."

"Why should she?" Cordella questioned, having listened quietly for as long as she could. "What is there for her here, or for any of us? But Brenna? Ha! You have not seen pride 'til you have seen hers. She will never accept this enforced slavery. Look at her now. She will not even speak to you, let alone serve you. You will have to kill her first!"

Heloise smiled, her eyes hard as she gazed at Cordella. "Whether she serves or not will not be my concern. She has been given to Garrick and will go to his home. You, on the other hand, fall under my domain, since Hugh has chosen you, and he and his wife live here in my home. Hugh owns you now, but I rule this house, and you will be answerable to me."

Cordella's face turned ashen, but she said no more. She did not care to be under this woman's rule, but she had seen the look the mighty Hugh had given her. Mayhaps all was not lost.

"Will I be allowed to accompany Brenna?" Linnet asked anxiously.

"Nay. My husband desires to keep you for himself. You will stay here also."

Linnet's cheeks burned hotly. "I—I am . . ." She could not finish.

"Do not worry, Linnet. I am not a jealous woman. 'Tis common here that our men will pleasure themselves with their women slaves. I believe that we are not unique in this, that 'tis the same the world over. Some women will not tolerate their husbands' concubines in their homes, but I am not such a one. So rest easy. I still say we shall be friends."

"Thank you."

"As for the rest of you," Heloise said, her voice filled

with authority again, "you will remain in my house for a time, but not for long. When my husband decides, you will be given to friends of his, those who have served him well. I do not think your lot will be as hard as you imagine. In time, all of you will adjust."

Chapter 8

BRENNA was put in a small boat resembling a canoe, and taken further inland. Only one man, Ogden, escorted her, and he had been given explicit instructions from Anselm's wife. The journey was a short one. Soon high cliffs bordered the fjord again, casting the water and the entire valley into murky gloom. Then she saw it; Ulric Haardrad's stone house, perched high up on the cliff, appeared like nature's own extension of the gray rock.

The Viking accompanying Brenna was not pleased with his task. As they approached the wooden landing, he rowed the small craft with increasing speed. He would have preferred, and thought briefly on it, to slit the girl's throat and toss her into the bottomless depths of the fjord; for hadn't she wounded his brother and so caused him untold shame? But then Ogden would have Anselm to answer to—not to mention Garrick, who owned the girl now. And to be honest, there was no honor in killing a woman, let alone one who was bound and helpless. Now she was nothing like the black fox who fought with such cunning against his brother. Still Ogden hated her, this woman who dressed and acted like a man and looked at him with the eyes of a tigress, hot and venomous.

The landing was not directly below the stone house, but further up the coast, where the cliff began its craggy decline. Here Ogden roughly yanked Brenna from the boat and dragged her up a steep, rocky path. The trail was a narrow one made by the slaves who hauled the great stones up to the site Ulric had chosen for his house. At the top was a huge boulder pushed to one side. If need be it could be used to block the way from the fjord. Ogden noted that Ulric's house would make an ideal fortress in case of war.

The house resembled the wooden domiciles of Norway only in one respect: it was windowless. Otherwise it was like the huge stone manors Ogden had seen on the Scottish coast; it had chimneys through which smoke could escape, and a second floor to live in. Rather than facing the sea or the fields behind it, the entrance to the house was on the side, where old, gnarled trees grew. A storage house and livestock sheds, as well as the stable, were behind the house; all were made of wood.

Before he died, Ulric had given this house and a few acres of fertile land to Garrick in Anselm's presence, so there would be no dispute afterward. Anselm had not wanted the house anyway, for its stone walls made it so cold in winter. For Garrick, however, it was an inheritance. Though but small, it was the only one he would receive, since by tradition all Anselm owned would go to his first born, Hugh.

Garrick was not a farmer like Ogden and other free men who had fertile land here, nor was he a fisherman, as most were. He was a hunter, skilled with the arrow and spear, his hunting ground the dense forests bordering his land. He liked to trek to the unpopulated lands further inland, where the lynx and elk abounded. In winter, he was not opposed to sailing north through the warm coastal waters as far as the North Cape, in search of polar bears. As proof of his hunting skill, he had a large cargo of furs gathered over two winters, which he took to trade in the East.

Although Garrick was not a farmer, he allowed his slaves to grow small quantities of produce; thence the onions and peas that graced his table, rye for bread, and barley for the honey mead consumed nightly.

Ogden had stayed a week at Garrick's house the winter before he sailed east. His hospitality was as generous as his father's. Lavish in supplying food and drink, he even gave Ogden a pretty slave girl to warm his bed, which sorely needed it in that cold house.

Ogden liked Garrick, and decided thoughtfuly that the young man did not need this gift from his father. This girl would be a thorn in Garrick's side, a veritable she-devil who would like as not slit his throat some night while he slept. Still, she was Garick's problem, and, for the moment, his housekeeper's.

The entrance to the house was open to let in the breath of summer. The weather was already turning cooler, a sign that the season of the midnight sun was drawing to a close and making ready for the long winter night, when the sun deserted her northern peoples completely.

"Ho! Mistress Yarmille!" Ogden bellowed as he stamped into the hall, tugging Brenna behind him as he would a roped cow.

"Ogden!" The surprised greeting came from the opening at the end of the hall.

This area had been closed off years earlier with a make-shift wall, for Ulric in his old age could not tolerate smoke from the cooking fires, and had ordered the cooking done behind this wall. Others had tried to do this, too, but not for long, for the warmth of the cooking fires was more desirable than the absence of smoke.

Yarmille stood by the opening, gowned in soft blue linen, a gold band securing her straw-colored hair in a tight bun at the nape of her neck, "I did not know Anselm had returned."

"Just this day," Ogden replied. "The feast is in progress now."

"Really?" Yarmille raised a tawny brow. This woman had been a beauty in her day, but no traces remained now that she neared two score and ten years. It was a wonder that this was so, since she had not led an overly hard life. "I trust the raid went well?"

Ogden grunted and released his hold on Brenna. "As well as any. There was treasure for all, and seven captives returned with us. One man went to Valhalla, praise his luck! My brother was wounded, though not badly." Ogden did not say how. "I believe Anselm will give him one of the captives, and one will go to the widow of the dead warrior."

"And this one?" Yarmile nodded toward Brenna, who stood erect, her raven locks falling about her shoulders in disarray. "He gave her to you?"

Ogden shook his head. "To Garrick. She was the one offered to him as bride."

That story had traveled far. "The Lady Brenna? Well, well. So Anselm kept his promise." At the Viking's questioning look, she explained, "I was there after that fool arranger left. I believe Anselm's words were, 'A bride is offered, a bride Garrick will get, though no wedding will take place.' "

Ogden laughed, for he knew of Anselm's hatred for the Celts, and that he would never allow such an alliance. "A bride with no wedding vows—I like that. But I doubt Garrick will."

"How so? She looks pretty enough. In something other than those awful leggings, she should be quite beautiful."

"Mayhaps, mistress. But her beauty does not disguise her loathing."

Yarmille moved to the girl and turned her face toward the door to see better in the light, but Brenna snapped her head away, not even deigning to meet the woman's eyes.

Yarmille frowned disapprovingly. "A stubborn one, eh?"

"To be sure," Ogden answered sourly. "She has the look of a runaway, and will no doubt try to bolt at first chance. She is a fighter too, this one; in truth, she is trained in warfare. So be careful, mistress."

"What am *I* supposed to do with her?"

Ogden shrugged. "I have done as instructed by Mistress Heloise. I have delivered the girl to you. She is in your care now, since you run Garrick's house in his absence."

"This I do not need," Yarmille snapped irritably. "When Garrick left he took almost all of his slaves to sell, leaving me with only a few to care for this iceberg of a house. And now I have this one who will have to be closely watched."

"Mistress Heloise suggested you leave the girl be until Garrick returns and decides how he will handle her. She will come herself in a week's time to see if the *lady* has accepted her lot."

"Heloise come here? Ha!" Yarmille laughed. "She must

be most concerned about the girl if she will venture here when Garrick is not home."

Ogden knew of the dislike the two women had for each other. Both had given Anselm a son. "My task is completed. Will you return with me to the feast, mistress? You have been invited by Anselm."

Yarmile's light blue eyes lit up with pleasure. "I will." She walked to the opening which led to the cooking area and the stairs. "Janie, come here."

A moment later, a tiny young woman dressed in a rough woolen shift appeared. "Mistress?"

"Janie, take this girl with you. Bathe her, feed her, then put her to bed in the master's chamber—for now. Later I will decide where to put her permanently."

"Yea, mistress," the woman answered, looking curiously at Brenna.

"Now, Ogden, if you will take this girl up to Garrick's chamber and watch her until a slave comes to guard her, I would be grateful."

For Brenna, the week slipped by like the flight of a butterfly, ever so slowly. She had no awareness of time. The room she was kept in was large and cold, with no windows, and two doors that remained closed. Her anger reached an unholy state when she was tied to the large bed in her room after the first day, for the haughty Yarmille decided it was a waste of manpower for a slave to guard her.

Brenna was untied from the bed only to eat, bathe and relieve herself, but at these times a male slave accompanied Janie, though he was left outside the room. For the first two days Brenna refused to eat, knocking the tray of food to the floor in a burst of rage. She finally spoke, screaming curses of the devil that made Janie turn pale and sent her fleeing from the room, leaving the young male slave to tie Brenna to the bed. She fought and cursed him, too, but could do little with her wrists still bound.

After the third day, Brenna felt weak from lack of food and began to eat again, though grudgingly. She continued to be withdrawn, and ignored Janie when the girl came. The two meals she received daily were widely spaced. One was served before Janie began her duties; the other after she was finished for the day. During this long interval, Brenna was frustrated nearly to tears with her inability to move; her fury was not helped by her hunger, which grew as the day wore on.

She felt guilty, then maddened, because she was such a burden to poor Janie, who had to wait on her. She knew the girl worked hard the whole day long, and since Brenna's arrival toiled even harder. Janie had kind words for her in the morning, but by the end of the day she was exhausted and as silent as Brenna. Brenna could hardly blame the girl for her abruptness at the day's end. Though she had yet to make any overtures to Janie, she felt pity for her, an unusual emotion for Brenna.

Janie spoke Brenna's tongue, but had also, by necessity, taught herself Norwegian. She had not mastered it fully yet, but knew enough to understand her orders without having to receive a beating. Brenna assumed Janie had also been taken captive, though how long ago she couldn't guess and wouldn't ask, for she resented the girl even though she knew Janie was only following Yarmille's orders that Brenna be kept bound. That her own fate was destined to be the same as Janie's was a certainty. She could never adjust to a life of servitude—she knew that. She would deal with that when the time came. If only it would come and she would be released!

Her thoughts turned to Garrick Haardrad—once her betrothed, now her master. She had often wondered about him in the past. She knew that he was young, having seen but twenty-five winters. That he had not married yet was her misfortune, for it drew Fergus to his clan to arrange a wedding that was never meant to be. She also knew now, after listening to his brother Hugh, that for some reason he hated women. This she could count as a blessing, she hoped. It might mean that he would leave her be, or he might cruelly mistreat her. She prayed for the first possibility, that his hatred would make him shun her. But if it was the other way, what then? Bound as she was now, she would be completely at his mercy. Beaten, unable to protect herself, perhaps killed. Damn Yarmille for her precautions!

After a week, Heloise came as promised. Brenna recognized her voice and that of Yarmille as they approached the room. As they entered, Heloise stopped short when she saw Brenna trussed on the bed, but Yarmille continued to walk into the room.

"You see," Yarmille said, her voice condescending. "As I told you, she is but a nuisance."

Heloise came closer, her eyes cold. "Is this the way you treat my son's property, to tie her up like an animal?" she demanded angrily.

"Ogden said she had the look of a runaway," Yarmille explained. "I only made sure she would be here on Garrick's return."

"Runaway?" Heloise shook her head in exasperation. "Where would she go? There is no place. Nor do we know when Garrick will return. It could be months yet. Would you keep the girl like this indefinitely?"

"I—"

"Look at her!" Heloise said sharply. "She is pale and has grown thinner in only a week's time. Have you no sense, woman? This girl will be a valuable asset to my son. He can sell her at market for a high price, or he can keep her for his own pleasure, but he will not appreciate the way you have taken her under your care in his absence."

Yarmille could see the truth in this and she paled slightly. It would not do for the girl to waste away during her confinement. At once she became furious with the girl for putting her in this predicament, but she hid this successfully beneath the tight smile she gave Heloise.

"You are right. I will see to the girl myself henceforth. This one will greatly please Garrick. She may even make him forget about Morna, do you not agree?"

"That, old friend, is doubtful," Heloise replied stiffly before she turned to Brenna. "You will be untied, child, but you must not attempt to escape from here. Do you understand?" she asked softly. "There is nowhere for you to go."

Brenna could not respond to the kind words, for they offered little hope, especially after these two women had just discussed her as if she were a piece of property. She turned her head away.

Heloise sat down on the bed. "This stubborn silence does you no good, Brenna. I had hoped you would be at least a little reconciled to your new home by now. Anselm thought you would please Garrick. If you make the effort, 'twill go well for you."

Brenna would not face her, but Heloise did not give up. "If you have fears, speak to me of them. Mayhaps I can relieve them. Brenna?" She hesitated, then added, "My son will not be difficult to serve. He is not demanding or cruel. Mayhaps you will even like him and find happiness here."

Brenna's head snapped around, her eyes glowing like polished silver. "Never!" she hissed, surprising both women with the force of her tone and the fact that she did indeed have a tongue. "I have no fear, mistress. 'Tis you who will have reason to fear, for you will rue the day you tried to make a slave of me! Blood will flow from it, no doubt that of your precious Garrick!"

"What did she say?" Yarmille demanded.

Heloise shook her head and sighed. "She is still overly bitter, but 'twill not last. She will soon find she has no alternative but to bend—a little, anyway."

"And in the meantime?" Yarmille asked.

Heloise looked at Brenna thoughtfully, meeting her defiant gaze. "Will you behave if you are given the freedom of this room?"

"I make no promises!" Brenna retorted hotly and turned away again.

"Can you not be reasonable?"

Brenna would say no more, and Heloise gave up at last and left. Yarmille, however, remained.

"Well, Brenna Carmarham, now that her highness has departed, there is no need to free you just yet. This eve will be soon enough," Yarmille said woodenly, though she spoke for her own benefit, never dreaming that Brenna understood her perfectly. "Tomorrow you will be given extra food to put some meat on your bones, and taken out to air —just like a rug, you might say." She laughed at her own jest before she walked out of the room.

Brenna would have killed the woman if she had a sword in hand and was not still hindered by the cursed ropes. Of all the hypocritical, vile, loathsome creatures! Later she would be freed, at least, and on the morrow she would make plans to escape. They were fools to trust her!

Chapter 9

THE great Viking longship moved up the fjord like a huge dragon with oars for wings, and floated peacefully to its home. The men wished to cheer and make a ruckus as they passed Anselm's landing, but Garrick stopped them. Though the midnight sun hovered like a large ball of fire on the horizon, it was still the middle of night, and nearly everyone would be sleeping soundly. There would be time aplenty on the morrow for revelry and the greetings of old friends. But for now Garrick wanted to be home, to sleep the remainder of the night in his own bed.

The men would stay the night at Garrick's house. In the morning they would go on to their homes, collect their families and return to Garrick's for a gala celebration. Exhaustion lay heavily on them all, for they had fought a storm that ended only hours earlier.

Two men elected to stay on the ship, since the cargo would not be unloaded that night. The others followed Garrick up the narrow cliff path, carrying only essentials with them. The house was dark and silent, for the weather was not yet cold enough to leave fires burning through the night. Sunlight streamed in through the open door, giving them ample light to make their way about without banging into the long tables and benches which filled the hall.

Garrick made his way up the darkened stairs with little difficulty, for he knew this house well, having spent a good part of his youth here with his grandfather. On the second floor were four rooms: his own, the large master chamber on one side of the stairs; a small sewing room on the other side; across the wide corridor, a guest room furnished with two large beds; and the room given to Yarmille, his housekeeper. At the end of the corridor at the rear of the house was a door which opened onto stone steps leading outside. The door was there mainly to let in the fresh air of summer, but Garrick was rarely home at that time to enjoy it.

He opened the door now to light the corridor, then returned to the hall for some of his men, Perrin included, to show them to the guest room. The others would bed down in the hall on benches, hard beds being more to their liking.

Finally Garrick entered his own chamber. Here the backless couch, reportedly from the Orient, and the two thronelike chairs he had purchased at Hedeby would be brought. At present, the spacious room was poorly furnished by only his huge bed, a single high-backed chair, and a large coffer. No rugs, save an old bearskin, warmed the cold floor, and no coverings adorned the walls. This would be rectified once the cargo from the ship was unloaded, for Garrick had purchased extravagantly for his home in order to give the cold stone chambers some semblance of comfort.

Scant rays from the corridor lit the room. Garrick made his way to the large door opposite, which opened onto a small stone balcony. A majestic view met his eyes. The fjord lay far below in shadowy splendor. To the west was the deep blue of the ocean; the dark purple and gray of the mountains spread to the east. But most stunning of all was the orange fireball of the sun which hung low on the horizon.

Garrick stood there for many minutes before he again felt the exhaustion of his body. Leaving the balcony door open, which flooded the room with light, he crossed the chamber to close the door before turning to his bed. There, on the white ermine spread made by his mother from skins he brought her, lay the small form of a girl curled into a ball, looking ever so tiny in the center of the large bed.

Garrick stopped in his tracks. Her long black hair fanned out on the white ermine and hid her face. Her figure was obscure, wrapped in a woolen nightdress many sizes too large, so that he could not begin to guess the age of this sleeping creature.

Yet he was not curious, only angry that his bed was not available to him when he so greatly desired its comfort. He turned and stalked from his room. He went straight to Yarmille's chambers, entered without knocking and shook the woman roughly from her sleep.

"Mistress, wake up!"

Yarmille opened cloudy eyes to stare at the tall figure looming over her small bed. His face was in the shadows, but she knew him instantly. "Garrick! You have returned!"

"Obviously," he answered dryly, the anger unmistakable in his tone. "And to find you have sorely overstepped your authority!"

"I—what are you talking about?" she asked indignantly, pulling the embroidered coverlet up about her neck. "You accuse me falsely."

Garrick's brows narrowed. "By what right do you allow a guest in my chamber when the room allotted for such lay empty?"

"A guest?" It was a moment before she made the connection, and then she laughed softly. "Nay, she is not a guest."

Garrick was close to losing all patience. "Explain, Yarmille, and keep it brief. Who is the female?"

"She is yours. Your mother bid me take her in hand, so I did not put her with the other women. And I knew that when you returned, the guest room would be put to use. I did not think you would mind over much if she shared your chamber."

Garrick stiffened in frustration. "First, I do mind!" he said harshly, not caring who heard him now. "Secondly, what do you mean, she is mine?"

Yarmille was not used to seeing Garrick this angered. She should have remembered his recent dislike of women, and put the girl someplace else.

"Your father raided in the British Isles this summer and

returned with seven captives. This girl was one of them and your father has given her to you. She was the daughter of a lord, and thought she would be your bride."

"My bride!" he exploded.

" 'Tis only what she and her people thought, Garrick," Yarmille added quickly. "Anselm played them falsely, to make the raid go easier. 'Tis a long story that I am sure Anselm will be pleased to retell."

"What is wrong with the girl that Hugh should not take her?" Garrick asked, knowing that his brother always took the choice females for himself now that Anselm no longer kept the young and pretty ones.

"The girl is a hellish vixen. You must be in your father's disfavor for him to saddle you with such a gift. She is a fighter, I have been told, and thirsts for blood."

No doubt she would also be hard on the eye, and this was why Hugh did not want her. Why *would* his father give him such a girl?

Garrick sighed, too tired to ponder further. "She is sleeping, so you may leave her be for now. But on the morrow you will move her elsewhere, I care not where."

"She will attempt to run away, Garrick. I cannot leave her in the women's quarters while they tend their duties. 'Tis too easy for her to sneak off from there."

"By Thor, woman! I said I do not care what you do with her, but she cannot stay in my chamber!"

With that, Garrick stalked back to his room.

The cool breeze ruffled the hair on Brenna's cheek and caused her to wake. She blinked sleepily at the sunlight filling the room and moaned. Morning already? It seemed as if only a few hours had passed since she had been untied and warned not to leave the room. She assumed a guard had been posted outside her door, but it did not matter. She was not ready to leave yet. Her body was still sore from the long confinement, and she knew she was in no condition to brave the unknown. She must get her strength back, and then see what avenues of escape were open to her. It would be foolish to leave without knowing something of the land.

She got up and closed both doors, sealing the room in darkness again, then crawled back into the bed. She had almost drifted back to sleep when she heard a voice raised

in anger. A few moments passed, then the door opened
and a very tall young man walked into the room.

Brenna was instantly alert, every nerve in her body at-
tuned to danger. She did not move, but watched the Viking
warily through half-closed eyes, prepared to dash for his
sword if the need presented itself.

The stranger did not look in her direction or move toward the bed, but went to the chair against the wall and
started to remove his clothing in a rough, angry manner.
First the sword, then a short knife, then the sleeveless tunic
was thrown on the chair seat. Next a leg was raised and
the foot placed on the chair to unlace the leather garters
and remove the soft skin boot.

Brenna scanned the man's features with eyes that seemed
almost possessive. A man this pleasing to look upon she
had never seen before. Long, wavy hair of a golden color
curled about exceptionally wide shoulders. The nose was
long and straight, the chin firm and smooth. The strong
bare arms were corded with thick muscles, as were the
broad chest and back, muscles that rippled and danced with
each movement. Blond curls covered the chest, ending at
the tight, flat abdomen. Narrow hips led to strong, tapered
thighs. The whole body spoke of strength and power. It
was superb, marred only by a few minor scars on the lower
torso. Such a body was a dangerous weapon in itself.
Brenna felt a strange and unknown sensation course
through her.

The man started to unfasten his trousers, and Brenna
stiffened. One part of her wanted to see the rest of this
beautiful physique, but the practical side of Brenna knew
no good could come from this. Fortunately, the man
glanced at the bed and changed his mind.

Brenna held her breath. She had yet to think about what
the Viking's presence here meant. Why he should come in
here and make as if to prepare for bed was beyond her.
She did not consider that this might be Garrick Haardrad.

The man turned now as if puzzled, and stared at the
balcony door. Then he moved to open it again. After this,
he closed the other door, shutting them in the room together, and returned to the bed.

Brenna no longer pretended to be asleep, for she had a
feeling he knew she was awake. She rolled to the end of

the bed, for it was placed in a corner with one side against the wall, and she needed an avenue for flight. She crouched there, her long tresses flowing about the woolen nightdress, her body tense.

Both of them froze when their eyes met and locked for a long moment. Brenna felt as if mesmerized by those aqua-colored eyes, so light, a gentle blending of both green and blue. Annoyed, she found she had been holding her breath, and released it.

"I think you have been playing a deceiving game, wench." His voice was deep, neither angry nor gentle. "You do not seem a wild vixen intent on escape, but a frightened child—though cunning mayhaps, for your game has gotten you a comfortable room."

She laughed boldly. "Frightened? Of you, Viking? Your first description was accurate."

"You are still here," he pointed out.

"Only because I was kept tied to this bed until last eve," she replied.

A tight smile formed on his lips. " 'Tis a convenient story, but one that can easily be proved false."

Brenna's dark brows narrowed. She was not accustomed to being accused of lying. Like a cat, she jumped from the bed and landed facing him, feet apart and arms akimbo.

"Know this, Viking!" she said furiously, looking at him with dark, steady eyes. "I am Brenna Carmarham and I do not lie. Were it not the way I said, then you can be sure I would not be here now!"

A glimmer of amusement came into Garrick's eyes as he watched this proud beauty. He ignored the implication of her words, and took them as an empty threat.

"Since Yarmille seems at a loss to know what to do with you, 'tis fortunate that I have come to take you in hand," he said lightly.

"How so?" she asked, raising a brow. Before he could reply she added suspiciously, "Who are you, Viking?"

"Your owner, so I have been informed."

Brenna gasped. "Nay, I will not be owned!"

Garrick shrugged. This was no meek slave he had been given: that at least was obvious. "You have little choice in the matter."

"I—said—nay!" Brenna shouted slowly, her entire being

rebelling against the idea. Flashing eyes reflected her outrage. "Never!"

Impatience crept into his voice. "I will not debate the issue."

She surprised him when she replied haughtily, "Nor will I."

Garrick laughed despite himself. Never had he had a slave such as this one. Such glorious jet-black hair, almost blue in its richness, such creamy white skin—and a face that was a vision. He was almost tempted to inspect her further, to see what lay beneath the unbecoming nightdress.

Brenna watched him warily as he sat down on the bed and ran long fingers through his wavy hair. So this was Garrick Haardrad, the man she was supposed to have married, the man who now assumed he owned her. He spoke her own tongue, which surprised her. But then, so did his mother, who must have taught him.

She wished he had not returned so soon, and that she had had time to assess her situation first. She didn't know whether to fear this man or not. He was decidedly pleasing to look upon, and she found herself almost wishing that things had turned out differently, that she was here to be his bride, not his slave. Anselm had ruined that, and she could hate him all the more for it.

"What do you mean, you will take me in hand?" she asked.

"I do not tolerate useless property. My slaves earn their keep one way or another, or I dispose of them."

The very coldness of his voice, coupled with the heartless words, sent a shiver down her back. "You would attempt to sell me?"

"Attempt? You imply I do not have the right."

"You do not!" she snapped, unnerved by his callousness. "I told you I will not be owned."

"Odin help me!" Garrick implored in exasperation, then turned a stormy eye on her. "You will desist, mistress, lest I am tempted to prove the issue!"

She started to ask how, but decided quickly that she would rather not know. She would not concede, but since he had made no demands on her as yet, she could let the matter pass for now.

"Very well, Garrick Haardrad," she said matter-of-factly.

He looked at her suspiciously, not sure whether she relented because of his threat, or because she was his. If he was not so exhausted, he would not have put up with her haughtiness this far. This slave most assuredly would need taming. He realized he might enjoy the effort. This surprised him. It had been a long time since he had felt an instant attraction to any female. He wondered if it was her beauty or her proud defiance which intrigued him most. He wished now he were not so utterly exhausted. But no matter. He could wait. She would be here when he was ready for her.

"You may resume your sleep, mistress," he said tiredly. "We can discuss your position in the morning."

She turned baffled eyes towards the balcony. " 'Tis morning now."

"Nay, 'tis the middle of the night, wench, and I am sorely in need of sleep."

"I am not blind, Viking," she replied tartly. "I can see the sunlight clearly."

He had lost the will to argue. He peeled back the ermine spread and lay beneath it. "We are far in the north. Our summer has no night as you know it, our winter no day."

Now she recalled her lessons with Wyndham. He had told her that the sun did not set during the summer here, rose for but a few hours during winter, and for a while not at all. At the time she thought he was just spinning wild tales to make her lessons more interesting.

She looked at Garrick on the bed, his eyes already closed. "Where am I to sleep then?"

He did not open his eyes to answer. "I have never shared my bed before, but I suppose I can make an exception this once."

"Your generosity is not welcome!" she retorted. "I will not sleep with you."

"Suit yourself, mistress. I'll wager the floor will not be to your liking, though."

She held back the curse that was on her lips and started toward the door. His raised voice stopped her long before she reached it.

"You do not have my permission to leave this room, Mistress Brenna!"

She swung back to face him, her eyes dangerously wide. "Your permission? I did not ask it!"

He propped himself up on one elbow. "Nay, but henceforth you will."

"You insufferable oaf!" she snapped irately. "Has not one word I said entered your muddled head? I will not be told what to do by—"

"Cease your prattling, girl!" he commanded. "Loki must be laughing at the fates that gave you to me. You are sadly mistaken if you think I want to share my bed with you, but I can see no other way this night if I am to get any sleep."

She let the insult pass. "Have you no other rooms in this house?"

"Yea, but they are taken. My house is full of men, mistress—those who returned with me. I am sure they would not mind you stumbling upon them in the dark, but your screams for release would not aid my sleep."

"The screams of your men, Viking, not mine," she replied.

He sighed loudly. "You greatly overestimate yourself, wench. Now give me peace and come to bed."

Brenna suppressed another retort and approached the bed slowly. It *was* more appealing than the floor, she admitted to herself. She crawled onto it and lay next to the wall, a good two feet away from the Viking. Indeed, the ermine spread that he lay under, and she on top of, was like a wall between them.

A moment later she heard his deep, even breathing. Sleep evaded Brenna for a long while.

Chapter 10

BRENNA was rudely awakened when Yarmille burst into the room. "Wake up! Wake up, girl, before he returns and finds you still abed."

Brenna raised her head and saw that Garrick was no longer beside her. Then she looked at the stern, hard-faced woman standing by the bed and shot her a look of contempt. She wondered what the woman would do if she attacked her. Probably run screaming to her master, and she had yet to judge his merit—to learn whether or not she had need to be wary of him.

"Be quick, girl, and dress yourself," Yarmille continued, handing Brenna a rough woolen shift. "Garrick no longer wants you in his room. To be sure, he is not pleased at all with you. 'Tis no wonder, with your evil eye."

Brenna gave her a piercing look, but said nothing. She had decided to continue to pretend ignorance of their language. If they spoke in her presence believing she could not understand them, she might be able to gain useful information. It was difficult to act thus, when already her lips were burning to snap this woman's head off, but she would try.

Yarmille started for the door and motioned for Brenna

to follow. Sounds of revelry drifted up from the lower floor as they passed the stairs, then entered a small room on the other side. When Yarmille lit several whale oil cups for light, Brenna saw that she was in a sewing room, where all manner of things were made.

The chamber was not so different from the sewing room at home, though Brenna had never spent time there. Her curious eyes took in the yarn reels weighted with soapstone, a loom for rug making, wooden boards for weaving ribbons, long-toothed combs and shears. Piles of animal skins were stacked high in one corner, and dyes sat on a shelf. This was a woman's room, and Brenna felt completely lost.

"Garrick has gone to fetch his father here, but he was most adamant that you remain in this room and not leave it," Yarmille said, making signs to explain the words she spoke. "I have much to do below to prepare for the feast, so I cannot stay to watch over you. Here." She crossed to a large loom in the corner, on which sat a crude, half-finished rug. She made it clear that Brenna was to work on it. "This should keep you busy."

"It shall rot with mold before I touch it," Brenna replied in her own tongue, a smile curving her soft lips.

"Good, good," Yarmille said, returning a tight smile. "Garrick seemed to think you would give me trouble, but I think not. You will make yourself useful, and all will go well." She turned to go, then added sternly, "You stay here—stay—here." Then she left, closing the door behind her.

Brenna looked menacingly at the rug loom, then said contemptuously, "Humph! If she thinks she will force me to do woman's work, that old hag will have more trouble than she can handle."

Brenna rummaged idly around the room. She found several strips of wide leather and wove them together to fashion a crude belt for herself. Then she braided her hair in a long single plait which fell to her hips, and interlaced it with a thin strip of leather to hold it in place.

The sounds coming from the lower floor reminded her of home, when her father entertained guests. This recalled her grief. Until now, anger and frustration had forced it below the surface. The memory of her father's death and the bloody scene she witnessed at home only increased her outrage.

"Oh, father, you were a fool," she whispered. "You drew them to us with your offer. You sought to save us, but you have destroyed us instead."

Brenna would not cry again. She would harbor her grief deep inside, but she would not moan over it, for she had other things to occupy her thoughts.

She firmly resolved that she could not stay here. Somehow she must find a way to leave this Godforsaken land and return to her home. She would need time to learn the way of the land, and to discover a way to escape. She hoped for revenge also, and would be more than pleased if she could accomplish both.

Her thoughts unwillingly turned to the Viking. Garrick Haardrad was a puzzle. He had no part in the deception played on her people, yet he posed the greatest threat to her. In his mind he owned her and could do with her as he pleased. That she would not allow this, he would find out.

This tall, virile man did not look on her with lust, and this, though a bit disconcerting, was a blessing. Brenna knew he expected her to make herself useful. If only she could think of something she would not mind doing, she would have no difficulty staying here for a while, and this would buy her the time she needed. But what was there for her to do?

Brenna opened the door quietly. She supposed if she left the sewing room, she would incur Yarmille's wrath. But then, she could always plead ignorance, saying she did not understand Yarmille's instructions.

The sounds from the lower floor grew louder. She wondered if Garrick had returned yet. If so, then Anselm would be there. That man she would take immense pleasure in destroying, just as he had destroyed her people. Poor Fergus and Wyndham; Dunstan, who had been reluctant to fight; and sweet, dear Alane, who had been like a mother to Brenna—all dead. Not by Anselm's hand, certainly, for he stood at the hall entrance and only watched the bloody battle, but he was responsible nonetheless. Besides, it was he who cut her treasured sword in two, rendering her helpless for the first time in her young life. Yea, Anselm must die. She would find a way.

Brenna stepped into the wide corridor and closed the door so that no one would know she had left the room. At the end of the passage another door opened to the outside, and she headed that way. Her eyes scanned the buildings below, but no one was about. In the far distance she could see the brilliant blue of the ocean; a cloak of diamonds seemed to shimmer on its surface. To the left was the fjord and the meadows that extended from the opposite bank. On the downward slope to the right were fields and forests; small houses occasionally dotted the landscape.

Brenna considered going down to the fjord to see if a ship lay there. She would most assuredly need a ship when she was ready to leave, but how could she sail it alone? Perhaps she could hide on one when it left to raid her homeland. That would not be until spring. Could she wait that long?

Brenna descended the stairs and walked briskly to the small buildings behind the large stone house. The grunts of animals met her ears, and she entered one building whose doors were wide open. It was a stable, with four fine horses inside.

Brenna was delighted. A magnificent black stallion caught her eye and she walked over to him, then gasped in alarm when she saw an old man rubbing the beast down.

The old man straightened up, groaning, a hand pressed to his back. A full beard covered his face. It was streaked heavily with gray, as was his sandy-colored hair. Mellow brown eyes regarded her intently.

"And who might you be, lass?" he asked in her own tongue.

"Brenna, Brenna Carmarham. Do you work here?" she questioned as she put a hand out gently for the horse to smell.

"Yea, almost two score years now I've tended the horses," he replied.

"Does no one help you?"

He shook his head. "Not since the master took most of us to sell when he sailed east. He left me behind since I am too old to bring a goodly price."

"You speak of Garrick, the Viking?" she asked. "Is he the one you call master?"

"Yea. He's a good lad. I served his grandfather before him," the old man said with pride.

"How can you speak kindly of the man who owns you?" she demanded.

"I am treated well, lass. Garrick is an ambitious young-blood trying to make his way in a hurry, but he is a fair master to us all."

Brenna did not pursue the subject. "Are these the only horses?"

"Nay, there are a half dozen out to pasture. And three others were borrowed by Garrick's friends, those who sailed with him and have gone to collect their families for the feast. These here," he pointed to the others horses in the stable, "they belong to Anselm Haardrad, who just came with his family." He rubbed the stallion's flanks. "A finer animal than this one I have never seen."

"Yea, he is," Brenna readily agreed. She looked with longing at the sleek animal. The man gently wiped the stallion's back. The horse had obviously just come from a run.

"The master brought him home with him. Found him in Hedeby, he said. A fat purse this one cost him, to be sure."

Brenna nodded, but her thoughts were no longer on the great steed. So Garrick was at the house, and Anselm with him. No doubt his brother Hugh was there also, that vulgar animal who had dared to maul her before all.

A frown creasing her brow, Brenna walked to the stable door and stared apprehensively at the stone house. How much time did she have? Was he looking for her already, or would he even bother, thinking she was safely tucked away in that sewing room? And why should he make the effort? He already showed that he had no interest in her, that she was only a nuisance to him. Even Yarmille said she did not please Garrick.

Brenna preferred it this way. She must keep out of the way and not draw attention to herself.

She walked back. "What do they call you?" she asked the old man, who was still grooming the stallion with tender care.

"Erin McCay."

"Well, Erin, do you know the girl Janie?" she questioned, her smile warm.

"That I do. A pretty lass, Janie."

"Where can I find her now? She took care of me when I was confined, but I was ungracious and needs must make amends."

"You were confined?" He looked at her curiously. "So! You be the one the tongues are wagging over, Garrick's new—"

"Yea!" Brenna cut him short, stopping him before he spoke the word she detested.

"And they have released you?"

She nodded. "They have. Now, whereabouts is Janie?"

"The lass is at the big house. She will be busy all the day and most of the night, serving the feast."

Brenna frowned. "This feast. How long will it go on?"

Erin smiled amiably. "It may last for days."

"What?"

He chuckled. "Aye. There is much to celebrate. The master has returned a wealthy man, and the family is reunited again. Truly there is much to celebrate."

A look of disgust crossed her features. Was she to be tucked away from sight all this time? Why did Garrick not want her to be seen?

"May I help you, Erin?" she suddenly pleaded.

"Nay, 'tis a man's work."

Brenna refrained from debating this and asked instead, "If I obtain Garrick's permission, will you let me work with you here in the stable?"

He raised a brow. "You know horses, do you?"

"Aye," she grinned, "As well as you, I'll wager." She was silent a moment; then in a soft voice she continued, "I rode every day when I lived in my father's home—out through our fields, over the streams and stone walls and into the forest. How free I felt . . . then." She stopped, and a look of great sadness passed over her face. She shook it off and looked once again at Erin. "If I work with you in the stables, will you let me ride the horses?"

"Aye, lassie. Nothing would please me more. But I must secure the permission of the master. Otherwise I can do naught."

"I will speak to him, then."

"You had best wait until the feast is finished. The master

will be well into his cups by now and may not remember your request or his answer."

She would prefer to have it done with, but perhaps Erin was right.

"So be it. I will wait."

"And, lassie, I suggest you remain away from the hall 'til the guests have all gone. 'Twill not go well for you if you are seen."

Curiosity made her eyes sparkle. First Garrick left instructions that she should stay in that small room. Now this old man warned her to stay out of sight.

"What is wrong with me that I should not be seen?"

"Brenna, lass, you must know you are a comely wench. These Vikings are a lusty lot, with an eye for a fair maid such as you. The master is generous with his female slaves. His friends need not even ask permission to have one of his wenches, for his hospitality is well known."

"You cannot be serious!" Brenna gasped, appalled.

" 'Tis true, lass. At one particularly boisterous affair, a poor wench was tumbled before all, right there on the floor of the hall."

Brenna's eyes opened wide; they were filled with repulsion. "Garrick allowed it?"

"He would have stopped that form of entertainment, but he was passed out on the table—or so the story made the rounds—thoroughly besotted."

"It happened nonetheless?"

"Aye, so take care, lass. I would not see the same happen to you."

"Have no fear, Erin. *I* would not allow it!"

The old man shook his head doubtfully as he watched her walk away.

Chapter 11

GARRICK sat at the head of a long table. His father was on his left, facing the room, and his mother sat on his right. His brother Hugh was also there, his plump wife by his side. Around the rest of the table were Garrick's closest friends, those who had sailed with him. And at the foot of the table sat his half-brother Fairfax.

Garrick eyed his brothers thoughtfully. Although he resembled his older brother in height and build, he and his younger brother had in common only their eyes, which were like those of their grandfather, Ulric. Fairfax was less than a year younger than Garrick, but he was a good head shorter; in that regard he took after his mother, Yarmille.

Garrick and Hugh enjoyed the normal rivalry that exists between brothers, even if it was sometimes a bit too earnest. Still, the bond of brotherhood was strong between them. With Fairfax, Garrick enjoyed a different relationship, of companionable friendship, just like the one he shared with Perrin, his closest friend.

Between Hugh and Fairfax, however, there was genuine dislike, and tensions were usually high when they were in the same room together. Hugh begrudged Fairfax their father's love, and Fairfax reacted to that animosity as any man would, with equal hostility.

Garrick, unlike Fairfax, had gained Ulric's admiration and thus this house and surrounding lands. Fairfax had nothing but his mother's small house and a fishing boat. It was a wonder the youngest brother was not bitter. His life was a hard one, and each day he worked to ensure he would survive a little longer. Yet Garrick knew he preferred it this way. Fairfax enjoyed the simple life of a fisherman.

The *skald* finished a humorous song of Loki's exploits, to which he added mischievous antics of his own making, and left the crowd roaring its approval. Even Anselm had tears in his eyes from laughing so hard.

Heloise leaned close to her son when the noise died down somewhat and whispered teasingly, "You know, Garrick, your tale of the Slavic tribe you encountered was almost as amusing as that one. Are you sure you did not dress up the truth some little bit?"

"For shame, woman!" Anselm roared, having overheard her. "My son does not need to embellish his tales as I do." Then he laughed at his own jest.

"Nay. With you, 'tis not known where the truth ends and the tale begins," Heloise retorted, then added thoughtfully, "As with your tale of the Celtic girl. I wonder now if all you said was true."

Anselm scowled across the table at her. " 'Twas true, mistress! I did not need to elaborate *that* tale."

Garrick looked on curiously. He had related his travels at length. But he had yet to ask about that stubborn wench he had found in his bed the night before.

"How is the girl, Garrick?" his mother asked. "I saw her but yesterday and she was still so bitter. She would hardly speak to me at all."

"Well, she has found her tongue, I'm sorry to say."

Anselm chuckled at this. "So you have tasted a bit of her spirit, eh?"

Garrick turned to his father. "Spirit? Nay, obstinacy is a better word. She is mine?"

"Aye, yours alone."

Garrick grunted. "Well, she will not concede this."

"I did not think she would." Anselm grinned, making his son scowl.

He told Garrick of her capture, a story he had already related many times with pleasure. It did not interest the others, but Garrick listened most intently.

"So why did you give her to me?" Garrick asked finally. He refilled his tankard from the large cauldron of mead on the table.

"The girl surely hates me, for she must blame me for her plight. I have seen her wield a weapon, and I do not want her around me so that I must always be wary of her. Nor does your mother, at her age, need to put up with the kind of tempers that girl will throw. Hugh wanted her but had second thoughts when she showed her claws. He knew I wanted to give her to you and so chose her step-sister instead. You, I believe, can tame the girl if you will but try."

Garrick scowled. "If she is all you say she is, why should I give the effort? She will be more trouble than she is worth, and is better sold."

Now Anselm frowned. "You are not pleased with her, then? Any other man would be."

"You know how I feel about women," Garrick replied acidly. "This one is no different. As a piece of property, aye, she is valuable. But for my pleasure?" He shook his head slowly, denying the attraction he felt for her. "Nay, I have no need of her."

Brenna had just returned to the small sewing room when the door opened and a young woman entered with a tray of food. Dull, disheveled orange-colored hair hung about her shoulders, and the blue eyes that met Brenna's were tired.

"Janie?"

"So you will speak to me now?" the woman said with some surprise. "I was near to doubting you ever would."

"I'm sorry," Brenna said guiltily. "I did not mean to make you the brunt of my anger. I know I only added to your burdens."

Janie shrugged wearily. " 'Twas not right that Yarmille should have you bound. You had reason to resent it. It seems I am still to tend you, even though you have been released."

Brenna felt additional guilt, for the small woman looked utterly exhausted. "I would tend to myself, but I was told to stay here."

"I know." Janie attempted to smile. "A girl as pretty as you would cause a commotion down there. You must be famished by now. Yarmille forgot about you, and so did I, until a few minutes past. Here," she added, handing Brenna the tray of food. "This should hold you until I can bring your meal tonight."

"Can you stay and talk awhile? I wish to thank you for all you have done for me."

"You need not thank me. I was ordered to care for you, but I would have done so anyway. We are of the same kin, you and I."

"Stay then, for a while."

"Nay, I cannot, Brenna—may I call you Brenna?" At her nod, Janie continued. "There is too much to do down there. Already half my morn has been wasted in the guest room," she said with a grimace. "These men do not care what time of day it is when they want their pleasure."

Brenna watched her leave. Were Linnet, Cordella and the others also suffering this kind of treatment? Would it be forced on her too?

"Nay! Never!" she said aloud before she sat down on the floor with a tray of food, suddenly conscious of her hunger. "Let them try!"

She attacked the meal with gusto, and silently thanked Janie for remembering her, since no one else had. The plate held two plump pheasant legs, a half loaf of flat bread spread with rich butter and a small bowl of creamed onions. The fare was delicious, spoiled only by the drink given to her to wash it down, a tankard of milk. Milk, bah! Did Janie think her a child? She craved ale—at the very least, wine—but never milk.

Before Brenna finished the meal, the door opened again and she looked up to see Garrick Haardrad, leaning casually against the frame. He was handsomely attired in a form-fitting tunic and trousers made of soft blue linen trimmed with sable. A wide gold belt with a large buckle studded with blue gems went around his waist and crossed his flat stomach. Resting on his broad chest was a huge silver medallion.

Brenna's eyes moved unconsciously to his bare arms. She saw much strength in the corded muscles under bronzed skin. She imagined those powerful arms gathering her to him, and her pulse raced wickedly at the thought. But this was quickly overshadowed by thoughts of the outcome Cordella had so often taunted her with.

She finally met his eyes, and her face flamed at the amusement she saw there. He had watched her appraise him; she sensed he had also read her thoughts.

"What do you want, Viking?" she asked sharply, to hide her embarrassment.

"To see if your disposition has improved."

"It has not, nor will it!" she replied vehemently, recalling all the vile things she had heard about this man. "So you needn't ask again."

Despite her sharpness, Garrick smiled, revealing white, even teeth, and two deep dimples in his cheeks. "I am glad to see you heeded Yarmille's orders and made use of your time. Is that your work?" He nodded toward the loom.

She followed his eyes and would have laughed if she did not believe him to be serious. "Nay, I would not touch that thing."

He was no longer smiling. "Why?"

" 'Tis woman's work," she shrugged and continued her meal.

"Will you tell me now you are not a woman?"

She cast him a look that implied he was daft. "Of course I am a woman. But I have never done women's work."

" 'Tis beneath you, I suppose?" he asked in a sarcastic tone.

"Aye," she answered, unabashed.

Garrick grunted and shook his head. "They told me you were offered as my bride. Would you have come, neither knowing how to run my house nor how to assume a wifely role?"

"I can run a house, Viking!" she snapped, her eyes stormy. "My aunt taught me all there is to know about women's work. But I never put those lessons to use. And for my being offered as your bride, 'tis so. But know that the prospect was loathsome to me, and I agreed only because my father had given his word that an alliance would be made. At least *we* honor our word when 'tis given!"

Her implication was not lost on him. "I played no part in the deception that was used. Do you blame me for it?"

"Nay, I know where the blame lies!" she spat. "He will pay one day!"

Garrick smiled at her threat. So his father was right when he said she hated him. From her defiant attitude, he could almost believe the other things Anselm had said also. He let his eyes travel over the length of her. Could this small girl have wounded a Viking? Nay, 'twas not likely. Her slim form was made for pleasure, not wielding a sword. Again he felt a strong attraction to her, and it rankled him. She was indeed dangerous—not in her threats, but in her beauty. He did not trust women, and only took them when the need was strong. Otherwise he shunned them, and he determined that this woman would be no different.

"If you do not blame me for your being here, then why do you direct your anger at me?"

"You are a fool, Viking, if you have to ask! I am brought here and then you come and say you own me. Well, no man owns *me!* No man!"

"So we are back to this again?" he sighed, folding his arms across his chest. "I am not yet ready to prove the issue, mistress, but when I am, you will know for a certainty who is master here."

She laughed, feeling that his reluctance accorded her a victory. "I know you are master here, Viking. I did not think otherwise."

The twinkle in her eyes made him smile. "As long as you concede me that, mistress, then I think we can get along without too many disputes." With that he left.

Chapter 12

THE sharp teeth of a nightmare woke Brenna with a start and she jumped up, ready to do battle. Upon seeing her surroundings by the dim light filtering through the half-open door, she relaxed in her improvised bed of furs and stared thoughtfully at the dark walls.

Was it morning or still night? How could those Vikings drink all night and still be at it?

The rumbling of her belly prompted Brenna to rise. Was she supposed to starve while waiting for them to remember she was here? To the devil with them! She would search out her own food. Anger and determination lighting her eyes, she left her place of confinement. She was not so foolish as to venture down the inside stairs, for they ended within sight of the hall. Instead she went the way she had gone before, down the stone steps that led outside, then to the open door at the rear of the house, where fragrant smoke was coming out.

Brenna peered nervously inside. She saw two women, one old and the other not much younger, turning a whole pig over a roasting pit. Behind them, Janie removed two loaves of flat bread from a long-handled iron tray and placed them with several others in a large basket sitting on a table. Yarmille was nowhere in sight, so Brenna stepped carefully inside the long, narrow room.

Janie's eyes widened when she saw her. "Brenna! Oh, Lord, I forgot about you again. I have been so busy," she apologized, "ever since Yarmille roused me from my sleep."

" 'Tis all right, Janie. I only just woke anyway. What time of day is it?"

" 'Tis afternoon, and many others are just now waking too," Janie replied tiredly, pushing her stringy hair away from her face.

"No wonder I am so famished," Brenna said, surprised that she had slept so long. "Have they been like that the whole night?" she asked, nodding toward the hall and the raucous sounds coming from it.

Janie sighed. "Yea, it has not stopped. Some passed out from overindulgence, but most were wise enough to retire for a while before continuing the celebration. Still there are those who are bleary-eyed and still singing in their cups."

"When will it end?"

Janie shrugged. "Mayhaps on the morrow, hopefully. But you had best return upstairs quickly, Brenna. The men drift in here from time to time to bother us. 'Twould not go well for you if you were seen. They have had their fill of me and Maudya, who is even now in the guest room. They go wild over a new wench who they have yet to try."

"I understand," Brenna replied, sure that Janie was exaggerating. After all, Garrick had not once looked at her like that.

"I will make you a platter now and bring it up."

"Very well." Brenna turned to leave.

But she had lingered too long. Behind her came a roar that sounded like a wild beast. Alarmed, she glanced over her shoulder and saw a burly giant stomping toward her. Two others stood by the opening to the hall, laughing and cheering him on.

"Brenna, run!" Janie screamed.

Although it was against Brenna's nature to run from anything, her common sense told her this was not an opportune time to take a stand, for she had no weapon and was unquestionably outnumbered. She bolted for the door, but had lost too much time debating with herself. The Viking grabbed her long braid and jerked her back against him.

"Unhand me, you bloody heathen!" she stormed.

But he only laughed at her outrage and futile struggle; besides, he did not understand her words. She had to bite her lip to keep from snapping his head off in his own tongue. To do so would not aid her plans, so she hissed at him in her own language, although it gave her little satisfaction, as he carried her back inside. He had her hooked under one arm like a piece of baggage as he passed through the closed-off cooking area to join his two friends by the hall next to the stairs. She noticed that Janie was no longer in the cooking area, but Janie could not help her anyway.

"Well, Gorm, a fine prize you have captured. I swear you have the luck of the gods this day."

"She would be Garrick's new slave. I wonder why he has kept her hidden until now," another said.

The man holding Brenna guffawed. "You can look at her and ask that?"

"Nay, Garrick does not care for women anymore, not since Morna played him falsely."

"Aye, but this one is different."

"I agree, Gorm. Still, Garrick would not make use of the wench as I would. Nor is he possessive of his property. So why did he keep her hidden?"

"I think she did herself. I would say by the way she fought me that she did not want to be found."

"Anselm says this one fights like a man."

"With a weapon, yea, but she has none—ouch!" Gorm cried and dropped Brenna to the floor, his hand going to his thigh where she bit him.

"She may fight like a man with a sword in hand, but she fights like a woman without one!" Another man roared with laughter.

Brenna was on her feet in an instant, but she stood in the midst of the three men, with only the hall at her back. The big one who had held her scowled his displeasure and reached for her again. Brenna had already suffered from his strength and was not about to be caught once more. Feigning a show of fear, she dodged Gorm's outstretched hand and collided with one of the other men. In so doing, she lifted a knife from the man's belt, then slipped from his light hold and stepped back, making sure they could see the metal gleaming in her hand.

"Thor's teeth! You have been duped by a crafty wench, Bayard."

The man whose knife she held shot his friend a murderous look. "She needs to be taught a lesson!"

"Then do so. For myself, I have no desire to return to my wife with a wound I could not explain easily."

"Gorm?"

"Aye, I'm with you, Bayard. She'll make the liveliest tumble I have had yet."

"Then I will take the arm with the knife, while you grab hold of her."

Brenna divided her concentration between the two of them. Fools, she thought contemptuously. Their free talk in front of her was a better weapon than her knife. She was ready for them when they came at her. She held the knife before her, and when Bayard jumped for her arm, she lowered it quickly and slashed at his middle, making a narrow rip in his tunic that was instantly soaked crimson.

"For your effort, pig!" she spat at Bayard even as she pointed the knife at Gorm to ward him off.

The animosity on their faces made her wary now, and she backed away from them slowly. However, she stopped short when she came up against the hard frame of yet another Viking. She realized her mistake too late. She was in the hall, and a group of men surrounded her. She turned in a flash before the one behind her could lay his hands on her, and quickly stepped into the open.

The hall was wrapped in a cloak of silence. Brenna's eyes darted all about her and met stunned faces. No one moved accept Gorm and Bayard, whose intent was still clearly malicious. If they all rushed her at once, she knew she was lost. Still, a few would die in the process and at least she would have revenge of a sort.

At least Brenna was in control of her actions. She had not panicked as would most who were so grossly outnumbered. When one sodden drunk sidled up to her, patted her buttocks familiarly and uttered a scurrilous jest, she whirled on him but stayed the knife. Instead she raised her skirt and gave him a kick that sent him sprawling backward. Once again she faced her two antagonists, who had taken advantage of the diversion to move in closer.

Everyone in the room suddenly roared with laughter at the drunk's thorough humiliation. Some of the tension was gone as comments about Brenna were bandied about. Many there knew her, and they were amazed to see her ready to fight again. All curiously watched her and the two men pursuing her, and noted the blood that stained Bayard's tunic.

"I applaud the entertainment, Bayard," Anselm's deep voice roared from across the room. "But do you think it wise to arm a slave?"

At the obvious jibe, Bayard's face turned bright red. Rather than challenge a man as powerful as Anselm for his taunting remark, he went along with the mockery. "Nay, but 'twas the least I could do to liven up the feast. Too many were wont to sleep rather than drink."

More clamorous guffaws followed, and Brenna watched warily as her two adversaries gave up the pursuit and blended in with the crowd. She turned toward the voice she recognized all too easily, her eyes smoky gray, ignited by the fires of hatred. She saw Anselm instantly, seated at a corner of one of the two long tables. Their eyes met, and it took all of Brenna's will to keep from screaming in rage and attacking him like a wild animal does its prey.

"Put down the knife, Brenna."

She tensed when she heard the voice. "Nay, I keep it!"

"What will it gain you?" Heloise asked.

" 'Twill keep me from being mauled by those bungling asses!" she snapped, looking around her once before she stuck the knife in her belt.

"Yea, I suppose it will. But Garrick won't allow you to keep it."

Brenna's eyes narrowed dangerously, and her hand rested on the hilt of the knife. "He will regret trying to take it away," she said acidly, then nodded towards Anselm. "Speak for me and tell your husband that I challenge him. He may choose the weapon, for I am adept at all."

Heloise sighed and shook her head. "Nay, Brenna. I will not tell him that."

"Why?" Brenna frowned. " 'Twill be my words you speak, not yours."

"A Viking will not fight a woman. There is no honor in it," Heloise replied softly.

"But I must see him dead!" Brenna cried, frustration in her voice. " 'Tis not my way to lay in hiding for my enemy, so I must fight him fairly. He must face me!"

"He will not fight you, girl. Rest assured, he knows how you feel towards him."

" 'Tis not enough! Can you not understand that I am torn apart and your husband is responsible. My people are dead because of him—men that I grew up with, that I broke bread with and cared for. My sister's husband— dead! Even one of your own who was there—" she caught herself before she revealed too much. "Who was a friend. He was also cut down. And my servant, an old woman whom I loved dearly." Brenna's voice rose, and she became distraught with the memory. "She fell with an axe in her back! Why her? She posed no threat. If a Viking will not fight a woman, why is she dead?"

"The men grow a little wild when they raid," Heloise answered sadly. "Many die who should not, and 'tis unfortunate that this happens. There are many regrets afterward. Anselm also has regrets."

Brenna looked at her with disbelieving eyes. "How can he when he keeps my aunt and stepsister as servants?"

"And yourself?"

"Nay, I will not serve."

"You will in time, Brenna."

"I will die first!"

Brenna's outburst had caused the hall to grow quiet again. Her words were not understood, but the men around her knew rage when they saw it. Hugh Haardrad moved in close, fearing for his mother's safety.

"Does she threaten you, mother?" Hugh asked.

"Nay, her anger is for your father."

"I do not trust a slave with a knife, especially this one," Hugh replied gruffly. "Keep her attention and I will take her from behind."

"Nay, Hugh, leave her be," Heloise ordered. "She is prepared to fight right now. Indeed, she wants to."

Hugh laughed. "So? What chance has she?"

Brenna shot him a murderous glance. This was the man who had dared to touch her intimately when she was bound and helpless.

"Swine!" she hissed, and spat at his feet.

Hugh's look grew venomous, and he instintctively raised a hand to strike her. "Why you—"

"Hugh, stop it!" Heloise demanded.

At the same time Brenna drew the knife from her belt and faced him with outstretched arms. She grinned, daring him to come at her.

"The bitch!" Hugh growled. " 'Tis fortunate I did not choose the hellcat, or she would be dead now! And likely he feels the same, from the looks of him," he added, nodding toward the rear of the hall.

Brenna turned to see Garrick standing in the doorway she had come through earlier. His face was set in a dark scowl, and his eyes told of his cold rage. How long had he been there? How much had he heard?

Janie stood behind Garrick, her expression anxious. It was obvious she had brought him. Oh, Janie, Janie. You thought to help me, but I fear you have only brought me more trouble, Brenna moaned to herself.

Garrick approached them slowly, his displcasure written all over his face. When he reached them he ignored Brenna and addressed his mother, though not in his Norwegian tongue.

"What is she doing here?"

"Ask me, Viking!" Brenna snapped. He gave her a steely look.

"Your friends Gorm and Bayard chased her in here, Garrick," Heloise explained quickly.

"And the knife?"

"She took it from Bayard."

"I can blessed well speak for myself!" Brenna interjected angrily.

"I am sure you can, wench," Garrick replied in a tight voice. "So tell me then. How were you found? I will not believe my friends entered the sewing room."

"I came below."

"You were told to stay put!" he reminded her harshly.

"Is it your intention to starve me then?" she asked indignantly, feeling a tight knot in her throat. "No one brought me food so I sought it myself."

His features softened only slightly. "Very well. So 'twas someone else's forgetfulness that caused you to be found. But that did not give you leave to steal a weapon, mistress!"

"I did so only to protect myself!"

"From what? he asked brusquely. "No one would harm you here."

"Mayhaps not harm, but what they intended was as bad!" Brenna returned.

"What they intended is permissible in this house, mistress," Garrick said, his brows narrowed.

"You would allow them to take me, then?"

"Yea. I have not denied my friends their pleasure before, and I will not start now."

Brenna's eyes widened, her confusion obvious. "Then why did you keep me hidden from them?"

"I would have given you time to adjust to your new life," he replied easily, as though his thoughtfulness should be appreciated by her. "I will still give you time."

She glared at him contemptuously, her eyes a stormy gray. "Again you show yourself to be a fool, Viking, for I will never adjust to the life you would force on me! I will not whore for your friends!"

His eyes brightened with barely controlled anger. "I think the time has come, wench, to prove who is the master here."

Heloise finally interceded. "Garrick, nay. Not here before all." She spoke in their tongue, assuming Brenna could not understand.

"She needs be taught a lesson!"

"Yea, but privately, son. She must be handled differently from the other slaves, for her spirit is too proud."

"Spirit can be broken, mistress."

"You would do that to such a beautiful creature?"

He crooked his head at her. "Why do you take her side? Do you expect me to tolerate her tantrums?"

"Nay, but I feel a sort of kinship with her," Heloise admitted. "At one time I felt much the same way as she does now. But I was won with love."

"What do you suggest, then?"

"You could try kindness, son," she said softly.

"Nay, 'tis not my way."

"There was a time when you were not so hard, Garrick. Has Morna destroyed you so?" Seeing that his eyes narrowed, she added quickly, "Forgive me. I did not mean to remind you of her. But this girl is not Morna. Can you not practice a little tolerance for her sake?"

"Is she mine?"

"Yea," she replied reluctantly.

"Then leave me to handle her as I see fit."

Brenna bristled. That they assumed she could not understand them was what she wanted, but it was becoming exceedingly difficult not to retaliate when the conversation was about herself. Garrick had proved himself to be a cold, heartless adversary, no better than she expected. At least she knew for sure now.

She found him looking at her with icy eyes. "Give me the knife, mistress."

His voice brooked no refusal, yet she shook her head vehemently. "Nay, you will have to take it."

"Garrick, for God's sake, let her keep it for now!" Heloise said earnestly. "Would you chance a wound here?"

"By Thor!" he stormed. "Her words are brave, but you greatly overestimate her, mother, as she does herself. She is no match for a man."

"Please, Garrick!"

He battled quickly with his emotions, but finally his mother's pleading won out over his instincts. He turned to Brenna, who faced him defiantly.

"Will you come with me peaceably?"

"Yea," she answered readily, knowing the victory was hers. "I will leave this hall."

He motioned for her to precede him, and she did so proudly, looking neither left nor right. She returned the knife to her belt as she walked, assured that no one would accost her now.

At the top of the stairs, Garrick stopped Brenna when she turned left, and instead shoved her toward his room. She did not object. At least his chambers had a soft bed. But as soon as she stepped through the doorway, he took her by surprise, lifting her off her feet with one arm, while the other snatched her knife away. He then swung her viciously across the room, and she fell hard against the cold floor.

"I should have done that below," Garrick snarled cruelly, "to put you in your place properly."

"Liar!" she hissed as she got to her feet. "You were afraid to face me when I was prepared for you. You had to attack me from behind like the cowardly swine you are!"

"Careful, wench," he warned her menacingly. "Or you will get the beating you so greatly deserve."

"So you also beat defenseless women? Is there no end to your despicable ways?"

"Not defenseless women, mistress—incorrigible slaves!" he said furiously.

"Ohhh!" she screamed and started to rush him.

"Hold, girl, if you value your life!"

She did not heed his words, intent only upon doing him harm. But she did stop in her tracks when she heard vicious growling coming from the bed. She turned fearful eyes in that direction and saw a huge white shepherd crouched on the bed, baring his sharp teeth at her.

"Had you struck me once, mistress, he would have been at your throat in an instant."

"Call him off," Brenna whispered fearfully, her face a deathly white.

"Nay, I think not. The dog is just what you need to keep you from mischief," Garrick replied, his lips turning up at one corner in a sneer.

She turned wild eyes on him. "You cannot leave me here with him!"

"He will not harm you, as long as you stay put."

Garrick stopped at the door, an amused smirk on his face. "We have not tangled yet, Brenna Carmarham. But when the time comes, I think I will enjoy it."

She forgot the dog for a moment and snapped, "So will I, Viking!"

Garrick laughed heartily and looked at the animal on the bed. "Guard her well, dog." He grinned, then closed the door, leaving the girl and the beast alone.

Chapter 13

A CHILL wind coming in through the balcony door woke Brenna. She shivered, then quickly tucked her cold bare feet under her shift. As she lay there tucked in a ball for warmth, the door opened and Brenna looked up. Garrick stood there holding a large tray of food. He ordered the shepherd out, then kicked the door shut with his heel and put the tray down on the table.

"What have you against fresh air, mistress?" he asked sourly, not looking at her, and opened the balcony door.

"What have *you* against a little warmth?" she returned flippantly.

Suddenly he grinned at her. "I fear you will perish come winter, girl, if you think this fine weather is cold."

She shivered at his words. How *would* she bear up come winter? Being so far north, the long, cold months would be nothing like those she enjoyed at home. And if what both Wyndham and Garrick told her was true, there would be no sun during that time to help melt the snow away.

"Come and eat, mistress," Garrick said, pulling the two new thronelike chairs over to the table.

"Have your *guests* finally departed?" Brenna questioned, saying the word with the disgust and loathing she felt.

"Yea, my household has returned to normal. We will eat first, and then we will talk."

She looked at him suspiciously. "About what?"

"You and your new life here—what will be expected of you. 'Tis time we settle things."

Oh, Lord! She sensed another battle was at hand, and in truth, she was not up to it. Would she always have to lock wills with this man? She had yet to have a day of peace since the day her father died, and she did so yearn for one.

Brenna sighed and joined Garrick at the little table. He had brought two large bowls filled with the normal daily breakfast, a porridge made of oatmeal. There was also warmed leftover pheasant and a full loaf of hard barley bread for them to share. When Brenna reached for her tankard and found warm milk in it as before, she grimaced.

She shot Garrick an accusing look. "What am I thought to be that I am given milk like a babe?"

"I have milk myself, mistress," he replied, raising a tankard like hers. " 'Tis thought to be a healthful drink."

"I hate milk!" she snapped. "Are women not allowed wine or mead here?"

He leaned back in his chair, a little smirk on his lips. "Yea, they are. But slaves are not."

She had a strong urge to throw the warm milk in his face to wipe away that smirk. She wondered briefly how he would react to that, then decided it would not go well for her. She damned the fates again, then attacked the meal, anxious to be done with it altogether.

Garrick watched her silently as he ate, noting the high color on her cheeks. It did not take much to ignite her temper. Just the mention of her new status was enough. He had never known a woman with so much misplaced pride and arrogance. That she belonged to him was something he had yet to decide he appreciated.

He remembered how she looked when he came late in the night and found her curled in a small ball on the bed. Her face had been so childlike, her beauty so unreal. But then he recalled how she looked when he found her below yesterday—all spit and fire, wildly defiant. Even then he had to admire her beauty, the fiery sparks reflected in her silver eyes, the high color of her face caused by her fury.

He was angered to his very core to find her arguing with his mother. But then he stopped to listen to her words describing the ordeal she had suffered, what she had lost at the hands of his father. Some of his anger died then, but was quickly rekindled when she threatened his brother.

To think that a slave of his would dare to accost his family! Then to have his mother defend her, to stay his hand from the beating the girl deserved. Still, it was fortunate that his mother was there, for as infuriated as he was, he would surely have hurt the wench seriously, only to regret it later.

"Well, are you going to lay your law down on me now?"

Her saucy question made him smile, which brought his dimples out. "Will you accept my law?"

"I will hear you out first, then you shall have an answer," she replied in a toneless voice.

"Very well," he said, leaning back in the chair again. "To begin with, there will be no more tantrums of the kind you have shown me thus far."

"I do not throw tantrums, Viking. I speak my mind," she returned calmly.

"The word Viking on your lips is a curse, mistress. I will hear it no more."

"I will not call you master!" she hissed, saying the word with loathing.

"I concede that," he replied. "I have a given name and you may use it."

"I also have a given name, though I have not heard you call me by it."

"Very well—Brenna," he grinned.

She let a smile cross her lips. " 'Tis not so hard to settle things with you."

"Oh? You should reserve your opinion till we have finished," he responded, watching the rare smile vanish. "Now," he continued in an authoritative voice. "Yarmille has suggested you be put with the two other young females. Janie and Maudya share a small house a short ways behind the stable. You will be quartered with them. You will sleep and pass your free time there. Is this agreeable to you?"

"Yea."

"Good. Your duties will be no different than those the other females share. You will help with the cooking and cleaning, the washing, milk the cows, grind corn. There is not really that much to do, since this is a small household and you have only me to serve. Yarmille will instruct you in your duties when she is here. When she is not, Janie will show you what to do. And since I have no wife, you will also help occasionally in the sewing room with the mending and making of new clothes."

"Is that it?" Brenna asked coolly.

"Yea. There will be no children to mind or a lady to tend, since I will never marry. You have only me to please," Garrick said quickly, assuming from her question that there would be no argument.

"All these duties you have described are woman's work."

"Of course."

She gazed at him levelly, trying to keep calm. "You were right that I should reserve my opinion on the outcome of this meeting, for if this is the only course you offer me, we will never be in accord."

Garrick looked at her sharply, frowning. "Do you refuse to work?"

"I have told you I will not do woman's work!" she said haughtily. "I never have and I never will!"

He leaned forward, his eyes forming narrow slits, his anger building. "You will!"

"Nay, Viking!" she snapped, ending the short truce between them. "I won't!"

"The food you eat, the clothes you wear, they come from me! The house you sleep in is mine!" he stormed, coming to his feet. "If you will not earn your keep, mistress, then you are useless to me!"

"I will earn my keep," she said in a suddenly calm tone that surprised him.

"How? 'Twill not be in my bed, if you have that in mind."

"With certainty, *that* will never happen. Nay, Erin has agreed that I may help him with the horses if you will give him your permission."

Garrick scowled at this. "When did you speak with Erin?"

"Your first day back."

"You were told to stay in the sewing room that day!"

"I am not accustomed to inactivity, Viking," she replied hotly. "Nor to taking orders!"

"Well, you will have to learn, wench," Garrick returned brusquely. "And as for working with Erin, that is out of the question."

"Why?" she demanded. "You said I must earn my keep. Well, I have told you what is agreeable to me. I know horses as well as I know weapons, and I am not opposed to cleaning a stable, for I have done so before. If that is not enough, I can also hunt game. I provided meat for the table at home; I can do as well here."

"Is that the extent of your talents?" Garrick asked sarcastically.

Brenna suddenly grinned. "Nay. If you have an enemy, I will kill him for you."

Garrick burst out laughing. "You are amazing, wench. You would really try to be a man?"

She glared at his mockery, her voice breaking. "I cannot help the way I am. 'Twas the way I was raised."

"Well, you will have to change your ways, mistress."

"You will not concede?"

"Nay, you will work in the house."

Brenna drew herself up, her shoulders stiff, her chin held at a proud angle. "Then you leave me no alternative but to leave."

"What?" He looked at her incredulously.

"You heard me, Viking. Since I will not work as you dictate, and you will not allow me my choice, then as you said earlier, I would be useless to you. So I will leave."

Garrick shook his head slowly, his arms crossed. "Nay, wench, that is impossible. You forget that you are no longer free to come and go as you please. You belong to me now."

"You insufferable ass!" Brenna stormed, her fury evident in the glassy silver of her eyes. "Do you think *you* can stop me if I want to go?"

Garrick's body stiffened in anger. That he had put up with her obstinacy for this long amazed him.

"If you leave my lands, mistress, every Viking for miles around will be called to hunt you down. You will then be locked in a cell for your troubles—indefinitely."

She laughed at him. "Once I go, Viking, I will not be found, so your threats do not frighten me."

"I have tolerated much from you," Garrick said in a voice as cold as ice. "But no more. 'Tis time you learned fully what being owned entails."

Brenna looked at the closed door, but refused to flee—not when she could secure the knife in Garrick's belt and win the upper hand.

"What have you in mind, Viking?"

"A sound thrashing to begin with," he said and started to approach her.

Garrick expected her to run and so was not prepared when she threw herself at him, then dipped away easily under his arm. Uttering an oath, he turned to grab her, but stopped short when he caught the glint of the knife in her hand.

She laughed at the absurd look on his face. "You were saying?"

"Give me the knife, wench!" he growled menacingly.

"Come and take it, damn you!" she retaliated, her eyes as stormy as her tone.

"You will suffer worse for this!"

"Careful, Viking," she grinned tauntingly. "Your dog is not here to protect you now."

A low growl escaped his lips as he came at her. Brenna kept the knife before her, intent on merely warding him off rather than killing him. He was an arrogant beast, but he had yet to do her harm. It was his father's blood she wanted, not his.

However, it proved a mistake not to attack him, for Garrick leaped at her and grabbed the wrist that held the weapon. The pressure he applied to make her drop the knife was excruciating, but she bit her lip and withstood the pain, then deftly maneuvered the knife in her hand until the point of the blade jabbed his arm and he released her. She stared at the blood for a moment, noting that it was only a small nick. But in that moment Garrick's fist came down hard on her wrist, and the knife clattered to the floor. Then he back-handed Brenna viciously, the blow almost making her lose her balance.

Blood trickled from her lip. She wiped it slowly with the

back of her hand as she glared defiantly at him. She stood proud and unafraid before him.

"Do your worst, Viking."

He said nothing, but looked at her for a long moment. Some of his anger drained away. She did not prepare to run when he took off his belt and held it in his hand, but her eyes glowed with hatred when they met his.

Then unexpectedly he dropped the thick belt on the floor. She looked on with a puzzled frown that became even more confused when he proceeded to remove his tunic. When he bent to untie the leather garters that held his trousers tight against his legs, she gasped.

"What are you doing?"

A cruel smile touched his lips. "Disrobing."

Her eyes widened. "You would beat me without your clothes on?" she asked incredulously.

"Nay, mistress," he said coldly as he finished with the garters and removed his soft-skinned boots. "I have decided to deal with you differently."

"How?"

He crooked a brow at her. " 'Tis obvious, I would think. I will master you in the one sure way a man dominates a woman. I will have you."

She stared at him for a long moment before the meaning of his words became clear to her. For the first time real fear entered her eyes. The color left her face and she took a step backward.

A terrifying panic gripped Brenna. This was not supposed to happen. Everyone had said he hated women. Bayard said Garrick would have no use for her in that way. And he had not once looked on her with lust, as the other men had. How could she endure the agony that Cordella said would accompany the act? Would she shame herself by screaming her pain aloud? She had no idea how intense it would be.

Garrick watched Brenna with a puzzled frown. He saw the conflicting emotions that crossed her features. But what surprised him was the terror in her eyes—she who had shown only courage thus far. She had stood defiantly, awaiting a sound thrashing, but now she was cowed at the prospect of his bedding her.

Such a dramatic change was baffling. He had surmised

by her rebellious stance that no amount of pain inflicted would gain him the end he sought. But that her resolve should be broken by the means he chose to humble her did not fit her character, at least not before the deed was completed.

"Have I found the means to tame you?" he asked in a quiet, curious tone.

At his words, a spark of anger was lit despite her fear. "I am not an animal to be tamed!"

"But you are a slave whose arrogance cannot be tolerated," he returned softly.

"But you do not want me, Viking. So why this?" she said in a subdued tone.

Garrick looked at her thoughtfully. "I agree I have no use for women. I do not take them often, only when my body demands it. And so a shapely wench does not turn my eye as she used to. But it seems this is the only way I can put an end to your haughtiness."

He took a step towards her and Brenna's face whitened even more. She stood petrified for a moment, then dashed madly for the knife on the floor. But Garrick had anticipated her move and caught her to him before she neared the weapon.

Brenna fought like a trapped wild creature, that knows it will soon die. Her sharp claws assailed his rock-hard chest, but only amused laughter met her ears.

"You have no weapon now, wench. You would match your strength to mine, but you know you will fall the loser."

Her answer was to sink her teeth into his arm. She quickly gained her release when he cried out. She made to dash for the door, but his hand caught the back of her shift. When she pushed on, the garment ripped to the waist. There her belt stopped the fabric from tearing further, and he pulled her back to him. She turned, and with a closed fist swung for his face. He caught her arm in a viselike grip and twisted it behind her back, crushing her breasts against his chest as he did so.

"Release me!" she cried, hysteria in her voice.

"Nay, I think not."

She thought to plead again, but then she looked up at him and saw the desire that was finally in his eyes. Her whole body was pressed to his and she could feel his swelling manhood against her belly. The fear that gripped her made her weak, and she could only thrash her head from side to side when he bent to kiss her. Finally he held her head still in his mighty hand and lowered his mouth to hers. But before the kiss was met, she grabbed a handful of his golden mane and jerked his head back.

"By Thor, wench!" he growled. "You fight me as if you were a virgin still, when you are not!"

"I am," she said in a whisper against his chest, grimacing from the pain in her arm, which he had not released.

He looked down at the top of her head, seeing the thick black braid trailing down her bare back and across both their arms. He loosened his hold somewhat, but still pressed her to him.

"I cannot believe that my father's men did not lust after you as my own have done."

"They did not come near me," she said quietly, praying that this knowledge would change his mind. "Your father kept them away."

Suddenly his laughter filled the room. "So this is why you fear me now?"

"I do not fear *you*, Viking!"

"Yea, you do," he returned, his voice softening considerably, "for I am the man who will bed you. I will be gentle with you, Brenna, as the issue will be proved no matter how I take you."

At that he lifted her into his arms, but she thrashed and kicked wildly again and it was indeed an effort to get her to the bed. There he dropped her down, then fell on top of her and pinned her firmly beneath him. She heaved and bucked to remove his great weight from her, and clawed his back until he secured her arms at her sides.

"Why do you persist, wench? I have said I will be gentle. 'Twill hurt this first time, but not overly much."

"You lie!" she cried, trying in vain to free her arms. "Another vile trait to add to your others!"

"Be still!" he commanded sharply when her knee rose dangerously close to his groin. "You would welcome the lash which effects much pain, but you scorn this, which gives only pleasure. Or is it only the humbling that you fear, for once done, there will be no doubt that you belong to me?"

"Your lying tongue will not make me submit!" she cried out in frustration. "I know of the agonies you would inflict on me!"

"Agonies?" he looked down into her terrified eyes and wondered at the demons that were planted in her mind. "The truth will come out in the doing, mistress."

With that he moved from her, and Brenna thought briefly that he had indeed changed his mind. But she was fooled, for in the next moment her belt was pulled open and her shift yanked from her shoulders and down her hips, then thrown to the floor. She moaned softly at the humiliation of having her young body bared in its entirety to a man's lusting eyes. And this man's eyes did feast hungrily upon her nakedness, making her close her own eyes in utter shame.

"So this is the body you would deny," he murmured huskily. "I would think to find a boyish form, not these perfect curves and mounds. Yea, you are a woman proud and true. Such beauty as the like I've never seen—and mine for the taking."

Brenna started at his words and her eyes flew open. "Cease your mumbling, Viking! I am not yours, and you have yet to prove otherwise!"

He grinned down at her stormy gray eyes, her bright crimson cheeks. "I will do so with pleasure, Brenna." He said her name like a caress. "Yea, much pleasure indeed."

He leaned over her, his hands securing her arms by her sides, one leg covering both of hers, thus holding her immobile. Then he brought his lips down to the firm mounds of her breasts thrust proudly before him. He took one deep in his mouth, then sucked gently on its delicious peak until it rose impudently beneath his tongue. Brenna jerked at this assault. She had never dreamed that a man's lips could be so hot. They seemed to sear her tender skin where they touched her. Was this intense heat part of the agony that she knew would come?

She looked down on him with wonder, at his golden head resting over her breasts, the wavy hair tickling her skin. His enormous shoulders met her eye, and she saw many little trails of blood from her scratches. She watched the iron muscles ripple on his back when she tried to move her arms and he stayed her. Brenna admired strength and courage; she always had. But this man's strength was unbelievable. He held her with such ease when she tried her mightiest to move him. Though such a powerful body was magnificent to behold, that she lay at the mercy of its strength was unbearable.

"Garrick—Garrick."

He looked up at her, puzzlement in his eyes. " 'Tis the first time you have used my name. I like the sound of it on your lips."

Brenna steeled herself for her next words. "Garrick, release me." Her tone of voice was the closest she could come to pleading.

He smiled softly, his eyes afire with passion. "Nay, my beauty. 'Tis too late for that."

At that he moved to kiss her, but she turned her head away. He released one arm to hold her head still. He instantly regretted his decision when her nails dug into a tender area of his chest like sharp teeth.

He bellowed in pain and quickly grabbed her hand again. "I see you have a weapon after all, my bloodthirsty wench!"

"Yea, but I regret it cannot reach your heart, for I would take that from you if I could and feed it to the wolves!"

"Well, vixen, there is something I will give you instead, though 'twill not go to the wolves, but between your legs," he growled angrily, and pulled her arms together to hold them with one hand while his other removed his trousers.

With her legs free for a moment, she kicked wildly, but could do no damage. And then his hard and swollen member pressed against her thigh. From his position at her side she could see it clearly, and she gasped at the huge size of it and knew that Cordella had not lied. That proud beast would surely tear her asunder and render her screaming for mercy. Yet even as a horrifying fear spread through her, she could not voice the words to beg again for her release.

Her rising panic nearly choked her, and she squirmed and heaved to such a degree that she was not aware he had thrust his knees between her legs and now loomed over her. When he lowered his weight slowly, stilling her futile efforts once and for all, she knew she was trapped without the slightest hope of escape.

"You act as if I would slay you, girl," he said, still amazed that she fought so fiercely. "Put your fears to rest. You will not perish in my bed."

"The words of a sly fox to his chosen meal!" she hissed between clenched teeth. "I warn you, Viking. If you persist in this deed, you will regret it. I do not take injustice lightly!"

He ignored her threat and buried his lips in the curve of her neck, then whispered close to her ear, "Relax, Brenna, and I will still be gentle with you."

"How can a bungling oaf be gentle?" she snapped.

Brenna did not see his face tighten in anger, but his voice gave testimony to his annoyance. "Then you shall have it your way!"

Her legs were spread wide by his hips. His huge member was like a thick steel pole pressing to enter her. It met the hard resistance of her maidenhead, a sturdy wall meant to keep out intruders. But like a battering ram, he broke through the fortress wall, tearing her flesh so she felt a stabbing white-hot pain. Her body was stiff with expectancy as she waited for the terrible agony to continue. She could feel the offending weapon deep inside her womb and then it left her completely, only to thrust into her even deeper. Again and again it teased her, departing, then returning quickly to bury itself within her. Where was the pain that she feared above all else? And what was this strange sensation that was slowly speading through her loins, which made her feel as if she were floating, somehow soaring on a mystical cloud that was lifting her ever higher—and to what end?

Brenna did not know that Garrick was watching the confusion which crossed her features. Finally he closed his eyes and thrust so deeply it seemed he would join them together for all eternity. Then he was still. Though he wanted to relax his guard and revel in this closeness, to take more pleasure from it, he could not trust her even now.

Brenna was deep in thought when he looked down at her, a frown creasing her brow. Garrick wondered briefly at her mood, why she was now so still and not demanding that he leave her. She had proved to be a greater pleasure than he had thought possible, and he found with some small bit of amazement that he already looked forward to having her again.

"Why did you stop?" Brenna asked him in a haughty tone.

He looked at her confused eyes and laughed. "Because you have my seed and 'twill be awhile before I can give you more."

"But you are still hard within me," she replied unabashedly. "I can feel you. Can you not continue?"

Garrick stared at her in utter amazement. "Do you want me to?"

She considered this for a moment, then answered flatly, "Nay, the mood has passed."

He grunted in irritation at her answer and wondered if he had won the battle after all. "I take it you found it was not so terrifying, eh?" he asked as he moved to her side and reached for his trousers.

"Nay, not in the least," she answered, stretching lazily before him. Suddenly a look of anger crossed her features. "But someone will answer dearly for what I was led to expect!"

"Who?"

" 'Tis my concern, not yours," she replied, then her laughter rang through the room, completely confounding him. "I have learned much this day, Viking. My thanks."

Chapter 14

SINCE neither Yarmille nor Garrick was about to tell her nay, Brenna spent the day lazily in the house, getting to know the servants. Garrick had stormed from the room after he dressed, in a thoroughly black mood. He returned only long enough to throw a new shift at her, then left again without a word. She knew he was sorely vexed at the outcome of their lovemaking. He had expected her to be humbled, when in truth she had mastered the situation. This did not sit well with him. Mayhaps even now he was scheming other ways to bring her down, but she would handle them in turn.

After he left, though, surprise at the new experience wore off, and Brenna brooded about her stepsister. She was almost tempted to take one of Garrick's horses and go seek out Cordella. What the bitch had done was unforgivable. The terror and panic Brenna had succumbed to were bad enough, but what rankled the most was that she had shown that fear to the Viking. Against her will she remembered the pleasurable feeling that had spread through her when he entered her. Then quickly she pushed the thought away. Why Cordella had filled her mind with lies was beyond her—but she would find out one day soon.

Brenna sat at the table in the long, narrow cooking area and watched Janie prepare loaves of bread for Garrick's evening meal. Maudya was by the fire, stirring a thick soup full of large chunks of chicken. Maudya was a tawny-haired woman of about two score years, short and pudgy, with a quick smile and florid complexion.

Both women had confided to Brenna how they came to be here. Surprisingly, their account was without rancor. They had been neighbors in their homeland, living in a village that was raided four years past. It was Garrick himself who had captured and brought them here. In those years he served his father, and went on many such raids. The two women did not mind their life here, for it was no different than they would have had at home, and they were well provided for. Maudya did not mind as Janie did the fact that any guest of Garrick's could bed them whenever he desired, simply because they were slaves and had no rights of their own. This was the only aspect of living here that Janie complained about. At least it did not happen often.

They both listened eagerly while Brenna explained her story, and were a bit overawed to learn the manner in which she was raised. She was doubly grateful now that her father had cared not a whit for custom or tradition, else she too might be like these other women, passive behind the yoke. She would never bend, either, and Garrick Haardrad would learn that truth in time, even if he did not accept it.

"Tell me about Garrick," Brenna prompted as she nibbled on some wild nuts Erin had brought them that morning. "Is he a fair man?"

"Indeed he is," Maudya answered easily.

"Except when he gives us to his friends," Janie added, the days of the feast still uppermost in her mind.

"Methinks you complain too much," Maudya chuckled. "I have heard you giggling the same as me when tousled in the hay."

"I do not mind one man at a time, but not one after another as it is at a feast," Janie returned in irritation. "Tell me you like the soreness 'atween your legs the next day?"

Brenna tried quickly to change the subject, for her own

experience with a man was still too new, and she did not want to think of it yet. "What of the slaves he sold? Does he not care what becomes of them?"

"He had to sell them, Brenna," Janie explained. "He had too many here—those he took himself, those from Ulric and those his father gave him. He sold only the hardy ones who would fare well and, of course, those who were troublesome."

Brenna blanched at this, but Janie and Maudya did not notice. She soon regained her composure. "How many does he have left?"

"About twelve, I would say. There's us, and the two old ones you saw here yesterday. Then there's Erin and old Duncan, and five younger men. Of course, there's the children too."

"Children?"

Janie beamed proudly. "I have one: Sheldon, who is two. Maudya here has three, two of them twins."

"The old ones watch them in the day," Maudya said. "You will meet them later, when you come home with us. I do hope you like children."

"I do," Brenna smiled. "I used to take the little ones from our village hunting while their fathers worked the fields. Mayhaps I can take yours also, when they are older."

Brenna realized with a shock that she had spoken of a future here, when she had no intention of staying overly long. She would have to guard herself and not become too friendly with these people, else she might regret leaving.

She continued her quest for information about the Viking. "Are they Garrick's children?"

"The master never touched me," Maudya pouted, "though I tried hard enough to catch his eye."

"He took me to his bed a few times after he first brought us here," Janie replied. "He lost interest in me, though, and would journey to his father's house to taste his slaves. Perrin is Sheldon's father; of this I am sure."

"Perrin?"

"He is Garrick's closest friend. They became blood brothers to bind that friendship. They combined their blood by sprinkling it on the ground in a fertility rite. This was six years past, when Garrick was but ten and nine, and Perrin two score and three."

115

"Perrin told you this?"

"Yea, he comes to see me often and tells me much."

"Does Perrin know that Sheldon is his child?" Brenna questioned.

"Of course."

"Then why doesn't he marry you?"

Both girls looked at Brenna as if she were daft. Maudya answered, "A Viking cannot marry a slave. 'Tis not allowed."

"What if the slave were freed?"

"Freedom will not come to me here, Brenna. There is only one way I know of that a slave can gain his freedom, and that is to help during a feud, to kill an enemy of the clan. Even then, freedom can be denied. 'Tis only a generous master who gives it. Perrin has thought to buy me from Garrick; he is waiting for the right time to make the offer, when Garrick's hardness mellows somewhat."

"Garrick was a cheerful young man when first we came, kind and gentle to all. Perrin's sister changed that three years past. Now he scorns all women and would scoff at Perrin for loving me. Perrin's sister has caused us much anguish, especially Garrick."

Brenna's interest was aroused. "Is this the Morna I have heard mentioned with distaste?"

Janie looked to the doorways to be sure they were alone before she answered. "She is surely the one. A cold bitch if you ask me—nothing like Perrin. Well, Garrick fell in love with Morna and thought she returned that love. They were to be married, in fact. But then a rich merchant came through here and Morna ran off with him, preferring wealth to love, so it seems. Garrick has not been the same since. He has vowed to scorn all women and never marry. He rants and raves about the smallest thing. He became cold-hearted and cruel and picked fights, and lost many friends.

"For two winters he took to the forests and sailed north to hunt, driving himself to exhaustion to accumulate hundreds of furs. These he sold with the slaves when he went east the spring before last. His quest for sudden wealth was intense. At least he has accomplished that. Perrin says he is a rich man now. And he is also not so violently harsh with us as he was before he left. But he is still cold and distrustful."

"Do you think he means to win Morna back with these new riches?" Brenna asked.

"Mayhaps," Janie replied. "I have no understanding of his mind. I only know what Perrin tells me, and that is that Garrick will never lose his heart to another woman. He guards it carefully. The only woman who has his love is his mother. That woman can do no wrong in his eyes."

"Yea, I saw the respect he gave her in the hall," Brenna remarked. "Tell me, why did she teach Garrick our language, and not her other son?"

"Hugh was her first born and is the heir, so he must be a Viking true. She could not show her love for him in public, for this is frowned upon, and he was always watched by the clan. She gave him up to them. Garrick was her second son, and she doted on him as only a mother can. He speaks our language and knows of our god, as well as his own. His kind and gentle ways came from that love she poured on him, until Morna killed it."

"I find it hard to believe that a broken heart can do so much damage," Brenna said thoughtfully.

" 'Tis easy to see you have never lost your heart, Brenna, or you would know of the devils that can wreak vengeance on a grieving mind. In Garrick they turned him mean. 'Tis not in jest they nicknamed him Garrick the Hard-hearted."

Chapter 15

BRENNA braided her hair as she walked up the path to the stable, then entered to find Erin busy applying a poultice to a mare's injured leg.

"I was beginning to wonder if you had lost interest in the stable, lass," he said as she approached him. "I could have used your help this morning to quiet this filly after that beastly stallion kicked her in his eagerness to be off."

Brenna rubbed the mare's nose gently. "I thought you would not accept my help unless Garrick gave his permission."

"He did that, last eventide."

"Really?" Brenna asked in surprise, then she laughed heartily. "So I have won!"

"I don't know about winning," Erin replied with an amused chuckle. "He said I was to work you till you dropped."

"Well, I did not think he would lose gracefully," Brenna grinned, feeling thoroughly pleased with herself. "I am willing to work hard, however. Here, let me finish that for you."

Erin stood up slowly and she dropped to her knees to take his place beside the mare. He watched her with a

119

critical eye as she worked, but she did not mind. She knew it would take a while to prove to the old man that she was capable.

"Winter is fast approaching," Brenna speculated. "The wind was chill on my bare arms as I came up the hill."

Erin chuckled. "You will be pleased with this fair weather, lassie, after you have had a taste of winter here. But aye, 'twill soon be upon us. The crops were harvested a fortnight past, and the sun sinks lower on the horizon. Before long, you will wish for the fires of Hell to warm you."

"Never that," Brenna admonished. "Mayhaps I can sleep here with the horses once the snow comes."

"Humph!" he grunted. "The notions you get, lass. Master Garrick would never allow that."

Brenna smiled slyly. "You thought he would not allow me to work here, but he did. Garrick is not so hard to persuade." Curiously she asked, "What does he do in winter, to occupy his time?"

"There is not much for anyone to do once the snows come. The master hunts mostly and gathers with his friends for drinking bouts. Usually he joins his brother Hugh for a month, to sail further north in search of the polar bear."

"Where is he now?"

"Gone for his morning ride."

"Does he ride every morn?"

Erin looked at her oddly. "Why so many questions, lass? Have you an eye for the master?"

"Certainly not!" Brenna retorted. "But if I am to stay here, then I would know all I can about the man who is master here."

"If?" he cocked an eyebrow. "You have no choice, lass."

Brenna rose, her task with the horse finished, and dusted straw from her skirt. "I have a choice, Erin. Do not doubt it," she said confidently.

A frown added to the wrinkles already on his brow. "What devilment is in your mind, girl? I warn you now for your own good, the master deals harshly with those who run away."

"*If* he finds them. Have no others from here sought their freedom?"

"Aye, two have. The female Hope tried to escape to the

hills in the heart of winter, but the master found her easily and brought her back. She spent two days in the punishment cell and was nearly frozen to death when finally released. She was taken with the other slaves who were sold."

"You said two?"

"A young man ran just last year. Hugh dealt with him since Garrick was not here. The lad was whipped to death before all. Hugh likes to make a warning well remembered."

Brenna shuddered. "This punishment cell. There is really such a place?"

Erin nodded grimly. " 'Tis below the house, facing the fjord. Ulric had it built for punishment, since he did not care for the whip. 'Tis just a small room carved in the cliff with a heavy door to seal it. A tiny square opening is in the door, with iron bars affixed, and this allows the only air to enter, but it also lets in the cold in winter. 'Tis not a pleasant room, but the master has made use of it on occasion."

"Well, never fear, Erin. I will not see that room. When and if I go, I will leave the land and not be found."

"By ship?" he laughed shortly. "How, lassie? There are only three ships on this fjord. The master's, his father's and one belonging to the clan across the fjord. None of these will sail again till spring, and you alone could never handle one by yourself."

"I did not imagine I could," Brenna replied stiffly, feeling a certain despair descend on her.

Just then they heard a rider approaching. A moment later the great black stallion pranced his way into the stable. Garrick sat straight and tall on the stallion's back, dressed in dark brown tunic and trousers, his blond hair tousled from the ride.

Brenna's eyes appraised the horse and rider appreciatively. The horse was powerfully sleek, a magnificent animal. But then, so was the rider, she admitted shamelessly. His was a body whose great strength was obvious from the bulging muscles in the bare arms, a body that was immensely pleasing to look upon. And his face could make a weaker wench swoon, so boyish when smiling, so ruggedly handsome when serious. Indeed, Brenna had never known such a man as this. She thought, a bit unsettlingly, that she could look at him for hours and not grow bored with what she saw.

Garrick sat motionless for a long moment, wondering at Brenna's bold perusal of him. He noticed quickly that she seemed overly pleased with herself. No doubt she thought she had scored a victory over him. Had she?

Gradually a smile made Garrick's lips curve and he dismounted, then tossed the reins to Brenna. She took them, and without being told, led the stallion to the stall she had previously seen him in. Erin came forward to remove the heavy saddle, but Garrick held up a hand and dismissed him. The old man returned to the back of the stable, mumbling that his bones could well use the rest.

"The horse needs grooming, mistress," Garrick finally spoke, his tone condescending. "See to it."

"You think I cannot?" she retorted, slightly piqued. "Is this a test then?"

"Nay, 'twas an order, wench. You have been given a task—do it."

"You—ohh!"

She stilled her tongue and gave him a murderous glare instead, before she tackled the saddle. Several strenuous pulls were needed before it gave way, then the heavy weight nearly toppled her backward. She then swung with maddening force to place the saddle over the stall rail. Her breasts heaving with the effort, she looked at him triumphantly.

"There!"

Folding his arms across his chest, Garrick leaned against one of the stall beams. "There what? You have not finished. Must I tell you what to do next?"

"I can care for horses better than you, Viking. I wager I can handle them better too!" she snapped, grabbing a rag to rub down the stallion's sweaty coat. "Were I atop him this morn, he would not have kicked the mare!"

"You grasp every opportunity to act the male," he sneered at her. "But I have seen the other side of you, wench."

"Be gone with you!" Brenna shouted furiously, her face reddening. "I do not need you to watch over me!"

Garrick laughed heartily. "Now you would order me from my own stable. Does your audacity have no bounds?"

122

She looked at him and could not help but grin. She *had* overstepped her limits this time, she knew.

"You are right," she said, her anger gone. "Stay if you like, though I do not know why you would wish to."

He refrained from pointing out that he did not need her permission. Instead he watched her quietly, noting that she did indeed know what she was about. When she brought oats to the stallion, Garrick spoke again.

"How fared you last night?"

She looked at him out of the corner of her eye, wondering at his concern. "Well enough."

"You did not miss the softness of my bed?" he asked her, his eyes gleaming mischievously.

She grinned at his question. "I find my new bed much more to my liking, since I need not share it."

He moved closer to her, taking advantage of her lightened mood, and tilted her chin up. "What makes you think you will not share it?"

Before she could answer, his arms enclosed her and he lowered his mouth to hers. The kiss was a shock to her senses. It was her first kiss, for she could not count the one given by Hugh. Garrick's mouth was gentle against hers, and moved softly. Then his tongue parted her lips and sweetly explored her mouth, giving yet another jolt to her senses.

Brenna found to her amazement that this tender closeness was immensely pleasing. Her blood seemed to be speeding through her veins and making her light-headed. She also found she wanted to be even closer to this man and wrapped her arms about his neck, pressing her body firmly against his hard one. She felt him jerk in surprise, and then his arms seemed to crush her while his kiss became more demanding, as if he would devour her whole.

Had her simple movement spurred him to this ardent attack? She liked it and didn't want him to stop. She felt the fires of passion burning in her. He was the enemy, but that didn't seem to matter to her traitorous body. The feel of him was like a drug, blinding her to all else.

This was not right, she told herself, even as she delighted in the reeling of her senses. She must stop him; she must. Finally she gathered the strength to pull her lips away and gain the time she needed to recover her wits, which she did quickly. When he would not release her, she laughed softly in his ear.

"Would you take me here, tumble me in the hay with Erin about?"

His arms left her so quickly she fell back a step. He stared at her for a long moment, a dark scowl on his face. Then he turned on his heel and stalked away, and she had to suppress her laughter so that he would not hear it and become even further enraged. She had won another round, though this one had been much more difficult.

Chapter 16

A FORTNIGHT had passed since Brenna began to work at the stable. She and Erin had become close since then, for he treated her like a daughter, and she enjoyed working with him.

Brenna finished currying the white mare and patted her flanks. When her work at the stables was done, Erin sometimes let her take one of the horses out for an hour or so. She chose the brown stallion this time. Waving to Erin, she mounted the horse and left the yard. She urged the animal into a canter, and when they passed through the flat meadow, pressed him into a hard gallop. For the first time that day she felt free. With her dark hair secured in back and the reins held loosely in one hand, she flew past the row of trees to her left toward the land that lay between the cliffs and the fjord. She forgot her captive status and her struggles in this strange and alien land. An exhilaration that she had not felt in months took hold of her. The sky was blue, and in the distance she could see the waters of the fjord glistening in the sun as she and the steed beneath her raced effortlessly across the hard ground. A smile was on her lips, and she felt her whole body alive with new-found freedom and joy. She lost all sense of time. It seemed that she had been riding for hours, for days, yet she felt not at all tired and the horse seemed as eager and fresh as he did when they first left the stables. The smile left her face an hour or so later when, in the distance, she saw two riders fast approaching her. They were still too far away to identify. Who could they be? she wondered. Not Garrick, for he had returned from his morning ride shortly before she left and she attended to his winded stallion. Hugh perhaps? And Anselm? Her face hardened at the thought that she would confront her sworn enemy. But as they came closer, she saw with surprise that they were unknown to her. They were upon her now, and as they saw the woman with the dark hair they looked at each other, smiled and reined in their horses. They were tall and blond. Brenna did not like the looks of them. One had darting eyes which she did not trust, and the other, a long jagged scar running across one cheek which gave him an evil look.

"You are no Viking with that hair," said the one with the scar. "A captured slave, perhaps?"

A look of rage passed over Brenna's face. She reached for the knife she kept hidden in her boot and held it low, waiting for the right moment to attack. They saw the glint of the knife's blade and nodded to each other, then rode quickly on either side of her, one grabbing her horse's bridle, the other attempting to wrest the knife from her hand. She lashed out with the knife, but the one she lunged for threw up his hand, which was slashed by the blade. He swore as blood flowed from the wound.

An ugly, angry scowl appeared on his companion's face. As Brenna turned, he dragged her from her horse. She hit the ground and lay stunned for a moment, while he grabbed the knife from her and pinned her arms behind her head. The other wrapped a piece of cloth around his hand and now, a cruel look contorting his face, he brutally tied her arms tightly together above her head.

"So you would provoke me, wench," said the wounded one with a snarl as he lowered himself on top of her and, securing her legs with his, began to move against her. Brenna felt his manhood against her and kicked furiously, but his weight pinned her and she could not move him. He pulled fiercely at the top of her shirt and ripped it down

126

to the waist, exposing her white, perfectly shaped breasts. She kicked and she bit, but this only increased his pleasure, and he fumbled at his pants to free his swollen member. As he made to enter her, he heard the sound of pounding hooves nearby and looked up in alarm.

Please, dear God, let it be a friend, not a foe, prayed Brenna silently. She took advantage of his hesitation and tried to buck him off, but his great weight still would not be moved. A second later, to her surprise, his bulk was off of her and she heard him say to his companion with fear in his voice, "Let us be gone." He grabbed his pants, pulling them up as he ran to his mount. The two of them gave the spur to their horses and galloped off.

Brenna turned her head and saw Garrick rein in his steed a few feet from her. She lay without moving, red-faced with humiliation, her fear of a minute ago forgotten. Oh, that he should have to rescue her as though she were one of those weak, helpless women she despised. And trussed up like a turkey, too. She closed her eyes in shame for a moment. When she opened them she was surprised to see Garrick bending over her with a look of concern in his aqua eyes.

"You are not harmed, Brenna?" he asked softly as he reached down to touch her face.

"Leave me alone!" she cried, blushing with fury.

He pulled back as though he had been slapped, and a hard look settled over his features. "Get up," he said and pulled her to her feet. He gave her the torn shirt to cover herself, then pushed her toward her mount. "That's the last time you ride alone," he said tightly. "Who gave you permission to leave the yard at all?" She did not answer him.

He looked into the distance. "I did not get a close look at your attackers, and though I will send men after them when we return, they are likely itinerant traders or brigands. Chances are they will have left the fjord by then and will not be found. You could have been killed," he added angrily, turning back to her. "Now get on your horse," and he pushed her toward the stallion. "I'm beginning to think I would be well advised to sell you at the next slave market in Hedeby."

He did not speak to her or acknowledge her for the

rest of the return ride, and when they entered the yard he tossed the reins of his horse at her and strode away.

Brenna saw Garrick daily now, in the mornings when he went for his customary ride, and most days in the afternoon too. Each time he returned, he would turn the sweaty stallion over to her. They did not talk. In truth, he had not said one word to her since that day when he had rescued her. He did not even acknowledge her presence, except to toss her the stallion's reins; then he would walk away stiffly.

Brenna often puzzled over why he ignored her so purposely, and wondered if what he had said was true, that he did not bother with women except when his body demanded he must. It rankled her some that she had no effect on him, for she had begun to think otherwise. He, on the other hand, still had the power to make her immensely aware of his presence. She would find at the oddest times that she had him on her mind, and this did not sit well with her. Most annoying was the fact that she could not forget that day he had sought to humble her, but had accomplished naught. Garrick had obviously dismissed it from his mind completely.

Brenna soaked in a small tub. Her head rested on the rim, and her thick black hair floated all about her in the warm water. Her thoughts were gentle, her mood relaxed.

She was alone in the small house; a fire blazed in the hearth nearby. Janie and Maudya were still up at the big house, no doubt serving Garrick his evening meal.

Brenna did not hear the door when it quietly opened, but she sensed the intrusion when cold air touched her face and made her shiver. She looked up to see a very tall Viking standing just inside the doorway, and surprised emerald eyes looking down at her.

"Go back the way you came, Viking, and close the door before I catch a chill."

He closed the door, but from the inside, then moved closer to her. Brenna looked down to make sure her hair covered her body from view before she looked back at the intruder suspiciously. She had not seen this man before, but his height and build reminded her of Garrick, and her eyes admired him slowly. His face was pleasingly handsome, and she noted humor and even kindness there. The smile on his lips reached all the way to his eyes and crinkled their outer edges.

He obviously had not understood her order. This language barrier was indeed a nuisance. She could make herself clear, but still she would not. Instead she motioned with her hands for him to go, but he just shook his head, his smile broadening.

"Be gone, damn you!" she shouted in frustration.

"There is no need for you to get upset, mistress."

Her eyes widened. "You speak my tongue."

"Yea, Garrick taught me when we were young," he replied, amused at her confusion.

"Who are you?" she finally asked.

"Perrin."

Her expression became knowing. "If you have come for Janie, she is not here."

"I can see that," he replied and moved even closer. "So you are Garrick's new slave." He stated this as a fact, not seeing the hot fury that leaped into her eyes when he spoke. "I have heard much of you."

"And I of you," Brenna retorted angrily. "I do not respect a man who does not claim his son, or take the mother of that son to be his own."

Perrin looked astonished; then he frowned. "So Janie has a loose tongue."

"Do not blame Janie," Brenna replied coldly. "She spoke of you only with love and pride, and does not hold your cowardice against you. You do not mind that other men bed the mother of your son?"

A look of deep hurt crossed his face. "I mind. But there is naught I can do about it yet. She belongs to Garrick."

"And you fear to ask him for her," Brenna said with obvious contempt.

"What I fear, wench, is his refusal, for then I could not ask again."

"If I were you, I would take what I wanted. You Vikings seem ever willing to do that."

Perrin suddenly laughed, surprising her. "So you are as arrogant and outspoken as they say. I see Garrick has not tamed you yet."

Brenna smiled at this despite her earlier anger. "If you

look closely, you will see that Garrick is the one who has been tamed. He was no match for me."

"I wonder if Garrick agrees with that," he replied, and finally moved next to the tub.

Brenna stared up at him impishly. "You like what you see, Viking?" she teased, amazed at herself for doing so.

"Most assuredly," he answered.

"Well, if you have in mind to see more, you can forget it now. I will choose my own lovers, not they me. And you, to be sure, will not be one of them."

He laughed heartily, his green eyes twinkling. "Those are brave words for a wench who finds herself at my mercy." He ran a finger through the water, grinning down at her.

"Careful, Viking." Her voice grew cold. "Janie would never forgive me if I had to harm you."

"Ha!" he chuckled. "And you would no doubt tell her, wouldn't you?"

"I would."

He stepped back. "Well, you have naught to fear from me, wench. I will not touch you."

She smiled at him. "I did not fear you, Perrin. I fear no man."

He crooked a brow at her. "Not even Garrick?"

"Especially not Garrick."

"You would be wise to, mistress," he replied seriously. "Do not take him as lightly as you seem to."

With that he turned and departed, leaving her wondering over his unexpected warning.

Garrick sat alone at the long table, finishing a hearty stew and brooding on his solitude. Dog lay at his feet, his tail thumping noisily on the cold floor, waiting patiently for a scrap of meat. Most times Garrick enjoyed the peaceful quiet, but at other times like now, he almost wished he had remained at his parents' home instead of moving to this cold, empty house. He missed the warmth of his family, of good talk and companionship. He did not even have Yarmille to keep him company at meals, for she only stayed at his house when he was away. When he was here, she lived at her home with her son. And now that he had fewer slaves for her to supervise, she only came twice a week to give them instructions.

Garrick absently speared a chunk of venison and gave it to the shepherd. Soon the servants would finish their duties in the house and return to their quarters for the night. Then he would be completely alone in this big house, with only Dog to follow him to bed.

Three years ago he had thought it would be different. How wrong he was. He had hopes of a new family that would add pleasure to his life. Sons that he could watch grow, a loving wife to warm his bed. A bigger fool never lived than was sitting at this table! Now he would never have a woman to share his life. He would never trust one enough to give his love to her. He would not ever leave himself open to that hurt again.

Dog perked up his head when Janie's shrill giggles came from the cooking area. A moment later Perrin came into the hall, a satisfied smile on his lips. He hailed Garrick and joined him at the table.

"I swear you spend more time with that wench when you come to visit than you do with me," Garrick said good-naturedly, glad to be interrupted in his brooding.

"I admit I find her company more pleasing than yours. Your disposition is usually too sour, when hers is oh, so sweet." Perrin laughed.

"Humph! I should have known she was the only reason you came," Garrick replied, pretending to be affronted. "Off with you, then. I free her from her duties to await your pleasure."

"You wound me, Garrick," Perrin said, bringing his hands to his heart to emphasize his point. " 'Tis a sorry day when a man seeks a woman's company over that of a trusted friend."

"Aye," Garrick returned, no longer teasing. Then he smiled. "So what has kept you away so long? I missed you at the feast and have not seen you since we returned home."

"I have been harvesting what few fields I have. Unlike you, I have not so many slaves that I need not bother with the crops myself."

"You should have asked for help, Perrin. My fields were

harvested a month ago. The slaves had naught better to do, nor had I."

"Mayhaps next year I will—but for a price."

"Bah! You wish to put a price on friendship? Now 'tis you who wounds me!"

"I will hold you to it then, Garrick, if you return from the East in time."

Surprise crossed Garrick's features. "You will not sail with me in the spring?"

"I have not decided yet," Perrin answered soberly. "My mother did not fare well during the winter with me away."

"We did well our first time at trading," Garrick replied. "Mayhaps we did tarry too long with the Slavs so that we had to stay. But that should not happen again."

"That, only Odin can say for sure," Perrin admitted. "We will see."

Janie came in with tankards of ale and both men fell silent. Garrick saw the look that passed between Perrin and the girl, and almost envied the relationship they shared. He wished he could take a wench so lightly, without committing himself.

When Janie left, Perrin grinned and leaned closer to Garrick. "I happened upon your new slave on the way here."

"Oh?"

"Aye. I stopped by the women's quarters first to see if Janie was there, but instead I found that black-haired beauty at her bath."

Garrick's eyes darkened. "And?"

"I wonder why you put her from you when your bed is big enough for two."

"Humph!" Garrick grunted. "You must not have had words with her or you wouldn't have asked that. She is a rose indeed, but her thorns are too sharp for my liking."

"Oh, I had words with her—quite a few," Perrin smiled. "She boldly teased me, in fact, only to turn around and threaten me if I should touch her."

"Did you?" Garrick scowled.

"Nay, but I'll wager the next man will who comes across her. You do not mind sharing that one?"

"Why should I? Mayhaps *that* will put her in her place," Garrick said sourly.

Perrin laughed. "You have yet to keep the promise you made at the feast? The wench is not tamed, eh?"

"You do not have to remind me of that drunken promise," Garrick grimaced. He recalled it clearly, for he was not *that* drunk at the time, merely angered by his brother's constant teasing that he could never handle such a termagant as Brenna. Placing his hands on the yule boar dedicated to the god Frey and drinking from the sacred cup, he had promised before all that he would tame her.

Little did he know then what a difficult chore he set for himself. The course he decided on had failed. She was not humbled by the outcome, but quite pleased, and since that was not the objective, it rankled him sorely. Yet to mar her with the lash would be useless, he knew; besides, his heart would not be in it. Although she would not bend to his will, at least she served him, even if it was not as he had first ordered.

"So she will not work for you?" Perrin asked.

"Nay, she works in the stable."

"You allow that?" Perrin looked surprised.

" 'Tis the only thing she would agree to," Garrick admitted grudgingly, his scowl deepening.

Perrin's laughter rang through the hall. "So the wench was right! 'Tis you who has been tamed, not her."

"She said that?"

Perrin's laughter died and he frowned at the black rage that gripped his friend. "Come now, Garrick. I would not cause the wench harm because of my words."

"She will not be harmed, but by Thor, she will not be so pleased with herself on the morrow!"

A dark cloud seemed to have enveloped Garrick. Perrin watched him and sighed inwardly. He sorely regretted his rash words, and hoped the girl would not fare too badly because of them.

Chapter 17

GARRICK made his way to the slave quarters, a brooding anger eating at him every step of the way. Stealthily he opened the door to the women's house and went inside. A soft reddish glow from the dying fire aided him in finding his quarry, and he moved to her.

Brenna was fast asleep on a mat by the hearth, curled under an old woolen blanket. Her silken hair was loose and flowed behind her, looking as if bedecked with rubies from the firelight. Long black lashes shaded her cheeks, and her parted lips were moist like dewy pink rose petals.

The sight of her so sweet and innocent in sleep stirred Garrick's blood. That she was a she-devil when awake was forgotten. He bent and gently removed the blanket. When the chill air from the open door touched her bare feet, her face puckered in a frown and she pulled her legs up closer to her chest to seek the lost warmth. Her small form was hidden beneath a rough, voluminous nightdress no doubt given her by the plump Maudya, asleep across the room.

Garrick well remembered the silken limbs that were now wrapped up so snugly, the soft arms and long, tapered thighs, the firm twin mounds of her breasts and taut flatness of her belly. He thought too of the delicate curve of her waist and the gentle, rounded buttocks that begged to be patted, the velvety smoothness of her back and the satin hollows of her neck that he had kissed.

Garrick quickly shook the imaginings from his mind before they got the better of him, and he acted like a rutting stallion with no care for privacy. With a deft movement he clamped his hand over Brenna's mouth to still her cry of alarm, for it would wake the others. Her eyes opened instantly, but before she could see who was abducting her, he picked her up and crushed her against the rock hardness of his chest, then carried her squirming form out into the night.

When he reached the stable, he put her down. She faced him angrily, her hair flowing over her shoulders to her waist like a raven's cloak. Then she recognized him and her temper cooled completely.

"Oh, 'tis you," she said in a tone that implied he did not merit her concern.

"And who else would it be?"

"One of your friends," she retorted. "That one called Bayard I wager would like to pay me back in turn for what I did to him. Your brother too would like to lay me low."

"And you fear them?"

"Nay, but I am not fool enough to take them lightly," she answered.

" 'Tis only *me* you take lightly, eh?" he growled.

She looked at him in surprise. "Why should I fear you, Viking? You have shown me your worst, but in truth, 'twas not so bad."

He stepped closer to her, his anger mounting again. "Do I carry you the rest of the way, mistress, or will you walk?"

"Nay, I will not go with you. I do not like being roused from sleep for your pleasure."

" 'Tis not my pleasure we're about, wench."

"Oh? What then?"

"Will you come?"

Before she could say yea, for her curiosity was pricked, he took her elbow and pushed her roughly before him. She pulled away and halted when the rocks on the ground made her aware of her bare feet.

"Why do you stop?" he asked, his tone impatient.

"Is it your wish to have my feet bloodied? It seems you must carry me after all," she said with an impish smile.

He hesitated for a long moment, staring at her darkly before he yanked her to him and lifted her off the ground. At once she wrapped her arms tightly about his neck, and heard him grunt his disapproval as she did. With quick strides he reached the back of the house and the stairs leading up to the second floor. He mounted them rapidly, taking two steps at a time. Her weight seemed to be no more than a sack of feathers in his arms.

Once inside the house, he let her slip to the floor, but Brenna purposely kept her arms about his neck a moment longer than she need have before she dropped them at her sides. His face was impassive as he pushed her on ahead of him.

She had not been in this house since the day he took her innocence, and she immediately noticed the changes that had taken place since then. Ornate gold candle-holders were now affixed to the walls at intervals, and between them hung small, brightly stitched tapestries with gold-fringed borders. On the floor a narrow rug ran the length of the wide corridor. It was black and silver, with gold stitching spiraling along the edges. The atmosphere was quite an improvement over the gloomy one that prevailed before.

Brenna hesitated when she saw that they were approaching Garrick's chambers, but he shoved her inside, then closed the door behind them. She whirled on him, arms akimbo, her eyes flashing stormily.

"Have you deceived me, Viking? For what purpose are we here?"

"Our purpose, as you put it, I expect will be lengthy. Knowing your aversion to drafts, I chose this room since 'tis the warmest in the house at present."

"How thoughtful," she muttered sarcastically.

Indeed, the room was cozy. A fire blazed in the hearth, and warmed the large room entirely. Brenna noticed that here too improvements had been made. Two identical huge rugs that nearly joined, covered the cold floor in a bright blue and gold pattern. Two large tapestries hung on the walls. One was of peasants toiling in a field under a brilliant sky, and the other told a detailed story in miniature against a yellow background. A backless divan had also been added to the room. Covered in rich blue and white brocade, it had carved lions' paws for legs.

Brenna took all of this in with surprise before she eyed Garrick again. "Well, will you tell me now why I am here? And why did you come for me the way you did, in such secrecy?"

He shrugged and walked to the small table where a skin of wine and a plate of cheese rested. "I did not know your mood, so I chose not to risk your making a ruckus and waking the other women. There is no point for them to lose sleep just because you and I have things to settle."

Brenna stiffened. "We settled everything. What else is there?"

"We settled naught, mistress."

"Yet I work for you," she replied, her voice rising. "I earn my keep! What more do you want of me?"

He walked over to the large coffer set against the wall and took from it a gray silk robe trimmed elegantly with white fur. Then he came to stand before her, only inches away, so that she had to tilt her head up to look at him as he spoke.

"Aye, you worked, gladly, but not as I wanted. I gave in to you because at the time I could see no other way. Slaves are not supposed to enjoy their labors, mistress, yet you surely did." He paused. "No more."

"Oh?"

A cold smile crossed his lips. "We will start anew. You will do the tasks originally set for you, and you will begin with this," he said, handing her the short robe. "There is a small tear under one arm that needs repairing."

She stared at him, aghast. "Lord in heaven!" she cried in exasperation.

"Your god cannot help you, wench, nor will mine. You have only me to deal with."

"I won't do it, Garrick!" she replied furiously, throwing the robe to the floor. "You know I won't!"

He shrugged again, unperturbed, and walked back to the table. "Then you will remain in this room until you change your mind," he said over his shoulder.

"Nay, only until you sleep, Viking."

"Then it appears you must be guarded again. Dog," he called, and the white shepherd came from the bed. Brenna had not even noticed him, his fur coat blended so well with the ermine. "Stay by the door and see that the wench does not leave," Garrick commanded.

The animal seemed to understand every word. He turned his head and looked at Brenna inconsequentially before moving to the door, where he lay down to rest again. Brenna cast the dog a murderous look, then turned that same look on his master.

"I have tried not to hate you, Viking, since you were not personally to blame for my being here, but you are making it difficult!"

His lips turned up in a cynical smile. "Hate me all you like, mistress. 'Twill not change a thing. My feelings for you are not much different, for you have been naught but an ill-tempered, troublesome wench since you came, a thorn in my side that I can do without. At least we know where we stand." He took a long draught of wine, then began to remove his clothing.

"Now what?"

"We have reached an impasse, so there will be no more discussion this night. To bed, mistress."

"I am no longer tired," she said sourly.

"So?"

"You may force me to stay in this room, but I will not sleep in that bed with you!" she stormed.

"Oh?" he crooked an eyebrow at her. "I thought by the game you played since last you lay there that you would be more than willing to do so again."

"You thought wrong!" she snapped, her cheeks reddening.

"Well, no matter. Since I do not mind sharing my bed, you *will* sleep there. But never fear, mistress. I will not take advantage of you, for you will not find pleasure in this room. Now to bed, and if not to sleep, then to think on your stubbornness."

Brenna's body urged her to consciousness. It seemed to cry out, Wake up, wake up and see what pleasures await you. The dream was dispelled and her eyes opened slowly in surprise at the strange sensations she felt, then they widened fully when she understood what was happening.

She lay on her side facing the wall, her arms resting on the pillow under her face, one leg raised and bent at the knee, the other leg straight. She was on top of the soft ermine spread, as she had been before she fell asleep with Garrick beside her. But now her nightdress was pulled up and bunched about her waist, leaving her hips and legs completely bare.

She lay perfectly still and managed to keep her breathing even as if she continued to sleep. Garrick's chest was pressed against her back, the warmth of him seeping through her nightdress. His arm rested on her waist, his hand beneath the material was squeezed between her breasts, gently teasing one. She could feel his breath on her neck, hot and tickling, and his hand moved slowly downward, trailing over the taut curve of her belly, then on to her hip and down her thigh. The sensation caused goosebumps to spread over her legs. Then his hand moved deftly to her inner thigh and began to ascend with maddening slowness until it finally stopped on the soft mound of black curls between her legs. There the hand lingered, the fingers gently parting the curls, nudging their way into the moist, hot flesh that already quivered with delight.

With startled wonderment, Brenna heard a soft moan escape her lips. She knew she should run, flee, but instead she slowly turned onto her back to lay the way open for those questing fingers. A seductive smile curled on her lips when she saw the ardent look in Garrick's turquoise eyes.

"It took you long enough to wake, wench," he murmured in a teasing manner.

It amazed her that he could be so warm and tender, when he was usually so abrupt and harsh. But she did not mind, and this amazed her also; she actually looked forward to this moment. The last time they had laid thus, she had experienced genuine pleasure, but she also sensed that even more intense delight could be reached.

"I could have sworn, Sir Viking, that you said I would find no pleasure in this bed," she said, running her fingers through the golden hair on his bare chest. "You cannot keep your word for a single night?"

"It seems, mistress," he replied huskily, lowering his parted lips to hers for a gentle kiss, "that I spoke in haste. But you have yourself to blame, for in truth, your mannish ways do vanish once you are abed." He grinned down at her. "Why is that?"

She shrugged, then smiled impishly. "I find that being a woman on occasion has its merits. And I am not too timid to admit it."

"Timid, ha!" he laughed. "Never that!"

" 'Tis well you know it, Viking," she returned, her hand moving to his neck to pull him closer. "Now you will not be surprised by my actions."

She kissed him hungrily, and even though she had said the words, he was amazed. That her nearness had tempted him beyond control was a fact. That she was driving him wild with passion now was even more true. She urged him to take her, and he did, without hesitation. She opened her legs to him and he thrust deep into her inner recesses. He clutched her buttocks to press her even closer to him and rode her like a stallion rides the wind. Before the final thrust, he felt her legs wrap around his hips and then he was lost in that white sphere of fire and delight that had spurred him to break his word and make her his.

Breathing heavily, Garrick rested his full weight on her small form, his head nestled against her neck. Finally he moved to get up, but her arms locked behind his head and held him tight, and her legs still circled his hips. He looked down, questioningly, and noted the alluring slant of her eyes, the sensual twist of her lips.

"Show me your strength, Viking," she breathed, squirming her body enticingly beneath his. "Continue."

"By the gods, woman, have you no shame?" he asked in disbelief.

"Why?" she returned undaunted. "Is it shameful that I like this? Am I supposed to pretend otherwise?"

"Nay, but no woman has ever asked more of me."

"Do not compare me with your other wenches, Viking!" she said hotly, and released her hold on him. "Leave off then if you have not the strength to satisfy me!"

He grabbed the hands she pushed against his chest and stretched them out at her sides. "The tactics you use are unseemly, vixen," he sneered.

With deliberation he started to move in her again, and at the same time crushed her lips with a painful kiss. It took but a moment for the spark of desire to be rekindled. Garrick thrust with a steady, purposeful rhythm and at length released her arms and cupped her face in his hands. His kiss became more intense, more demanding. He could feel her hands roving over his back, kneading the hard muscles there. She began to moan softly and her arms circled his neck again, tighter and tighter she squeezed as if she would hold on for dear life. Even in his own fiery haze, he noted her wild abandon and at last the breath caught in her throat and she went rigid, her nails digging into his shoulders like cat's claws. His name escaped her lips in a throaty whisper. At that moment he joined her in that most sought-after realm of explosive delights.

This time she did not protest when he moved to her side. They both lay exhausted, breathing heavily. When she touched his shoulder softly, his mind rebelled, for he feared that she would dare demand more of him yet.

" 'Tis not yet morning, mistress," he said tiredly, his eyes closed. "Go back to sleep."

"I only wished to thank you, Garrick. That is all."

He opened his eyes to see the tender expression on her face before she turned away from him and pulled her nightdress down. He stared hard at the back of her head, wondering anew at the many different temperaments this woman possessed. This one he liked best.

His features softened. "Come here, wench," he said huskily and pulled her back into his arms.

He knew she wouldn't resist, and this pleased him even more. She snuggled close to him, and he knew without a doubt that he could grow accustomed to this woman without much effort.

" 'Tis nice, Garrick, not fighting with you," Brenna breathed softly against his chest, already half asleep.

He smiled to himself and unconsciously held her closer. The effect she had on him was startling. If she kept this up, he would want her again.

"Yea, Brenna, 'tis nice indeed."

Chapter 18

BRENNA sat across the small table from Garrick, her morning meal before her. She was slumped back in her chair, moodily picking at her food, every few moments flashing Garrick a furious look. But he was too intent on his meal to notice.

For one week now he had kept her confined to this room, with only the cursed white shepherd for company. Garrick brought Brenna her meals himself, but left her alone for the length of the day, only returning at night. He did not touch her again after the night he carried her here, even conceding when she insisted she would sleep on the divan instead of next to him in the large bed.

Awakening that first morning after their night together, she was appalled at the memory of what she had done. It was not Brenna who had acted no better than a wanton whore, but her contemptible female body. That traitorous instrument had demanded to know the full fruits of its awakening, had even teased and cajoled Garrick to show her. He had stirred a fire within her that she never dreamed existed, but never again. The delicious pleasure she had experienced could be denied. Yea, that kind of ecstasy she did not need, for she would have to give up too much to attain it again. . . .

Though it was too late to change what had happened, she would be damned before it was repeated. She had been a fool to think Garrick would change his mind because of it; he was still determined that she would serve him as he demanded. She could not forgive him for that, not after the tenderness that had passed between them.

With Dog resting between their feet, Brenna absently offered him a morsel of meat, accustomed to doing the same at home with her father's hounds, which romped through the manor. When the white shepherd nuzzled her hand for more, she realized what she had done and looked up to see Garrick scowling at her. Good, she thought viciously. It was better than the self-assured smirk he had worn so often of late.

"What displeases you, Viking?" she asked in an innocent tone, though her eyes were alight with mischief. "Do you fear I have taken the dog's loyalty from you?" When his countenance darkened even more, her grin widened and she pressed on. "You did not know he and I have become friends, eh? But what did you expect when you keep us locked together? 'Twill not be long before he does not even raise his head when I walk from this room."

Garrick stared at her coldly for a long moment before he finally answered. "If you speak the truth, mistress, then 'tis time I put a lock on the door."

Brenna's face turned ashen. "You wouldn't!"

"I would indeed," he replied, an icy tinge to his tone. "Tonight, in fact, since I have naught better to do."

"I was only teasing you, Garrick," Brenna said, trying to make light of it. "You can trust your dog to do your bidding."

"'Tis *you* I don't trust," he returned pointedly and made for the door with angry strides.

"How long will you keep me here?" she demanded furiously.

He turned at the door, the old sneer coming to his lips. " 'Tis not I who keeps you here, wench, but yourself. You have only to serve me as I desire and you may enjoy the same privileges as the other slaves."

"You pompous, overbearing ass!" she stormed, coming to her feet, her fists clenched. "You will rot in hell first!"

"You are a stubborn wench," he sneered disdainfully. "But you will find that I can be more so."

With that he left the room, leaving Brenna so thoroughly maddened that she picked up her full tankard of milk and hurled it at the closed door. Seeing the damage done, she did not stop there. With a destructive glint in her eye, she toppled over the small table; the platter of food crashed to the floor and sent Dog scampering out of her way. Determinedly she went to the bed and tore the covers from it, then moved to Garrick's coffer. With malicious pleasure, she flung its contents about the room.

So intent was Brenna on her task that she did not hear Garrick return. She was grabbed from behind and thrown on the bed.

"Your tantrums are those of a child, not the woman I know you to be!" he stormed, and followed her onto the bed.

When Brenna turned to face him he was on his knees, with one hand raised to strike her. She stared at that fist without flinching, daring him to do his worst. But Garrick hesitated a moment too long and the impulse passed. He lowered his arm with a curse and left the bed, then looked down on her with heartless fury.

"You have set your own task, wench. You will put this room to rights before eventide, or you will go hungry to bed this night. And if you have it in mind that one meal will not matter, then think again, for you will be denied sustenance until the task is done." And with that he left the room, slamming the door behind him.

"What shall I do, then, Dog?" Brenna asked softly as if the powerful animal would have a solution to her problem. "Shall I starve myself for spite? 'Tis not to my liking, but 'twould show that domineering jackal he cannot order me about. Damn him!" she cried. "Why does he do this to me? He would break my pride and grind it in the dirt!"

Everything was going so well before this, she thought. And now he would starve me. Aye, he has said the words and so cannot relent. 'Tis I who will have to concede this time.

Chapter 19

GARRICK topped a small hill and rested the stallion there. He dismounted and ran his hands through his tousled hair. His shoulders erect, he gazed up at the northern lights shining in the otherwise black sky, those mystical colors that cast a strange light on the land.

He had ridden hard for most of the day, at times not even aware of where he was, giving the great stallion his head to take him where he would. Still Garrick had not resolved the turmoil of his thoughts, and they had weighed heavily on him ever since he left the haughty Brenna. Her fate, the one he had set, hung like a dark cloud over his head.

He cursed himself a hundred times for the words he had spoken in anger, the words that might very well end the girl's life. Could she really be that stubborn? And over such a trivial matter? He should have followed his first impulse, which was to beat her. But he had been appalled at the thought of striking her lovely face. If he returned to his room and found it still in shambles, what then? If he backed down this time, he would never be able to handle the girl. If neither of them gave in, the girl would die. . .
If only he knew more of her character, then perhaps he

could predict how she would react. But who was there to enlighten him?

"Imbecile!" he said aloud. "There is such a one who can shed some light on the stubborn woman I have found myself harnessed to."

Garrick turned his mount in the direction of his father's house. After only a short ride, he entered Anselm's smoky hall and found his father and brother engrossed in a game of dice. His mother was busy sewing.

"Ho! What brings the merchant prince to our humble door this late of a night?" Hugh teased when Garrick joined them. "I would think you would need all your spare time to count the riches you have amassed."

"Nay, only half of it," Garrick rejoined, though he was in no mood for this light banter. "I came to have a word with one of the new slaves."

"Is it only a word you would have?" Hugh asked, then slapped his knee and guffawed at his wit.

"Enough, Hugh," Anselm said solemnly. His curiosity pricked, he turned to Garrick. "Which one?"

"One of the kin to Brenna," he answered. "It matters not which one."

"Oh?"

Garrick grimaced. "Father, I see the question on your face, but do not ask it. 'Tis I who have questions that need answering now."

"From Brenna's kin?" Anselm replied, grinning. "You would know more of her, eh?"

"Aye, I would know to what limits her pride would take her," he admitted.

"You do not make sense, Garrick. Have you problems with the girl?"

"You are a fine one to ask me that—you who praised her spirit," Garrick retorted. "Did you really think she would adjust to her new life here?"

Anselm sighed. "So the girl does not please you?"

"I have yet to decide if the pleasure she gives me in bed is worth the trouble she gives me out of it."

"Give her to me," Hugh broke in. "I would know what to do with the vixen."

"You would break her spirit as well as her will," Anselm remarked to his oldest son. "A woman with spirit is worth having, and must be tamed gently, not broken. Ah, Garrick, if that one ever gave you her loyalty, there would be none like it."

"You speak from experience?" Garrick asked, casting his mother a tender glance.

"I do," Anselm chuckled, "though I know I do not deserve the loyalty I have gained. Go find your answers, son. The women are out back."

When Garrick left the hall, Anselm shook his head and commented to Hugh, "Your brother seemed deeply troubled."

"Would that I had his troubles." Hugh grinned, but Anselm could find no humor in the situation.

Cordella quickly answered the forceful knock on the door before the noise woke the other women, who were sleeping. She assumed it was Hugh at the door, for she was expecting him. He had not come round to see her for the last few days. That Viking's amorous ways she had become well acquainted with in her short time here. She knew what he expected of her—resistance at every turn—and she played this new role easily. She could not afford for the Viking to lose interest in her, not if her plans were to be fulfilled.

Hugh Haardrad must believe himself to be the father of the child she suspected she was carrying. She would give him a son, and so assure her own future. Hugh's weak-kneed wife was thought to be barren; so Cordella had learned from Heloise, who said he had no bastards as yet either. Mayhaps one day she might even gain marriage from her deception. She knew the child could not be Hugh's, but she would swear it was, and his own mother would concur, for Cordella had purposely complained bitterly to the older woman of the trials of the ocean voyage, how the cramps of her monthly time had made it worse. Yea, she had wisely thought ahead. At least *she* would not have such a hard time of it here.

She was careful not to look overly anxious when she opened the door. It was not Hugh who stood there in the cold, but his brother Garrick. She had seen this one before on occasion, when he came to visit his father, and she had been entranced by his handsomeness. He was a striking man, much more so than Hugh. Still, Hugh would be head of the clan one day, with power and wealth, and so she preferred him.

"You are Brenna's sister?" Garrick asked her. At her slow nod he continued gruffly, "Then I would have a word with you, mistress. Will you walk with me?"

Cordella hugged her arms and shivered as the chill wind ruffled her coarse skirt. "I will get a wrap."

"Nay," he replied. Shaking off the heavy fur cloak he wore, he wrapped it over her shoulders. "I am impatient."

She bit her lip as she walked with him away from the house she shared with the other female slaves. She was a bit fearful that this tall Viking wanted her and was taking her away from the others to have his pleasure. Though she would indeed relish the experience, it would not suit her plans. No one but Hugh had bedded her since she first arrived and he put his claim on her.

"I have a problem, mistress," Garrick said as they walked slowly about the settlement. "I seek your help if you can give it." He went on to explain about Brenna's attitude and her stubborn refusal to serve him, ending with their last confrontation this morning. "I would know if she will prove stubborn on this also. Does she value her life so little?"

Cordella wanted to laugh, but she dared not. So Brenna was acting true to form, just as Cordella knew she would. The Viking showed real concern, which Brenna certainly didn't deserve. Mayhaps there was a way to further her own revenge, Cordella thought maliciously.

" 'Tis typical of Brenna," Cordella answered. "But she would never do anything to risk her life," she added firmly.

"Yet she fought against my father when he attacked your home. She risked her life then."

"Brenna never really believed real harm would come to her that day," Cordella explained with a convincing expression. "She assumed you Vikings would not kill a woman. As for Brenna's stubborness, 'tis only a ruse to see how much she can gain. She feels that menial labor is beneath her, and in truth, she is lazy and would be happy if she need not lift a finger to do anything. All her life she has had servants to wait on her."

"She did work in my stable," Garrick argued. "She says 'tis only women's work she will not do."

"Did you see her do the work?" Cordella asked. "Or did she coax someone else to do it for her? Nay, 'twas the same at home. Brenna expected everyone to serve her, even her family, while she spent all of her time diverting herself with the village men, tempting them away from their wives."

"'Tis a different Brenna you describe, not the one I know who shuns men."

"'Tis only what she wants you to believe," Cordella said slyly. "Nay, the real Brenna is a tease with a whore's heart. She knows she is comely and would have every man she knows fall for her charms. She even coveted my own husband, who was smitten by her also."

"But she was a virgin!"

Cordella smiled. "Is she still?" She saw his dark scowl, yet this did not stop her from adding, "If you want her only for yourself, Viking, then you had best keep a watchful eye on her, for she would never be content with just one man. I know my sister well."

"I did not say I want her for myself, mistress," he said brusquely.

Garrick left his father's house feeling more disgruntled and confused than when he came. Cordella's words did not sit well with him and he returned home in a dark mood.

A few minutes later Garrick stood before the door to his chambers. He hesitated a moment, wondering again what he would find inside. He held a tray of food awkwardly with one hand and threw open the bolt with the other, then went inside. Dog came to his feet immediately, his tail wagging. "Go on, Dog," Garrick said, "your food is below." He waited until the shepherd trotted from the room, then closed the door with his foot. Only a single candle burned on the mantel, but in the dim light he could see the room was in order. Surprised, he searched further until he found Brenna sitting on a chair staring into the fire. He set the tray down, then went over to her. He looked at her, wondering anew if what her sister said was true. Was Brenna just playing a game with him? Why should her sister lie?

"Why did you take so long?" Brenna asked. "I am famished."

He wondered bitterly if she had only put the room to rights after hunger had gnawed at her belly for a while.

"Aye, 'tis late," he replied. He built up the fire, then stood up and waited for the tirade to begin. When it did not come immediately, Garrick eyed her speculatively and moved toward the table to join her, finally feeling his own hunger. Brenna was deep in thought as she ate, a frown creasing her brow.

"You were detained, then?" she finally asked.

"Nay, I simply forgot that you would be waiting on my return," he answered rather sharply.

Then suddenly she laughed, causing Garrick no small amount of confusion. "Good. I am glad that you can forget me so easily, Viking."

"Why so?"

"Why not?" she countered, a smile on her lips. "You think I want myself bandied about in your thoughts? Nay, for I know not the direction of your thinking. Whether 'tis good or bad, I do not wish to weigh on your mind."

He grunted. "You have odd ways of proving that, mistress, what with your behavior thus far."

"So I have been on your mind?" she asked innocently, humor in her voice. "I *am* sorry, Garrick. I suppose I will have to change my ways, then."

He put down his food and looked at her hard. "What game are you playing, wench?"

"No game."

"Am I to understand you will serve me now?" he questioned, bewildered by this sudden change.

"Aye, is it not what you wished? I bend to your will, Garrick. How does it feel, to win this victory?"

He felt the loser for some reason, but he would not tell her that. "I am glad you finally came to your senses."

"Did you give me a choice, Garrick?" she replied, a slight note of bitterness in her voice now.

He watched her as she continued eating, her eyes averted from his. Still he could not fathom this change. After such stony resistance, after the way she would have defiantly faced a beating, he would have expected her to endure at least a few days without nourishment before finally giving in. Was it really just a test all along, as her sister had said, to see how much she could gain?

"Your chamber is in order, Garrick," Brenna said, breaking into his thoughts. "And your robe is repaired." She pushed her empty platter away and stood up. "If you have no further need of me this night, have I your permission to return to the women's quarters?"

He hesitated before answering, his clear aqua eyes riveted to hers. "Nay."

"Oh? What is there needs be done, then?"

"There is naught to do, mistress, but you will not stay with the others any more. From now on you will sleep in the room Yarmille uses when I am gone. 'Tis across from the sewing room."

"Why?" she demanded curtly, her eyes darkening to a stony gray, her hands on her hips.

His brows raised questioningly, and there was a hint of mockery in his voice when he replied. "I thought you would bend to my will, mistress. Did you speak falsely?"

He could see her back stiffen, and her eyes sparkled with fury, but her voice was surprisingly calm when she answered. "As you wish."

Then she left the room with cool dignity, leaving him to wonder at his reasons for wanting her near at hand.

Chapter 20

BRENNA entered the cooking area tired and blurry-eyed, for she had slept little during the night. Janie was busy at the table, cutting up a hind of beef for a stew. The young woman looked exceptionally lovely in a clean gray shift, her coppery hair tied back neatly at the base of her neck. She looked serene and fresh, which made Brenna feel even more tired. Dog perked up when he saw her and left his perch by the roasting pit. He came and nudged her hand until she petted him. Then, his tail wagging, the big animal returned to its resting place.

"Good morn," Brenna said finally, to get Janie's attention.

"Oh, Brenna!" Janie exclaimed as Brenna joined her at the table. "God's mercy, we have been so worried about you. When the master locked you up, we did not know what to think. And we dared not ask him why, for he has been in such a mean mood of late."

" 'Twas only that my working with Erin did not agree with Garrick. Nor my long rides," she added. "He would have me work here instead. 'Twas my own fault that he kept me confined to his chamber, because I refused to do as he wanted."

"But you have agreed now," Janie stated. "Master Garrick said this morn that you would help us henceforth."

"Yea, I will."

"You do not sound pleased," Janie replied. "There is really not that much to do, Brenna."

" 'Tis not the work I am against, Janie, but that Garrick would have me serve him as a slave when I was prepared to serve him as a wife. This is what galls me, that I must bend to him without the benefit of marriage."

"Pretend he is not the one you would have married," Janie suggested.

Brenna grinned. "I doubt that would help very much." She ladled herself a bowlful of oatmeal from a small pot over the fire and returned to the table. "You said there is not much to do. Why then were you so tired all the time when I first came here?"

Janie made a grim face. "That was when Yarmille was here all the time, as she is whenever Garrick is away. She owns no slaves herself, and so takes delight in her authority over us. She is also a woman who cannot abide idle hands. She would have us clean a room that is already spotless, just to keep us busy at all times. 'Tis fortunate she only comes once or twice a week when Garrick is home."

"Does Garrick know what a hard taskmaster she is?" Brenna asked.

"Nay, but 'twould bode ill to tell him. In a sense, Yarmille is family. Her bastard son is Garrick's half-brother."

"I see."

"She is also the only one around who has no family or farm to tend, so Master Garrick needs her. Others have a wife to leave in charge of their household when they are away—Garrick has Yarmille."

"So he would think twice before he would reprimand her for her severity."

"Yea, I would imagine so."

"But that is terrible!" Brenna said in outrage. "He really should be advised of the situation."

" 'Tis not so bad, Brenna. He is home more than he is away. Except for last winter, of course. That should not happen again, however. Besides, he does not demand much of us when he is here, only that he be served according to his needs, and that when he has guests, they be treated with respect."

"And their every wish granted," Brenna added in obvious disgust.

Janie smiled. "Ah, these Vikings do like their pleasure."

"Lusty bastards is what they are!" Brenna spat, her gray eyes sparkling with contempt. "A servant I will be, but not in that respect. He can starve me if he will, but I will *not* be his whore!"

"Is that what he did?"

"Nay, but he threatened to," Brenna admitted. "He plays the game most foully."

"Mayhaps you need not worry," Janie offered. "When guests come, you can hide as you did before. They come to our quarters looking for us, but you could stay in the sewing room again."

"I will not be going back to the quarters," Brenna replied. She still did not understand why. "Garrick has bid me stay in Yarmille's room."

Janie grinned. "Mayhaps you really have no cause to worry. It seems Garrick would keep you for himself."

"Nay, if that were so, I would have had a hard time this last week in his chamber, but I did not. He has no interest in me that way."

"He has not taken you yet?" Janie asked in surprise.

Brenna's face reddened considerably. "Yea, but only twice," she snapped in embarrassment. "And he will surely regret it if he tries again!"

"No doubt 'twill be awhile before he does," Janie remarked. "The man tries hard to do without women, he distrusts them so. And if you recall the reason for it, mayhaps that is why he has been in such a dark mood of late. Morna has returned."

"Returned?"

"Yea, a few days past. Perrin told me of it. It seems her rich husband perished of consumption. She has returned to her family a wealthy widow. It can mean only trouble."

"Why so?"

Janie frowned. "Perrin thinks she has it in mind to turn her attentions to Garrick again."

Brenna's back stiffened. "And he would take her back?"

"She was his first love and not easily forgotten. Yet in

157

truth she hurt him badly," Janie said, then shrugged. " 'Tis my opinion he would be a fool to want her again after what she did to him. But who can say what is in a man's heart?"

"Only the man, and most times he will not," Brenna murmured with a slightly bitter edge to her tone. She would give anything to know Garrick's thoughts.

Janie and Brenna spent the rest of the morning and afternoon doing the wash. Brenna did the scrubbing while Janie kept water boiling from the huge vat of rain water beside the house, and then hung the clothing to dry. Brenna rubbed Garrick's clothes over the scrubbing board with a vengeance, tearing seams that she only had to repair afterward. As there were not many hours of actual daylight, the clothes did not dry with the help of the sun, but had to be thoroughly wrung out and hung in the cold wind. It was near eventide when the clothes were brought in, and it was then that Brenna saw the northern lights for the first time. She was frightened at first by the strange formless glow until Janie explained that the greenish yellow light appeared frequently in the sky. She also warned Brenna that the light took different shades, and was sometimes white. The more beautiful lights were blue, red or even violet. Brenna was enthralled, and looked forward to seeing more. This land of many mysteries, so different from her own, was another world entirely.

It was late when Garrick finally came in for his meal. Brenna's eyes were drawn quickly to his blood-stained trousers, the crimson red standing out on the tanned deerskin, and then she peered questioningly into his face.

"I did not know you had enemies in your own land," she said speculatively, her voice husky.

" 'Tis the truth, but I met none this day," he replied, his lips turning up in a slow grin as he came closer. "I must disappoint you, wench, and tell you that the blood is not mine, but that of the doe Avery is now skinning."

"Avery?"

"He is another of my slaves."

Garrick's patent reminder of her status was not lost on Brenna. Color flushed her cheeks hotly and her silver gray eyes flashed at him.

" 'Twould appear you bungled the kill," she remarked derisively, her gaze returning to the blood stains. "Are you not aware that an arrow through the head makes a cleaner wound and a finer pelt?"

He laughed. "First you wager you know horses better than I. Now you would instruct me on the merits of hunting. When will you cease to amaze me, Brenna?"

She was rankled for a moment. She did not like it when he used her given name. He had only done so before in a tender moment.

"Your meal awaits you," she said woodenly, anxious to be away from him as soon as possible. "Where will you have it?"

"Does this mean you will serve me?" he asked, his eyes looking over her body much too boldly for her liking. "Where are the others?"

"Mayhaps you do not know 'tis late, Viking," she retorted irritably. "The others have retired for the night."

"And you waited patiently for me?" He was behind her now, removing his heavy fur cloak. "This change in you is truly remarkable, Brenna. I find it odd that you did not seek your bed and leave others to see to my needs. Could it be you yearn for my company?"

"Ohh!" she gasped and sprang to her feet to face him. "You conceited jackal! I would sooner spend my time with a braying ass than with you!"

She started to stalk from the room but his sharp command stopped her after only a step. "I did not give you leave to retire, mistress!"

She turned furious, smoky eyes on him, but gritted her teeth and waited for him to continue. She bristled at the mocking smile that curled his lips. He was enjoying this!

"You will serve my meal," he said in a level tone. "First you will prepare water for my bath."

"A bath? Now?" she asked incredulously.

At his nod she groaned. Her hands were stiff and sore from the washing, for they were unaccustomed to the chore, the scalding water and abrasive soap. Now she would have to lug buckets of water up to his chambers! She balked at the thought.

"Why do you hesitate?" Garrick questioned, seeing the

fleeting emotions cross her face. "A bath is a simple matter."

"Then you do it!" she hissed. "I will not carry water up to your chamber."

"I did not ask you to," he replied. "I will have the bath here. Will that suit you?"

Indeed it would, she almost sighed. Instead she answered stiffly, "As you wish."

She picked up two large buckets and went outside to the huge vat of fresh rain water at the side of the house. The cold wind lifted her skirts and sent a chill up her back. She filled the buckets, then almost dropped them when the handles bit into her sore fingers as she hauled them back into the house.

Garrick had moved the barrellike tub that had been beneath the stairs over in front of the fire. He stood back and watched her silently as she emptied the cold water into the tub. Her unconscious grimace left Brenna's face when the buckets were light again. She reluctantly walked out of the warm cooking area of the hall to fill them again.

On her return this time Garrick met her at the door. "Prepare my meal!" he barked impatiently and took the buckets from her. "At your pace I would wait all night for my bath!"

Brenna hurried across the room to the hearth, grateful for his impatience, though she would not admit it was a kindness. It took many more buckets of water to fill the tub halfway. The amount of water Garrick brought was more than was needed for a bath, but Brenna said nothing.

She kept her back to him and filled a wooden platter with the stew Janie had prepared earlier. A loaf of flat bread and a tankard of ale were placed on a tray beside the stew, for Brenna did not know yet where he would eat. Right here, most likely, since the fires in the main part of the hall were low, thus making it an unwelcoming room. Nor had she thought to kindle a fire in his chamber—or in her own, for that matter.

With the cauldrons set to boil over the fire, Garrick came to the table and sat down on the long bench before his food. This time Brenna stood behind him, staring at the wide expanse of shoulders, the light gold hair that curled up off his neck, the huge, powerful bare arms that bulged with corded muscles. Brenna shook her head to avert her gaze, which had become almost hypnotized. The very sight of this man stirred something in her that she could not explain, and it frightened her.

"Have you eaten?" Garrick asked over his shoulder.

"Yea, long ago," she murmured.

Brenna bit her lip as he continued eating. His meal was fixed and his bath prepared, but she was loath to leave the warmth of the room, yet even more reluctant to stay here and ponder the strange effect Garrick's presence was having on her this night.

She came around the table so she could face him. "May I go now—Garrick? I will kindle a fire in your chamber before I retire."

Garrick stared at her for a long moment before answering. His eyes left her face to rest on the soft mounds of her breasts that moved gently with her breathing beneath the rough material of her shift. His eyes then moved to the swell of her hips, accentuated by the crude belt she had tied about her waist. The shift was coarse and unbecoming, but there really was not much that could take away from her slim beauty.

"Well?" she prompted stiffly, flushed from his bold scrutiny.

His eyes locked with hers again and he smiled humorously. "You may light the fire in my room, mistress, but then return here."

"Why?"

His smile widened at the confusion on her face. "You are not to question my orders, but to carry them out without delay, Brenna."

She repressed the angry retort which came to mind, and instead stalked from the room. She would find out why soon enough, she supposed. She struck up a fire in Garrick's chamber and in her own, then slowly made her way back to the cooking area below, hugging her bare arms as she came down the drafty stairs.

She had purposely taken her time, and when she entered the hall, Garrick was finished eating and had already added the boiling water to the tub. He was standing with his back to the fire, removing his tunic. She had brought him a robe to don after his bath; it was slung over her shoulder.

When Garrick saw her, he grinned and threw his tunic at her. "Soak this before 'tis ruined. You will have the rest in a moment," he said, and bent to unlace the criss-crossed leather garters which molded his trousers to his legs.

She shot him a murderous glance that he did not see, then dropped the tunic into the one bucket he had left water in. When he started to remove his trousers, she quickly turned her back on him, her face blushing hotly. She had assumed he would want privacy for his bath. How dare he bare himself before her when she was fully clothed? Had he no shame?

"Here," he said behind her, but she would not turn. Then, "What ails you, woman?"

When she still would not turn, he laughed and tossed the trousers by her feet. She heard the water splash as he got in the tub, and only then did she pick up his trousers and put them in the bucket. When she finally turned cautiously to look at him, her eyes were drawn to his bronzed torso, the thick, sinewy muscles beneath the blond mat of curls on his chest, the powerful arms that could surely squeeze life from a bear if need be.

"Would you join me, Brenna?"

Her eyes flew to his head and she saw that he had been watching her stare at him. Her face turned three shades of red and she gasped, "Nay! I bathed this morn!"

Indeed, she had even used the same tub, after Coran, the slave who helped the women with heavy chores, had filled it for her. But Garrick was only teasing her—he must be.

"If you will not join me, will you scrub my back, then?"

She saw the humor in his eyes and it infuriated her. "Nay, I will not!"

"And if I order it?"

" 'Twill be my nails your back will feel, not the sponge!" she warned him, then continued to take her stand. "You have me serving you in normal ways. Do not press me for more, Viking. If you overtax what you have gained, you will lose it all!"

"Now she threatens me again," Garrick said in mock exasperation. "So you have not changed overmuch, as you would have me believe?"

"I agreed to serve in your house, but not in this intimate

162

capacity," she returned in a calm tone, though her eyes were broodingly dark. "May I go now?"

He sighed. "Yea, go. Coran will empty the tub in the morn."

Brenna left the room quickly and ran up the stairs. She entered her own small chamber and slammed the door soundly. She immediately regretted doing so, for Garrick would hear the noise and no doubt laugh that he had upset her so. Why did he insist on continuing with these small battles of will? Would he persist until finally she would do anything he asked of her? Nay, that day would never come!

Brenna pulled off her shift and laid it neatly over the single chair in the room. There was a small coffer at the foot of the narrow bed but it was empty, and she had nothing of her own to put in it. The nightdress and one shift that had been given her came from the storage house and were slaves' clothing. She had also been given a bone-handled comb and a pair of soft-skinned shoes that were too big for her delicate feet. A fine lot of possessions, she thought with some humor, remembering how she had scorned the lovely gowns she once owned.

She donned the nightdress that was laid across her bed, and immediately regretted that she had washed it earlier, for it was even more starchy than before. Then she sat on the bed, unbraided her long silken hair, and combed it till the firelight was reflected in its gleaming softness. Finally she climbed beneath the embroidered coverlet and tried to sleep.

But sleep eluded Brenna and she knew why. She could not relax, not until she knew Garrick was abed. She tried to let the crackling fire lull her, but it was no use. Her body was tense, stiff as a board. She waited and waited, for what seemed like hours, to hear the door down the corridor open and close. Why was it so imperative that she know Garrick had retired before she could find sleep herself?

When her own door opened, Brenna found her answer. How did she know he would come? Was it the bold look he had given her earlier that unconsciously warned her?

He stood there by the door, wearing only the short silk robe she had brought him. Tied at the waist, the garment extended in a deep V to the belt, baring the curls on his chest. The firelight danced over his bare legs, the strong thighs and muscular calves. Long, powerful legs that would soon lay between her own.

Brenna shook her head, stunned at her own thinking. She would not let it happen. Garrick had the strength, but she could outfox him.

"What do you want, Garrick?" Brenna asked in a throaty whisper.

"You," was all he said.

She propped herself up on one elbow, her hair cascading over her shoulders. "I suppose this is one of those times you mentioned before, when your body craves a woman?"

He grunted at her, not pleased with her question. "You remember well."

"Why should I not? After all, 'tis not the man Garrick who wants me, only his body," she said lightly. "Will you have me here, or do you prefer your own bed?"

A frown crossed his brow as he puzzled over her compliance. Brenna felt nowhere near the calm she displayed, though his hesitating helped her.

"I see you cannot decide, Garrick. Well, this bed is much too small to fit your frame, so I will come with you."

She slipped out of her bed gracefully and walked to the door, a sensuous smile playing on her lips. She stopped next to Garrick and placed a hand gently on his chest.

"Have you changed your mind, Garrick? Tell me now, before I go any further."

His bafflement at her acquiescence turned to a dark scowl. "Nay, I have not changed my mind."

"Well, come then," she breathed and left the room before him.

Her heart was pounding in her chest almost like a throbbing pain. He would be furious with her for tricking him, but she would not bear the brunt of that anger unless he caught her, and she was determined he would not. When she reached the stairs, she dashed down them with frantic speed and raced for the back door. Outside in the black of night, she would find somewhere to hide until Garrick's anger and his desire had cooled.

But Garrick had locked the door, which she had not counted on, and before she could throw the heavy bolt, he was behind her. She screamed when he hefted her in his arms and tossed her over his shoulder, rendering her breathless, but only for a moment. She kicked and twisted until he nearly dropped her as he made his way back up the stairs. A sound whack to her behind did not stop her struggles; it only increased them.

In his chamber, he kicked the door shut, then crossed the room and dumped his bundle on the bed. He stood and watched her scramble away from him to the foot of the bed, poised to jump if he pursued her. A cynical sneer played on his lips and he made no immediate move for her.

"From one extreme to the other, eh?" he remarked, his hands on his hips. "And here I thought you would fit comfortably between the two."

"You speak in riddles," Brenna said warily, relieved to see he was not blustering with rage.

"Do I? Explain to me then about your performance of a few minutes past. What was that all about, mistress?"

"I don't know what you are talking about," she said defensively, holding her chin high.

He shook his head, letting his hands drop to his sides. "I should know better than to expect honesty from a woman. I should have realized you were playing me falsely. You were just too obliging, which puzzled me, but then I was not expecting tricks from you. Nor did I expect you to run from me again like a frightened virgin. What game do you play, Brenna? Explain the rules to me."

"I play no games. Do you really expect me to open my arms passively to you?"

"Yea, our last encounter did lead me to believe you would." He grinned at her.

"Conceited cur!" she snapped, her courage returning twofold. "Have you forgotten that you lied to me that last time? You said you would not take advantage of me, but you did. And 'twas only my curiosity that allowed you to."

He laughed derisively. "So 'twas curiosity that made you turn to me in passion."

"You lie!" she gasped. "You woke *me,* Viking, not I you!"

"But you did not try to escape. And by Thor, 'twas you who would not let me go and who brazenly taunted me to continue. Do you deny that?"

She shrugged, then grinned impishly. "You could not

understand that, could you? You see, for you the act was completed, but I found it lacking." At his dark scowl, she quickly added, " 'Twas not your fault though. It just took me longer to solve the mystery."

"The mystery?"

"Yea, to reach the end, as you did. To find out what made the act so desirable. How is that for honesty, Viking?"

"And you did enjoy it?"

"Yea, I admit it."

He frowned at her and demanded, "Then why in thunderation did you now run from me?"

"Just because I enjoyed it once, Viking, does not mean I crave it again, as you men forever do. My curiosity has been appeased, and so I can do without a repetition of the act."

"The act!" he grunted, thoroughly vexed. "There is a better word for it."

"What?" she sneered. "Surely not lovemaking, for there was no love in what we did. Not for me, and especially not for you. You, the man, do not even participate. You have readily admitted 'tis only your body that craves release. So do not come to me for that release, when any woman will do."

"But I *have* come to you," he replied, a decidedly wicked smile turning his lips.

Brenna's eyes clouded with fury. "I refuse! I will not be used to satisfy your body's cravings!"

"So you refuse," he said lightly, the evil smile still on his lips. "That will not stop me from having you."

Her eyes lit up with cunning. " 'Tis fortunate, I suppose, that your body does not get these urgings often. But tell me, do you, the man, ever seek a woman?"

"Why should I?"

"Not even Morna?"

She expected to arouse his anger by her question, and possibly even to suffer a reprieve because of that anger. But she did not expect the icy rage that contorted his features and sent a cold chill down her back.

"How came you to know of Morna?" he asked in a deadly calm tone.

"Have you not learned that you should never do battle

with an enemy until you know all you can of him? I made it a point to know of you."

"You consider me your enemy?"

"You are certainly not my friend or ally. So, yea, we are enemies."

"Nay," he returned coldly. "We are master and slave. We make war with words, not weapons. And now I grow tired of the words."

"You will let me leave, then?" she asked hopefully.

"Yea, you can leave—after the act, as you call it, is finished."

Garrick's sudden leap across the bed took her by surprise, and in a panic she jumped away from him. But she was not quick enough and he grabbed her foot, holding it secure while the rest of her tumbled forward to land flat on the floor. The impact knocked the breath from her, and her elbows, which hit hard, smarted terribly and brought tears of pain to her eyes. She cursed herself silently for allowing the glistening drops to well up and make her eyes glassy. A woman's weapon, tears; she would not use them to aid her cause.

"Are you hurt?"

"Would it matter?" she snapped.

"Are you?" he repeated harshly.

"The only thing that hurts is your grip on my foot!" she lied, quickly wiping her eyes on her palms. "Release me, damn your hide!"

"Nay, Brenna," he said softly. "Not yet."

One hand holding her ankle, he moved his other hand up her calf and lifted her nightdress. When she kicked out at him with her other foot, he laughed and grabbed it too, then twisted her until she was forced to turn over on her back. He was crouched at the foot of the bed, holding her ankles, one in each hand. She stared in disbelief as he slowly started to stand, pulling her legs up with him as he straightened.

"Cease, Garrick! Stop it, I say!"

But he continued to lift her up off the floor, up and up until he had her dangling in the air above the bed. Brenna was torn between whether to use her hands to brace herself, or to try to push her nightdress back in place, for it fell about her head, baring her limbs for his view. Before she could decide, though, he lowered her gently on the bed till she lay on her back. But he kept her legs raised and slowly spread them wide.

When he fell to his knees, she tried to pull away from him, but he yanked her back. Then in a swift movement he dropped her legs over his shoulders and fell forward on top of her at the same time, pinning her legs high with his arms so that she could not lower them. He did not even need to remove his short robe, for it had opened with his exertion, and his throbbing member pressed against her, searching for the moist cavern of her womanhood.

"You are a depraved beast!" she gasped.

"Nay, I am determined to have you, Brenna, that is all," he murmured.

She glared at him murderously. "So far you have only gained my anger, but if you force me now, Garrick, you will have my hatred as well. 'Tis not a pretty thing, my hate. You will never find peace with it."

His answer was to plunge deep within her, bringing tears to her eyes again at his brutal onslaught. He took her without mercy, quickly, while she whispered her loathing in his ear. When he finished, he let her legs down one at a time and then moved to her side. The moment he released her, she scrambled off the bed as if it burned her and ran from the room, slamming first his door and then her own down the corridor.

Garrick pounded his fist into the bed. "Loki take her!" he growled.

What he intended as a pleasing encounter had turned into a hollow victory indeed.

Chapter 21

THE first snowfall was long in coming, and did not occur until late fall. With it came a storm that lasted a full week, froze lakes and ponds and left snowbanks four and five feet in height. The land was blanketed in dismal white, and few were wont to brave the icy wind and falling snow. Garrick was one of the few. He had been gone a fortnight before the snowstorm began, and even with it finished, he had yet to return.

On the very day the winds settled, Anselm came to Garrick's home, bringing with him an extra mount, a fine-bred silver-coated mare. His wife had told him (as related to her by Linnet) that this particular animal had belonged to the Lady Brenna. For three long months now he had brooded over the raven-haired girl. His own son's displeasure with her did not make him feel any better. He regretted giving her to Garrick, for though he had not come to see her personally over the months, he feared she had not fared well with Garrick's dark moods.

Anselm had given the girl to Garrick with the hope that her spirit and beauty would turn his mind from the bitch who had changed a cheerful young man into a cold cynic. When Garrick sought out the girl's sister, and then a month later spoke at length with the aunt, Anselm assumed his desire to learn more of the girl was a promising beginning, and soon he would have back his son of old. But after that, Garrick's foul disposition did not improve, it actually worsened. Why, Anselm could not guess. Now Garrick took to the hills for weeks at a time, and Anselm saw little of him.

Garrick's absences grew more lengthy, and this last trek north had already extended to three weeks. Though Anselm had begun to worry slightly over Garrick's welfare, he would wait a few more days yet before he began a search, as Heloise had nagged him to do ever since the snowstorm started.

"Ho, old man, where are you?"

Erin came from the back of the stable, wrapped from head to foot in a cloak of multicolored furs. "I hear you," he grumbled in his crusty voice.

Anselm eyed him with displeasure. "I see Garrick still wastes his furs on you servants."

"Aye, we're warmer clothed than the poor souls you own," Erin replied, grinning.

Anselm would not have taken that remark from anyone else, but he was genuinely fond of old Erin. He had served Anselm's father, and now his son, and for many years they had enjoyed heckling one another good-naturedly when they met.

Anselm grunted, repressing his humor. "I brought a new filly for your stable. Have you room?"

"Have I room, indeed," Erin mumbled, taking the reins of both horses. "Of course there's room."

"She is not for Garrick, mind you."

"Oh?"

"Nay, she's a gift for the Celtic wench," Anselm said gruffly. "And you be sure and tell my son that when he returns."

"By the saints!" Erin cackled. "Since when do you bestow such fine gifts on a slave?"

"Never mind that, old codger. Where is the girl? In the quarters below?"

"Nay, she lives in the house."

Anselm was surprised by this news, then he chuckled. "Mayhaps I was not such a fool after all."

"Do you ask my opinion?" Erin returned, his old eyes alight with laughter.

"Get about your work!" Anselm barked, and made his way to the house.

Brenna was in the cooking area, where she spent most of her waking hours, since it was the warmest and most pleasant place in the house. On the table were the remains of her breakfast. Beside it was the rabbit she had started cutting up for her dinner, but had left on the chopping board.

With Garrick off on a hunting trek, Yarmille had come to stay. She drove Brenna mad with her insistent demands. But a week past, the older woman had returned home, and when the snow came, Yarmille did not come back. Without her authoritative presence, Janie and Maudya stayed in their quarters, and Brenna was not wont to venture from the house to seek them out. Not even Erin came to keep her company, for he had brought her enough provisions from the storehouse to last a fortnight, and preferred to keep to his warm stable.

Brenna had reached the point where she would almost welcome Yarmille's return. Even though they did not communicate, Yarmille's constant chattering to herself was amusing, at times enlightening.

On one occasion, Brenna discovered that Yarmille harbored a deep, abiding hate for Heloise, and that hatred reached out to include both of Heloise's sons. This Brenna found confusing, since Yarmille worked for Garrick. She wondered if Garrick was aware of Yarmille's true feelings.

Brenna dropped another log on the fire, then leaned back in her chair and stared at the flickering flames. She hated to admit it, but she actually missed Garrick. When he was around, she lived in a constant state of apprehension, not knowing when he would demand something of her, or if she would comply or not. When he was there, she never noticed how the hours dragged by. She was alert at all times, alive as she had never been before. And at night, merciful Lord, she was a bundle of nerves at night waiting and dreading for Garrick to come for her again. But he never did, not after the night he had raped her.

She was bitterly hurt by his treatment of her. Perhaps

171

she could have forgiven him if he had been tender like before. The one night he had been gentle and she had softened to him, it had been wonderful. She could not forget the beauty of it, or the pleasure, like no other, that he had given her. Afterward he had held her possessively, as if he might really care for her, and she had reveled in the closeness they shared.

But that last time, for him to be so cruel—God, how she hated him for it. She had escaped the house the next day, and tried to dispel her anger with a wild ride on the fastest horse Erin would allow her. It had helped to a degree. She actually felt a little better when, returning, she came across Coran and offered him a ride back to the house. She remembered that now with a grin.

He had shook his head sternly, eyeing her horse with apprehension. "I will walk, Mistress Brenna," he informed her.

"What are you doing out here in the fields?" she asked, walking her horse beside him.

"Avery and I were sent to find a cow who wandered from the pasture."

"Did you?"

"Yea, Avery is taking her back now."

"Come on, Coran," she coaxed him. "I cannot bear to see you walking when 'tis unnecessary. 'Tis a good distance back to the house yet."

"Nay," he refused again.

Finally she guessed at his reluctance. "Have you never ridden a horse before?"

He shook his head and lowered his eyes to the ground. Coran was only a year or two older than Brenna. A lanky youth with a pleasing face, he never grumbled over his enforced servitude. She liked Coran and couldn't help laughing at his reluctance.

" 'Tis time you learned, Coran. Now come on. I will think you do not like my company if you refuse again."

Finally he relented with a sheepish grin and she helped him up behind her. Brenna had not felt so carefree in ages, and with a mischievous glint in her gray eyes, she dug her heels into the horse and they shot forward. Coran grabbed hold of Brenna for dear life, mumbling prayers in her ear. But Brenna laughed heartily and spurred the horse on, making Coran grip her that much tighter. She did not see the rider on a hill who sat in a black fury and watched her antics with Coran. She didn't care about anything except that her mood was made lighter for a little while, at least. But it didn't last. As soon as she saw Garrick's angry countenance, and found that no apology was forthcoming for his harsh treatment of her, she was enraged again herself.

Brenna sighed wistfully. For two long months he ignored her. Then he began to go hunting and stayed away for days. When he was home, he would come in very late. She would wonder then if he had been with Morna. Or perhaps he had gone to Janie or Maudya in their quarters. Mayhaps his father's women—slaves, even Cordella—were more to his liking! Brenna would pace the floor at those times, building up a fine steam. She told herself she had every right to be upset. She could be sleeping instead of waiting for the master to find his way home.

One night in particular, when Garrick was overly late for the third night in a row, Brenna went to bed to spite him. He finally came home in a wild, drunken mood, and despite the fact that his food was simmering over the coals, he woke her and dragged her down the stairs to serve him.

His attitude was belligerent and brooked no refusal, but Brenna was too furious to fear him. She filled a large wooden bowl with steaming soup, then dropped it on the table, spilling half the contents over him. She knew it pained Garrick, but the fact that he didn't show it cooled her temper. He dismissed her then and she left him quickly. Not a word was said of it the next day.

Brenna started at the loud pounding on the door. She felt her pulse quicken, for only Garrick would knock like that. He would wonder why the door was locked. Indeed, all the doors were bolted and had been ever since she went for water one morning and found a stray dog slaughtered and left on the stoop. Yarmille had turned white when she saw the dead carcass but she said nothing, leaving Brenna to wonder who would do such a thing.

She opened the door wide, prepared to tell Garrick why she had locked it. But it was Anselm standing there, wrapped in a heavy fur jacket, which made him look twice as huge as he was. Seeing him gave her a shock, but it took only a second for the white-hot fury to flash in Brenna's eyes.

She did not think twice before she ran for the table and grabbed the long knife she had used earlier to butcher the rabbit. In her blind rage she was careless. She turned to attack, only to find Anselm behind her. He grabbed her wrist, and with his other hand, pried open her fingers until the knife dropped to the floor. He then swung her away and she fell back against the chair by the hearth, nearly knocking it over.

She stayed there, breathing heavily, and watched him pick up the knife, then look about for any others before he closed the door. When he faced her, their eyes locked, mellow blue with stormy gray, and it seemed like hours before he finally moved again. Undaunted, he walked over to the table, pulled the long bench out, and straddled it.

"I mean you no harm, girl," Anselm's words came out gruffly, and he cleared his throat before he continued in a softer tone. "Can you understand me? Have you learned to speak my language yet?"

Brenna did not blink an eye at his question, but remained perfectly still. She watched him suspiciously. What reason did he have to be here when Garrick was away?

Anselm fiddled with the knife in his hands, his head bent as he watched the long blade gleam in the firelight. "I expected no less from you," he said in a soft whisper.

Brenna frowned. What was he talking about? She had to strain to hear him as he continued. "I should not have come, I suppose. 'Tis too soon for you to forget what I did, or to understand why. I hated your people, girl, for what they did to my son. When you have a son of your own, you will understand. Garrick could forgive them, for he learned compassion from his mother, but I could not. We are a proud and vengeful people, but I was wrong to exact my vengeance from you and your family, who were not to blame.

" 'Twas your northern Celts who held my son prisoner in a murky dungeon for nigh onto a year, and he only a youth of ten and seven then. They denied him nourishment, except for gruel not fit for dogs. They tortured him for sport, but were careful not to kill him, for 'twas their intention to use him against other Vikings who came to raid them. When Garrick escaped and returned to us, he was but a shell of the boy he was. It took over a year for his full strength to return and the scars to heal."

Anselm finally looked up at Brenna, his blue eyes sad. "I know you do not understand what I am saying, girl. You hear my voice, but do not comprehend my words. 'Tis just as well," he sighed. "I like you, girl. I admire your spirit and I regret that I took you from your land. You will never know this, though, for I am a man with fool pride like any other. I could never say these words to you if you understood them. But I can at least try to make amends and hope that one day you will no longer hate me as you do now."

Brenna was tempted to speak to Anselm in his own tongue, to let him know she understood every word he said. It would give her some satisfaction to humiliate him thus, but she was reluctant to give up the one secret that might help her when she was ready to escape. Besides, she was disturbed by what her own people had done to Garrick and could see why Anselm might want revenge (even if she could not forgive him for what he and his men had done in her land). After all, Garrick had risked being captured when he chose to raid her people. Still, he should have been killed when taken, not kept to torture just for sport.

Anselm stood up and dropped the long knife on the table. Brenna watched it fall, then looked quickly back at the huge Viking.

"Aye, I know you would run me through if given the chance." Anselm spoke again with his customary gruffness. "But do not try it. I have no wish to die yet, not with many years of fighting before me, accounts to settle, and grandsons to see and hold before I join Odin in Valhalla."

Anselm moved to the hearth to warm his hands by the fire. It was as if he was daring Brenna to run for the knife on the table. Either that, or he was showing that he was willing to trust her. Wisely, she stayed where she was.

Still he continued to speak, perhaps clearing his conscience. "Ever since I first laid eyes on you, girl, you have weighed heavily on my mind. But I see you have fared well here in my son's home." He glanced at her slyly. "Aye, you have fared well, while Garrick's moods have a darker edge to them. Are you the cause?" Suddenly he grunted. "Bah! As if you would answer me even if you could. I am seven times the fool for talking to a wench who knows naught of what I say. And even more of a fool to give a prized horse to a slave girl. What possessed me to make such a decision—ah, 'tis done. Garrick will not like it, but mayhaps he will allow you to ride the silver mare when he learns she was yours in your land."

Brenna had to lower her eyes so he would not see the sudden joy reflected there. She could not believe it. Willow here? And given to her—not Garrick—her!

Anselm crossed to the door to leave. Brenna stared curiously at his back. Why would he do such a thing? After all that he had put her through, it was inconceivable that he should be kind now.

As if in answer to her silent question, Anselm turned at the door. "Erin will tell you of the horse. I do not expect this to change your feelings for me, girl, but 'tis a beginning." He chuckled. "My action will certainly give you cause to wonder at my motives."

Whatever his reasons, Willow was here and hers again. She now had a reason to venture out into the icy breath of winter. She would need trousers, though, to ride comfortably and protect her from the cold.

Brenna suddenly twirled about the room in her excitement. She had not felt this happy for a long time. The fact that Anselm was responsible did not hinder her pleasure. Garrick, on the other hand, might forbid her to take Willow out after her run-in with the two men. A frown crossed her brow, but only for a moment. He could not stop her when he was not here to do so. And when he returned, well, the devil take him. Just let him try to stop her!

Chapter 22

BRENNA entered the stable and quickly closed the large door to keep out the cold. She was tightly wrapped in the heavy bearskin cape that Garrick had tossed at her one day when the last hints of summer had vanished. All of the slaves here had their own capes or jackets made of old furs stitched together and considered worthless for trading.

Brenna was certainly not happy with hers. Although the fur was clean, the skin was rough and terribly heavy. She was sure Garrick had given her the heaviest cape he could find, just for spite. But it was all she would have unless she raided the locked storehouse where clothing, provisions and Garrick's treasures were kept. This she was determined to do one day with Erin's help. For her escape, she would also need the weapons kept there.

The stable was warm, and the pungent odors of horse and dung filled her with nostalgia for home. As a child, she had spent most of her time in her father's stable—whenever she was not practicing with her weapons or tagging along behind Angus.

Erin was nowhere in sight. He was probably sleeping in the back, but Brenna was not eager to wake him, not yet. She could hardly contain her excitement as she scanned the stable for Willow. When she saw the silver-flanked mare, Brenna ran to it, tears glistening in her eyes.

"Oh, Willow, my sweet Willow. I thought to never see you again!" Brenna cried.

In truth, she had begun to doubt she would ever see anything from her home again, including her aunt and stepsister. She had asked Garrick once to take her to see them, but he had refused without explanation, and she was too proud to ask again.

Brenna hugged Willow's neck tightly; the horse snorted and shook its head in return. "I am so glad to see you," Brenna said softly, "that I will even forgive you for throwing me the last time I rode you. It has been hell here, but you will make it bearable."

"Who is there?" Erin called from the back of the stable, then came forward. "Oh, 'tis you, lass. What brings you here?"

Brenna chewed her lower lip nervously. She hated to fool Erin, but she couldn't trust her secret to anyone, not even this old man she considered her friend.

"Anselm came to the house yesterday," Brenna finally said. "He talked long, but I did not understand anything he said. I came to ask you what he wanted." Brenna turned to Willow again, and the joy that entered her voice was genuine. "I found my horse, Erin! What is she doing here?"

Erin chuckled, unaware of Brenna's deception. "The filly is yours again, lass, given by Anselm himself."

"Did he say why?"

"Nay, only that I was to be sure Garrick understood that the horse was yours, not his."

Brenna could not suppress her laughter. "Do you think Garrick will be angry?"

"Of course he will, just as he has been angry about everything of late. I cannot guess what is the matter with that boy. He is worse now than he was a few years back, when his temper first surfaced."

"You mean when Morna first ran off?"

"Aye."

"Do you suppose Garrick's foul moods are because Morna has returned?" Brenna ventured.

"Truly, I cannot say."

Brenna understood Garrick's harsh attitude no better than anyone else. He had not been so forbidding when she first met him. He had humor then, and teased her often. Now she never heard him laugh, and when he spoke, it was harshly. But then, he had hardly talked to her at all before he left this last time. It was as if they had begun a silent battle, speaking only with their eyes.

Brenna had hoped at first that she was the cause of his dark moods, but she could see no conceiveable reason why she would be. No, Morna was the cause, she was sure. Morna was a part of Garrick, even though he hated her now. Yet the only reason he hated her so much was because he had loved her that much. This thought disturbed Brenna greatly and she shook it off, not wanting to ponder it.

"I am going to ride my horse, Erin," she announced with determination. "Have you any objections?"

"Nay, but—"

When he did not continue, she smiled. "Will I return?" He nodded sheepishly, and she added, "I have not been provoked to leave Garrick's house yet."

"But you have your horse now, and a sturdy horse she is, one you know and trust. She could take you anywhere you wanted to go."

"She cannot take me home, Erin," Brenna murmured, and some of the joy left her eyes for a moment. "Come now, help me saddle her. It has been months since I have ridden, and even longer since I have ridden Willow. I will not ride long, for I am sure the cold will chase me home."

"At least you admit this is your home now," Erin said as he hoisted a saddle over Willow's back.

"Home is where the heart is, and my heart is across that black sea."

"For your own sake, lass, I hope your heart will be here some day."

Garrick broke through the forest of dense pine from the east, but stopped his mount at its edge when he saw the rider crossing the open field of tall grass covered with thick patches of snow. He could see the rider clearly, for the dusky sky was a mellow blue, affording him enough light without the sun's rays.

Garrick sat back and admired the grace of the silver-gray horse as it raced swiftly across the field, but he did not recognize the animal as one of his own or one of his neighbor's. However, he did recall seeing such a horse in his father's stable.

The rider was small, surely not his father or Hugh. His mother perhaps? Garrick's curiosity was piqued until the rider's fur hat flew to the ground and he saw the jet-black hair beneath it. Then he felt his fury rise.

Brenna had stolen his father's horse. There was no other plausible answer—she was escaping. His first impulse was to chase her and show her immediately that she had failed. But the shifting of his own mount reminded him that the stallion was weary and in no condition for a spirited race.

Before Garrick could make a decision, Brenna reined her horse in a wide arc and circled back toward the fallen headdress, but she did not stop to retrieve it. Instead, holding tightly onto the horse's mane, she swooped down to try and grab the hat as she passed.

Garrick stiffened. She could have broken her fool neck if she had lost her hold on the animal! With fresh anger he watched as she circled to try again. This time she succeeded. Now she pulled in the horse and stopped, tossing the hat high into the air and then catching it, just like a child who has won a coveted prize. Even with the great distance between them he could hear her laughing uninhibitedly as he had heard only once before from Brenna.

Before Garrick could recover from his confused emotions, Brenna surprised him further by galloping off in the direction she had come. Garrick relaxed and his temper cooled. His concern about why she was riding his father's horse was forgotten. Uppermost in his mind was that she was not trying to run away, as he had first imagined. He would not have to mete out the punishment due a runaway slave. He was pleased about that, at least, for he had no desire to hurt Brenna.

He could no longer see her now, for she had descended the sloping hills that led to his home. The sound of her merry laughter continued to echo in his mind the way it had the day he saw her offer Coran a ride home. It still rankled him that she had enjoyed the company of a slave more than his own.

In many ways, Brenna was still a child. Her tantrums and utter defiance gave proof to that fact, as did the foolishness he had just witnessed in the field. And she still clung stubbornly to the past, to her childhood days when she was given a free rein to live out her desire to be Lord Angus's son, not the daughter she was. Linnet had told him much about Brenna, things that contradicted most of what Cordella said. He did not know which of the two women to believe. He was inclined to believe Cordella's description of Brenna, for she reconfirmed his own opinion of women as a whole. But he had seen the proof of the aunt's words that Brenna had yet to grow up completely.

By the gods, he was bewitched! He could not chase the little vixen from his mind even when he tried. He had hoped this long absence from home would help, but even when he was stalking prey, Brenna and her willfulness were in his thoughts. It was little consolation that Brenna had dispelled his brooding over Morna, for his thoughts now were just as dark. From the blonde bitch to the raven-haired termagant—both were the same, for they could not be trusted.

Garrick urged his horse toward home. He was returning with a variety of furs that would be cured and readied for spring, when he would again sail for the trading markets of the East. He had startled two black bears from their hibernation and had felled one.

This was a perfect excuse to call out his neighbors and have a feast for all to share. Brenna would not like that, but Loki take her. The bearskin would be sold come spring, and perhaps Brenna would too. This was one way to rid his thoughts of the Celtic wench. Or was it?

Chapter 23

BRENNA stood before the fire in the cooking area with a warm woolen blanket draped over her shoulders, and briskly rubbed her hands together to dispel the freezing numbness. It was doubtful she would ever get used to such icy weather, but the next time she went out into it, she would be better prepared.

Light tapping sounds drew her attention, and she walked slowly away from the hearth to open the back door, wrapping her blanket more tightly about her. She hid behind the door to avoid the sudden rush of cold wind, and quickly closed it as soon as Janie, Maudya and Rayna plodded in.

The old woman clucked her tongue, peeled off her cloak and hung it by the door. "Why do you bar this house, girl? The master will not like it."

"Have you not heard of the slaughtered dog found on the door stoop?" Brenna retaliated caustically.

"We have all heard of the dead mongrel, but 'tis no reason to bar the door," Rayna returned, and moved to the hearth to add wood to the fire. "Yea, 'twas the deed of the Borgsen clan, there is no doubt," she continued. "The feud between them and the Haardrads has not reached the point of bloodshed again. They merely slaughter the livestock."

"What feud?" Brenna asked.

"There is no time for that story now," Janie interposed, taking off her own wrap. "Master Garrick has returned and has ordered a feast."

Brenna's pulse quickened at learning Garrick was home, but at the same time, the thought of a feast like the last one made her cringe. "Where is he?"

"Gone to gather his neighbors to bring in the bear he felled," Maudya answered cheerfully, obviously looking forward to a large gathering of men again. "Erin sent us up here to put the pots on to boil and prepare the hall. Coran is bringing kegs of ale from the storehouse."

"And how long will this feast last?"

"There is no telling. Since 'tis winter with naught better to do, it could last for weeks."

How would Garrick act after being gone for three weeks? Would he be glad to see her? Brenna mused. She pinched herself for her foolish wonderings and began to sweep the hall with a vengeance. She must remember that she had sworn to hate Garrick. She could concede him nothing, not even a smile of welcome.

So when Garrick entered the hall, Brenna had worked herself into a fine temper. Yet catching sight of him standing at the end of the makeshift wall which separated the cooking area from the drafty hall, she felt her heart beat faster and her anger was momentarily forgotten. He was arm in arm with Perrin, and laughing at some comment the other had made. Then he saw her and their eyes touched like a gentle caress.

She lost herself in those aqua eyes, which still twinkled with laughter, but not for long. Some wicked voice inside her head upbraided her, and regretfully she turned away.

Only a few seconds passed before she felt Garrick's presence directly behind her. He took her elbow and without a word, escorted her from the hall. They passed Perrin, who grinned but said nothing, and saw Gorm and two others just coming in the back door. Garrick ignored them all and pulled her up the stairs behind him. When they reached the top, she finally jerked away from him.

"Where are you taking me, Viking?" she demanded in a harsh whisper.

"To bed," he replied and grabbed her quickly, sweeping her off her feet before she could escape him.

"But you have guests below!" she protested.

Garrick laughed heartily, a sound Brenna rarely heard. "They can wait; I cannot."

Cradled in his arms as he carried her into his room, Brenna felt overwhelmed by the desire that flooded her senses. She squeezed her eyes shut and fought the urge to succumb to Garrick's advances.

"Put me down!"

He grinned devilishly. "As you wish."

He dropped her on the bed, then followed her there, straddling her hips with his knees. She sat up with all her force and pushed him with both arms, but did not even knock him slightly off balance.

"Can it be you have not missed me, wench?" he teased her as he removed his belt and threw it aside. She leaned back on her elbows and stared up at him haughtily.

"Why should I miss you? You are not the only man around here, Viking."

The coldness that came instantly to his eyes shocked her. "You will not dally with any man save me."

Now anger flared in Brenna and black smoke gathered in her eyes. "And what of your friends? I was told you allow them to bed any female slave you own!"

He grinned at that. "Do you at last agree I own you, Brenna?"

"Nay, but your loathsome friends think you do!" she retorted hotly.

"Well, you need have no fear on that score, mistress. They will not bother you."

"You will tell them to leave me be, then?" she asked in surprise.

"Aye."

"Why will you do this?" she questioned skeptically. "Certainly not for me."

" 'Tis enough that I do not choose to share you yet," he admitted in a careless tone.

Brenna's eyes darkened even more. "Yet—*yet!* You are contemptible! When you tire of me, you will just throw me to the wolves, eh? Well, let me tell you something. You have given me your warning not to dally. Now I give you mine. If I find a man I desire, I will have him, be he slave or freeman. *You* will not stop me!"

"I will have you whipped, mistress," he said coldly.

"Then do it now, damn you, Viking!" she stormed. "I will not be threatened!"

"You would like that, eh?" He took her wrists and spread her arms out on the bed, leaning down close to her. "You have a clever way of distracting me from my purpose, wench."

"That was not my intent!" she cried in frustration, squirming beneath him.

"Then be still."

Brenna felt tears well in her eyes as he released one hand to raise her skirt, then moved to lower his trousers. She felt like a whore. She felt dirty, but he wouldn't understand.

"I hate you, Garrick!" she hissed, trying desperately to stop her tears of weakness.

He said nothing as he nudged her knees open, then fell between them. But when he finally looked down at her face again and saw the tears, he froze.

"Why do you cry?" he asked in a surprisingly soft voice. "Did I hurt you?"

"Nay, I can stand what pain you inflict."

"Then why are you crying?"

"I never cry!" she snapped childishly.

"You deny the tears that fall from your eyes, Brenna?" He shook his head. "Is it because I am intent on making love to you again?"

"You do not make love, Viking. You force yourself on an unwilling victim."

"Would you let me make love to you?"

"I—nay, I would not."

He bent down and kissed the tears that fell on her temples. "Then why do you mention it?" he asked softly.

"You would not understand."

"Ah, but I do," he said, and held her face between his hands, then kissed her softly. "You would rather I made love to you gently than force you." He lowered his lips to her neck. "But more than that, you would rather I not have you at all." He kissed her lips again, passionately this time, and her arms circled his neck without her knowing it. "Is this not so, Brenna?"

She felt like a puppet in his hands and answered mechanically. "Yea, you are right."

"Then go."

Brenna opened her eyes wide, the sensuous spell now broken. "What?"

He rolled to her side and fastened his trousers. "You may go. Is it not what you want?"

"But I do not understand," she replied, her surprise evident as she quickly got off the bed and faced him. "You don't want me anymore?"

He laughed. "You tell me you hate me, that you do not wish my attentions, and when I grant your wish, you argue with me. Make up your mind, Brenna. Have you had a change of heart?"

Her gray eyes widened even more. "Oh!" she gasped and stalked from the room.

Brenna hurried down the stairs and met Janie on her way into the hall, her hands full of empty tankards. On hearing Garrick leave his room, she stopped Janie and offered, "I will take those in." Quickly she took the tankards, before Janie could refuse.

When she entered the hall, she groaned inwardly as she saw who the tankards were for. Anselm and Hugh had arrived, along with Bayard and two other men. Brenna gritted her teeth and continued to the long table where the men were gathered.

When she passed Perrin, he winked at her, which made her smile despite herself. She handed tankards to the two men she did not know. They dipped them into the enormous cauldron filled with foaming mead that sat on the table. Then she set one beside Bayard, who was, fortunately, involved in a discussion with Gorm, and did not notice her. When she came at last to Anselm and Hugh, her expression was filled with loathing as she set the tankards down by them, but this quickly changed to a tight smile when she met Garrick's eyes as he took his place at the table.

In the next moment Brenna gasped as Hugh grabbed her about the waist and pulled her down on his lap. "So you tamed the vixen after all, brother," Hugh said to Garrick, chuckling. "I would not have thought it possible."

"Did I not say I would?" Garrick replied.

Brenna forced herself to remain still. If it were anyone but Hugh who held her, she might even consider flirting with him. But not with Hugh, whom she despised.

"You have had her for three months now and you are seldom home to make use of her anyway. Why not sell her to me?" Hugh offered. "I will give you three of my finest horses—four if you insist."

Brenna watched Garrick closely for his answer. His brows were knitted together in thought, his hands clasped over his middle as he slouched back in his chair. When he did not answer immediately, Brenna felt panic rise within her. She had not considered that he might sell her. She realized with dread that he really did own her. He had the right to sell her and she could not say yea or nay.

Brenna was about to disclose her secret, that she knew what Hugh had offered and plead with Garrick to refuse him. But Hugh's impatient voice stopped her. "Well, what say you, brother?"

"You could have had the girl for naught, but you chose her sister instead," Garrick reminded him.

"In truth, I did not think she would ever be manageable. I wanted a spirited wench, but this one nearly bit my tongue off when I tried her out. But yet you have tamed her, it appears."

"So you have changed your mind, eh? Methinks you would start a harem as those caliphs have in the East. 'Tis fortunate you have a timid wife who does not mind your dalliances, Hugh."

Laughter resounded round the table from those who were listening, and even Anselm joined in. All but Hugh were amused, and Brenna cringed as his hold tightened around her waist.

"You have not given an answer, Garrick," Hugh said in a cold voice.

"Why do you want the girl?" Garrick asked seriously. "She is not as agreeable as you believe. Her tongue is as sharp as the blade of your sword, but of course, you would not understand her. She is obstinate, defiant, stubborn to a fault and decidedly hot-tempered. Her only attribute is that she is comely."

"The reasons you have just given are why I want her. I admire her spirit."

"You would cripple her, Hugh, for you would not have patience with her stubbornness," Garrick said sharply, then softened his tone and added, "Still, it matters not, for I have no desire to sell her yet."

"Then I will take my pleasure with the vixen now," Hugh said and rose from the table, one huge arm still around Brenna's slim waist.

Garrick came to his feet also, his countenance darkly threatening. "Nay, brother, I will not sell her or share her either."

Hugh hesitated for a moment. Then he chuckled nervously and, releasing Brenna, sat down again. Brenna stood frozen, feeling the tension in the room like a weight around her neck.

Anselm had been quiet while his sons argued, but now he cleared his throat and addressed Hugh sternly. "Be content with the fiery-haired wench you have at home and forget about this one. She belongs to Garrick by my word, and if he ever decides to sell her, 'twill be to me, for I can offer him more for her than you would care to part with."

Both sons looked at their father incredulously.

"You have already said you could not trust her in your household for fear she would try to kill you," Garrick reminded his father. "Why would you want to buy her back?"

"I gave her to you with the hope you would want to keep her, but if you do not, then I would see her free rather than have the wench belong to someone else."

"You would pay me the fortune I would demand, just to set her free?" Garrick asked.

"Yea, I would."

" 'Tis unheard of, father!" Hugh protested.

"Nonetheless, I would do it."

Brenna stared at Anselm in astonishment. Again she must be thankful to him. Damn him! How could she kill him now, knowing this?

"Go see to the food, mistress!" Garrick ordered in an unreasonably sharp tone.

Brenna turned to see him scowling at her and reasoned that he was not too pleased with his father's words.

"You need not shout, Viking. There is naught wrong with my hearing," she admonished him haughtily and turned to leave. She stopped by Perrin first and leaned over to whisper in his ear. " 'Twould appear you must wait forever to find him in a good mood. Poor Janie."

"Poor me," he whispered back at her, his expression full of woe. Then he grinned. " 'Twould help matters if you would but smile at him."

Brenna straightened and laughed aloud. "Shame upon you, Perrin, for even suggesting such a thing."

She then left for the cooking area, unaware that Garrick followed her with his eyes, now become the dark color of turbulent waters in the deep sea.

Chapter 24

IN all her years, Brenna wondered if she would ever again see anything as beautiful as the northern lights. She gazed in wonder at the swirling violet mist in the sky. The ground, the buildings, everything about her was painted a bright, glowing violet. Who would ask for a sun to light the way, when they could have such magnificent displays of color instead. If only it were not so cold, Brenna would have stayed and watched the glowing mists indefinitely. But it was cold—freezing, in fact.

"Come on, Coran, before my feet turn to ice and me along with them."

She hurried along with the young man. He too was bathed in violet and looked as though he belonged on a tapestry.

It was a stroke of luck when Coran asked her if any more supplies were needed from the storehouse before he retired for the night. There was really nothing needed that couldn't wait till morning, but Brenna made the excuse that they were low on rye for bread, and if they fetched it now, Coran could sleep later in the morning.

Brenna made him wait while she got two sacks from the small storage area behind the stairs where food and spices were kept. She hid one of these sacks beneath her cape, then told Coran she would accompany him in case she saw something else they might need.

This was the opportunity she had hoped for. She could get weapons that she would hide away until she needed them. And if she could find a lighter cape she would exchange hers, though she had to admit now that the heavier one did keep her warm.

Brenna was thankful it was late and the other women were busy in the hall, clearing away the remains of the roasted bear that had been served earlier.

Coran unlocked the sturdy door to the storehouse and quickly lit the candle that was just inside. Brenna was disappointed to see that the room contained only foodstuffs, but was amply filled indeed. A large vat like the one outside the house in which rain water was collected in warmer weather was full almost to the brim with barley, and another was filled with oats. Salted meat was hung from the rafters—small game that Garrick had caught. There were barrels of rye, and one full of mountain apples and other dried fruits. Large sacks containing peas, onions and nuts, and many smaller sacks of herbs and spices were on shelves built on the walls. What Brenna was after was obviously behind another locked door, the one at the back of the storehouse, where a smaller room had been added.

"What is back there, Coran?" Brenna asked innocently enough, pointing to the closed door.

" 'Tis where Master Garrick keeps his wealth."

"Do you have the key?"

"Aye," Coran answered. "But 'tis forbidden to use it unless ordered."

"Have you never used it?"

"Of course," he replied proudly. "Four times each year I clean and polish the weapons kept there. And 'tis where I put the furs after they are tanned."

"Could you open the door now, Coran? I would love to have just one look."

"Nay, I cannot."

"Please, Coran," Brenna said very sweetly. "The master need never know. I could look about while you fill the sack with grain."

Coran shook his head slowly. It was obvious he was terribly afraid to do as Brenna asked. However, she was determined to get inside that room.

"I must not, Mistress Brenna. 'Twould mean a whipping if the master found out, mayhaps worse."

"But he won't find out, I promise," Brenna persisted. "He is making merry in the hall at present, and does not even know we are here. Please, Coran—for me."

He hesitated only a few seconds more, then smiled timidly. "Very well. But only for as long as it takes me to fill this sack." He moved to the door and opened it. "And you must not touch anything."

Impulsively, she leaned over and kissed him on the cheek. "Thank you, Coran. I will not forget this."

His cheeks reddened, and he ducked his head bashfully and went to fill the sack.

Brenna threw the door open wide to let the candlelight filter into the smaller room. She had expected treasures, but not the abundance that she could see even in the dim light. There was a small pile of furs, which would grow high before spring, and beside this was an open coffer filled with exquisite material: silk, brocades, velvets made of the finest fabrics. On a shelf against the wall were beautiful chalices made of brass, silver and even gold, and inlaid with jewels. Beside them were carved and engraved silver platters and tankards.

On a long table were many oddities of value, statues of marble and ivory, gold candle-holders, tiny brass incense burners, a jeweled cross a foot in length, ivory chessmen, and many other treasures. In a carved teakwood chest lined with velvet that sat on the center of the table, Brenna saw jewelry that dazzled her senses: necklaces of rubies and diamonds, armbands of gold and silver studded with gems or delicately carved. Another chest was open on the floor, and filled with gold and silver coins.

Finally the weapons caught Brenna's eye. Hanging from the two side walls were arms of every description. Crossbows and arrows, spears of different lengths, axes and broadswords, spiked clubs and, on a special rack, jeweled daggers. Brenna went over to these and took one inlaid with amber stones. Perhaps the amber, which was reputedly

193

Thor's favorite stone, would protect her. Not that she would need Thor's help.

Brenna looked at the crossbows, which she was expert in handling. She took one, along with a supply of arrows. She put these in the sack tied to her belt, and stuck a sword through her belt. It was not as lightweight as her own had been, but that precious sword was no more.

Brenna started to leave the room, her sack full, but a pair of black leather boots caught her eye. Her own! Next to these on a shelf were her clothes, the ones she had worn to bury her father. She was still wearing them when she lost the most important battle of her life to Anselm Haardrad.

Brenna quickly grabbed these, then pulled her cape tightly about her and left the room just as Coran approached.

"I had not realized Garrick was such a rich man," Brenna commented uncomfortably. She prayed Garrick would not notice the missing weapons.

"Aye, 'tis not many who know this."

"But he is so young to have accumulated so much wealth. He must have raided often in his youth."

Coran grinned. "Nay. Most of what you saw he brought with him from the East. Our master is a crafty tradesman."

After Coran locked the doors, they returned to the house together. Hearing the sounds of revelry still coming from the hall, Brenna bid Coran goodnight and went quickly upstairs to the sewing room.

Though it was the middle of the night, Brenna was still wide awake. She turned over and burrowed deeper into the furs. There was a small fireplace in the room, but she had not bothered to light a fire in it. Now she wished she had. It was odd, but she could not remember ever being cold at home. Yet there had been chilling winters there too.

Home—so far away. No one was left there to make it home for her. She missed her father terribly. If he were alive, he would be moving heaven and earth to find her. A comforting thought, but not realistic. She missed Linnet, too, who was so close, yet unreachable. And God forbid, she even missed her stepsister.

If these self-pitying thoughts do not stop, I will be crying soon, Brenna chided herself. A moment later, she heard the stairs creak under a great weight and Garrick bellowed out her name from down the corridor.

"Brenna!" he yelled again.

"By the saints, Viking, must you shout the house down?" Brenna said to herself as she went to open the door. She called out to him in a soft whisper, "I am here. You have no doubt aroused your mother with your blustering," she added as he came over to stand before her. "Did you consider that?"

"That good woman is used to being roused from sleep during a feast," Garrick answered in a loud voice which made Brenna grimace.

"By her husband, yea, but not by a drunken son," she scolded quietly. "Now what did you want?"

"I am not drunk, mistress," he said evenly enough, his dimples showing as he grinned. "To answer your inquiry, I want you," he added as he laughed and grabbed her about the waist, lifting her from the floor and carrying her against his hip to his room. Once inside, he set her down. She backed away from him toward the divan while he closed the door. When he faced her he grinned, but did not approach her.

"Will you have some wine with me?" he asked pleasantly enough.

Brenna hesitated, wondering at his mood. It was the first time he had offered her wine. She recalled him saying once that slaves were not allowed it.

"Yea, I will drink with you."

She curled up against the armrest on the divan while he filled two chalices from a wineskin. A single candle lit the room and cast a flickering, dim light, but Brenna could see Garrick clearly. He did not appear drunk as she first suspected. He had changed from the clothes he wore earlier to dark-green trousers with soft-skinned boots trimmed in white fur. His short robe was of white silk, with green thread shot through the hem and the long sleeves. On his chest rested a gold medallion with a single large emerald in the center, instead of the engraved silver medallion he usually wore. He looked terribly handsome this night, and Brenna found it hard to take her eyes from him.

Garrick brought her a chalice. She took only a small

sip of the bittersweet liquid, savoring the taste, then held the vessel in her lap as she watched him move to light a fire in the hearth. She had forgotten how chilly it was, forgotten everything except Garrick's presence.

The fire caught, and added more light to the room. Garrick picked up his wine and joined Brenna on the divan. He leaned back against the wall and raised one leg, on which he rested his arm, then took a long draught of wine.

Brenna was so nervous waiting for Garrick to make some kind of move that her hands would have trembled if she were not gripping the chalice so tightly in her lap.

"The wine is not to your liking?"

She started when he spoke, then looked guiltily at him. "Nay—I mean, 'tis fine."

He grinned at her knowingly. "If you have it in mind to delay me with the excuse you have not finished your wine, 'twill not work. Still, I am not in a hurry, mistress, so relax and drink your wine. You may have more when you finish."

Brenna took his advice and downed the intoxicating liquid, hoping it would steady her nerves. Yet she could not relax, even as the wine warmed her blood.

Finally she leaned back, beginning to feel the effects of the wine. "If you were to die, Garrick, what would happen to me?"

He looked at her with amusement. "Are you contemplating foul play?"

"Nay, I fight fairly. But suppose you did not return from one of your hunting trips?"

Garrick sighed and stared thoughtfully at the chalice in his hand. "Since I have no bastards nor a wife, all that I own will fall to my father. That should please you, Brenna," he added dryly.

Brenna knew what he meant, but she could not let him see that. "Why should that please me? I hate your father even more than you."

"Would you still hate him if he set you free? That is his wish," Garrick said in annoyance. "He regrets now that he gave you to me."

Brenna finished her wine and looked at Garrick seriously. "Then give me back or sell me to him."

Garrick picked up a lock of her hair from her shoulder

and twirled it slowly around his finger. "And what would you do for me, sweet Brenna, if I agreed?"

She stared at him in surprise. What price freedom? "Anything," she breathed.

"You would make love to me?"

She did not hesitate. "Yea, even that."

Garrick set his wine down and pulled her onto his lap, supporting her back with his arm. He grinned down at her before he buried his head in the hollow of her neck. His lips felt like a searing brand, and she moaned softly until his mouth claimed hers in a kiss that demanded more than a mere response.

Brenna dropped her empty chalice on the floor and gripped Garrick's head, pulling him even closer. She was lost to him. She did not know if it was for freedom or for herself, and she didn't care. She wanted him.

Brenna protested when Garrick moved her and stood up, but smiled when she saw him begin to remove his clothing. She stretched languidly, contentedly, before she got up to do the same. On her feet she swayed dizzily, then giggled.

"Too much of your precious wine, I think."

Garrick said nothing, but smiled at her and helped her out of her shift, then lifted her in his arms and carried her to the bed. He set her down gently, and laid by her side. Then she felt his hands on her, surprisingly tender for one so powerfully strong. He caressed her intimately, his fingers doing strange and wonderful things to her.

"You can be as sweet as honey when you want to," Garrick said huskily, his lips brushing against hers.

"As can you," she murmured, running her fingers through his wavy hair.

"My Celtic beauty," he murmured, running a hand up over her belly. His lips descended to her breasts. The sensations tingling through her made her weak, but still she tried to resist him, though feebly. When she brought her knees up, he stilled them with one leg. When her nails dug into his shoulders, he withstood the pain and instead of securing her hands, he kissed her, a wildly savage kiss that seemed to suck away the last remnants of her will and blot all else from her mind.

All that mattered was Garrick, his kiss, his hands caressing her urgently, his body as it pressed closer, on top of her now, his warm, throbbing member probing for an entrance, finding it at last, and then that first exquisite thrust, which drove Brenna to distraction.

She called out his name again and again as he moved in her, holding him to her as if she would mold his body forever to hers. She kissed his neck, his cheek, his lips, with wild abandon. Then all sensation gathered into her lower region, closing around his swollen member with his final deep thrust. A moment later, she felt a delicious throbbing of her own.

Having reached the heights of pleasure, Brenna succumbed immediately to the effects of the wine and lovemaking. She slept, not even stirring when Garrick rolled away from her to fetch a cover. Then he lay beside her on his belly. Propping himself up on his elbows, he watched her for a long while as she slept, his expression unusually tender. Finally he threw an arm over her possessively and fell fast asleep himself.

Chapter 25

THE noise of a fight woke Brenna from a sound sleep. Seeing that she was alone, she jumped out of bed and grabbed the first thing at hand, Garrick's white silk robe, and donned it even as she ran from the room. The robe barely reached her knees, but she was not concerned with her appearance.

At the bottom of the stairs, she hid in the shadows and observed the scene in the hall with growing alarm. Both long tables were turned over; benches were broken into pieces. The large cauldrons of mead had spilled onto the floor along with the remains of a morning meal.

Brenna's eyes scanned the room frantically. Several men were lying unconscious or dead on the floor. Some were fighting fist to fist, others with sword or axe. How in heaven's name could a brawl like this happen so early in the day? And where, dear Lord, was Garrick?

Quickly her eyes searched further until they lighted on Hugh, sitting on a bench against the wall. He was holding a swollen jaw with one hand, yet chuckling with a companion on the floor. Brenna looked down and gasped. Garrick was sprawled on the floor, with one arm resting on the bench. Her eyes saw nothing but the bright red blood splattered all over his fawn-colored tunic and trousers.

In a moment of anxiety, Brenna forget everything else and ran to Garrick. He had been laughing over something Hugh had said, but when Brenna reached him and knelt by his side, the laughter died. He turned to her in astonishment, and then anger took hold and his furious glare made her flinch.

"Have you no shame, woman?" he asked her harshly, grabbing her arm in a painful grip. "What is the meaning of this?"

She had no idea what he was talking about. "You are hurt."

"Nay!" he growled. "But were I dying 'twould not be cause for you to come before these men dressed as you are. Leave here before bloodlust turns to pure lust!"

She glanced nervously about her and saw that many had stopped fighting and were staring at her. With her unbound hair flowing about her shoulders in disarray, and the deep V of the robe nearly exposing her breasts, she presented a very tempting picture.

"I did not think, Garrick" she murmured, her face reddening. "I wanted only to help you."

"You never think, mistress!" he said cruelly, shoving her away from him. "Now get from this hall!"

Brenna bit her lip to still the trembling of it. She felt a knot swell in her throat and nearly choke her, and tears glistened in her eyes. She ran quickly from the hall before the tears fell and she was further shamed.

She would not think of last night. Brenna ran into the sewing room and slammed the door shut, then fell on the pile of furs and gave way to a torrent of tears. But after a few moments she wiped viciously at her eyes.

"I never cried," she hissed aloud, "until I met him! No more tears will I shed for any reason. If he can abuse me like that when I only wanted to help him, the devil take him! I will not be here for it to happen again!"

Brenna dug into the furs and pulled out the sack she had hidden there just last night. She had not dreamed she would need her stolen articles this soon, but neither had she imagined Garrick could be so heartless.

She dressed slowly in her own fine clothes, reveling in

the feel of the rich black velvet against her skin. Donned in her male apparel, her hurt pride healed somewhat. Her confidence was restored, and she felt as if she could accomplish anything. She stuck the sword through her belt and stuffed her sack with extra furs and leather straps to make leggings and coverings for her hands later on. Then she went into Garrick's room and took the extra blanket from his bed.

Wearing her cape to conceal her apparel, she made her way to the upstairs door but nearly tripped over Dog, who was sleeping there. Brenna knelt and tickled the shepherd's ears.

"Did he banish you from the hall also?" The animal licked her hand. "Never mind, old friend. Have you been out yet this morn?"

She opened the door and Dog followed her out into the crisp late-morning air. She was learning to judge the time of day by the stars. Strange to call it morning when the sky was so dark. Perhaps on the tip of southern Norway, the sun was lighting the land, but up here, further north, the sun only teased the horizon near midday, turning the sky a dusky blue.

Brenna slowly approached the open door to the cooking area, but Dog charged right in to scavenge for food. When Brenna saw that only Maudya was at the table, chopping onions for a soup, she came halfway into the room.

"Have you a loaf of bread I can take with me?"

Maudya looked up in surprise. "Aye, but where are you off to? There is much work to be done. They made a fine mess earlier that needs cleaning."

Brenna could hear laughter from the hall. "So the brawling is over? What was the cause, do you know?"

" 'Twas Garrick himself," Maudya replied with a shake of her head. "Janie was there and said Bayard made some remark that Garrick did not like. The master attacked Bayard like a wild boar, and 'twas the excuse for all hell to break loose. Everyone joined in."

"Bayard and Garrick are now enemies then?"

"Nay, Garrick made amends. 'Tis the way with a friendly brawl."

"Humph! What was it Bayard said to rile Garrick? Did Janie say?"

"Nay." Maudya sighed, smoothing troublesome hair away with the back of her hand.

"Did you have a rough night of it?" Brenna asked sympathetically.

Maudya grinned. " 'Twas not so bad."

"And Janie?"

"She was lucky this time. Perrin took her away and no one was the wiser."

Brenna could not understand Perrin. Garrick was supposed to be his closest friend, yet Perrin was afraid to approach him on a matter so important as Janie. Was Garrick really so forbidding, even to his friends?

"Well, have you a loaf of bread to spare, Maudya? I'm famished, but I feel like riding for a while to ease my pain first."

"What pain?"

"You did not hear Garrick upbraid me harshly in front of all his friends?"

Maudya looked shocked. "He did that to you?"

"He did."

Maudya clucked. She got a fresh loaf from the fire and wrapped it in a clean cloth. "You go ahead then, lass."

"If Garrick asks for me, do not tell him how his words have wounded me. Just say I felt like a brisk ride and will be back shortly."

"As you wish, Brenna. But if you ask me, he should know."

A grin curled Brenna's lips as she headed for the stables. Maudya would tell Garrick everything she had said, for Maudya was that way. He would assume hurt pride was keeping her from the hall so long. Later, when he finally realized she had run away, he would think his harsh words were the reason for it.

But that was only the half of it, Brenna admitted truthfully. She could no longer trust herself to be near Garrick, not after last night. In his hands she turned to clay, to be molded anyway he wished. His kiss drove away her resistance, her will. She could not tolerate that. She was a woman accustomed to having complete control over her reactions. Yet when Garrick touched her she became a puppet. She had to get away from him—far, far away.

Erin was not in the front of the stable when she entered and went straight to Willow. She saddled the mare quickly, praying Erin was sleeping or absent. She did not like lying to Maudya, but to Erin it would be even worse, for she had come to care for the old man a great deal. Fortunately, he was not about.

Brenna took two large sacks of oats for Willow and tied them across the mare's flanks, then filled four water skins from the water bin. She was ready.

She urged Willow down the path behind the stable, but stopped when Dog came running after her, yelping and raising an alarming commotion.

"Go back!" she snapped at him, fearing he had alerted someone. "Go on, Dog."

She rode on, but still he followed. "Go back, I say! You cannot come with me." He bent his head curiously and wagged his tail. Brenna sighed. "Very well, if you are set on adventure, come along. We three will make a strange trio. A dog, a horse, and a runaway slave."

She raced out into the open field, with Dog trailing close behind. She had no idea where she was going, but she was free, and answerable to no one.

Brenna stopped at the edge of the forest and looked back at the stone house on the cliff. "Farewell, Garrick Haardrad of Norway—Garrick the Hardhearted. I will remember you, no doubt forever."

Again she felt that choking lump in her throat. "You should be happy, Brenna," she chided herself aloud. "You are free now."

The coast could offer her little game, and she knew nothing of fishing. The south, which was the most desirable direction, was cut off by the fjord. The east, which she would have preferred, was where Garrick would search for her, for he would never dream she would go north, where the winds would blow even colder than here. So north it was.

"Can we survive up there till spring, Dog? By then I will have many furs and we can find another settlement near water. We will buy passage on a ship bound for home, or at least away from your homeland. What do you think?"

He regarded her solemnly.

"Aye, I think we can do it. Or die trying—there is no other way," she answered herself.

Garrick mounted the stairs just as Maudya was coming down. "Where is Brenna?" he barked at her. "If she has turned stubborn because of this morn, I will take a switch to her."

Maudya blanched at his anger. "I was just coming to find you, Master Garrick. She has not returned yet. She has been gone all afternoon, and I fear some—"

"Gone where?" he interrupted her, his eyes narrowing.

Maudya became all flustered and started weeping. "She said she was going riding—to ease her pain—because of the way you chastised her this morn."

"Did she tell you that?"

"I was not supposed to tell you, but only to say that she felt like riding for a while, and would soon return. She has not, and I fear some harm may have come to her."

"What harm?"

"The Borgsens slaughtered a dog while you were away. Some of us feel that soon they will tire of killing animals and the slaves will be next."

"What is it, Garrick?" Anselm asked from the foot of the stairs.

Garrick joined him, his brows knitted together. "The girl says Brenna has been gone since morn, riding on that horse you gave her, no doubt."

"She is pleased with the gift, then?"

"Pleased, aye. Pleased enough not to return. Maudya thinks the Borgsens may have done her harm."

"Nay, I know Latham Borgsen too well. He would not resort to such foul play. I would stake my life on it."

"I agree, which can only mean Brenna has run away," Garrick said acidly. "You give her to me, then you give her the means to escape me."

"You cannot blame me for this, Garrick," Anselm returned angrily. "You forget I was in the hall this morn. I do not know what you said to the girl, but I recognized your tone. You were overly harsh, I think."

Garrick stared furiously at his father. "You saw how she was dressed! She came into the hall nearly naked.

And 'twas intentional, I'll wager. She is the tease her sister claimed. She would have every man besotted by her."

"I saw none of that, only the concern in her eyes for you. And how do you greet her? With naught but anger. You have much to learn of women, son. 'Tis no wonder she ran away from you."

Garrick stiffened at his father's words. "You act as if you care more for the girl than you do me. Is this so?"

"Nay, but I understand her better than you."

"I have no doubt of that, for I understand her not at all." Anselm chuckled. "I will help you find her."

"Nay, this I will do myself," Garrick replied adamantly. "She needs a lesson taught that she will not soon forget."

"Garrick!"

"Do not interfere, father. You washed your hands of Brenna when you gave her to me."

Anselm sighed, staring after Garrick's retreating back. He had been amused this morn when Garrick had taken exception to Bayard's jesting remark about Brenna, saying she had changed too quickly from a wildcat to a purring kitten and that it could only be a ruse. 'Twas obvious Garrick did not like that possibility, even though it was said in jest.

Garrick's reaction gave Anselm reason to think Garrick really did care for the girl. Only yesterday he had said to all that he would not share her. Now this. Ah, would the two young people forever be at odds with each other?

Chapter 26

BRENNA stirred her small fire and added more sticks before she lay down for a few hours' sleep. She was pleasantly sated after sharing a plump, roasted hare with Dog. Willow was covered and settled for the night, and Dog lay at her feet on a pallet of old furs.

She had encountered no difficulties thus far. Game was plentiful in the wooded areas, and she had found a few flowing springs where she could replenish her water supply. The only discomfort she suffered was the icy north wind that whisked through her camp. Even next to the fire she could not get thoroughly warm. At least no snow had fallen to add to that still on the ground from the last storm. Here in the forest, there were many areas free of snow like the place where she was camped.

Four days had passed since she left Garrick. After three days of riding, she had come upon another fjord which blocked her way. So she was forced to turn east after all, but she didn't think it would matter now. She had covered Willow's tracks for two days. Garrick would never find her.

Another two days' distance should be enough. Then Brenna would look for a comparatively sheltered area—

dense woods perhaps, or a deep glen. There she would build a hut where she could wait out the winter.

It all seems so easy, Brenna thought, as sleep drew near. She should have left Garrick months sooner.

Garrick came upon the camp in the middle of night, but he was too exhausted to feel anything but mild satisfaction that his search was over. His stallion was near collapse, for Garrick had rested only twice since starting out, and had wasted a day searching through the eastern hills.

He had expected to find Brenna near death; starving and frozen. He was relieved to find her well enough, but that she glowed with contentment while she slept did not sit well with him.

Garrick dismounted and secured his horse beside the gray mare, then moved over to the fire. He lay down beside Brenna without waking her. Tomorrow would be soon enough to have it out with her. He slept.

Brenna stirred when the weight on her chest hampered her movements. As consciousness came she realized that the heavy weight she felt was not a dream, and her eyes flew open to see an arm slung across her chest, pinning her to the ground.

She fought the urge to cry out and slowly, fearfully, turned to see the rest of the long body beside her. She nearly screamed with exasperation. This was too much, too much to bear!

"You!" she stormed, throwing his arm off her and scrambling to her feet.

Garrick woke in surprise, and reached instinctively for the hilt of his sword. Upon taking in his surroundings he relaxed, then frowned when his eyes fell on Brenna, standing with legs astride, hands on her hips, her dark eyes smoldering with rage and fury.

"So you are awake?"

"How did you find me?" she demanded, her body nearly shaking with outrage. "How?"

He ignored her for a moment as he threw off his heavy cloak and dusted his clothing. Then he did not answer her question, but said contemptuously, "You have effectively confirmed my opinion of the female sex. There is not one of you who can be trusted."

"You form judgments too soon. I did not say I would stay with you. If I had, I would not have run away. Now how did you find me?"

"You forget that I am a hunter, Brenna," he said in a surprisingly even-tempered voice. "I am good at what I do. Neither beast," he paused, his eyes darkening, "nor runaway slave can escape me."

"But I covered my trail! You should be south of here. What brought you north?"

"I admit I lost a day riding towards the mountains, but with no sign of you there, I turned around." He shot a murderous glance at Dog, who hung his head guiltily. "Since I could not find that traitorous mongrel anywhere, I knew he had gone with you. You covered the mare's trail well enough, but you forgot about the dog."

It was too late to cry over her mistake. Brenna could see that Garrick was furious with Dog, however, and she did not want the animal to suffer because of her.

"Do not blame him for coming with me. I coaxed him to come," she lied, "so you could not use him to find me."

Garrick laughed shortly. "Yet 'twas Dog who led me to you after all."

She faced him squarely, her bearing defiant. "And now, Viking?"

"Now I will take you home."

"To be punished?"

"You were warned what would happen if you chose this course. Did you think that because you warmed my bed on occasion, I would be lenient with you?"

She felt that painful lump in her throat again. "Nay, I did not expect that of you," she said softly, her lower lip nearly trembling. "I thought you would not find me. Are all your neighbors out searching too?"

"I came alone," he replied in a gentler tone, almost a whisper.

"Well, I will not return to face your punishment, Viking," she replied, her voice deceptively quiet.

He shrugged and picked up his cloak, ready to leave. "You have little choice."

"You are wrong."

209

The words came out slowly, for it made her heart ache to say them, but he left her with no other course. She threw off the heavy fur cape that had concealed her weapons and placed her hand on the hilt of her sword.

"I have a choice, Garrick."

He looked at her in genuine surprise, his eyes covering her body from head to foot, coming at last to rest on the weapons. "Where did you get those?"

"I stole them."

"Who aided you?"

"No one," she lied. "I took Erin's keys to the storehouse when he slept, then returned them afterward."

"And those clothes, they are yours? But of course they are," he sneered. "They fit so well. Not a seductive gown, but tempting just the same."

"Stop it!" she cried, seeing desire mix with the anger in his eyes.

"So you wish to play the man's role again, Brenna," he speculated, amusement in his voice. "You want to fight for your freedom?"

"Leave me, and we need not fight."

"Nay," he grinned, and drew his sword. "The challenge is met."

Brenna groaned and brought her sword to hand as Garrick came at her. Her heart was not in the fight to come. There was no anger in her now, only regret that it had come to this.

He attacked quickly, trying to knock the sword from her hand, but Brenna moved aside. His side was open for her thrust, but she could not do it. He attacked again. He was skilled with the sword, and he had strength behind his blows, but he did not have her expertise, nor her cunning. Yet she could not take advantage of him. She could not bring herself to draw his blood though he gave her many opportunities to do so as he tried to disarm her.

To kill him, to see Garrick dead—the thought sickened her. She would only disarm him, as he was intent upon doing to her, and then she would move on.

Brenna was not given the chance, for at that moment a huge bear, the likes of which she had never seen before, stood up directly behind Garrick. She cried out, but she was too late. The bear had taken them so unawares that he was only inches from Garrick when he turned to see what had so frightened Brenna. With a powerful swipe of his paw, the bear knocked Garrick sideways. He fell against a tree trunk, striking his head.

Garrick did not move. Brenna stared in disbelief as the bear approached him, roaring victoriously. Brenna screamed and attacked the bear in blind fury. She held her sword in both hands and raised it over her head, then thrust it into the bear's back with all her might. But the beast didn't fall over or even stagger. He roared in bloody rage and swung round to Brenna, who turned ashen with the worst fear she had ever experienced.

Her dagger was useless, so she ran in a panic to Willow and got the crossbow from the sack. The bear was nearing her too quickly. She ran to the left, away from the horses, and readied the crossbow as she moved. Finally she crouched and took aim. The arrow pierced the bear's throat and after several agonizing moments, he fell at last.

Her relief was so great that Brenna fell on her knees to give silent thanks. Though her whole body was trembling, she made her way on shaky legs to Garrick's side and held her breath till she made sure he was alive. His shoulder was bleeding where the bear had swiped him, leaving deep grooves in the skin. But the blow to his head had not broken the skin, though it had begun to swell.

Brenna went to the horses and tore a strip from Willow's blanket, soaked it in water and returned to Garrick. She wet his face and began to clean away the blood from his shoulder.

He groaned and felt the back of his head, then eyed Brenna warily. "Do you always minister to your enemies?"

She ignored his question and inspected his cuts. "Does it hurt?"

"Nay, 'tis numb. Did the bear run off?"

Brenna shook her head. "I had to kill him."

Garrick's eyes widened. "The beast attacked you?"

"Nay, 'twas you he wanted," Brenna said calmly, avoiding his eyes.

Garrick took this news with displeasure. "First you try to kill me, then you save my life. Why?"

"If I had tried to kill you, Garrick, you would be dead now. I could not do it."

"Why not?" he asked harshly even as she bandaged his shoulder. "You would have gained your freedom."

Brenna looked at Garrick with eyes that were a soft gray. "I do not know why. I just could not find it in me to cause your death."

He grabbed her wrist and pulled her to him, then quickly lifted the dagger from her belt. "In case you have second thoughts on the matter, I will keep this."

She said nothing as he came to his feet and shook the dizziness from his head. With his hand still around her wrist, he pulled her with him over to the bear. He recognized the animal as the one he had disturbed from slumber a few days past.

" 'Twould seem I did underestimate you, Brenna," he said grudgingly, surveying the dead carcass. "You are as capable as you declared." He looked at her sternly. " 'Tis a pity I cannot trust you from my sight."

"If I were loyal to you, then you could trust me, Viking," she said almost bitterly.

He cocked a questioning brow at her. "Would you give loyalty?" Then he pulled her to him, gripping her shoulders painfully. "What do you want of me, Brenna?"

"Freedom!"

He shook his head angrily. "A free woman has many rights, among them the right to refuse a lover."

" 'Tis unlawful to rape a freewoman?"

"Aye."

Brenna stiffened. "That is all you care about—raping me! Why is it so important that you have me and not another? You do not care for me as a woman. You have no thought for my feelings. You have proved that many times. So why must it be me?"

"Your body is most pleasurable, Brenna. 'Tis enough that I enjoy having you when I want you."

"Mayhaps if you were a kindhearted man, 'twould be enough, Garrick," she said quietly. "But you are harsh, and cruel in many ways."

The look that came over Garrick's countenance was frightening. He crushed her to him, the pressure of his powerful arms excruciating.

" 'Tis me you have, mistress. I will have your word that you will not escape me again."

"You cannot force my word from me, Garrick, for if you do, 'twill not be given freely, and I will not honor it."

"Then you have set your own fate," he said.

He pulled her over to the horses and set her atop Willow. There she waited obediently while he gathered their cloaks and weapons.

When Garrick mounted, he took her reins, not even trusting her to follow him. What fate had she set for herself with her stubborn pride? Brenna shivered, staring at Garrick's stiff back. She would know soon enough.

Chapter 27

THE huge stone house loomed up before them, bathed in soft blue by the northern lights. It was night when Garrick led them into the stable. Erin came out hastily from the back, joy and relief glowing on his weathered, old face. This quickly turned to fatherly gravity.

"Shame on you, lass, for running away from us!" he said gruffly, though his eyes still gleamed his welcome.

"I did not run away from you, Erin, but from him," Brenna replied, ignoring Garrick's presence.

"Well, you gave me a mighty scare," Erin continued. "You could at least have waited till spring, so you would have had less chance of freezing out there."

"That is enough, Erin!" Garrick commanded, and took Brenna's arm roughly.

She did not even have a chance to bid Erin farewell as Garrick pulled her along in the direction of the house. As they approached the back entrance, he turned to the right, toward the side of the house, and Brenna halted immediately.

"Where are you taking me?"

He did not answer, but yanked her along. Brenna held back, thus making it more difficult for him. She knew where he was taking her, yet she could not believe it.

On the side of the house facing the fjord was a small wooden door. Garrick threw it open. Cut in the door was a little square with iron bars affixed over it. Because of its nearness to the fjord, the room inside was dark and damp like an icy wet cavern.

Garrick stood aside. "Your quarters, mistress."

She looked at him with horror in her eyes. "You would really put me in there?"

" 'Tis the kinder of most punishments for running away," he said in an impatient tone.

"How can you do this to me after I saved your life? Does that mean naught to you?"

"Yea, I am grateful."

"You show it admirably, Viking," Brenna said sarcastically.

He sighed. "If I took no action against you, Brenna, 'twould be an invitation for the other slaves to run away also. I cannot allow that."

She would not plead with him. "How long will you keep me in there?"

"Three or four days—until you have learned your lesson."

She shot him a contemptuous glance. "And you think *this* will teach me anything, Viking? You are mistaken. Here my hatred will grow and I will be even more determined to escape you."

He jerked her to him, and his lips crushed hers possessively. She returned his kiss, but only for spite. He must regret doing this to her. She would make him regret it.

"You need not stay here, Brenna," he breathed against her neck, "if you will give me your word you will not leave me again."

She put her arms about his neck and said provocatively, "But then the other slaves would think I am special to you."

"You are special."

"Special, yet still you could shut me in that cold cell."

"Will you swear, Brenna?"

She kissed his lips lightly, teasingly, before she pushed him away. "The devil take you, Viking. I will not be your prized toy."

With that she held her head high and walked into the dank cell, gritting her teeth as he closed the door behind her. She began to tremble immediately. She almost screamed out and called him back, but then she clamped her hand over her mouth. She would not beg to be released.

It was cold—freezing, in fact. Fortunately she had her cape and her arm coverings and fur leggings. There was also an old woolen blanket on a narrow bench, the only furniture in the room. But there was no fire, and the incompletely enclosed room could not keep out the icy cold.

No food had been left for her, either. All at once she felt ravenous, though she and Garrick had shared some venison only hours earlier. He would reutrn. He could not possibly leave her here to freeze.

She sat down on the bench and covered her legs with the blanket. The first three days of leisurely riding with Garrick he had been coldly silent. But the last two days his mood lightened, and she began to think he would do nothing to her when they returned. Still she could not believe he would really make her stay here.

An hour passed, and then another. The blue mist in the sky disappeared, leaving only a depressing black gloom. Brenna shivered and felt the first signs of a fever. A while later she grew hot and threw off her cape, along with the strapped coverings on her legs and arms.

He was not going to return. That unwelcome lump grew in her throat again, and tears stung her eyes. After all they had shared, even after she had saved his life, he could so mercilessly lock her in here. She would freeze to death. Then he would be sorry. A fine way to have revenge, when she would not be there to revel in the fruits of it.

She started shaking again, and lay down on the hard bench. She dozed fitfully, alternately waking to cither throw off her cape and blanket, or to pull them back over her again.

"I am ill and he doesn't even know it," she reasoned, half asleep. "I should have told him. But it wouldn't have made a difference to him. He is a beast. He doesn't care." She turned over, tears making her eyes glassy. "You will be sorry, Garrick, sorry . . . sorry . . ."

Chapter 28

GARRICK turned fitfully on his bed and smashed a fist into his pillow. Try as he might, sleep would not come. The devils in his mind were having a fine time of it. Hour after hour, self-recriminations kept churning.

Finally he could stand it no more. He leaped out of bed and threw on his cloak, then stormed from the room. In the hall, he lit a torch quickly, then braced himself for the icy cold outside. He reached the small cell in seconds and rapidly fumbled with the keys to unlock it.

The door creaked open and he stooped to enter the dank chamber, then straightened, setting the torch in a wall holder before he approached Brenna. She was asleep on the floor by the bench, curled childlike in a ball, devoid of covering, including her velvet mantle.

Garrick gritted his teeth in anger. The little fool! With no covers, she would catch her death in this weather. No doubt that was her intention.

He knelt down beside her and shook her roughly, but stopped as he felt the heat that permeated even her thick velvet tunic. He put his hand to her face and drew in his breath sharply. She was burning with fever.

"My God, Brenna, what have you done?"

She opened her eyes and stared at him in confusion. "Why do you speak to my god? Your pagan gods will be angry."

"Does it matter which god I speak to?" he asked angrily. "They are one and the same, I think. But I ask them and you, why did you try to kill yourself?"

"I am not dead," she said in a soft whisper before her eyes closed in sleep again.

Garrick's face was ashen. "You will be if you do not fight this, Brenna. Wake up!"

When she did not stir, he picked her up and carried her swiftly into the house and up to his room. There he laid her on the bed and covered her with the warm ermine spread. He stirred up the fire, then came back to the bed.

"Brenna. Brenna!"

She would not wake. He shook her shoulder, but still she did not open her eyes. He began to panic. He knew nothing about fevers. Yarmille must be called. She knew much of herbs and potions. She had cured Hugh when he was a boy, taming a raging fever he had.

Garrick left the room. After waking Erin and telling him to send the women to the house, he himself rode to fetch Yarmille. They returned within the hour and Yarmille closeted herself in the room with Brenna, forbidding anyone else to enter.

Garrick paced tirelessly before the fire in the hall. Maudya came in quietly, bringing food and drink for him, but he did not touch them.

Erin sat at the table watching his young master with deep concern. "She is a strong lass," he said encouragingly. "I have seen many fevers in my day. 'Tis only a matter of cooling her when she is hot, and warming her when she is cold."

Garrick looked at him stonily, as if he had not heard a word the old man said. He continued to pace, the loss of sleep affecting him not at all. Hours passed and day turned to night again.

Yarmille came into the hall, looking tired and haggard. Garrick held his breath as she stared at him for a long moment without speaking.

Finally Garrick could not stand the suspense any longer. "The fever has passed?"

Yarmille shook her head slowly. "I am sorry, Garrick. I have done all I can."

He came forward. "What are you saying? That she has not improved?"

"She did for a while. The fever dropped. She took my potions and ate some broth. But then the fever returned and everything I gave her, she vomited. She can keep nothing down and now she is much worse than before."

"There must be something you can do!"

"I will make a sacrifice for her," Yarmille suggested. "That is the only thing left to do. If the gods are pleased, they may spare her life."

Garrick blanched and ran from the hall up the stairs to his chambers. Erin, who had stayed with Garrick the whole day, got up from the table, tears glistening in his eyes.

"Is the girl really so ill?" he asked.

Yarmille looked at him disdainfully and said in a haughty tone. "She is. And the gods won't help her. Why should they? She will die before morn."

With that Yarmille left the hall to return to her home. Once outside, a contented smile came to her lips. She would make a sacrifice all right, but to insure the girl's death—though she doubted help from the gods would be necessary. With Yarmille's potions and an open balcony door in Garrick's chamber, her death would be assured.

If only she had seen the threat the girl posed sooner, she could have gotten rid of her before Garrick even saw her. She had been sure that Garrick would not take to the girl, that he would shun her as he did all the others. Still, all things come to those who wait—and she would not have to wait much longer . . .

Erin entered Garrick's chamber to find him standing beside the bed, a defeated man. A fire was burning in the hearth, yet the room seemed terribly cold.

"Would that I could do it all over again, it would be different, Brenna," Garrick said in a hollow voice. "I will never forgive myself for this."

Erin moved beside him, his face drawn with worry. "She cannot hear you, lad."

"She was speaking when I came in the room," Garrick told him. "In such a childlike manner."

"Aye, she is no doubt reliving her past. I have seen this

221

deep sleep before, where devils play havoc with the mind. For some 'tis not so bad; for others it can be a living hell, where death is welcome."

"She cannot die!"

"So you love the girl, Garrick?"

"Love? Love is for fools!" he answered heatedly. "I will never love again."

"Then what does it matter if the girl dies, if she is only another slave to you?" Erin said wisely.

"It matters!" Garrick said forcefully, then all anger suddenly left him. "Besides, she is too stubborn to die."

"I pray you are right, lad," Erin replied. "Myself, I would not give a fig for Yarmille's opinion. There is always a chance, with God's help."

Brenna sat on her father's lap, her new sword with sparkling gems clutched tightly in her tiny hand. "Did I thank you, father? Oh, I thank you again! My very own sword, made especially for me. I could not have asked for a better present!"

"Not even a pretty gown, or a fancy trinket? Your mother loved such things."

Brenna made a face. "Those are for girls. Girls are silly and cry. I never cry!"

Alane pushed Brenna into the steaming bath. The water was scalding hot. Steam filled the room, making a white fog which hid Alane from sight.

"What would your father say if he knew you were fighting with the village boys, and in the mud no less?"

"Father would be proud of me. I won, didn't I? Ian has a black eye, and Doyle a swollen lip."

"They let you win only because you are Lord Angus's daughter."

"I am not his daughter. I am not! And I won fairly. Now let me out of this bath before I boil to death!"

"You must get clean and pretty, Lady Brenna."

"But the water is too hot. Why does it have to be so hot?"

Brenna's stepmother's disembodied face came out of the foggy steam. "Brenna, you are a disgrace to your father. When will you learn to be a lady?"

"I do not have to do what you say. You are not my mother!"

Alane blew away the steam. "She is your mother now, Brenna."

"Nay, nay, I hate the widow, Alane, and her daughter. Why did father have to marry her? Cordella is always teasing me. And the widow is a witch."

"You must show them respect."

"Why should I? They hate me too. They are both jealous of me."

"Mayhaps they have no kindness in their hearts, girl, but you do. 'Tis up to you to make them welcome here."

Brenna was duly chastened. "If I must, I must, but I won't like it."

Snow began to fall, heavy thick sheets of it, covering the land in a blanket of ice. Brenna ran across the frozen lake, skidding and sliding. She waved to Cordella, who stood by a tree, wrapped in a mantle of silver, her red hair like a flame against the white snow.

"For shame, Brenna. A young woman your age acting like a child. The ice will break and you will fall in. Then what will you do?"

The ice cracked with a deafening sound and Brenna tumbled into the icy black water just as Cordella had predicted. She began to shake uncontrollably. Her hands were numb with cold, and she could not crawl back onto the solid ice.

"Help me, Cordella. I am freezing."

"Did I not say you would fall?"

"Della, please help me out. The water is so cold. It hurts, it hurts terribly."

" 'Twill hurt also when your husband first takes you. Then you will know real pain."

"I saw an act of coupling in the village. 'Twas not so horrifying as you would have me believe, Della."

"Wait and see. Soon your future husband will come for you. Then you will suffer."

"I will not marry a Viking. I will marry no man. Did I not shun two score of wealthy suitors?"

"You will be married, Brenna. Your father has given his word."

Linnet came from a great distance, walking slowly toward Brenna out of the dark. Finally the woman reached her. Her face was tired and sad as she pulled Brenna out of the freezing water and began to wrap blanket after blanket about Brenna's shoulders until the girl felt as if she would suffocate in the warmth.

"Angus is dead, Brenna."

"Nay!" Brenna screamed in agony. "My father cannot die! It is not so!"

The village was weeping. Angus was laid to rest. The sun was not up yet, but it seemed terribly hot for so early in the morning.

"The Vikings come, Lady Brenna."

"Wyndham! Is this the way your kinsmen come for a bride? To attack and kill? Alane, no! You must not die too! I cannot help you, Aunt Linnet. He has broken my sword. I cannot help any of you. I will kill him for what he has done to my people, I swear!"

"I am Heloise, wife to Anselm. You will be given to my son Garrick."

"I will not be owned!"

"Have I found the means to tame you, wench?"

"He will rape me. My God, how will I endure the agony Cordella said I would feel? Where is the pain? Cordella lied! She made me show fear to the Viking when there was no need. But 'twas beautiful. He is beautiful. Such a magnificent body, so much power and strength. He makes me forget that I hate him. He makes my will his own."

Laughter came from far away. Cordella and Yarmille laughing. Anselm and Hugh laughing.

"He is a beast! He cares naught for me. How could he abuse me so before his guests? I am free of him now. He will never find me. I could not have stayed with him any longer, not when his touch turns me to honey."

Swords clanging together. The noise was deafening, and hurt her ears, finally she screamed.

"I cannot kill you, Garrick, even for my freedom. I do not know why, but the thought of you dead hurts so terribly."

Brenna trembled. "I am so cold. I am ill and he does not even know it. He will be sorry when he finds me dead.

How could he do this to me after I saved his life? 'Tis so cold, so cold."

"Yarmille, close the door before . . . before . . ."

Brenna floated in the warm lake, her eyes closed to the welcome sun. Not a care creased her brow. Not a thought disturbed her peace, gently floating, the warm water a natural balm.

She awoke and the warm lake was replaced by a soft bed which felt uncommonly hard for some reason. She blinked her eyes several times before she recognized Garrick's room, then turned her head to find him sitting beside the bed in one of the thronelike chairs, looking terribly haggard and unkempt. Yet he was smiling at her. And his eyes were warm.

"You do not look well, Garrick. Have you been ill?"

He laughed at her concern. "Nay, wench, I am fine. But how do you feel?"

She tried to sit up, but groaned. "I feel sore all over, as if someone took a stick to me." She glanced at him suspiciously. "Did you beat me while I slept?"

He looked affronted. "How could you think such a thing? You have been gravely ill for two days. 'Tis no doubt the sickness that has made you weak and sore." He got up and pulled the covers up about her neck. "The women have kept soup warmed for when you woke. I will bring you some."

Brenna relaxed in the big bed when he left. Is he sorry? He shows concern, but does he really care?

She could not wait for the food. Sleep took hold again and pressed her into peaceful darkness before he returned.

Chapter 29

THE last month of the year was a bitterly cold one, bringing snow and ice to the land in abundance. Brenna spent a good deal of the month in bed, having her every need pampered by Janie and Maudya. Even Rayna grudgingly brought her a special soup full of herbs known for their healing powers.

The women served Brenna eagerly. She was one of them, one who had narrowly escaped death. Yet she was also the master's favorite, which became more apparent every day, though Brenna did not see it so.

When Garrick finally pronounced her well enough to return to her chores and her own room, Brenna was hard pressed to hide her relief. However, the most strenuous task she was allowed to perform was to baste the hind quarter of a small boar with honey, and she was thoroughly annoyed that she was still being cosseted by the other servants, under Garrick's orders.

Brenna threw open the door to Garrick's chamber without knocking. He looked up from his evening meal, more startled by her presence in his room than by the loud banging of the door. He ignored her rigid stance and the stormy gray of her eyes and continued eating.

"You should be abed, mistress," he said sternly, without looking at her. "You have no doubt had a trying day and need your rest."

She came further into the room. "What I need is for you to relax your concern. I am not a cripple, Garrick," she said tightly, trying to control her temper.

She knew it was pointless to argue with him when he was so damned benevolent. She hated his new attitude. He was like a forgiving father with an errant child, when forgiveness was the last thing that was needed.

"Do you doubt that I am well?" she continued.

He shook his head, still not looking at her. "Nay, but you cannot be allowed to overdo things, Brenna. You nearly died, but were granted life. Is it not reasonable that you begin that new life with a measure of caution?"

"Nay, 'tis most unreasonable!" she snapped, forgetting herself. "First you keep me confined to bed longer than necessary. Now you treat me like a fragile doll that will break if moved. I am well, I tell you!" Brenna threw up her hands in exasperation. "God's mercy! I am not an idle person. I was ever willing to work in your stable but you said nay. If all you will allow me to do is work here, so be it. Yet I must have something to do."

"This is not what your sister would have me believe."

Brenna was startled out of her anger by his words. "You spoke with Cordella?"

"Yea, at length."

Brenna clenched her fists. The thought of Garrick and Cordella talking, laughing, making love together, drove everything else from her mind. So she was right. Those many nights Garrick had come home late, making her wait up for him, he had been with Cordella!

"Brenna, come here."

"What?" she asked without hearing him.

"Come here!" he repeated.

Still she did not move or look at him. Finally he came to her and touched her cheek.

His fingers against her skin were like a shock, and she slapped his hand and backed away from him.

"Don't you touch me!" she cried, pain and anger in her voice. "Don't you ever touch me again!"

Garrick stared at her in confusion. "Thor, help me! What is wrong with you, woman?"

"You—you are mad if you think I will share you with my sister! If you want her, then you can have her, but don't you ever come near me again, or I swear I will kill you!"

A twinkle came into Garrick's eyes and he grinned in amusement. "Why would I want your sister when I have you? And why would you even think that, when I said only that I talked to her?"

"You have not made love to her?"

"Nay, I have not. But if I had, why should this upset you, Brenna?"

She felt her face redden deeply and realized how foolish she must have sounded, almost like a jealous wife. She turned away from him, wondering at her own reaction.

"Brenna?"

"I would not mind if you take another woman," she replied quietly, feeling that unwelcome lump rise in her throat. "If another can take care of your needs, I would be glad of it, for then you would leave me be. But 'tis not right that you should have both me and my sister. Can you not see the wrong of it?"

"Is that the only reason you will give me?"

Her eyes shot open wide. "There is no other."

"Very well, I will not press you for it."

She glared at him. "I tell you there is no other reason!"

Garrick grinned at her, his dimples deepening. "You take offense easily this night," he said with humor in his voice, and moved to his coffer. "Mayhaps this will lighten your temper."

She fixed her gaze on him, entranced for a moment at the way his golden hair fell over his forehead, making him look so boyish and harmless, not at all like the Viking warrior, ravisher and coldhearted master she knew him to be. She was loath to take her eyes from his face, but finally she looked at the box he took from his coffer and her eyes lit up with curiosity. As he came toward her, she could see that the box was a miniature chest carved in an Eastern design and inlaid with ivory. It was quite lovely.

She met his eyes as he handed the chest to her. "What is this for?"

"Open it."

She lifted the lid. Inside, on a bed of blue velvet, were a matched pair of gold arm rings in the shape of coiled snakes, with bright red rubies for eyes. She knew that for the Vikings, rings like these were prized. She had seen Hugh's wife wearing gaudy bands on her bare arms, and even Heloise wore arm rings. The men did too. The wealthier the man, the more costly the arm ring.

These that Garrick showed her were tasteful. She lifted one and found it was heavy—made of solid gold, no doubt.

Brenna met his eyes again. They shone softly with aqua lights.

"Why do you show me these?" she asked, handing the chest back to him.

Garrick kept his hands at his sides. "I do not show them to you, Brenna. I give them to you. They are yours—the chest too."

She looked at the rings again, then stared at him incredulously. "Why?"

" 'Tis my wish."

"To give a slave such costly trinkets?" She became incensed. This was his way of assuaging his guilt for locking her in that horrible cell. But she would not forgive him for that. "When do I wear them, Garrick? When I am washing your clothes? When I sweep the hall? Nay, I will not wear your gift."

"You will!" he said sharply, his eyes darkening. "And you will also wear the gown my mother is now making for you. You will wear them when you come with me to the feast at my father's house to celebrate the winter solstice."

Brenna was thoroughly taken aback. "Your *mother* is making a gown for me?"

"At my request," he answered curtly.

Brenna was amazed that Heloise would agree to make a gown for a slave. She knew Heloise was Christian and kindhearted, but still, to spend her time sewing for a servant was incredible. Just as surprising was the fact that Garrick would take her to Anselm's settlement, and for a feast, no less.

"I do not understand, Garrick. Why will you take me to your father's house now, when every time I have asked you to take me there to see my family, you refused?"

"You needed time to adjust to your new life, without re-membrances of home. You have done that."

"You honestly think I have adjusted, after I only just tried to escape you?"

"I did not say you have adjusted to me, mistress, but to your new life."

"But why will you take a slave to a feast? Is that ordinarily the custom?"

"Nay, but I do not conform strictly to custom. You will come along to serve my needs."

She gasped at his meaning. "And if I refuse?"

"You cannot refuse, Brenna," he laughed. "You go wherever I take you."

"Mayhaps. But I can make it most difficult for you," she remarked slyly. "Still, I will go on one condition—that I have a dagger to wear."

"Agreed."

She smiled and crossed to the door, his gift still in her hands. She felt she was the winner this time. Garrick was getting soft.

"As to my taking care of your needs while there, we will discuss that when the time is at hand."

"There will be no discussion."

"You can be sure there will be," she countered, and left him to brood on it.

Chapter 30

THE day of the solstice feast came sooner than Brenna would have liked. Though she was eager to see her aunt again, and she had many choice words to say to Cordella, who would rue the day she had lied to Brenna, she was not looking forward to being in Anselm's house, wanting to hate him, yet knowing she had much to be grateful to him for. And to go there with Garrick, before all, not as his slave but as his woman, wearing his gifts. She wondered if she could bear the humiliation of it.

Brenna wanted desperately not to go, but knew she must. Garrick was in high spirits over the whole affair. He was adamant that she accompany him. He would drag her there if she offered resistance.

Brenna looked down at the beautiful gown that clung delicately to her slim body. It was rich red velvet, not too heavy, and shot through with gold thread. It was a simple design, sleeveless, in the Viking fashion, with a gently curving neckline. Most startling was the wide gold belt studded with rubies to match the arm rings she wore.

Janie helped Brenna with her hair, twining thick braids interlaced with red ribbon about her head for a becoming effect. She was not at all jealous of the fact that Brenna would be a guest at Anselm's house, but was quite excited for her and chatted aimlessly about her good fortune.

Brenna did not feel that way, and became even more apprehensive when Garrick called for her. She met him in the hall, and was stunned by his appearance. He was dressed also in velvet, the fine, gold material molded to his muscles like a second skin. Red thread contrasted with the gold, and large rubies studded not only his belt, but also a gold medallion around his neck. She wondered if he had planned it this way, that they should look like a matched pair.

His wavy hair glistened gold in the firelight, but his eyes were cloudy when she noted him staring oddly at her.

"You are a jewel in a black sea, mistress," Garrick said softly, coming toward her.

She felt herself blush at the way his eyes looked her over. "The gown is lovely," was all she could manage to say.

"Yea, but 'twould not be as beautiful on another."

Now she was thoroughly ill at ease. " 'Tis not like you to play at flattery, Garrick."

"I speak only truth," he smiled. "There is much to me you have not yet seen."

"I am beginning to learn that."

All at once he was impatient. "Let us go. The feast has no doubt begun."

She nodded and followed him through the cooking area to where their cloaks hung by the back door. But hers was not there. In its place was a beautiful cloak of ermine, with a wide hood. She stood still while he draped it over her shoulders, then carefully placed the hood over her hair.

She looked up at him, her brows raised questioningly. "Another gift?"

He grinned. "Aye. Rich apparel becomes you. You shall have more of it."

" 'Tis not like you to be generous either, Garrick. Why have you changed?"

"It suits me," he replied with a shrug, and at last handed her the dagger he had promised her.

She stuck the jeweled weapon in her belt, then looked at him in exasperation. "God's mercy! 'Twas better when you would brood and were predictable. I hate inconsistency!"

she snapped, then stalked from the house, but not before she heard him chuckle at her sudden outburst.

A thick cloud of smoke from the cooking fires hung heavy in the hall, but Brenna preferred stinging eyes to the cold that they had just come from outside. She was still too chilled to give up her cloak, and it was just as well that she had that excuse, for as she looked about the room at the other women there, she saw that not one of them had a gown as rich as hers.

She blushed nearly crimson at the thought of their reaction to Garrick parading her before them. A mere slave adorned better than freewomen—it was unheard of. Brenna felt like Garrick's pampered whore, and knew that all would come to the same conclusion.

These thoughts plagued Brenna, and she grew increasingly bitter. She said nothing when Garrick left her at one table while he went to greet his family. She sat stonily silent, fixing her gaze in her lap, knowing that many eyes were turned her way. She continued to brood, and was startled when Heloise joined her.

"Are you pleased with the gown, Brenna?"

Brenna met the kind eyes and began to relax. "Yea, I thank you."

"Then come, let me have your cloak. I did not spend many hours on such a lovely gown to have you hide it."

Brenna gave up the ermine cloak reluctantly, but found that she was not nearly so self-conscious with Heloise beside her. She was immensely grateful that the mistress of the house was taking the time to make her feel at ease.

"Yea, 'tis indeed lovely on you, child," Heloise smiled.

"You are very kind."

"Nay, I speak the truth. And I owe you my thanks, Brenna."

"I have done nothing."

Heloise glanced at Garrick standing with his father and some other men, then looked back at Brenna and placed a hand affectionately on her arm. "I have not seen my son so relaxed and actually in good humor for a very long time. For this I have you to thank."

Brenna blushed once again. "Surely you are mistaken."

"I think not. Oh, he did not want to fall prey to your

235

charms and fought against it, but he has nonetheless. Have you not noticed the difference yourself?"

Brenna nodded slowly, avoiding Heloise's eyes. She could not agree with the other woman, yet surprisingly, the thought warmed her. Could that really be the reason for the startling change in Garrick since her illness? Could he have fallen in love with her?

Brenna was afraid to pursue such thoughts or speak of it further, so she quickly changed the subject. "My aunt. May I see her?"

"Of course. Ah, she comes now. I will take my leave, so you may speak privately."

Brenna rose with Heloise just as Linnet reached them, but Brenna did not see her leave. Her eyes were on her aunt, and her tears fell as they embraced. All that Brenna had endured during the recent months came to her mind now that she finally had someone to confide in, but it did not seem half so bad in light of her aunt's situation.

They sat down together, but Brenna would not release Linnet's hands. She took in her aunt's appearance with a critical eye, and saw that the older woman still did not look her age. In fact, her blue eyes sparkled with youth and vitality.

"You fared well, Aunt?"

"Heloise has made me feel as if I am part of her family," Linnet confided easily. "Yea, I fared very well."

"I am glad. So often I worried for you, but Garrick would not let me come here till now."

"He is very possessive, I think, and would like to keep you close to his home. I have heard much of you, Brenna, from Heloise. I know that you were terribly stubborn in the beginning, but I knew you would be. I know that you ran away, and also were deathly ill. I was frantic at the time. But here you are, well and honored. I am so pleased."

"Honored?"

"You are here as a guest, not as Garrick's slave. Yea, he honors you in this."

Brenna laughed dryly. "I know his reason, Aunt. I am here only to see to his needs."

"Come now, Brenna," Linnet reasoned. "There are many here who could do that. Also, he did not need to give you such beautiful gifts for what you imply. I was with Heloise when Garrick bid her make that gown for you. 'It must be in the Viking fashion,' he said, 'for she is one of us now.' "

Brenna knitted her brows in thought. "I have given him no reason to believe I am happy here. He knows I will escape again if given the opportunity. Why would he say I am one of them?"

"You must have given him some cause to believe so. But truly, Brenna, you must not try to escape again. If you succeeded and Garrick could not find you, I would forever worry over you."

"When I go, Aunt, 'twill be by sea, and I will take you with me," Brenna said hastily, doubtful that she could ever accomplish such a feat. Though she had tried to put her aunt at ease, what she said seemed to sadden the older woman instead.

"Ah, Brenna. I thought surely, seeing you here this day, that you had finally outgrown your wild ways. A mature woman would accept the fates that brought her here. She would be thankful she is alive and adjust to her new life, knowing there is no longer an old life to return to."

"As you have done?"

"Yea, as I have. 'Tis the only way, Brenna. If we mourn the freedom we lost, we will suffer unduly. In truth, my life has improved, so I cannot complain. I have a kind, dear friend in Heloise. She does not begrudge me Anselm's occasional visits, and so I have a man too, who is quite kind in his way."

"Cease! I wish to hear no more."

"Be sensible, Brenna. Garrick cares for you, 'tis plain to see. Make your life with him something special."

"By being his whore!" Brenna hissed, the heart of her unrest coming to the surface.

"Yea, I know he cannot offer you marriage, but you will be as a wife to Garrick. His splendid gifts are proof of that. 'Tis said a bastard can inherit from his father if there are no legitimate heirs. Mayhaps Garrick will never wed, but keep you as his only love. Your future with him would be just as secure, even without vows spoken. You may birth bastards, but they would have a place here."

"My pride demands better. I once scorned marriage, yet that is the only way I could live with Garrick in peace."

"But 'tis forbidden to marry a slave."

"I know," Brenna said softly.

She looked at Garrick across the room and smiled. She had said the words aloud. She would marry Garrick, yea, she would do so gladly. The thought of marriage to him, without the constant battle of wills, filled her with warmth. Yea, she did love him!

Brenna greeted this realization with laughter clear and joyous. She leaned over and hugged her aunt. "I love him. I did not know it until now, but 'tis truth. I love him. If he cares for me as you have said, as his own mother has said, then he will marry me. 'Tis the only way I can live with Garrick."

"Brenna, you are surely Angus's daughter. Stubborn beyond good sense. If you truly love Garrick, then you will take him as he is and not demand more of him."

"And decency be damned? Nay, Aunt. 'Twill be my way, or not at all," Brenna replied sternly and stood up. "Where is Della?"

"She complained of an illness, and took to her bed in our quarters."

"Did she know I would be here?"

"Yea, we all knew. Garrick had to obtain permission from his father to bring you as a guest, so as not to insult Anselm."

Brenna bristled at this. *She* was the one insulted. To obtain permission indeed!

"We will speak later, Aunt," Brenna said stiffly. "I hope by then you will be more supportive of me, rather than of these pagan barbarians."

Chapter 31

Johanna Lindsey

HUGH joined Garrick, refilling both their tankards from the huge, foaming cauldron of mead in the middle of the long table before he sat down. Men masked in animal heads danced and ran about the room, playing tricks on each other and various guests.

Garrick was hard-pressed to keep a stoical countenance as a man hidden beneath the head of a ram, whom he knew for a fact to be his half-brother Fairfax, snuck up behind Hugh and emptied a bucket of snow atop his head. Garrick watched in amazement as Hugh merely laughed and shook the snow from his shoulders, not even turning to see who the culprit was, even though Fairfax had run for dear life after completing the deed.

Finally Garrick laughed boisterously. "You have mellowed, brother. I know you have never liked the merry antics of the winter solstice feast. I was prepared to battle you to the floor just now, once you rose in a rage, drawing your sword."

"And I disappointed you, I see," Hugh chuckled, his golden mane shaking.

"Nay. I am in no mood to do battle."

"Nor I. So we have both mellowed, eh?"

239

Garrick leaned back and studied his older brother speculatively. "I thought I was in high spirits, but you are even more so. You are as a man who has been granted a glimpse of Valhalla and has found it to be just as anticipated. Enlighten me."

"Toast me, brother," Hugh grinned. "I will at long last have a child."

Garrick was indeed surprised. He pounded his brother on the back. " 'Tis welcome news, Hugh!" He raised his tankard. "May the child be male, and blessed with the strength of his—uncle."

Hugh roared with laughter. "I will settle for that."

"Your wife must be ecstatic in her joy," Garrick remarked. " 'Twas a long wait."

"Nay, she is furious. She always placed the blame on me for her barrenness, but she is still barren. 'Tis the new slave Cordella who is breeding."

Some of Garrick's pleasure was lost at this disclosure. "Are you sure 'tis your seed?"

"Yea," Hugh answered proudly. "As you have kept your wild vixen for yourself, so I have kept mine."

Garrick frowned at the mention of Brenna, remembering the grudge she harbored against her sister. He cursed himself for giving her a dagger, and prayed she would not use it against her sister.

He looked about the room quickly to find her, but she was nowhere to be seen. She was no doubt with Cordella.

Garrick rose quickly. "Your pardon, Hugh. I would find Brenna before our father's feast is ruined. She has a talent for trouble."

"Sit down, Garrick, 'Twould take more than a little vixen to ruin this feast. I would discuss with you your voyage this spring."

"Can it not wait until later?" Garrick asked impatiently.

"If you leave now, Morna will be sure to think you are afraid to face her."

"Morna?"

Hugh motioned toward the door and Garrick turned to see Perrin, looking justifiably embarrassed, and beside him, his sister Morna. She looked as lovely as ever. Her flaxen hair was pulled back tightly, accentuating the strong bones of her face, and her full curves were pressed hard against the dark green silk of her gown. Their eyes met, and Garrick's were as dark as a stormy cove.

Hugh was right. He could not leave now. He turned his attention back to his brother and sat down slowly. He would just have to trust Brenna not to do something that they would all regret.

In the sky, a red mist was gathering, tinging the white landscape. An ominous color, red—the violent color of blood and anger.

Brenna stared at the northern lights for several seconds, imagining the shafts of violet-red mist to be bloody arms reaching out to unseen enemies. Her stormy thoughts and the vivid memory of her humiliation because of Cordella's lies brought out such imaginings. Her anger was barely controlled as she opened the door to the women's quarters.

Numerous oil cups glowed with light, and a fire burned in the center of the room. Pallets lined the walls, and on one lay Cordella, an arm draped over her eyes, her fiery red hair spread out on the pillow beneath her head.

"Who is there?" Cordella asked in a bored voice. "Hugh?" She waited for an answer, but none came. "Linnet?"

"Nay, 'tis me, Della."

Cordella sat up immediately, her face slowly losing all color. "Brenna—I—"

"You what?" Brenna demanded sharply as she came closer. "You are sorry? You meant to admit to your lies before I was humiliated because of them?" Brenna stood directly in front of Cordella, her hands planted on her hips, her eyes stormy with rage. "Why did you lie to me about what happens between a man and woman?"

Hot color returned to Cordella's cheeks. " 'Tis what you deserved!"

"Why? What have I ever done to you to make you so vengeful? I would know the answer, Della, before I take my *own* vengeance!"

Again Cordella blanched. Quickly she tried to justify herself. "Dunstan wanted you, but you were not even aware of it."

"Dunstan?" Brenna's brows narrowed. "That is absurd. He was your husband."

"Yea, my husband!" Cordella shrieked bitterly. "But 'twas *you* he coveted. If you had known, you could have put an end to it. You were too wrapped up in trying to prove yourself worthy of your father's pride. You were not aware of how others felt."

"If what you say is true, why did *you* not tell me? You know I wanted no man, least of all Dunstan."

"I could not have admitted to you or anyone that I could not hold my husband's love."

"And for this you would make me anticipate a nightmare? You thought 'twould be with my new husband, but it being the enemy who first ravished me made it even worse. Not the experience, Della, but the fact that for the first time in my life my courage fled completely."

"I am glad if you suffered even a little humiliation, for I suffered much because of you!"

Hot fury flashed in Brenna's eyes and her hand struck out and slapped Cordella soundly across her face. Her other hand reached for her dagger.

"I am not to blame for your hurt pride, Della! If you had any sense, you would see that. Had I found you the night the Viking first took me, I would have killed you. 'Tis still a pleasant thought."

Cordella stared in disbelief at the blade in Brenna's hand. "You would harm a woman with child?"

Brenna was stunned, and she drew back. "Do you speak the truth, Della?"

"Linnet knows. Ask her if you doubt my word."

Brenna had not counted on this. She would not have killed her, for she could be generous in her new-found love for Garrick. She had meant to scare her greatly, however. Now she could only make false threats.

"You have trifled overmuch with my life, Della. If you ever do so again, I will forget that I am Christian and drive this blade through your heart—child or no child!"

As Brenna sheathed the dagger, Cordella smirked with new courage. "You do not frighten me, Brenna Carmarham! Hugh will protect me. And you will pay dearly for what you did to me this day!"

"Is more revenge worth your life, sister?" Brenna countered in a menacing tone before she turned on her heel and stalked from the room.

Brenna was furious. The meeting had not gone at all as she had planned. She could not believe Cordella's audacity. She would wash her hands of her stepsister, and never see the lying witch again. The one slap was hardly adequate retribution, but she would be satisfied with it.

The red mist had not stayed long to light the sky. It was dismally black again as Brenna hurried back to the hall. She now regretted the harsh attitude she had taken toward her aunt, and looked about the hall for her to make amends. Linnet was nowhere about, so she made her way to where Garrick sat.

As she sat down beside him, her self-consciousness returned twofold. Many eyes stared at her wonderingly, and Garrick's were the most curious.

"You saw your sister?"

"Yea, I saw her."

"She is well, I trust?"

"She is with child!" Brenna snapped irritably, then immediately regretted her harshness.

"But she *is* well?" Garrick persisted.

"She was in good health when I left her," Brenna conceded. She had too much on her mind to wonder about his concern.

Because of her new-found feelings, she looked at Garrick in a different light. She noticed quickly that he was not totally at ease, and wondered if she was the cause. She decided to convey some of her new feelings to him, but sensed she must do it in a subtle way. It would not do for Garrick to become suspicious and misconstrue her motives.

She smiled at him in a flirtatious manner. "Did I tell you how splendid you look this day, Garrick?"

As she had guessed, he looked at her skeptically. "I recall you had the opportunity to do so, but you let it pass."

Her smile brightened. "Then I tell you now: you do indeed look the noble lord. 'Tis a fitting title, but not used in your land, eh?"

He shook his head. "We are a feudal kingdom. Each clan has a chief. He is lord, even King, of his settlement."

"Like your father?"

"Yea," he replied, his eyes questioning. "Why do you ask?"

She answered with another question. "Do you not think it is time I became curious about your people—and you?"

He grinned. "I suppose 'tis reasonable."

"Is your family large?"

Garrick shrugged. "I have uncles, aunts and many cousins."

"I know you have two brothers, but are there no others? No sisters?"

A black cloud seemed to descend on Garrick. "I had a sister," he said in a voice edged with bitterness. "She was my mother's youngest child. She died many years past."

Brenna could feel his anger and pain like a sword piercing her heart, and it surprised her that she could be so touched by his emotions. "I am sorry, Garrick."

"You need not be," he said tightly. "You did not know her."

She touched his hand gently. "Nay, but I know the pain of losing one you love."

He took her hand in his and squeezed it. Then he gazed at her softly as the anger slipped away. "Yea, I suppose you do."

Brenna had an overwhelming desire to lean against him, to feel his arms encircle her warmly. Even as she thought of it, the raw wounds of her father's death seemed to heal somewhat. She no longer felt so alone, so lost.

Though Garrick was now the center of her life, she was not yet ready to bare herself before him. Brenna withdrew her hand from his. They had never before talked this way, and she was pleased with the new beginning. Yet she felt awkward and nervous as a short silence fell between them. She resumed her questioning, but on a new subject.

"Garrick, you never speak of the time you were captured by my people, nor do you appear to hate them for what they did to you. Why is this?"

He looked surprised by her question. "Who told you of that?"

"Your mother spoke of it when I was first brought here, to explain why Anselm attacked us."

She did not need to add that it was Anselm who had gone into greater detail on the matter. "Do you prefer not to speak of it?" she continued, seeing that his mood at least did not darken with the reminder.

"I prefer to forget that time. But since you are profoundly curious this day, I will tell you. When a Viking raids, he is aware that he risks a warrior's death, or capture and slaughter, which are not so valiant. These were the risks I took, and when captured I expected to die without honor."

"This is so important?" Brenna interrupted. "To die a warrior's death?"

" 'Tis the only way to reach Valhalla."

"A Viking's heaven?"

He shrugged. "A good comparison. But only warriors may enter Valhalla."

She remembered her lessons with Wyndham and would not ask Garrick more of what she already knew. "So you expected to die without honor?"

He nodded and continued. " 'Tis the truth that I was cruelly treated, and there are a few I would kill if I found them. But 'tis also the truth that I would not be alive today were it not for one of your people, an old guard who took pity on me and helped me to escape."

"And that is why you do not hate us all?" When he nodded again, she added, "Yet your father does not feel that way. Does he not know 'twas a Celt who aided your escape?"

"He knows. But my father is a man of quick judgment. He decided to blame all of you for what I endured. Once his course was set, he would not deter from it—until he met you. He regrets attacking your vilage and bringing you here. You do know that, Brenna?"

"Yea, I know. Your mother has said as much."

"Do you still hate him?"

Brenna was torn, for she did not really know. "If it had happened to you, Garrick, if a Celt had come here deceitfully and killed most of your clan, taking you prisoner, would you not hate him?"

"With certainty," he admitted, surprising her. "Nor would I rest until he was dead."

"Then do you blame me for how I feel?"

"Nay. I only asked if you still feel that way. A woman is usually more forgiving than a man, nor does she think like a man. But then, you are the exception to that rule, are you not?" he teased.

She smiled, anxious to be done with the subject she had unwillingly led herself into. "Not as much as before."

"Oh? How have you changed, mistress? Did you not insist on carrying a weapon before you would come here? And will you not use that weapon against me when I claim you later?"

"Nay, not against you, Garrick," she answered softly.

He leaned closer and tilted her chin up to search her eyes. "Will you give your word, Brenna?"

"I give it."

He leaned back and laughed. "Then indeed you have changed."

She grinned slyly. "Not as you would think, Garrick. I may not use a weapon, but you still will not claim me easily."

He sobered, then complained good humoredly, " 'Tis not fair, wench, to give me such a brief moment of victory."

Her eyes twinkled with merriment. "Who was it, Viking, who told you women played fairly?"

He grunted and purposely turned his attention away from her to Hugh, who was bragging to a few others that he would win the horse race planned for the next day. Brenna did not care to listen. She felt extremely good. It was the first time she had ever spoken to Garrick without anger coming between them.

That she had fallen in love with this Viking was not so surprising, now that she thought on it. He had everything that she admired in a man: courage, strength, a strong will. He could be gentle at times, she knew. And that he was so undeniably pleasing to look upon did not hinder his cause.

She was certainly aware that he wanted her. In small ways he had shown that he cared. Others had noticed this too, so it must be so. The only difficulty, then, was to tell him that she also cared.

Oh, Garrick, somehow I will make you trust me, Brenna thought, filled with determination. She smiled again and moved aside as servants laid huge platters of roasted boar and beef on the table, along with bread and honey.

She stood and filled a tankard with foaming mead. As she did so, her eyes met those of Anselm, who was at the head of the table. Brenna quickly turned away, missing the warm smile he gave her. She saw Perrin next, and returned his rather reserved greeting. Then her eyes were drawn to the woman beside him, a stunning creature in dark green silk, with a haughty bearing and vivid blue eyes. She would be truly lovely were it not for the cold venom in those eyes. Brenna was held by the silent message that passed between them.

She was shocked at first that she aroused such strong emotions in one she did not know. But then she realized she did know this woman, or knew of her. Morna—it could be no other.

So this was the ambitious woman who had hurt a younger, more vulnerable Garrick, who had made him distrust all women. Indirectly, Morna was responsible for many of Brenna's difficulties. This was a woman without scruples, and with unbelievable audacity.

It was obvious Morna wanted Garrick for herself again. Why else would she look at Brenna with such contempt and loathing? She had gained her wealth and was aware now that Garrick had wealth of his own, so she wanted him. Did Morna truly think the past would not matter?

She gave Morna a tight, calculating smile. The blonde beauty would not have Garrick, not as long as Brenna still lived and breathed.

Chapter 32

THE feast progressed, and with it, the usual outrageous antics. In the Viking manner, tempers flared and brawls ensued continuously. Garrick had a bout with Hugh; fortunately Anselm interceded, and soon the argument was forgotten. Hugh and Fairfax also had words, but again it was Anselm who eased the tension between his sons before a challenge was met.

Still, not all disagreements were interrupted, and many ended in bloodshed. One man, whom Brenna was grateful she did not know, lost his life in what had started as a friendly test of strength. It was deplorable that such things were allowed to happen, and even more so that the winner was cheered for his victory.

Brenna was learning well the importance of strength among these people. It was considered the highest virtue. Without strength, a man was a failure; he brought shame upon his family. Brenna supposed a Viking *would* rather die than lose a test of strength.

Tall tales were bandied about by one and all, and jests and chiding followed. Brenna became subdued as she heard Anselm repeating the tale of her capture. He had embellished it greatly, yet her courage could not be denied.

Brenna watched Morna listen to the tale with obvious disbelief. She would dearly love to get that blonde viper alone and teach her a thing or two.

Her wish was nearly granted a while later, when the hour grew late and most were sodden with drink. Morna persuaded her brother to escort her home, and waited at the door while he went for her cloak. Brenna quickly intercepted Perrin when he was alone.

"You have not enjoyed the feast, Perrin?"

He looked utterly embarrassed. "Nay. I know my sister was not welcome here, yet she insisted I bring her."

"Tell me, Perrin, is it true she has designs on Garrick again?"

"Yea, she has said as much," he admitted. "Does this displease you?"

"Only if Garrick would be fool enough to jump into a fire that has already burned him."

"Let us hope he never becomes such a fool."

Brenna grinned. "You do not favor an alliance between them?"

"Morna is my sister, an unfortunate truth I cannot undo. What she did to Garrick, my closest friend, I have never forgiven."

Brenna looked thoughtful. "You have not bid your host farewell. Do so, Perrin. I will take your sister's cloak to her."

He held back, alarm crossing his face. "Nay, wench. My sister begrudges you Garrick's attention. She would be more than pleased to remind you of your status."

"Do you fear for me?"

He shook his head and grinned. "I know you. 'Tis my sister who would be in danger."

Brenna laughed. "Then may I walk you to the door? With you there, surely no problems will arise."

He appeared reluctant, but finally Brenna's winsome smile won him over and he agreed. They met an impatient Morna at the door. By now she was thoroughly vexed, and turned on her brother heatedly.

"I cannot believe that you would keep me waiting here while you talk with this slave!" Morna hissed through clenched teeth, her face livid with anger. "How could you embarrass me this way, Perrin?"

"You did not wait long, Morna," he answered tiredly.

"If you had spoken with anyone else I would not have minded," Morna continued indignantly. "But that you should keep me waiting—because of *her!* Do you not consort enough with her when you visit Garrick?"

Perrin reddened. "That is not the way of it, Morna. Garrick will not share this girl with anyone. He keeps her only for himself." He said this truth with relish.

His words angered the blonde widow even more, and Brenna was hard pressed to contain her mirth.

Morna looked at Brenna with cold contempt. "Put my wrap on me, slave!" When Brenna stared blankly at her, she turned back to Perrin. "You speak her tongue. Tell her what I demand."

Perrin's eyes narrowed. "You go too far, sister. Brenna is not yours to order about."

Morna glared at him, her blue eyes smoldering. "She is a slave; now tell her!"

"What is your sister shouting about?" Brenna asked innocently.

Perrin sighed. "Odin help me. She demands you put her cloak on. She merely wishes to take her anger out on you, Brenna."

Brenna smiled. "There is no problem, Perrin. Simply tell her I refuse. Then hand her the cloak and leave. 'Tis an easy enough solution."

Perrin shook his head in doubt, but handed the cloak to his sister. "Brenna will not do your bidding, Morna. Now come along," he said and left the hall.

Morna was beside herself with rage, and turned fiery blue eyes on Brenna. "I will have you whipped for this!"

"I think not," Brenna replied, shocking Morna with words she could understand. "For one thing, Garrick would not allow it. But more important, and I pray you heed me well, Morna, I would cut your throat gladly before you call for a whip. You were an unwelcome guest at this feast. There is no one here who would seek out your killer."

"You would not dare to touch me!"

Brenna smiled wickedly. "Test the truth of my words. Call for a whipping."

Morna hesitated a moment too long. "You will rue the

251

day you dared to threaten me when I become Garrick's wife!"

" 'Tis a day you will never see."

"Do not be too sure, slave!" Morna snapped and stalked from the hall.

Brenna bit her lip. She should never have revealed her secret to Morna . . . But what if Morna's prediction came true? To Garrick's way of thinking, he could have them both, Morna as his wife to give him legitimate heirs, and Brenna as his concubine. Brenna actually shivered at the thought. Nay, it would not happen, she resolved. If she could not hope to become his wife herself, then she had no hope at all. Yet she had every reason to believe he cared for her.

She turned and found Garrick's back was to her. She prayed he had not seen her talking to Morna, for then he would question her, and she would not lie to him. This might bring on his anger, which was the last thing she wanted.

She joined Garrick at the table and waited nervously for him to notice her. When he finally turned her way, she held her breath in anticipation of his questions.

"I missed you," he said pointedly, leaning closer. "What were you about?"

"I bid Perrin farewell," she said after a moment's pause. When he grunted in response, she quickly changed the subject. "Will we leave soon?"

"Are you tired?"

She nodded. "It has been a long day, and I have had much too much to drink."

He grinned devilishly. "I remember fondly another time you had too much to drink. You were most agreeable then. Are you now?"

She lowered her eyes. "Nay, Garrick."

He ignored her answer and stood up. "Come. I have found us a place to pass the night."

Brenna remained seated. "Are we not to go home? 'Tis only a short distance."

" 'Twould only waste time, Brenna. The horse race begins early on the morrow, and I will be here on time for it." When she frowned, he added, "Mayhaps I will take you home on the morrow's eve, then we will return on the day following."

"Return?"

"Yea, this feast will continue for nearly a fortnight. Now come."

Brenna sighed, took the hand he offered and followed him to get their cloaks. There was still much activity in the hall. Only a few had taken to benches to sleep off their soddenness. Heloise had retired to bed earlier, as had Linnet, but not before Brenna was able to apologize to her aunt for her unreasonable sharpness. Anselm and Hugh were still full of vigor and were involved in a serious drinking bout, with many wagering on the outcome.

Garrick bellowed his farewells, but no one paid much attention, and he quickly slipped out the door with Brenna under his arm. The icy fingers of the wind went unnoticed as Brenna snuggled in the warmth of Garrick's closeness. She felt as if she were floating, gliding smoothly over the cold ground. As her head began to swim dizzily, she rested it on his chest and felt total contentment.

When he led her into the stable and to an empty stall where many blankets were piled on top of a bed of straw, Brenna drew away from him with slight annoyance. She watched him close them in with a large wood panel, making the stall a tiny private room.

"This is the place you spoke of?"

" 'Tis the warmest I could find," he said without looking at her, and shrugged off his cloak.

"And you expect me to sleep here?"

He ignored her indignation and grinned at her. "You will not be alone."

"But—"

"Be quiet, wench," he interrupted softly and came to stand before her. "This is indeed better than a hard bench in the hall. Will you not agree?"

She looked down at the improvised bed and grudgingly nodded. "I suppose."

His warm fingers grazed her cheek. "And we will not be disturbed here."

Brenna felt something akin to pain take root in her chest. She wanted to throw herself into his arms, yet she would not gain her ultimate goal that way. She would indeed find pleasure, but for how long? He would not make her his wife if she became his devoted slave.

Reluctantly she stepped away from him and sought a topic that would delay what she knew would soon come. "The race that is planned for the morrow—can anyone enter?"

"Yea."

"Can I?"

Garrick started to laugh, but thought better of it. "Nay. Any man may enter, but no woman."

"And I imagine no slaves either?" she asked, rather piqued.

Would this woman ever let pass a day without showing her temper? he wondered. " 'Tis true."

"But I could conceal my appearance, Garrick. At home I was oft mistaken for a boy by those who knew me not. And 'twould give me great pleasure to best your brother."

"How did you know my brother will race?" he asked her pointedly.

Brenna blanched and quickly turned away. How could she admit she overheard them talking of the race without admitting she understood their tongue quite well? "Will he not?"

Fortunately, Garrick let her question suffice for an answer. "He will, but then, so will I. Do you wish to best me also, mistress?"

Brenna glanced at him sideways. "I suppose it would not do to beat you where all could see." Then she added with an impish grin, "As long as you know that I could do it, that is enough."

Garrick burst into laughter. "I will accept that challenge one day soon, wench. But for now, I have a much more interesting sport in mind."

He reached for her, but Brenna ducked beneath his arm and moved to the entrance of the stall, ready to push aside the panel and flee. She faced him and put up a hand to try and halt his pursuit.

"You know I will not lay down with you willingly, Garrick. I will sleep outside if I must."

Garrick moved one step closer, but that was all. "I have enjoyed your presence beside me this day, Brenna," he said in a level tone. "I had hoped for even greater pleasure this night. But I will not chase you for it." He lay down on the straw and motioned for her to join him. "Come. You had best sleep while you can. The morrow will be a long day."

Brenna had not expected Garrick to give up, certainly not so easily. She let down her guard and almost sighed in regret. She doubted she would get much sleep being so near him, but she was determined at least to try. However, Garrick was on top of her before she was even fully prone, his weight pinning her securely beneath him.

She glared up at his look of triumph, her eyes darkening quickly. "You tricked me!"

"Nay, wench," he chuckled. "I only said I would not chase you, and I have not."

His lips came down on hers to silence any further arguments. She tried to turn her head aside, but he cupped her face between his large hands as his tongue plundered her mouth. The very pressure of his body, his strength, his desire—these were intoxicants that helped melt away her objections. And then even these were quickly forgotten as he moved to her side and slipped one hand into her bodice.

Her belt was opened and her long skirt raised, and before she even had time to think of the folly of it, they both lay devoid of clothing. His hands moved gently over her body, caressing, molding with skillful fingers that set fires where they touched and brought moans to her lips. She did not care. Her love for him was all that mattered, her desire, her intense need to feel his hard, throbbing shaft inside her.

And when at last he drove deep into her, Brenna cried out with the ecstasy of it. It was as natural as if they were made only for one another. She drained him of his strength, and her will was his. Even the after-glow was beautiful as they lay pressed together in exhaustion, breathing heavily, contentment flowing through them.

Several minutes passed, but Garrick did not move from her. Brenna finally opened her eyes to find him staring down at her, a soft yet strange expression on his face. She wondered about that expression only briefly before the words she had cried out in passion came back to her.

Her first reaction was panic, and she pushed at Garrick. She wanted to flee, to hide. She had not planned to declare her feelings this way, and certainly not this soon. She was not sure of him yet.

Her hands could not budge him, and at last he bound them at her sides to still her. "Did you speak the truth? Do you love me, Brenna?"

She closed her eyes against his penetrating stare. She could lie, but that would not gain her his trust. And she needed that above all else if they were ever to be truly happy.

"Yea, I love you." She whispered the same words she had cried earlier.

There, it was done, and now she felt good about it. She opened her eyes and found he was smiling tenderly at her. She took heart from this.

"Are you sure, Brenna?"

"I know what I feel, Garrick. I am most sure."

"Then you will give me your word that you will never run away from me again?"

His question surprised her somewhat, but she answered readily, "You have my word."

"Good. This has been a remarkable day that I will not soon forget."

He rolled to her side, and Brenna lay with her eyes open wide in disbelief. When no further words from him were forthcoming, she propped herself up on an elbow and faced him.

"Is that all you have to say to me, Garrick?"

"I am pleased that you have softened to me, Brenna," he replied, then turned his back to her. " 'Tis late and I am tired. Go to sleep."

His words were like a physical blow. He said naught of returning her love, only that he was pleased that *she* had softened to him. She stared blankly at his hard back. "Methinks I have given you more pleasure than you deserve this night."

"Eh?"

Garrick's back remained to her and suddenly Brenna saw red, blind red fury. She shoved him forcefully, gaining his attention again.

"I would know your intentions, Garrick. Will you wed me?"

He frowned at her. "A Viking cannot wed a slave. You know that."

"Your father would free me! You can free me!"

"Nay, wench, 'twould serve no purpose. I will not wed you. If I set you free, I would lose you." Then he tried to calm her. "As my slave I will keep you always, Brenna. You will be like my wife."

"Until I am old!" she snapped. "Then you will put me out to pasture as you would a mare!"

" 'Twould not be that way."

"Words, Viking!" she cried, pain making her unreasonable. "If you know me at all, you know that I have more pride than most. I can never come to you freely without sacred vows between us. You are the only man I will wed. If you refuse, I will never be content."

"You will in time."

"In time my love will die through bitterness. Do you not see that?"

"You ask too much, woman!" he said curtly. "I have sworn never to wed!"

"Or to love?"

"There is no love in me. It was destroyed long ago." He took her hand and held it tightly. "But 'tis you I come to, Brenna," he said, his voice soft again. " 'Tis you I care about above all others. I can give you no more than that."

"But you can change."

He shook his head slowly. "I am sorry, Brenna."

"So am I," she murmured and added to herself, "for you give me no hope, Garrick."

Pain and regret brought tears to her eyes and she turned away from him to hide her misery and spill her tears silently.

Chapter 33

THE stars of early morning were sprinkled across the black sky. A lone woman hurried furtively down the fjord where two small canoes were tied to a wooden landing. The fjord was calm, cast in murky shadows, and the woman shivered and pulled her cloak tighter about her.

She quickly untied one of the small fishing crafts and jumped inside. In a second it floated slowly away from the landing. She grasped the oars and they sliced through the water. Time to change her mind was swiftly fleeing.

The plan that had come to her the night before was daring enough, but dangerous. Her destination was the opposite bank of the fjord and the Borgsen settlement. Because she lived on the north side of the fjord, they would consider her their enemy. She hoped that a fat purse would make them forget that. She knew no one here who would do what she wanted—but a Borgsen would. At least that was what she was counting on.

The current hurried her along and she reached the opposite bank. Only once before had she ever set foot on this side of the fjord. That was long ago, when the two great clans were joined in friendship. She had come to a marriage feast held at Latham Borgsen's house, when his daughter was wed to a distant cousin. It was a grand celebration lasting nearly a month, and all were invited for miles around. She wondered now if she could remember the way to Latham's house. So many years had passed.

She started to walk inland. Her cloak was wrapped tightly against the cold. A bulky fur hood concealed her features, as she had intended. She did not want her identity known on the off chance her hastily concocted scheme failed. It was such a simple plan, she thought. How could it fail?

According to the woman's calculations, there was less than half a league left to walk before reaching the Borgsen settlement. She did not have to journey the full distance. In a dense crop of trees she was set upon by two riders who galloped to her in haste. Their mighty mounts pinned her against a tree trunk in her fright.

They laughed at her cowardice. From this and her short stature they knew her to be a woman, though they assumed they were making sport with one of their own.

One of the stout men dismounted. The younger of the two, he was wrapped in fur pelts; these made him look twice his normal size, which was immense to begin with.

"A wench out this early, and alone, must be meeting her lover. You need look no further, for you have found two instead of just one to satisfy you."

The other Viking still sat on his steed. He was not much older than the first, but just as large and menacing. His expression showed he was impatient with the other man's remarks.

"Ease off, Cedric," he said, though it was hardly a command. Then he turned to the woman. "Your name, mistress?"

"Adosinda," she lied.

"I know of no one with that name," Cedric remarked. "Do you, Arno?"

"Nay. From where do you come, Mistress Adosinda?"

She hesitated, her heart beating wildly. "From—from across the fjord."

Both men became deadly serious. "You are of the Haardrad clan?"

"Only distantly, very distantly."

"If you come from across the fjord, then you must know you are not welcome on this side!" Arno exclaimed.

"This is a plot, Arno," the younger Viking speculated. "I told you the Haardrads had been quiet for too long.

They have sent a woman to sneak into our homes and kill us while we sleep! Who would suspect a woman?"

" 'Tis not true, I swear!" she cried. "No one knows I have come here!"

"Do not lie, mistress. I am Cedric Borgsen, third son of Latham. 'Twas my oldest brother Edgar that Hugh Haardrad killed. If I sense deceit, you will die instantly!"

"I mean you no harm!" she insisted, fear gripping her. "I came without weapon."

"Why then do you trespass where you are not wanted?"

"I seek your help."

"You seek to trick us!" Cedric accused.

"Nay—nay! I know of no man who would help me, for 'tis my intention to slight a Haardrad, and what vassal or kin would do this? Nay, only a Borgsen would carry out my plan."

"Your words ring false. What Haardrad would seek to harm another?" Arno demanded.

"A woman—one with much to gain by it."

"Hear her out, Arno. I am most curious now."

"What I want done is very simple, and I will pay you well for it. There is a slave girl captured only recently— a Celtic beauty with raven hair and eyes the color of smoke. She stands in my way, and I want her gone."

"Killed?"

"I do not care what you do with her once you have her," the woman continued. "You can keep her for yourself as long as she does not escape—and she *will* try. You could also sell her far away from here and gain another fat purse. Or, yea, even kill her; I care not."

"How does stealing a slave girl slight a Haardrad?" Arno demanded.

" 'Twas Anselm Haardrad who brought her here and he gave her to his second son, Garrick. In a short time, Garrick has been bewitched by her. He treasures this girl and will be devastated when she runs away."

"Runs away?"

The woman laughed, an evil cackle. "It must appear that way. You see, Garrick will search for her far and wide, but he will give up eventually. However, if he thought she did not leave freely, that she was taken away by force, he would never rest until he found her."

"It sounds to me like a trap," Arno said. "We cross the fjord and find Haardrads waiting there for us."

"If you know anything of the Haardrads, you know they do not deal in trickery. They fight fairly, Borgsen."

"'Tis the truth," Cedric admitted reluctantly. "Hugh came and challenged my brother. 'Twas a fair fight."

"Mayhaps this is so," Arno replied skeptically. "But your father should be informed of this plan—he knows the enemy well. 'Twould be foolish to agree to this woman's scheme without Latham's advice."

Young Cedric was affronted. "Do you imply, Arno, that I cannot decide on this matter myself?"

"Nay, only that I think it wise that your father be enlightened. After all, there has been no bloodshed in this feud for years, naught but the slaughter of worthless cattle and scrawny dogs. This woman's scheme could well bring about vengeance of a different nature."

"It could also make us richer, with no one the wiser," Cedric responded greedily.

"And the slave?" Arno persisted. "How will you explain her presence here?"

"My friend, you search for a storm when it has yet to brew. We will keep the slave at your farm until we decide what to do with her. 'Tis that simple."

The woman stepped closer, glad to see that the greed of these men was overcoming their suspicions. "You need have no fear that bloodshed or vengeance will come of this," she assured them. "It must be made to appear that the slave has run away. Therefore, you and your clan will not be suspect. And you will have this to gain," showing them the sack of gold. "You will also have the knowledge that you harmed a Haardrad without him knowing of it. If you give me your word that you will do as I ask, you will have the payment now and see no more of me. Do you agree?"

The man on the ground did not consult his friend again, but answered readily. "First you will tell us how you think this plan of yours can be accomplished, then you will have our word."

The woman smiled, confident that she would soon have what she wanted.

Chapter 34

BRENNA woke to boisterous cheers and the sound of horses galloping away from the settlement. Her first observation was that she was alone. Then the sounds that had awakened her made sense in her turbid thoughts. The horse race had already begun.

She quickly donned her velvet gown, careful to shake the straw from it first, grabbed her cloak and left the stable. The crisp morning air helped to bring her fully awake, and she wondered now how she had slept through all the excitement as men readied their horses for the race.

The memory of the night before was like a cancerous sore festering inside her, and the thought of staying for more festivities was abhorrent.

In the crowd that had gathered for the start of the race, Brenna spied her aunt and sauntered slowly to her side. Linnet looked refreshed after a good night's sleep, and met Brenna with a warm smile.

"I thought you would be here to wish your Viking luck," Linnet said cheerfully. "He did look for you."

"If he had wanted any good wishes, then he should have woken me," Brenna replied in a listless tone.

"What is amiss, Brenna?" Linnet asked. "You do not look well at all."

"I am merely tired. I did not sleep well in the stable."

Linnet's concern was visible in the tightness of her expression. "My quarters are empty. You may sleep there for a while if you like. The men will not return until midday."

"Nay, Aunt. I will make my way home. I have no wish to see Garrick this day."

"But the feast . . ."

"Will continue without me. I will not celebrate when I have naught to be thankful for."

"What has happened, Brenna? You were so happy when last we spoke."

"I have been a fool."

"Because of Garrick? Does he not care for you as I—as we thought?"

"He cares, Aunt, but not enough," Brenna replied and started to walk back to the stable. "Not nearly enough."

"Brenna, wait!" Linnet called after her. "He will ask for you. What will I tell him?"

Brenna turned and shrugged. "The truth. I have gone home and will not return. I will see him when he has had enough of revelry."

It was a short distance from Anselm's settlement to Garrick's house on the cliff, but to Brenna it seemed an endless journey. She rode aimlessly for a while, brooding over Garrick's aloof attitude.

It took several moments after she had reached the stable, before she realized that Erin was nowhere to be seen. That was a stroke of luck. Now she would not have to explain why she was alone. The house was also empty, and as cold as the outside, if not more so. Brenna did not bother to light the fires in the lower half of the house, but went straight to her room. There she sat on her bed, staring dismally at a crack in the floor.

At last anger came to the surface and slowly took hold, searching for an outlet. Brenna was beside herself with this new anger born of hurt. Since Garrick was not there for her to vent it on, she chose the next best thing—his gifts. She yanked off the two gold arm rings and threw them at the wall, but they merely fell and rattled on the floor, coming to rest undamaged. Disappointed, she started a fire, then tossed the rings into it, but the process of melting the gold was too slow and not at all satisfying. Next Brenna tore off her beautiful gown, ripping it again and again till it lay in shreds on the floor.

The sight of what her destructive actions had wrought, brought tears that stung her eyes. " 'Twas too rich for a slave, so a slave should not have it!" she cried aloud. Then remorse overcame her as she thought of the kind woman who had made the gown for her. "Heloise will not be pleased." More tears fell. "Look what you have made me do, Garrick! 'Tis your fault and no other's," she said childishly, then threw herself on the bed. "Damn you, Viking! I do not like this hurt I feel!"

Sleep came unexpectedly and lasted most of the afternoon. It was late when a sound outside Brenna's door woke her. She immediately scrambled beneath her covers, hating to be found in this predicament. A second later, before she could completely hide her nakedness, her door was thrown open and Garrick bounded into the room.

His face was a mask of fury. "I did not give you leave to return here, mistress!"

"I am aware of that."

"Yet you did as you pleased!" he shouted before his eyes fell on the ruined gown. Then he turned on her with new rage, and yanked her from the bed. "I came here to drag you back with me if necessary, but I see you have made that impossible!"

Hot color burned her cheeks as he held her cruelly before him. " 'Twould not do to have a guest in your father's house wearing coarse wool, now would it, Viking?" she taunted him with sarcasm to hide her own humiliation.

"Nay, it would not," he answered coldly. "And since you prefer your slave's garments, 'twill be all you will have, wench, for you will receive no more gifts from me!"

"I did not ask for any!"

He made as if to strike her, but instead shoved her away from him, and she fell back against the bed. "You will stay in this house, since 'tis where you prefer to be. I will find another to entertain me at the feast."

His words struck her harder than his hand would have.

"Do you think I care?" she shouted, though her voice cracked with the lie.

"It matters little if you care or not," he replied, wounding her further. "And henceforth you will abide by my rules, wench, for I am through being lenient with you."

"What will you do, Viking?" she demanded recklessly. "Will you take my life as carelessly as you took my love?"

He stared hard at her for a long moment, his eyes moving over her soft curves, stopping at her heaving breasts, then resting on her face, seeing her proud beauty, her defiance, her spirit. She was like a wild, untamable creature, yet vulnerable.

"Nay, I will not take your life, Brenna," he said, deeply, thoroughly impassioned by the sight of her splendor. "I will take your love again—now."

Before she could cry nay, he fell on her, his only effort that of lowering his breeches to unsheath his manhood, which throbbed to be inside her. Brenna was shocked and repelled by this onslaught. She was too enraged to be stirred by the rape, and fought him wildly, clawing his bare arms till blood dripped on her bed. But he did not stop or try to stay her hands, pressing on until his gift of life poured into her and he collapsed.

When he left the small bed and fastened his breeches, Brenna trembled in outrage at the way he had callously taken her with no thought for her, only his own animal needs. She would never forgive him for that.

"Remember my warning, Brenna," he said as he crossed to the door. "Do not leave this house."

Even now he was asserting his power over her, reminding her that she belonged to him, that she could only do what he allowed her to. He scorned her love, yet he controlled her life.

"Did you hear me, mistress?"

She glared at him with malice, her eyes dark cinders. "The devil take you, Viking! May you never find your Valhalla, but rot in hell with Loki's daughter!"

Garrick seemed to pale. "Those are harsh words, Brenna, even spoken in anger. Another would slay you for such a curse."

"Do so! Kill me!" she screamed. "I don't care anymore!"

Garrick did not answer, but quickly left the room before he took his anger out on her again. He went directly to the stable, and for the second time did not notice that Erin was not about. He mounted the poor beast who had run his best that morn, though Garrick still lost to Hugh. Losing had soured his mood considerably, but finding Brenna gone was the last blow.

Garrick bolted from the stable, his temper boiling. "Damn fickle woman!" he growled at the wind. "First she cried her hatred so stubbornly, then she turned about and said she loved me—now she hates me again. I gave her all I had to give, but nay, 'tis not enough for her! Loki take her! I do not need this vexation."

Garrick spurred his horse on without pity. He would drown in mead this night and forget the stubborn vixen at his house.

Chapter 35

BRENNA started the cooking fire, then prepared a loaf of flat bread as she had seen Janie do so often. She was in a much better frame of mind now. After Garrick had left, she had cried some more, but then she realized how foolish she had been. Garrick was willing to share his life with her, to give her what he could. She must accept that and be grateful for it. One day he might change and love again. After all, she had changed.

The house was quiet, with only the occasional crackling of the fire to break the stillness. Dog was sprawled out beneath the table, so Brenna did not see his head when it suddenly perked up. However, she did hear the noise outside that had aroused the white shepherd.

Could Garrick have returned already? If so, then he must have missed her company. Brenna smiled at that thought and waited for the door to open. It did, although very slowly. Cold air rushed into the room and chilled Brenna, but not as much as the realization that Garrick would not enter his house in such a stealthy manner, nor would anyone that she knew.

A man stepped carefully around the half-opened door—

a tall man, nearly Garrick's height, with golden brown hair and light blue eyes. He was warmly wrapped in fur pelts of different colors, and a single-edged sword was clasped in his hand.

Brenna held her breath. She did not know this Viking, and from his look of surprise when he spied her, he did not know her either.

Dog came to her side, his low growl bringing back some of her courage. The dagger Garrick entrusted her with rested on her hip, and this also lessened her apprehension, though her weapon was little good against a broadsword.

"Brenna?"

She was bewildered. Did he know her after all? But no, his tone was questioning. He must only know of her, and so must also know Garrick. Perhaps there was nothing to fear, then.

"Who are you?" she asked, but his expression showed plainly that he did not understand her.

Brenna bit her lip in indecision, wondering if she should speak his tongue or not. Dog continued to growl threateningly. Did he sense danger?

"The wench is alone, Cedric."

Brenna caught her breath and whirled around to face the stranger who had come in from another part of the house. Before she could even appraise the situation, the young man called Cedric grabbed her from behind. She cried out in startled alarm, and at that moment Dog bared his teeth and attacked the Viking's leg.

Cedric yelled in pain as Dog drew blood, and he raised his sword to sever the animal's head.

"Nay!" Brenna screamed, and grabbed the Viking's arm to stay him. She forgot her own fear and mustered all her strength to keep the sword from reaching its target. Yet it was not through her efforts that Dog was spared, for she was like a mouse against a deadly hawk. The other Viking acted quickly and kicked Dog away from the descending sword.

"*She* would not kill the dog," he said warningly, "so neither can we."

"Ah! 'Tis a fool's errand, this trickery!" Cedric spat and released Brenna in order to tend to his leg. "We have the girl, Arno. That is enough."

"We will do this as the woman wanted it done," Arno replied. " 'Tis the only reason I agreed, because we will never be suspected."

Cedric grunted and remarked with sarcasm, "The purse of gold swayed you not a little, eh?"

Arno ignored that question and stared angrily at his friend. "Is revenge against a dog worth your father's wrath?"

"How so?"

Arno threw up his hands in exasperation, a coiled rope he held sliding up to his shoulder as he did so. "Must I remind you that your father loathes the feud you and your brothers started. 'Tis my thinking, and you know it too, that Latham would frown on this deed. If we are found out, 'twill bring the peace of these last years to a bloody end."

Brenna stood silently between these two men as they argued. She did not understand exactly why they had come here, but she knew it boded her no good. Though he would live, Dog was hurt, and could not come to her aid again—and Garrick was enjoying himself at the feast.

She felt a twinge of resentment that Garrick had left her here alone to fend for herself. Then she chided herself. It was not his fault, but hers, that she was here facing God knows what.

Before Arno finished his last words, Brenna slipped slowly from between them. In frantic haste, for this was her only chance as far as she could see, she turned and started to run. Suddenly her feet became tangled in something and she fell forward, scraping the palms of her hands against the hard floor.

With dread, she realized her error as she was roughly yanked to her feet. She glared at this Viking who had cunningly thrown his rope at her feet to stop her. Her eyes were as dark and wild as a tempest as she watched him gather the short rope and wrap it about her wrists.

He did not look at her once to see the fury and contempt she felt, but turned to Cedric once he finished binding her hands together.

"We have the horse and now the girl. Let us be gone before this plan goes awry."

He did not wait for an answer from the younger man,

but quickly grabbed an old cloak by the door and threw it over Brenna's shoulders, then left the house, pulling her behind him with the rope. She felt degraded and helpless, like a poor trussed-up animal. How dare they treat her like this?

Brenna was led along the side of the house, past the cell where she had spent one wretched night, to the front of the house. She was more confused than ever, and frustration and anger further prevented her from thinking clearly. They started down the steep cliff path to the landing below. There Brenna saw Garrick's ship, awesomely proud, floating on the smooth waters of the fjord like a sleeping dragon. Beside it and just as impressive was another huge Viking ship.

She was deposited on this second ship, and in no time at all it moved slowly away from the landing, away from possible rescue, away from Garrick. Brenna fought the panic that rose to overwhelm her. Where were they taking her? And more important, for what reason?

She watched the Vikings closely. The current carried the ship along with it, yet the two men still struggled with the oars. If they had come from the direction they were headed now, she wondered how they had possibly managed to fight against the current. Why bring such a large ship to steal a single slave when a small boat would have sufficed?

Brenna saw the reason for it when she surveyed the empty ship and found it was not so empty. In the shadows behind her she made out the shape of a horse. Since she was not tied to anything to restrict her movements, she moved closer and finally recognized Willow.

This was even more confusing. Garrick had many fine animals. If these Vikings were pirates, thieves in their own land, why did they take only one horse and one slave?

Brenna reached every imaginable conclusion about her predicament, and all were disheartening. She waited eagerly for the Vikings to speak, to give her more information, but they were silent, bent on their task. At least she was not being taken out to sea. They had gone inland and now reached a landing on the opposite side of the fjord.

As she and Willow were taken off the ship, she looked dismally out at the deep water of the fjord. Even if she managed to escape from these men, how could she possibly return to Garrick? She could never man this ship alone, nor could she attempt to swim back to safety, for she did not know how to swim.

Two horses were tethered near the landing. Brenna was lifted up onto Willow's bare back and after the men climbed on their own mounts, they started to ride in the direction they had come from, back toward the sea. After going only a short way they turned south, away from the fjord, further away from Garrick.

Garrick. What would he do when he found her gone? With Willow gone also, would he think she had run away again? The thought might come to him, but he would reject it. She had given her word not to escape him, so he must conclude that she did not leave of her own accord. He would search for her, but would he think to cross the fjord?

The night seemed cloaked in a shroud. Not one star blinked down from the heavens. It was not a night to find one's way in the dark, but the two men beside Brenna knew exactly where they were.

Less than an hour passed before the horses stopped. Brenna could just barely make out the silhouette of a house on flat land. She strained her eyes to see more, but there was no time, for she was pulled down from her horse and quickly taken inside the dwelling.

The house was dark, and the acrid smell of trapped smoke hung heavy in the air. The men started a fire and Brenna looked about the sparsely furnished room. There was only a single stuffed pallet on the floor, a small table with two benches, and a few cooking implements by the fire.

Many fur rugs covered the dirt floor and the walls, adding some luxury to the room. On closer inspection, she noticed too small personal items, though they did not number many. A brass tankard sat on the table, and four beautifully painted plates of glass were set on wall racks. Two fine axes with amber handles were crossed above the door. In one corner was a shelf full of clay pottery, thin cups, vases and bowls, all etched with heathen designs.

Brenna finally returned her attention to the two men. Arno was removing the many fur pelts wrapped around him, while Cedric was staring with apt interest at Brenna. She felt her blood turn cold.

"Mayhaps I will delay my leaving." Cedric said, his eyes still affixed on Brenna.

Arno looked up and frowned. "Your pleasure can wait. We discussed this at length while waiting to be sure she was alone."

"I know," Cedric said, then remarked, "the woman Adosinda said this slave was a beauty, but she is much more than I anticipated."

"Cedric."

"Very well!" he replied in annoyance. "I will return to my father's feast. But I will be back come morning. And she is mine first, Arno. Remember that!"

Arno shook his head. "I want no part of her. I have bad feelings about what we have done."

Cedric laughed. "I do not believe my ears."

"Say what you like. She belonged to another man, she did not want to leave his house, and I fear he will not rest until he has her back."

"What are you saying?"

"There will be blood shed yet because of this deed. I feel it—I know it to be so."

"If you know so well what the morrow will bring, then tell me how he will ever find her?" Cedric asked with sarcasm. "Ah, 'tis a coward I have for a friend."

"*Because* we are friends, I will not take exception to your loose tongue."

Cedric did not show even a little remorse as he stalked to the door. He took one last look at Brenna, and she cringed at the meaning she read in his cold eyes.

"Take good care of her for me, Arno," he said, then left the house.

Brenna was shaken. She looked at Arno hopefully, but he quickly ignored her. He would offer her no help. He would leave quietly while his friend ravished her. She could not let it happen; she would not!

Some of her old spirit returned. She had fought Garrick, and with some degree of success. She would overcome this Cedric also. He would expect her to be his victim, not his opponent. She would have that element of surprise on her side.

She also had her dagger. For some reason, they had not taken it from her. Either they did not imagine she would use it on them, or they thought the hilt of the weapon that glittered on her hip was merely an ornament. Whatever the reason, she was grateful.

Arno moved about the room preparing food. After he set a large pot of soup to boil over the fire, he gathered blankets for Brenna's bed. These he placed on a rug by the fire and motioning with his hand, indicated she would sleep there. Then he went outside to see to the horses.

Brenna walked slowly to her temporary bed. She felt sick to her stomach with apprehension. On the morrow she would either kill a man or suffer the consequences for trying. She did not look forward to the outcome, whatever it was to be.

The aroma of the soup was tempting. She had not eaten all day. But she was afraid to do so now for fear she could not keep the food down.

Brenna lay down on the fur rug. The rope about her wrists was annoying. She considered cutting it, but quickly decided against taking the chance. It would not do to lose her dagger just for her own comfort. Instead she unsheathed the weapon and placed it under the rug within easy reach. Before Arno returned, she was asleep.

Chapter 36

A S it turned out, the Viking called Cedric did not re-
turn the next day, or the day following that. In fact,
Brenna was left alone with Arno for more than a week.
Her endurance was tested to the limit those first few days.
Every little noise she heard was Cedric returning, even
the moaning of the wind.

To help her through those first days, she did not even
have the hope that Garrick would find her, for it snowed
the first night and for three days more. Now Garrick would
not know that she had left no tracks to follow. He would
never guess that she had been taken away by ship. He
would curse the snow for covering her trail, but it would
do her no good, for he would search north of the fjord
and never come close to her.

Damn the snow! Damn Cedric and Arno! Damn the
woman they spoke of who told them of her! Who was that
woman? Did Cordella make good her threat? But Cordella
could not speak to these men, nor would she know how
to find them. The ugly scene with Morna came to mind.
She was the only one who would attempt such foul play.
But then there were those who felt they had scores to
settle; Bayard, Gorm, even Hugh—and especially the Vik-

ing she had shamed in battle by wounding him. Any one of those men could have sent a woman to do their foul work in contacting Cedric and Arno.

The second day Arno took pity on her and removed the rope from her wrists. That night, after Brenna was sure he slept, she attempted to sneak away quietly. But he had cunningly left a trap for her just outside the door, a cart full of wood that she stumbled over in the dark. Before she could even get up, he was there, dragging her back into the house. She cursed him in her own tongue, and fought him with all her strength. In the end he subdued her, and after that he kept her tied at night, this time to the iron bar over the round fireplace in the center of the room, so that she could not reach her dagger if she needed it. At least he let her go during the day.

After a week passed, Arno also became impatient. He fretted and grumbled to himself, and this caused Brenna to relax somewhat. Perhaps something had happened to Cedric and he would not return at all. Arno had already shown that he did not want to bring Brenna here, any more than she wanted to be here. Mayhaps he would let her go.

After nine days passed, with still no sign of Cedric, Brenna finally broke down and spoke to Arno. She had nothing to lose now, for since there was no one there for him to speak to, she had no chance of overhearing something useful.

He was preparing bread for their morning meal and quite edgy when Brenna approached him.

"Your friend seems to have forgotten we are here," she began, gaining his startled attention. "How long will you keep me here?"

"You speak my language well."

"As well as you," she replied.

"I was told you were here but a short while. You must have had a good teacher to have grasped a new tongue so quickly. Was it your master?"

"He taught me many things," she remarked evenly and came closer. "One of which is you cannot keep what you take from another in this land, not without paying dearly for it."

Her warning struck home and Arno jumped up from

the table nervously, as if Garrick was already there to collect her. "Young Haardrad will never know you were brought here!"

"He will in time," Brenna reasoned hopefully. "He knows the land well and will search every inch of it. And when he does not find me there, he will at last look this way."

"Nay, he will give up before then."

"You think so, Viking? What you did not take into account is that I love Garrick Haardrad, and he loves me." She said the half-truth with conviction. " 'Tis love that binds us, and love that will conquer all obstacles."

Arno sat down and stared hard at her, making her uneasy. "Mayhaps, wench. But 'tis out of my hands. I am only keeping you here for another."

"You helped to bring me here!" she accused him with a pointed finger. "You stop me from leaving. You are just as responsible as your friend."

"Cease your prattling, woman!" he stormed. "I liked you better before you found your tongue."

"You know I speak the truth. Garrick will not forgive this slight unless you release me now."

" 'Tis not my decision to make. Save your arguments for Cedric. You are his now."

"I will die before I am his!" Brenna spat, thoroughly repulsed, then she lowered her voice. "Cedric is not here now. You can let me go before he returns."

"He is my friend, wench, the only one I have," he replied. "I may not agree with what he does, but he has my loyalty nonetheless."

"Your *friend* will bring about your death!" Brenna warned, grasping at anything to make him see reason.

"There is little truth in what you say, for Garrick Haardrad will not look for you here. And if he ever docs, 'twill be too late, for by then Cedric will have had enough of you and you will be sold away from here. Know this, wench. My loyalty is to Cedric and his family. I farm on their land. I am vassal to Cedric's father, Latham Borgsen. What you ask would get my throat cut sooner than your master would."

"Then take me to your liege. By your own words, I know he will not approve what you have done."

"Enough!"

Brenna steeled herself for one last try. "Please."

She humbled herself uselessly, for Arno stalked from the room, leaving her exhausted from trying and devastated at failing. When Arno returned, Brenna was silent once again. He did not attempt to change that. Then Cedric finally came, a little past midday.

From the moment he walked into the room, Brenna felt as if she was the long-awaited meal caught by the starving beast. Cedric's eyes did not leave her. His lustful intentions were so obvious that Arno was reluctant to demand an explanation of his absence, and looked away in embarrassment.

Cedric removed his cloak and Brenna's eyes were drawn to his bare arms bulging with muscle, and covered with scars. There was strength there, and Brenna knew the power of a man bent on having her, especially a man with strength. What chance did she have? But then, she had never wanted to kill Garrick, not even in the beginning. This man, yea, this man she could kill with no regrets.

"Has my pretty prize given you trouble?" Cedric asked Arno, though his eyes were still on Brenna.

"Not until this day."

"Oh?"

"She speaks our tongue, Cedric, and very well."

"Is this so, wench?"

Brenna did not answer, but moved closer to her temporary bed, where her one hope lay hidden. She must be in control of the dreaded situation when it finally came.

"She also knows us by name," Arno continued. "If Haardrad ever finds her, she will tell him all. I told you we should never have taken her."

"You sound worried, when there is no need. He will never find her."

"Will you sell her soon?"

"Nay, I think not. If Haardrad does look for her here, we will kill him. 'Tis that simple."

"Have you lost your senses, Cedric?"

"Enough! I have been delayed long enough by my father sending me on fool errands to collect a prized horse he bought from his cousin. The whole time I thought of naught else but her and I will wait no longer to have her."

Suddenly he laughed. "Will you stay and watch, Arno? Or is it not time you paid your respects to my father?"

Arno glared at Cedric, then looked at Brenna and saw her silent plea for help, but he quickly turned away. In exasperation, he stormed from the room, slamming the door soundly in his wake.

The closing of that door was so final, yet Brenna had expected no less. Arno was a man torn between his loyalties and what he felt in his heart. Unfortunately for Brenna, his loyalties came first. That was the way with all Vikings.

Now the test began. Brenna would either leave here with blood on her hands, or be violated by this young bastard and forever lose the hope of Garrick's love. Garrick was no different than other men, unwilling to share what they claimed as their own. He had proved that where she was concerned. He would never forgive her, even though she was blameless. How unfair was the judgment of men.

Still, it had not happened yet, though the moment was definitely at hand. Cedric moved in closer, slowly, like a snake about to strike.

"Come now, my pretty," he said cajolingly. "You speak my tongue. You know what I want."

She said not a word, but her eyes spoke for her. Dark, smoky gray eyes relayed her disgust and loathing, her profound contempt. Yet he was not daunted, not even surprised.

"Will you fight me, then?" he raised a brow, his lips curling repulsively. "I do not mind, wench. I am sure you put up an admirable struggle when you were a maid first taken, but you have naught to defend now. If you prefer to pretend the virgin still, 'tis fine with me."

Brenna could not contain her disgust any longer. "Loathsome pig!" she hissed. "If you touch me you will not live long to regret it!"

He laughed at her warning. "I will regret naught, but relish the touching. Do you truly believe your master will come bounding through that door to prevent me from having you? Nay, wench, there will be none here to stop me."

Brenna wisely held her tongue. Let him think she was

helpless. Let him fall into her trap unawares. It would be her only chance.

Cedric slowly began to remove his weapons. First his sword, then a crude ax with a chipped blade. How many skulls had split under that ax? How many men had fallen to this young braggart? Would her sin be great for killing him? Did she not have the right?

Cedric leaped at her all at once, taking her by surprise. Brenna screamed, not in fear, but in regret, for they fell many feet from her weapon and she could see no way of getting nearer to it.

"Now the victor claims the spoils," he murmured before he ripped her shift to her belt.

Then he fought to untie the belt, and Brenna fought desperately to stop him, her fists hammering at him. One blow brought forth a curse as blood oozed from his split lip. He slapped her, rendering her nearly unconscious. In her dazed state, her belt seemed to open magically and the rest of her shift tore effortlessly in half.

Blinding pain cleared her muddled mind as both his hands came down to torture her bared breasts, squeezing them cruelly, delighting in her anguished screams. He continued mercilessly, it seemed endlessly, until finally Brenna could stand no more and fainted to escape the pain.

Chapter 37

GARRICK stood in Brenna's room, a candle on the mantel his only light. He stared venomously at the cold fire and the remains of the two gold arm rings, now black, but still retaining their original shape. This was how she repaid his generosity. This was what she thought of his caring.

Garrick no longer held his anger in check—he had not for days. Why should he pretend to others that he was unaffected? He was furious, so much so that if he could find Brenna today he would kill her. But there was little chance of finding her—she had made good her escape.

Never again would he come close to trusting a woman. Having given him her word, he actually believed she would honor it.

"Fool!"

He drained the tankard in his hand and walked out of the room. He would order everything within it burned. He wanted no memory of the lying bitch left behind.

Garrick entered the hall, where Maudya was just placing his meal on the table. "Where is Erin?" he barked at her.

Maudya jumped nervously and scampered out of his

way. "He is coming." Then she added, hoping to pacify him, "Erin is old, Master Garrick. It takes him longer these days to cross the yard than it used to."

"I did not ask for excuses, mistress," he growled in return, then he pounded his fist on the table. "Odin and mighty Thor, help me! Will I have obedience from no slave under my rule?"

His call to his gods frightened Maudya more than his rage, and she ran from the room as if those very heathen deities were about to devour her. She passed Erin on his way in. He was vexed at seeing her white face and terror-filled eyes.

"You have no need to take your anger out on the poor wench," Erin said boldly to Garrick, taking more liberty than he knew he should. "She has done naught but serve you well."

Garrick was angered further. "You overstep your place, old man. You would do well to remember who is master here!"

"I know well enough whom I serve with love—and patience when needed."

Garrick was adequately chastised, but he hid this under a stern countenance and moved to the reason why he had called for Erin again. "Tell me once more what you recall of the day Brenna left."

"Again? Garrick, we have been over this four times thus far. I have told you everything."

At that moment Perrin strode into the hall, but his bone-weary expression relayed that he had no encouraging news. Garrick ignored him after a single glance and continued his interrogation.

"Just repeat your story, Erin."

Erin sighed. "I did not know the lass had returned that day, nor that you had come and gone. I curse myself for my weakness, for falling ill on a day that has since caused you such misery."

"Never mind what it has caused me, Erin!" Garrick said harshly. "Just repeat what happened."

"I did not expect to be needed that day, so I went early to Rayna's for her special potions. She put me to bed for most of the day, and God's truth, her mixtures made me feel well again. I returned to the stable late, and that was when I heard the shepherd howling as if he were a hound from hell. The storm had not yet begun and the air was still, so 'twas not hard to hear the animal from the stable, even with my old ears. I found him alone in the house, but thought nothing of it till I realized the animal could not have started the fire or made the bread that was then burnt to a crisp. I knew the other women had not been to the house, so that was when I sent Coran to tell you what I found. Since both your mount and Brenna's were not in the stable, 'twas only natural I assumed she was still with you at your father's house. Before you came with Coran, the storm had begun, covering the tracks you hoped to find."

Garrick gritted his teeth as he remembered cursing the heavens for the snowstorm that had thwarted any chance of finding Brenna quickly. He had not found her at all, and too many days had passed.

"And you said when you opened the door that night, Dog ran out and off to the front of the house?"

" 'Tis as I said," Erin replied.

Garrick slammed a fist into his palm. "I have searched every inch of land to the east, all the way to the base of the mountains, but there was no sign of her!"

"And the mountains?" Perrin finally spoke.

"Any fool would know they could not survive there in winter, yet I did cross the lower hills."

"And Dog? He would have more luck than you," Perrin said. "Did you not take him with you?"

"I could not find him when I left the first time. Erin says he returned the next day, wet and injured. He died hours later."

"I am sorry, Garrick. I know you raised him from a pup."

Garrick said nothing. He had yet to deal with that loss, or to think of anything save finding Brenna.

"I still insist she did not run away, Garrick," Erin said stoically. "She is out there hurt, perchance—"

"Do not say she is dead, old man!" Garrick cut him off with such vehemence that Erin quickly regretted his words almost spoken.

Perrin tried to ease the tension that suddenly filled the

air. "If Dog returned wet, the nearest lake is northwest of here. Have you been that way, Garrick?"

"Yea, and north. And my father is still looking west, to the coast."

"I have also been north and east, along with many others."

"You have my thanks, Perrin, for your efforts, but 'tis time to quit. Erin has told me naught different. There is no clue to the direction she fled, not one."

"You have given up?"

"That woman is as cunning as any man. She swore once that when she escaped I would not find her. 'Twas only because she had Dog with her the first time that I brought her back."

"But to just give up when, as Erin said, she might be injured, unable to return."

"Then I would have found her. Nay, my father will not quit, but I am through being the fool. She is gone, and I do not want her name mentioned in my presence again."

Chapter 38

THE icy water thrown on Brenna's face brought her back to consciousness. She choked and coughed, feeling she must surely be drowning. Then her eyes flew open. She was aware of immediate danger, but she could not recall what was threatening her until a tall form loomed before her.

Cedric stood at her feet, completely devoid of any clothing. She saw then that she was also bared to his view, her torn shift thrown open. He feasted his eyes on her with a libidinous grin and she moaned inwardly. Was it over? Were her most private parts already violated by this grinning whoremaster? Nay—nay! She could not believe her mind would so desert her, leaving her helpless in the face of danger.

"So you came back," Cedric said in a voice that held contempt. "You are like all my women, swooning when faced with a little pain. I had hoped you would be different, wench, that you could endure what I mete out."

The horrid memory of blinding pain shot through her mind. She looked down at her breasts and saw that small bruises had already formed where his fingers had dug into her skin. She quickly pulled her shift together, but it would not stay.

287

"You are an animal!" she hissed, her blood racing with poisonous hate.

Cedric chuckled evilly at her outburst. "You do not appreciate my methods of finding pleasure? You will, Brenna," he said confidently, his voice rising with excitement. "In time you will love what I do to you, and the many different ways I will take you. You will find pleasure in exquisite pain, and beg me to inflict more."

Her stomach churned in revulsion. She would have to kill him, there was no doubt of that now. But how soon? What would she have to suffer before she found her chance?

He was an evil monster with a warped mind. She stared at him in morbid fascination, revolted, yet unable to take her eyes away. The scars that covered his arms and torso were nothing compared to a long, horrid gash on his hip. And next to that was his protruding manhood, throbbing with anger—a shaft so swollen she knew it would indeed inflict much pain. Had it already? Was it now standing tall to have her again? She had to know. If the damage was already done, she could never return to Garrick without unbearable shame, knowing that what they might have had would never come to pass.

She bit her lip, her misery intense. "Did you—" She could not bear to ask it, but she had to. She closed her eyes and rushed on. "Did you have me yet?"

He laughed at her question. "Do you doubt it?"

She cried out in anguish, but then she heard him laugh even harder. "Nay, wench. I will not have a woman unless she can feel every inch of my sword. She must know who has mastered her, and you will know now."

Brenna sighed with a relief that she felt for only a second. She realized with dread that she was in the same position as before, no closer to her hidden dagger. This time he was not on her yet, though he was ready. When he bent down, Brenna quickly scrambled away from him, using her feet and elbows to push her backward. But she was still too close for her to try to rise and run. In the next moment, with the mighty yell of a victorous warrior, he leaped on her.

Brenna's breath was lost when his body fell on her full force. She fought the black waves that clouded her mind once again. She felt terror-stricken, sure she could delay him no longer. Instead of trying to ward him off with her hands, she reached frantically behind her, praying she had moved close enough to her weapon.

At first she felt nothing but smooth dirt beneath the rug, and she panicked. Cedric was already trying to pry her legs apart with one knee and he quickly succeeded. At the same moment, Brenna's fingers finally touched the cold blade of her dagger and she pulled it to her until she grasped the hilt.

Brenna would have cut his throat smoothly at that moment had he not become suspicious of why she was not resisting him. As it was, he saw her arm beneath the rug and the blade when she brought it out. He clasped her wrist and pinned her hand to the floor by her head, applying brutal pressure until she felt her own grasp weakening. She held on as if her very life depended on it, and as far as she could see, it did. She could not fail now, not when she was so close.

He raised himself up on his knees, and with his free hand, formed a fist and prepared to inflict a stunning blow. He was furious. In Brenna's mind flashed the further tortures he would mete out if she failed.

In a last effort, before his fist came down and rendered her unconscious again, she tried to dislodge him by finally utilizing the rest of her body. She brought her legs up forcefully, and even though only one struck him, this propelled Cedric forward with a cry of pain.

Brenna was startled by the outcome, for she knew not how her one movement had crumbled her mighty opponent. But finish him it did, for he fell forward onto the upraised dagger and lay motionless. Her relief was so great that she could barely breathe with his chest covering her face.

It required a decided effort to finally pull herself out from beneath him. Still he did not move. If he was not dead now, he soon would be, and she felt no regret. Her sin could not be that great, for if any man deserved to die, this one did. She thought of the many women he had bragged about misusing and thanked God she had escaped without too much damage. They would not mourn his death any more than she would.

These thoughts went through Brenna's mind, but her body reacted in a different manner. As she stared down at the blood slowly covering the floor beneath Cedric, she was overcome with nausea. She turned away and lost all the contents of her stomach, then continued to retch painfully even when there was nothing left to spill forth.

At last she rose, even though her stomach still rebelled. She realized that time was her new enemy. Arno might return at any moment, and then she would be in an even worse position than heretofore. She had killed a Viking, a freeman—and worse, the son of a chieftain. If she were found now, her life would be over. Arno would raise the alarm and she would be hunted down, but if she could reach Garrick first, he would protect her.

In a burst of speed, Brenna gathered up anything that would be useful, food, covers, Cedric's weapons, the rope that Arno had used to tie her at night, and to be on the safe side, flint. She put all this in a large rug and tied it into a bundle. Grabbing her cloak, she ran out of the house. She quickly found the crude shelter that housed Willow, but did not bother with the saddle that was there, only throwing a heavy blanket over Willow's back. She found a sack of oats and added this to her bundle, then mounted Willow and rode out of the shelter.

The sky was dusky blue, starless. She prayed Arno's house faced the fjord, for she rode in that direction. In the distance, to the left, she saw Arno astride his horse, coming home. He saw her too and Brenna suddenly felt as if all she had done was for naught. But he did not make to ride toward her. In fact, he stopped and simply watched her leave.

Brenna did not waste precious time wondering over this. Arno was no doubt in shock, realizing what had happened. She rode on, urging Willow to greater speed. Before she disappeared into a crop of trees, she looked back and saw Arno racing to his house.

How much time would she have now? Arno would call others to assist in the hunt, and that would give her a little time, for he would have to first convince them that a woman was responsible for Cedric's death. His death was an accident, even though she had wanted to kill him, but this would not help her cause. Dear Lord, to escape the smoke only to end in the fire!

Brenna rode on, endlessly, it seemed. She did not stop or slow her pace until she finally heard the rolling waters of the fjord in the distance. She began to fear that she might have gone south, instead of north. She could not bear to think of her chances if this were so. As it was, she was still at a loss as to how she would cross the fjord and return to safety. She would need Garrick's help. In her mind, she saw his house situated on the cliff, and wondered whether, if she called from the opposite cliff, she would be heard. It was possible, and this gave her hope.

She approached the fjord cautiously. She was on a flat bank that reached the water's edge. Across the water were dense woods. She could see no sign of a rising cliff that would lead home. Brenna was desolate. She did not know how far inland they had sailed on the ship, nor how far they had backtracked on land. She had ridden directly north, or at least she prayed it was north.

"Merciful God, show me which way I should go!" Brenna cried aloud.

As if in answer, Willow turned left and moved along the bank of the fjord. Tears came to Brenna's eyes.

"Please be right, Willow. Please!"

Brenna was unmindful of the cold, except when her cloak fell open and the icy air touched her bare skin. Her bundle was wrapped loosely enough so that it fell on both sides of Willow. Brenna did not have to worry over holding it in place, so she used one hand to cling to Willow's mane and the other to keep her cloak together.

The hour was unknown to her until stars finally appeared. She did not know how long she had ridden. One hour? Two? At last she recognized the landscape across from her, and very near, the stone house on the cliff. It was all she could do to contain her joy. Deep waters separated her from her love, but he would conquer that and she would be safe again.

She reached the top of the cliff, dismounted immediately and began to scream Garrick's name. Only after some time passed without a response did she begin to wonder if he were home. He could very well be out searching for her. Yet someone must be there, for smoke came from the chimney. With all the doors closed against the cold, could they hear her cries for help?

All of her earlier happiness dissolved. She was getting nowhere. Her cries were surely not reaching the house now, for her voice was hoarse, her throat so sore she could hardly bear the pain. To come this far and be this close, and yet not be heard or seen. Even if someone came from the house now, she doubted she could make a noise loud enough to draw their attention.

Brenna sank down on the ground and fell prey to despair. Tears fell unchecked, then she burst into ragged sobs. What should she do now? She could not stay here and wait for morning when someone might leave the house —Arno would find her before then. Yet how could she ever get home without help? She could not swim or man a ship. And to cross the fjord in a small craft would mean leaving Willow behind. Yet that seemed her only course. Already she grieved at the solution she had come to. But then, she would have to find a boat first.

Brenna mounted and rode back the way she had come.

Brenna did not sleep that first night. She rode on past the landing where the Viking ship floated in a small bay. There was no other craft there, so she continued east along the fjord, riding till her back ached and her legs lost all feeling. Her stomach had long since stopped demanding nourishment.

Finally, sometime the following morning, Brenna stopped, for Willow's sake, not hers. She quickly fed the horse and herself and rubbed Willow down, then cut thin strips from the fur rug before covering Willow with it. Brenna poked holes with Cedric's sword along the edges of her shift, then, using the leather strips, tied her shift together as best she could. Curling up in a ball beside Willow, she slept for a few hours.

So it went for days. Little sleep, hurried meals and a constant fear of being found. Soon her rations diminished and she was forced to hunt game. She thanked God now that she had taken flint for fire and would not have to eat raw meat. So far she had done without the warmth of a fire at night, too fearful that her hunters were close. Now she had no choice.

On the sixth day, Brenna gave up hope of finding a boat. She was not crushed, for this meant she would keep Willow with her. However, it left her only one other course, to reach the end of the fjord and circle around it. This would either bring her home eventually, or she would die in the wilderness. She had little hope left, and as more days passed and the fjord seemed to stretch endlessly, she lost even that.

She continued on without thinking simply because she had no other alternative. At times she walked beside Willow, wearing away the wool coverings she had made for her feet. She hunted game only when she became so weak from hunger that she could not go on. Twice she gave up and collapsed, only to have Willow nudge her back to life. That faithful beast was not ready to let her die. When at last her body, full of countless aches and pains, would move no more, Brenna fell into a sleep that lasted a full day and night. Even Willow's gentle prodding did not stir her.

She woke at last, not refreshed and ready to go on, but so disheartened that she would not move, preferring to wait where she was for death to come and claim her. She lay there, covered with blankets that did little to keep out the cold, her limbs so numb she no longer felt pain.

Willow tried her best to attract Brenna's attention, but the girl closed her eyes tight, willing her beloved mare to go away and leave her to die in peace. When at last Willow did trot away, Brenna looked up to see her go, only then feeling a sense of loss. It was then she saw the lake for the first time, magnificent in its size, nestled at the base of the mountains. It was the end of the fjord.

Chapter 39

IT took a full day to round the lake. This was the most hazardous and frightening part of her journey. In many areas she had to wade in the shallows, for jagged rocks from the mountain's edge blocked her way. The warm current did not reach this far inland, and Brenna was threatened with frostbite as she waited for her clothes to dry.

She crossed barren land where no game wandered. Through all this was the terrible snow, still clinging to the ground from the last storm. She had to dig through it to find nourishment for Willow once the oats were gone. Then she had to leave her course and go further north in search of food for herself. She passed streams and frozen lakes, and cursed the low mountain hills that slowed her pace. Once she found game, the journey was not so difficult, for she fashioned a crude bow by shredding her rope into thin strings, and with the ax carved adequate arrows. Finding game was the tiring task. She wondered how Garrick managed to bring so many pelts home in winter.

With each step closer to home, her disposition improved greatly. She no longer felt hopeless and lost, but sure that she would make it. The cuts and blisters, the aching joints, these nuisances had become so much a part of her that they went unnoticed. There would be time enough to tend all her hurts, to regain the many pounds she had lost. Garrick would care for her and nurse her back to health. She would quickly grow strong in his love. And he did love her. Even though he did not admit it yet, he would in time.

These thoughts urged her on whenever she began to despair. It made the hardships bearable, knowing that he would be there for her at the end of her journey. How he must have worried over her and scoured the countryside in search of her. He must have given up hope by now. It would make their reunion that much sweeter.

When she at last came to lands that she knew, her relief and joy gave her added strength. If Willow were not in the same poor condition as she was, she would have raced the remaining distance. As it was, it took her another two hours till she finally topped the last hill, at the bottom of which sat Garrick's house. Such a welcome sight, one she thought never to see again.

Erin was in the stable when she opened the door and dragged Willow inside. The look he gave her was not merely one of surprise, but disbelief.

"You have come back from the dead," he said fearfully, his old face pale.

Brenna found the strength to laugh feebly. "Nay, I did not die, though many is the time I wanted to."

He shook his head, staring at her with something akin to pity. "You should not have run away, lass."

"What?"

"Nor, having done so, should you have returned."

She smiled at his misconception. "I did not run away, Erin. I was taken away by two Vikings from across the fjord."

He wanted to believe her, but all evidence said she lied. Yet he would not be the one to accuse her.

"You look wasted away, lass. I will prepare food for you."

"Nay, I will eat at the house. Is Garrick home?" When he nodded uncertainly, she went on. "You know, I called from across the fjord, but no one heard me. I could not stay there, though, for I had killed one of the men who took me away, a chieftain's son, I believe he was." She looked dazed, trying to remember it all.

"Do you know what you are saying, Brenna?"

She did not seem to hear him. "I lost count of the days I traveled round the fjord. How long have I been gone, Erin?"

"Nearly six weeks."

"That long?"

"Brenna—"

"Care for Willow, Erin. She has endured as much as I and needs a gentle hand. I must see Garrick now. I can wait no longer."

"Brenna, lass, do not go to the house."

She saw his concern and it puzzled her. "Why should I not?"

"You will not be welcome there."

"Do not be absurd, Erin." Then she frowned. "Does Garrick also think I ran away?"

"Yea."

"Then more is the reason I should see him quickly. He must know the truth."

"Brenna, please—"

" 'Twill be all right, Erin," she cut him off and started for the door.

"Then I will come with you."

The house was warm from the blazing cooking fires. Tantalizing aromas filled the air, making Brenna weak with hunger. In all her weeks away, she had not had a single filling meal, always having to ration because she never knew when she would find more food.

Janie was the first to see her and immediately stopped what she was doing. Her eyes filled slowly with fear, but Brenna smiled and hugged her old friend. They said not a word, though, for Brenna was conserving her strength and Janie was too frightened to speak. Brenna went on into the hall, leaving Erin to explain.

Garrick was bent over the fire in the hall, jabbing at the burning wood as if he were attacking an unknown enemy. Brenna took a moment to look her fill at him before she moved closer and stood behind him. He turned quickly when he sensed her presence, and they stared at each other for a long while. She saw the surprise in his eyes, then

297

the anger, but she could contain herself no longer and she threw herself against him, clinging to him with what little strength she had left.

She felt his body stiffen, and his arms did not return her embrace. Slowly he pushed her away from him.

"So you returned."

She could not bear the look in his eyes or the tone of his voice. There was hatred there, not just anger.

"Did you lose your way?" Garrick continued in that same bitter tone. "Or mayhaps you finally realized that you could not survive in the wilderness alone."

"She claims she did not run away, Garrick," Erin said as he came into the room. "She was taken across the fjord by force."

"Is this what she told you?"

"I believe her," Erin said firmly in her defense. " 'Twould explain why the shepherd was wet and injured when he returned. He could have tried to follow her across the fjord."

"Or fell in a lake trying to follow her, which cost him his life!"

"Dog is dead?"

Garrick turned away from her question. She turned haunted eyes on Erin, who nodded sadly. Merciful Lord, why this too? Was not her suffering enough? Tears welled in her eyes as memories assailed her. She had won the shepherd's affection, only to lead him to death.

She could see Garrick was of the same opinion, yet she was not wholly to blame. She must make him see that.

" 'Twas Arno who hurt Dog," Brenna said in a grief-filled whisper. "He kicked him away when Cedric would have killed him."

"Cedric!"

"They were the ones who took me, Garrick!" She could see his doubt and she became frantic. "You must believe me! They brought a ship so they could take my horse too. They wanted you to think I ran away so you would never suspect them."

"Why?" he demanded.

"I never learned why, except that a woman approached them and told them of me. I was kept on Arno's farm, but I was to belong to Cedric. When he came and attempted to have me, I killed him and escaped. I sought your help first and called from the opposite cliff, but no one heard me. I cannot swim, nor could I find a boat, so I went around the fjord, the only way left to me."

"Get her out of here, Erin, before I do her harm!"

Erin put his hands on her shoulders, but she shrugged him away. " 'Tis the truth, Garrick! All of it! In God's name, why would I lie?"

"In hope I would forgive you and take you back," he said heartlessly. " 'Tis too late for that."

Unchecked tears wetted Brenna's cheeks and neck. "You could learn the truth if you would, Garrick. Cross the fjord. See for yourself that Cedric is dead by a woman's hand."

" 'Twould mean my death if I were found on Borgsen land. But you must know that, the same as you learned the names of the Borgsen clan, from the women. They know the story well and gossip often."

" 'Tis not so. Ask them!" she was crying hysterically now, but he turned his back on her.

"You give the lie in your own words, for no one could survive what you described in winter. Take her to my father's house, Erin."

"Why there?"

Garrick faced her again with such venom in his eyes that she cringed. " 'Twas my intent to sell you in the East if I found you, where slaves are treated as slaves, not with the liberties I foolishly bestowed on you here. But you were a gift to me, and so being, 'tis my father's right to have you back."

"Come along, Brenna," Erin urged her.

Brenna felt as if she were torn in two. Bile rose in her throat and nearly choked her. She was not strong enough to deal with this rejection. She would have crumpled on the floor if Erin had not supported her. She let him lead her as far as the wall dividing the hall, but there she stopped and looked back one last time at Garrick.

"Everything I have said is the truth, Garrick." Her voice lacked all emotion—she was dead inside. " 'Twas my love for you and my need to return to you that made it possible for me to survive rounding the fjord. I went without food because there was none, and I nearly froze many times. But I kept on because I thought you would be there for me in the end. I should have died. 'Twould have made you most happy."

She had spoken to his back, stiff and unyielding. Now she left, the pain in her chest agonizing. She had lost him. Nothing mattered any more.

Chapter 40

ERIN did not dare disobey Garrick. He knew his young master was wrong, he was sure of it now, but he was also certain that Garrick would never be convinced of his error. Erin grieved for Brenna. She did not deserve such callous treatment. Were it not for the other woman who had destroyed Garrick first, he might relent this time and trust in Brenna. But Garrick, a bitter young man, had closed himself off completely, and Brenna was suffering for it.

She said nothing on the way to Anselm's settlement. Erin had brought a cart for her to ride in, promising to bring her horse to her as soon as the mare had regained some strength. Brenna still said nothing, and it was with a heavy heart that he left her at his old master's home.

Brenna was fussed over by Linnet, who treated her like an invalid after exclaiming over her condition. She was not allowed to step one foot from the bed, nor did she try. Her every whim would have been catered to, but she demanded nothing. She ate very little of the food placed before her, even when Linnet scolded her severely. Brenna grew weaker instead of stronger. She would explain nothing, respond to nothing, until the day Cordella visited her.

"Linnet tells me you are wasting away, Brenna," Cordella said smugly, sitting on the edge of Brenna's bed. "This pleases me greatly."

Brenna appeared not to have heard. She simply stared at her stepsister with her expression unchanged. This riled Cordella more than a scathing response.

"Did you hear me, Brenna? I am glad you are dying. 'Twill mean you will not be around to tempt Hugh away from me. And he does wander with my belly so big."

Still Brenna did not bat an eye, and Cordella got up from the bed to pace around it.

"Hugh cannot do enough for me, nor can his father." Cordella paced more quickly, her huge belly preceding each step she took. "But I have not had such beautiful gifts as your Viking gave you. You are spoiled, Brenna! You are never satisfied! Why did you run away from him? Now you are here where you are not welcome. Always when you are near, I lose what is mine. Not this time, though. I will not let you take Hugh from me—I will kill you first!"

Brenna followed her with her eyes. "You are a fool, Della," she said in a weak voice. "I would sooner die than take Hugh from you. He disgusts me."

"You lie! You want everything that is mine!"

"Your ridiculous fears are groundless, and you sicken me with your jealousy. I want naught that is yours. I want no man, ever again."

"Not even your precious Viking, who cast you aside for another?" Cordella laughed shrilly. "Yea, I know of Morna, his one true love."

Brenna sat up in bed for the first time in days. "Get out of here, Della!"

Cordella crossed to the door, then surprised Brenna with a smile of genuine warmth. "So your spirit returns. Mayhaps now you will live just to spite me, eh?"

With that she left the room, leaving Brenna immersed in confusion. Did Cordella purposely make her angry? Did she in truth not want Brenna to die?

Linnet came into the room, relief on her features. "You are better finally?"

Brenna ignored her question. "What has come over Della?"

"She has changed greatly as life grows within her. She worried over you when no one could find you. She cried to me that she had wronged you terribly and she feared she could never make amends."

"I find this hard to believe."

"We all feared you were dead, Brenna. 'Twas a foolish, foolish thing you did!"

Brenna sighed and lay down again. "The only foolish thing I did was to return to Garrick."

"Nay, child. You are alive, and now you must make an effort to regain your strength."

"There is much that I have to tell you, Aunt."

"First you will speak to Heloise. She has been waiting many days to talk to you. I will find her and bring you food. And this time," she added sternly, "you will eat it all."

Brenna waited patiently. She *would* recover. She was hurting no one but herself by wallowing in self-pity and grief. She was through not caring whether she lived or died.

Suddenly Anselm's words came to mind. "I would see Brenna free, rather than belonging to someone else." She belonged to Anselm again, and by his words, he must set her free, even if she had to reveal to him that she had heard him say this. It would mean all her suffering was not in vain.

Heloise came into the room followed by Linnet, who carried a large tray of food. Brenna felt hunger gnawing at her belly, but that could wait a few minutes more.

"I have killed an enemy of the Haardrads, and in so doing, by Viking law, I demand my freedom."

Her words surprised both women to the point of speechlessness, and she quickly went on to explain what had really happened to her. "You may not believe me," she said in the end, "just as Garrick refused to accept the truth. But I swear, with God as my witness, that all I have said is true."

" 'Tis an incredible story, Brenna," Heloise said at last. "You must admit 'tis hard to believe you could survive such a long journey at this time of the year."

"Yea, I admit that. Were it not for my love for Garrick, I would have perished."

"I will agree that love can give added strength. It can conquer impossible obstacles," Heloise said, then added thoughtfully, "Yea, I believe you, Brenna. But others will not."

"I do not care what others think. Only your husband must believe me. I could not bear for all I endured to be for naught. I must have my freedom."

"I will tell him your story, Brenna, but 'twill not matter if he accepts it or not. You are already a freewoman. You were from the day my son relinquished his hold on you."

Chapter 41

THE enormity of Heloise's words and the seriousness of Brenna's position did not affect Brenna until she was fully recovered. She was free, yet here she was in Anselm Haardrad's care, eating his food, sleeping in his home. This dependency began to gnaw at her insides. She did not like feeling indebted to this man any more than she already was.

It was two months into the new year and spring was nearing when Brenna approached Heloise. She found her in the main hall, supervising her many servants while she skillfully worked a standing loom weighted with soapstone, on which a beautiful bedcover was almost finished.

It galled Brenna that she must ask to work in order to feel less burdensome, but she had nowhere to go in this foreign land, and so was forced to stay here. Yet she could no longer do so without paying for her keep.

"Milady," Brenna began reluctantly, "I cannot continue to accept your hospitality without some payment."

" 'Tis unnecessary, Brenna."

"Nay, I feel 'tis most necessary. I am a burden in your house."

"You are a freewoman and a guest, Brenna. Taking payment from a guest is unheard of."

"Then I must leave here," Brenna said adamantly, knowing her foolish pride was leading her on a course she could not alter.

Heloise frowned, shaking her head. "My husband said 'twould come to this."

Brenna was momentarily taken aback. "How could he know that?"

"He prides himself on being able to predict your actions. He thinks of you as a Viking maid, where courage and pride reign uppermost."

Brenna was nettled that she was so accurately speculated over, and more so that Anselm would relate her traits to his own people.

"So he knew I could not stay here long?"

"This is what he told me," Heloise admitted, "though I could not believe you would be so rash as to leave here with nowhere to go."

Her words stung Brenna. "I cannot help the way I am, milady. 'Tis my lot in life to be controlled by pride."

"I know, Brenna, and I am sorry I criticized you. I once had pride like you, but I learned to temper it, as I hope you will one day."

"I will leave on the morrow, and I thank you for my stay here."

Heloise shook her head and smiled weakly. "If you are determined to do this, there is a house on our land where you may live until spring."

Brenna was relieved and crushed at the same time. "Only until spring?"

"Nay, as long as you wish, Brenna. But my husband has bid me tell you that come spring, he will return you to your land if that is your desire."

Brenna took this news with mixed feelings. To leave this cold land had long been her only wish, then she had lost her heart to Garrick. And now? What would it matter if she put the distance of their respective lands between them? There was an ocean between them now as deep as any, filled with hatred and distrust.

"Brenna, is that what you want?"

"Yea." Her answer came as a whisper.

"But there is no one for you to return to—is there?" Heloise asked sadly.

"Nay," Brenna replied and lowered her eyes. "Yet there is no one for me here either."

"Your aunt is here—and your sister. And I have come to love and worry over you myself, because my son—"

"Do not mention him to me!" Brenna snapped, cutting her off. "He is the most hateful, mean, most distrusting person I have ever known!" Brenna stopped, biting her lower lip. "Forgive me. He is your son and I suppose he can do no wrong in your eyes."

"Nay, my son has done much that I am not proud of," Heloise admitted.

Brenna fought to shake Garrick from her thoughts. "My aunt? Would you release her to sail home with me?"

"I do not know, child." Heloise frowned. "She and I have become close friends, yet I suppose you will need her more than I. I will think on it and decide before you sail."

"And my sister, and the other women from my village?" Brenna persisted.

"The others have made new homes, Brenna. From what I know, they are happy here."

"As slaves?" She could not keep the sarcasm from her tone.

"You and I could argue endlessly over this issue, Brenna," Heloise smiled. "I know how you feel and you know my views. These other women are no worse off than they were." Brenna started to protest, but Heloise held up a hand so she could continue. "And your sister can never be released now, for she carries my oldest son's child. I do not think she will want to return to a ruined estate anyway."

Brenna cringed. She had not thought of that. She would have to build a new home to replace the old one. Even if the gray manor still stood, she could not bear to live there alone.

"You said there is a house where I may live until spring?"

"Yea, 'tis not far from here, near a small lake. And there is a well close to the house."

"I will of course pay for the use of the house."

"Of course." Heloise said diplomatically, knowing better than to argue with stubborn pride. "The family who used the house last gave a share of their summer crop. But since you cannot do that, I think two furs a week will do for payment. I understand you have hunted game since you were a child, so this should not be too difficult for you."

"Nay, 'tis too little. I will give three furs a week," Brenna returned adamantly.

"Brenna!" Heloise admonished.

"I insist."

The older woman shook her head, but smiled despite herself. "Then I insist you let me furnish you with salt, for you will end up with more meat than you can eat and will have to cure it. Also oats and rye, and some dried vegetables, for you cannot exist wholly on meat."

Brenna nodded, satisfied. "I agree. And I will also have enough furs by spring to pay for my passage home."

"Now *that* is not necessary, Brenna. Anselm will not hear of it."

"Nonetheless, that is the way 'twill be." And she turned and left the hall.

Heloise threw up her hands. "Foolish pride," she muttered under her breath before she again started working at the loom.

Chapter 42

THE little house was perfectly suited to Brenna's needs, and had been thoroughly cleaned before she arrived. It was small enough to contain the warmth of a fire, and very near the woods, where ample game roamed. In the house were iron pots for cooking, clean woolen blankets, a crossbow and snares for hunting, and even a change of clothing made of soft wool, and a warmer cloak.

The only thing that had not been provided was a tub to bathe in, but Brenna supposed that was because the small lake was so near. However, the lake was now covered with ice, and breaking that ice to wash in freezing water was not in the least tempting. She would manage with sponge baths until the weather warmed.

Brenna settled into her new home with the joy and excitement of a small child. She was independent now, solely responsible for herself. She luxuriated in her new freedom, but it did not take long for the novelty to wear off and loneliness to set in. With such complete solitude, she could not stop herself from thinking of Garrick constantly. When she saw him one day in the woods and they passed with the hostility of enemies, saying not a word, her brooding became even worse.

She would wear herself out hunting each day, then exhaust herself further by preserving the meat and treating the hides, finally making her meal for the following day before she would at last go to bed. Her days became monotonous, involving only work, as she tried desperately to keep her mind filled with immediate concerns.

The ice cracked and melted with the lengthening of daylight hours, but the weather seemed no warmer, so Brenna still chose not to bathe in the lake. Then new flowers began to take the place of winter blooms, and snow disappeared from most of the land. Spring had come to Norway.

Brenna was ecstatic when she saw the cart drawing near her house. She hoped it would be Heloise or Linnet, with news of how soon Anselm would sail. But she was so starved for company that she was not in the least disappointed when Janie and Maudya alighted from the cart that Erin had brought them in.

After warm greetings were exchanged, Brenna took them in her house, grateful that she had a generous meal stewing that she could offer them. Erin had brought a skin of wine which Garrick had given him over the winter celebration, and they all drank to each other's health. Erin then went to cut wood for Brenna against her protests, for he felt uneasy around so many chattering women. At first Janie and Maudya were distant, awed by Brenna's new status, but as they consumed more wine and felt Brenna's genuine warmth, their unease soon disappeared.

"Erin told us what happened to you, Brenna," Maudya started. " 'Tis a wonder you are alive."

Brenna only nodded. She rarely thought of the time she nearly died. It was best forgotten.

"Garrick is a true Viking now."

"What do you mean, Maudya?" Brenna asked. She found she was eager for information about him, no matter how little.

"He is the kind of man my mother used to scare me with tales of when I was bad. He has grown terribly mean, Brenna, since you left. 'Tis much worse then before, when that other woman left him for another. Now his temper is never below the surface. He scares me so."

"How is he otherwise?"

"If you mean his health, 'tis fine. Except he drinks more and more, until to everyone's relief, he sleeps."

"Surely you exaggerate?"

"Were it only so."

"Not even a little?"

"Nay, Brenna," Janie remarked sadly. "He has offended his friends with his temper—even Perrin. Words were spoken that could not be undone. Perrin no longer comes."

"I am sorry," Brenna offered.

"And if it is to be believed, Master Garrick turned even meaner after he crossed the fjord," Maudya added.

"When was this?" Brenna asked excitedly.

"Not long after you came back. He was thoroughly armed when he went, as if he prepared for war. But he was gone less than a day. He would tell no one why he went, or why he was not pleased with what he found."

What could he have found that would not confirm her story? Or perhaps he learned the truth, and was now furious that he had been wrong—too stubborn to undo the damage he had wrought with his doubt.

" 'Tis a wonder he came back that day at all," Maudya continued. "He could have died, had the Borgsens found him."

Some of her old curiosity returned to Brenna. "This feud between the two clans. Tell me about it."

"Don't you know?" Maudya gasped. "I thought Janie told you."

"I thought you did," Janie returned.

"Will one of you explain?" Brenna asked in exasperation.

"There is not much to tell," Janie replied.

"Then let me," Maudya cut in, for this fulfilled her love of gossip. "Five winters have passed since it all began. Before then, the chief of the Borgsen clan and Garrick's father were close friends, blood brothers if truth be told. Latham Borgsen had three sons: the youngest, who had just returned from his first sea voyage, was Cedric, the one you claim to have—"

"Yea, go on," Brenna interrupted quickly.

" 'Twas fall, and time to pay tribute to the gods and good harvest. A huge feast was prepared by Anselm, and both clans joined together to celebrate. The drinking and merrymaking went on for weeks—more mead was downed than ever before."

"But what could have happened to put an end to this long friendship?" Brenna asked impatiently.

"The death of Anselm's only daughter, Thyra. She was a pretty maid, from what we have been told, but sickly and terribly shy, except with her own family. She was fifteen summers then, but she never attended celebrations, even after she was permitted to. So 'twas understandable that Latham Borgsen's sons did not know who she was, having never seen her."

"What have they to do with her?"

" 'Tis not really known exactly how it happened, Brenna. The general agreement is that Thyra had gone out for a walk to get away from the noise of the feast. She was found the next morn behind the storehouse, her face badly beaten, her skirt still bunched up around her waist and her virginal blood covering her thighs. Her own dagger was plunged in her heart with her hand still clutching it."

Brenna was struck with horror at the plight of one so young. "She killed herself?"

"No one knows for sure, but 'tis the opinion of most that she did, because she could not live with what had been forced on her."

"Who could have done such a monstrous thing?" Brenna realized the answer from the other things they had told her.

"Latham's sons: Gervais, Edgar and Cedric—all three of them."

"How was this learned?"

"They gave themselves away that morn when they found out who Thyra was. All three panicked and fled. 'Twas a terrible time for all—the grief, and then the blood-lust for revenge. Master Garrick cherished his little sister, but so did Hugh. The two brothers fought over who would have the honor of avenging her death. Hugh won. It did not matter that the Borgsen brothers thought they had tumbled an unimportant wench, no doubt assuming she was merely a slave. A crime had been committed against the Haardrad clan, and the offenders would pay.

"Anselm, Garrick and many others crossed the fjord

with Hugh. Anselm was heartsick over what happened, and so was his friend Latham. Hugh first challenged Edgar and killed him fairly. When he would have challenged the other two in turn, Anselm put a stop to it, against both Hugh's and Garrick's protests. The Haardrads all returned home and waited for the Borgsens to retaliate. But they never did, except for the minor slaughtering of stray animals. Both families had suffered a loss and both chieftains were loath to add to that count."

"Such a tragic story. Did no one ever wonder why Thyra did not cry out when she was attacked? None of it need have happened."

"She was such a timid girl, frightened of everything," Janie answered. "She was no doubt too frightened to scream, or mayhaps they prevented her from doing so."

"They say she was always a weak child, even from birth," Maudya added. " 'Tis a wonder she was allowed to live when she was born."

"Allowed? What play on words is this?"

" 'Tis the right word, Brenna," Janie said with disgust. "Had I known of the Viking custom when I carried my son in me, I would have been terrified. But my baby was healthy, thank the dear Lord."

Brenna had turned a sickly white, "What are you saying? What Viking custom?"

"The ritual of birth," Maudya said with equal distaste. "A newborn baby must be accepted by his father, whether that father be wed to the mother or not. As you know, these people prize strength and deplore weakness. 'Tis assumed that a man or woman who is not strong cannot survive in this hard land. So a baby born deformed or weak is rejected by the father and exposed to the elements. It dies, of course, but the father absolves himself by reasoning that the child would not have survived anyway, and 'twould be wasteful to give it food and attention, when others are more in need."

"That is barbaric!" Brenna gasped and fought to control the nausea rising in her throat.

"What is barbaric?" Erin asked, coming in with a stack of wood in his arms.

"The custom of rejecting a weak baby and putting it out

313

to die of cold or starvation before a mother can even hold it in her arms," Janie answered.

"How is that barbaric?" he asked testily, dropping the wood by the fire.

"You think it is not?" Brenna snapped. "You are as heathen as these Vikings, Erin, if you can condone such a hideous custom!"

"Nay, 'tis not so. I only think it is the kinder of two evils. Ask Janie, she is a mother. Ask her if her love does not grow stronger for her child with each day's passing."

"This is so," Janie agreed.

"What are you saying, Erin?"

"The bond between mother and child is a strong one, but it does not grow strong until the mother knows that child."

Brenna was appalled. "So you think 'tis kinder to kill the child at birth, before a bond can be formed? What of the bond the mother feels while carrying the child? Do you discount that?"

"I know only that I lost a son at birth through none but natural causes. My wife and I grieved only a short while, and then the child we never knew was forgotten. I had another son whom I came to love, and I lost him after ten short summers. This son I grieve for to this day. carry memories that still haunt me."

"I am sorry, Erin."

"You are sorry, but do you understand, Brenna? Can you see that 'tis kinder to lose the child at birth, before the child knows what life has to offer, before the parents know what 'tis like to love that child, rather than lose the child later, when the loss will nearly destroy the parents?"

"Nay, this I cannot understand. A weak child can be made strong, a deformed child can be taught to do for itself."

"Mayhaps in your land, lass, but this is the North, where lives are governed by snow and ice. This is spring, and yet you still burn your fire for warmth. Look at the smoke, Brenna. A weak babe would die from that smoke, yet to keep it from the fire would cause it to die from the cold."

"I could never see the wisdom of it, Erin, so enough," Brenna said and turned away.

Her hands were shaking as she served her friends a meal.

She had been so delighted to see them, but now she wished they had never come. Their talk of the feud and killing babies had depressed her terribly. She could not touch her own food, her stomach was churning so.

The others chatted on as if they were unaffected by the earlier talk. Erin stared at Brenna thoughtfully. She tried to avoid his eyes, and finally left the table to tidy the room. After a while, she still found him staring at her, and could stand it no more.

"Why do you look at me so?" she demanded.

Erin was not abashed by her sharp tone. "Are you breeding, lass?"

Brenna had refused to admit it to herself. She would be damned if she would to anyone else.

"Nay, I am not!"

"I was going to ask the same thing, Brenna," Maudya said. "You *have* put on a little weight."

"I said nay!" Brenna shouted, unconsciously covering her belly with her hands. "I am not with child, I tell you!"

All kinds of disastrous possibilities tumbled through her mind. Garrick rejecting her baby because of his hatred. Being forced to stay here like Cordella. It would not happen! Spring was here. She would go home soon, very soon.

The others left after her outburst, unconvinced by her denial.

Chapter 43

BRENNA spent a sleepless night filled with terrifying imaginings she could not control. She was in a highly nervous condition by morning, exhausted yet wide awake. She had finally accepted the truth. A child was growing within her.

"A child for a child," she spoke aloud, feeling sorry for herself. "We can both play games, both throw tantrums. Lord, I don't want to be a mother! I don't know how!"

She cried, though she had done so all night long. Anselm must sail quickly, before anyone else noticed her plight. She must get far away from this heathen land and give birth to her child among her own people, where she need not fear for her baby's life.

Brenna prepared to leave. When she opened the door, she felt as if the heathen gods were conspiring against her. The ground was covered with a white cloak of freshly fallen snow. How did it dare snow this late in spring? she wondered unreasonably.

Panic gripped her, and she rode with careless speed to Anselm's settlement. She sought out Heloise and found her with Cordella. They were both sewing tiny clothes, clothes for a new baby. Did Cordella know what fate

Johanna Lindsey

awaited her child if it was not born healthy? Did Heloise know? Brenna stared at the little garments, forgetting momentarily why she had come.

"You look flushed, Brenna," Heloise commented, setting aside her sewing.

"It must be the light, milady," Brenna said guiltily. "I feel well."

"Would that we all did."

"Milady?"

"Oh, my husband has become ill. 'Tis not serious, but he cannot abide taking to bed." As if to prove her words, he bellowed from his room. "You see?"

"How soon will he be well enough to sail?" Brenna asked anxiously.

" 'Twill not be soon, Brenna, but not too long. The ship was being refurbished until this unexpected snowfall. Now the men must wait till the weather warms again to continue. By then my husband should also be well."

"But how long?"

"I would imagine early summer. That is a beautiful time of the year to sail."

"Summer! I cannot wait that long, milady!" Brenna's voice rose, though she did not realize it.

"Whatever is the matter, Brenna?" Cordella asked. "I was pleased when I knew you would not leave so soon. Now you will be here when I give birth."

How impending motherhood had changed Cordella. She was no longer spiteful, filled with thoughts of vengeance. At last she was actually happy.

"It seems I have no choice but to stay, though of course seeing your child before I go will give me pleasure, Della. If you will send for me when your time comes, I will help you all I can." I will see no harm comes to your baby, she added silently to herself, then bid them farewell.

When Brenna stepped outside to leave, she saw Garrick just riding into the yard. She stopped. Beside him, on a short-legged mare was Morna, her smile radiant, her laughter tinkling in the air.

Brenna met Garrick's eyes and cringed at the icy look he gave her. She turned to go back into the hall, to hide, to run, to get far, far away from that look that hurt her

318

worse than a physical blow. But the sound of Garrick's voice stopped her again, torturing her with his soft tone.

"Let me help you down, my love."

Brenna felt real pain choke her. He spoke her tongue, not his, so she would understand every word. He purposely flaunted Morna before her. How could he forgive her and not me? she cried inside.

"What did you say, Garrick?"

"Let me help you down, Morna," he answered in his own language.

"I knew you would come around," Morna said with great confidence. "When I learned you got rid of that Celtic witch, I knew you would be mine again."

"Did you indeed?"

Brenna could not bear to listen to any more. She ran through the hall, oblivious to Cordella's and Heloise's calls, and stumbled out the back of the house. She wiped viciously at the tears that blurred her eyes and ran, without stopping, to the stable to get Willow.

When Garrick saw that Brenna was gone, he quickly released his hold on Morna's waist. He stared murderously at the open doorway where she had stood, still picturing her there, wanting to put his hands on her, yet knowing full well if he came that close to her, he would kill her.

"Well, help me down then, my love."

Garrick turned his fiery gaze on Morna. "What I will help you do is feel the weight of my sword!"

"Wha—what is wrong with you?"

"Never approach me on the road and follow me again, Morna! If you value your life, do not ever come near me again!"

"But—but I thought all was forgiven!" she cried. "You smiled at me. You—you did not growl a moment before when she was—" Morna gasped, her blue eyes widening. "Was your congenial mood just for *her* benefit?"

"Take care, Morna," he warned coldly. "I do not have the patience to endure your presence."

"Garrick, please. You must forgive me for the past. We shared a love once. Have you forgotten that?"

"Nay, I remember you vowed your love." His voice grew lower, like the calm before a storm. "And also that you turned to the first man who dangled a purse before your greedy eyes."

"I have changed, Garrick. Wealth no longer has importance to me."

"You can say that easily, now that you have what you want," he said with contempt.

" 'Tis not true, Garrick. I want you. I have always wanted you."

"And I wanted you—*then*. Now I would sooner rot in hell than turn to you!"

"Do not say that, Garrick!" she cried.

"Begone, Morna!"

" 'Tis because of that foreign witch that you will not forgive me! What spell has she cast on you?"

"No spell. She is dead to me, as you are. Neither of you will find forgiveness in me!"

"You—"

He cut her off with a sharp whack on the rump of her horse. The animal bolted from the yard, with Morna fighting to control it yet trying to look back at the same time. Garrick turned away in disgust.

That he once thought he loved that woman was inconceivable now. He had been drawn to her beauty, and proud that he would marry the most desirable wench in the county. But these were not measures of love. When he lost her, it was wounded pride that had turned him bitter, the fact that she had chosen a fat merchant over him.

Morna's only true motivation had been greed. Brenna had needed freedom and was unable to share herself. She had gone to great lengths for that freedom and to control her own life. She had used lies, deception. She vowed love as easily as Morna once did, speaking words that held no truth. Well, Brenna was welcome to her freedom, welcome to return to her land and forever leave his life.

Garrick entered the hall and suppressed some of his anger before he approached his mother. But seeing Brenna's sister so satisfied and pleased with her new life here, only added to his bitterness. Why was Brenna the only one who could not adjust?

"Where is Hugh?" Garrick asked stonily.

Heloise did not look up from her sewing. "My youngest son is here, yet I would not know this since he has forgotten the common courtesies I have tried so hard to teach him."

Garrick was duly chastened and smiled despite himself, then leaned over and kissed her on the brow. " 'Tis easy to disremember when no other Viking son shows the respect due his mother."

"A truth that breaks many a mother's heart, I'll wager. But you are half Christian, Garrick, and though few know it, I raised you differently." She put aside her sewing and looked up at him finally, a gleam twinkling in her eyes. "You seek your brother? He took the cattle to pasture."

"When?"

"Before the snow fell."

"Then he will be delayed," Garrick said with irritation. "He had goods he wanted me to trade. Did he make mention of them to you?"

"Nay, Hugh bid me tell you wait on his return. He wants to sail north with you, to hunt the great white bear before you go east."

" 'Tis too late to sail north."

Heloise clucked her tongue. "You are too eager to leave, Garrick, just like—" She stopped and he raised a brow, but she shook her head. "You know that even one fur of the white bear will make your waiting worthwhile. Are you concerned with profit, or do you just want to be gone?"

"If I leave in midsummer, I will not return this winter," he replied.

"You need not sail as far east as you did before, Garrick. Hedeby is a fine trading center."

"Bulgar is better," he returned gruffly. "I will wait only as long as it takes my ship to be readied." He started to leave, then stopped suddenly and looked about the hall.

"She is gone, Garrick," Heloise said.

He looked back at her. "Who?"

"The one you were just looking for. She ran from the hall with tears in her eyes before you entered. Why does she cry when she sees you?"

Garrick stiffened. "She does not cry! She swore she never cries!"

"Why should this upset you?"

321

"Because *all* things that she swears to are false!" he said heatedly.

"In your own stubborn opinion. I happen to believe that what Brenna claims to have occurred when she was gone is true—all of it."

"Do you indeed, mistress?" he sneered. "Then let me enlighten you. She swore she killed Cedric Borgsen, yet I have seen Cedric with my own eyes and he is very much alive."

"How did you see him?" Heloise gasped. "You crossed the fjord?"

"I did. I had to see for myself proof of what she claimed. And I did—proof of her lies."

Heloise wrinkled her brow in thought. "She assumed Cedric was dead, that is all."

"You are kind, mother," Garrick said disdainfully. "Brenna does not deserve your trust."

"Would that you would trust her, Garrick, and believe in her," Heloise said with genuine sorrow. "We will lose her soon, and I for one will be sorry."

"Truly, I never had her to lose," he replied bitterly and walked away.

Chapter 44

IN the ensuing weeks, Brenna passed her days no differently than she had before, except that she had more energy. She felt a compulsion to fill each waking moment with strenuous activity. She tried not to think of her changing body and the life it was nurturing. She tried even harder not to think of Garrick and the last time she had seen him, with Morna by his side. She wanted only to be exhausted each night when she crawled into her lonely bed.

She waited eagerly for news of Anselm's health, but none came. The warming sun quickly melted the last snow that had fallen, so the ship that would take her home must be ready to sail. Spring came and went, yet still no one came to tell her to prepare.

Finally she could wait no longer for news to come to her. She was very late in her weekly payments to Anselm, for she had dreaded going to his settlement and perhaps encountering Garrick again. The furs she owed gave her a reason to venture from her seclusion now, but it also meant that she would risk revealing her condition to Garrick's family. She chose to take that risk, for she had to know why she was being forgotten.

Summer brought to the land a dazzling display of color.

Although spring had been beautiful when nature seemed to wake from the long winter night, summer was intoxicating. The sun warmed the skin, and heady floral scents filled the air.

The warmth had been most welcome until this day, when Brenna approached Anselm's settlement. She had thought herself most cunning by hiding her condition, which was quite obvious now, beneath her heavy cloak. But now she felt as if she had enclosed herself in an oven. She was debating whether to turn around and go home when she found herself in the yard before Anselm's house, and a young *thrall* had already taken Willow to the stable.

To Brenna's relief, the large hall was empty except for her aunt. "Brenna!" Linnet came forward and took her hands. " 'Tis such a pleasure to see you."

"And you, Aunt. I had hoped you would come to visit me now that the weather is much improved."

"Forgive me, child. I meant to come, but there has been so much to do here. The planting of crops, the first thorough cleaning after winter. So much to keep us all busy."

"And you helped to plant?"

"Yea, everyone helped. Anselm has many fields. Most are still being worked."

"A Viking farmer," Brenna said with sarcasm.

"He has many slaves and less fortunate kin that he must provide for. Besides, most Vikings are farmers. Surely you have learned this by now."

"Yea, or merchants like Garrick," Brenna replied in a quiet tone.

Linnet changed the subject quickly. "I see you brought your payment to Anselm, and extra 'twould appear. You have been busy too?"

Brenna nodded and set down the large bundle of furs. Sweat was pouring down her, but she did not make to remove her cloak. She could trust no one with the new secret she kept, not even her aunt.

"Did you come only to pay your debt, Brenna, or will you stay and visit a while?"

"I cannot stay, Aunt. I would know only how soon Anselm will sail. Can you tell me?"

Linnet frowned. "I do not know."

"Is he still ill?"

"Nay, what ailed him was not serious and passed quickly. He is not here."

"What do you mean, not here?" Brenna asked, her voice rising. "Did he sail without me?"

"His ship is here, Brenna. But he has sailed with Garrick and Hugh to hunt the great bears in the north."

"How could he do that now?" Brenna gasped. "He has promised to take me home!"

"And he will. 'Twas Hugh's idea to go north. Garrick was reluctant to delay his trading voyage, but since Anselm wanted this chance to hunt with both his sons as they used to in years past, Garrick agreed."

"When will they return?"

"Soon. Cordella has reached her time, and Hugh will not want to miss the birth of his first child."

"Of course not," Brenna said caustically. "After all, he must play God and decide whether the babe should live or die."

Linnet gasped. "Merciful Lord, Brenna! What wild notions have you in your head?"

Brenna wrung her hands beneath her cloak. "I am sorry, Aunt. I have been so touchy of late. I just want to go home. I long for the days before I met Garrick, before I learned to love and hate!"

Brenna ran from the hall, tears threatening to fall once again. She also longed for the days when she never cried. It seemed now that was all she ever did.

That night Brenna was roused from sleep by a fierce pounding on her door. She was not quite awake when she crawled out of bed to answer it and so she did not think to cover herself with more than a blanket.

To Brenna's surprise, Heloise stood in the doorway, her face anxious. "I came as quickly as I could, Brenna. Cordella is calling for you."

"Is it the baby?"

"Yea. I would not have come here, but I have never in my life helped with a birthing, and I am too old to start now. Yet I wanted to do something. This is my first grandchild!"

"I understand," Brenna said in bewilderment. She would

have thought this strong woman could face any aspect of life with a smile. It was difficult to see her so distraught now.

"Her pains began this morn," Heloise continued nervously, "yet she told no one until eventide. Now she screams for you. Hurry, Brenna."

Even as she said the words, Brenna unthinkingly threw off the blanket and grabbed her cloak. It was then that Heloise saw her fully. The five months of swelling could not be mistaken.

"In the name of God, Brenna!" Heloise gasped. "Why did you not tell us you were also with child?"

It was too late to regret her carelessness, but Brenna sighed miserably nonetheless. "We will speak of it later. There is a child to be born now. Mine will not come till winter."

"Wait, Brenna." Heloise put up a hand. "This is Cordella's first child. Mayhaps you should not go to her. 'Tis best not to know what you will also have to endure."

"I have seen birth before, milady, in the village at home. I know 'tis long and painful. Cordella wants me to be with her. She and I have never been close, but this is the least I can do for her."

Cordella's labor lasted through the night—long, tortuous hours which played on everyone's nerves. Heloise was especially fretful as screams from the servants' quarters drifted into the hall, cries so low and agonizing that they did not sound human.

Had she screamed so horribly the five times she gave birth? It would explain why Anselm was always so pale when she would see him afterward, as if he had endured more than she. Yet toward the end her suffering had lessened, thanks to a potion made by a loyal slave from the Far East. If only that slave had revealed her magic before she died, then Cordella too would be ignorant of her pain and not fear any future children.

Streams of sunlight followed Brenna into the hall. She looked pitifully haggard, as if she had suffered Cordella's pain as well. Her shift was soaked with sweat, her beautiful raven hair matted and stringy. Heloise barely recognized her.

"I did not notice that the screams have ceased. Is—is Cordella—the child—"

"All is well, milady," Brenna said, and collapsed into Anselm's thronelike chair. Her voice was weak, her eyes dull. "You have a fine grandson and Cordella now sleeps peacefully. My aunt and Uda are tending the child."

"A grandson! Hugh will be so pleased. And my husband, he will burst with pride!"

"More important," Brenna added bitterly, "the child is healthy. This baby will not be judged. He will live."

Heloise fell silent for a long moment, then she asked in a whisper, "You know?"

"Yea, I know. You asked me earlier why I did not tell anyone of the child I carry. This is why. I will not be forced to stay here and bear my baby in this land, where its life depends on its strength."

"I know 'tis a harsh custom, Brenna. I did not know of it myself until recently. I lost two children at birth before I had my fifth child," she said in a voice choked with memories.

"Did they die naturally?"

"I was told they did. When I learned of the custom, doubt was raised in my mind. Yet I could never bring myself to question Anselm. My third child that survived was born weak, but Anselm knew how much I wanted that baby, after losing two before it. That child lived for many years before she too died."

"I know the story, milady. I am sorry."

"I wanted to die when my daughter died," Heloise said hollowly. " 'Twould have been better if I had not known her. She was not meant to live."

"You are wrong!" Brenna snapped, overly harsh. " 'Twas cruel fate that took her from you. You must have fond memories of her. And she had the right to know life, however briefly. I cannot condone this custom. My baby will not be born here!"

"I know my husband, Brenna. He will not take you home now, at least not until after the child is born."

"In winter!"

" 'Twill have to be the following spring."

"Nay!" Brenna cried, standing up so quickly that her chair nearly toppled over. "He promised!"

"You must think of the child now. If there was a storm at sea, you could lose it."

"I *am* thinking of the child!"

"Brenna, you are a strong woman. Your baby will be strong. There is no reason to fear for it."

"Can you assure me of this? Can you promise me that Garrick will not be allowed near my baby?"

" 'Tis the law here that the father must accept the child and name it. You judge Garrick harshly. I have raised him with Christian love."

"He is a Viking and he—he hates me now. He would not want my child to live."

" 'Tis his child too, Brenna. However, I will tell you this," Heloise sighed. "Garrick sails east this summer and since his journey has been delayed, he may not return before next spring."

This was the most assurance she could give Brenna.

Chapter 45

ANSELM and Hugh returned from the north, but Garrick sailed on without stopping. Brenna had every reason to believe that he would not come home this winter. She could bear her child with peace of mind.

Heloise had predicted Anselm's reaction correctly: he refused to take Brenna home. He came to tell her himself, bringing Heloise along to translate. The meeting did not go well, for Brenna was bitter at having to spend another year in this land. However, Anselm was in an exuberant mood after seeing his first grandchild and learning he would soon have another.

He insisted Brenna return to his settlement. She refused stubbornly, taking offense at his offer.

" 'Tis for your own good," Heloise explained. "You can no longer live alone."

"I can and I will!" Brenna said hotly. "Naught has changed. I will never again be dependent on anyone!"

"You must reconsider, Brenna. You will grow bigger and more clumsy. You cannot go on as you have been."

"Nay!"

"For once, put aside your pride, girl. You have the child to think of, not just yourself anymore."

Johanna Lindsey

"Ah, she is as stubborn as ever," Anselm said sourly. "She would not be happy with us anyway. If only my pig-headed son were not so pigheaded, we would not have this problem!"

Heloise cleared her throat awkwardly. "Will you see reason, Brenna?"

"I will stay here, milady, and I will manage. My growing shape does not stop me from finding food. My aim has not changed. I will not be foolish and ride anymore, but the woods are near and game is plentiful. I will gather twigs for my fire instead of cutting wood. I will take care not to harm my baby."

" 'Tis not that we did not think you could manage alone, Brenna," Heloise said. "We know you are able. But accidents can happen."

"I will be careful."

The older woman sighed. "If you will not live with us, will you at least consent to have someone stay with you here? Your aunt said you would take this stand and asked if she could come here to live with you. I agreed. If you will also agree, I will not worry over you."

Brenna did not answer immediately. To have her aunt with her again would be wonderful. Someone to share her new experiences with, when the baby kicked or a new stretch mark marred her skin, someone she loved who she could talk to.

"Would you give my aunt her freedom?"

"Brenna, you are being unreasonable."

"Would you?"

Heloise turned to her husband. "Brenna will agree to let Linnet stay here if you will give her her freedom."

"Nay! Never!"

"What is more important here?" Heloise said, losing her temper for once. "Brenna could die here alone; the child could die! *She* will not see reason, so we must!"

"Thor's teeth!" Anselm blustered. "Our lives were simple before I brought that girl here!"

"Well?"

"Do what you think best, mistress. Whatever it takes to see this girl cared for despite her foolishness."

"Linnet will come on the morrow, Brenna—as a free-woman. I will also send a strong woman to help with the

330

more difficult tasks. You cannot expect your aunt to chop wood or lug water at her age."

Brenna smiled. "Very well, milady. But I will still make payments for this house. I will not live here on charity."

"You are the most stubborn girl I have ever known, Brenna. I can see you now, nearing your time, out in the woods hunting rabbit! You will be the scandal of the land."

Brenna laughed strongly, the first time she had done so for a long while. "I have been a scandal all my life, milady."

Brenna longed for the day it would all be over and she could hold her baby in her arms. She wanted a girl child, a little daughter like she had never been, with raven hair and gray eyes. She wanted to see nothing of Garrick in the child. Life had been cruel enough, and she needed no more of its disappointments.

With the end of summer the days grew shorter, but they still did not pass quickly enough for Brenna, who was quite large now. She still hunted in the woods, but not as often, for twice a week, every week, she found fresh meat or fish on her doorstep, and she could not very well throw it away. A cow had been left to graze in their back yard, and with extra time on Brenna's hands, she helped Linnet and Elaine, the servant Heloise had sent, make butter and cheese from fresh milk. Brenna enjoyed these times of sharing, but whenever Garrick entered her thoughts, she needed to be alone, to bear her hurt privately.

It was on such a day that Brenna went hunting, even though it was unnecessary. She walked deep into the woods, her brooding thoughts making her unaware of the distance she traveled. When at last she noticed her surroundings, she did not recognize them. She began to backtrack.

After she had gone a short way, Brenna had the gnawing suspicion that someone was watching her. She could not shake the feeling, even after looking about to see if anyone was there and finding no one. She continued on more quickly.

Then she saw the rider, too heavily cloaked for such mild weather, hood drawn so Brenna had no idea who it was. The rider just sat there atop a large horse, not more than fifty feet from her. Unreasoning fear made Brenna's hands begin to sweat. She loaded her crossbow, then moved on cautiously as if she were not disturbed in the least. She began to relax as she put distance between them until she heard the sound of a horse galloping at her from behind.

Brenna swung around just in time to get out of the way of the charging animal. It raced by, just barely missing her. Brenna could hardly believe what was happening. The rider had tried to kill her! When she saw him turn the horse about and come at her again, she began to run. She was too clumsy to run fast, and the sound of the horse approaching became louder and louder. She turned to fire her weapon, but she had waited too long, and the animal was upon her.

She was hit squarely on her shoulder and the impact knocked her to the ground, though she was able to brace her fall. She lay there breathing heavily and felt no injury. After a few seconds, the urge to reach safety returned. However, when she tried to rise, pains shot through her middle, making her scream from deep within. Then she heard the evil laughter, a woman's laughter, and the sound of the horse receding in the distance.

The pain came again and she screamed again, unable to stop. As she lay there feeling the black clouds of unconsciousness nearing, she could only think of one thing. Her baby was coming, but it was too soon, much too soon.

Brenna opened her eyes just a crack. Across the haze of bright sunlight filtering through the trees, she saw Garrick, his blond hair longer than usual, an unruly beard covering his face. Why would he look thus in her dream when she had never seen him this way before? He was holding her—no, he was carrying her someplace. She wanted to wake quickly, for even to dream of Garrick hurt her. Yet this was a different kind of pain, a dull, nagging ache.

"Go away, Garrick," Brenna whispered. "You are hurting me."

"Be still," he replied.

Garrick wanted her to suffer. He would haunt her dreams forever just to make her suffer. Dear God, the pain is real!

She screamed, a sound she did not recognize as her own. Then the dream ended.

"First the fever, then she nearly dies of cold and starvation, and now this! How many times can she face death and survive?"

" 'Tis not a question of how many times, but whether she can survive *this* time."

Brenna heard the low, whispering voices near her. First her aunt, then Heloise. Now she heard another voice, deeply masculine, coming from far away.

"Where is the child birther?"

"Who is that?" Brenna asked weakly.

Linnet came to her side and smoothed the hair away from her face. She was pale, and for once looked older than her years.

"Do not spend your strength with questions, Brenna. Here, drink this."

Linnet placed a cup of wine to her lips and she drank it all. Brenna stared at her aunt with growing alarm, feeling pain spreading through her body.

"Were you just speaking of me? Am I dying?"

"Please, Brenna, you must rest."

"Am I?"

"We pray not." Heloise came forward. "But you are bleeding, Brenna, and—and—"

"And my baby is coming now, too soon," Brenna finished for her, and a wave of fear made her skin crawl. "Will it live?"

"We do not know. Other babies have come before their time, only—"

"Go on."

"They were too small—too weak."

"My baby *will* live! It may be born weak, but I will make it strong!"

"Of course you will, Brenna," Heloise said to pacify her. "Now please rest."

"You doubt me!" Brenna became angry and tried to rise. "I will—"

She could not finish and fell back on the bed. Dull knives seemed to be digging away at her insides. She closed her eyes to fight the pain, but not before she had seen her surroundings. When the ache subsided, she glared at both women accusingly.

"Why have you brought me here, to *his* house? Why?"

"We did not bring you here, Brenna."

"Then who?"

"He found you in the woods. 'Twas closer to bring you here rather than take you home."

At that moment Uda, the woman who had helped Cordella birth her baby, came into the room and immediately started poking around Brenna. "This is not good," she clucked in her native tongue. "The bleeding is not much, but there should be none."

Brenna ignored her completely. "Who found me?" she questioned Heloise. "Did he see the woman who tried to kill me? I know it was a woman. I heard her laugh."

"Someone tried to kill you?"

"A woman. She came at me on a large black horse and knocked me down."

"No one wishes you harm, Brenna. Surely you imagined this. So much pain can make you think things that are not so."

"The pain did not start until *after* I fell!"

"But Garrick said no one was about when he found you," Heloise said.

Brenna paled as she remembered the short dream she had of him carrying her. "Garrick is back?"

"He returned a week ago."

All of the old fears returned twofold to Brenna. "You must take me home. I will not have my baby here!"

"We cannot move you now."

"Then you must swear you will not let him near my baby!" Brenna cried.

"Now cease this foolishness, Brenna!" Heloise said sharply. "Garrick wants your baby to live as much as you do."

"You lie!"

But then she was gripped by another stabbing pain more terrifying than the last, and there was no time left to plead as the pressure increased and demanded all her energy to propel her baby forward. And again, quickly, she felt the need to push with all her might.

Garrick stood in the open doorway to his room, feeling more helpless than he ever had in his life. He had heard all that Brenna had said, and her fears had cut into him like a steel blade. Still, he could not blame her for thinking him so cruel. When had he ever shown her differently?

Brenna's anguished cry shook him to his very soul. To think he had wanted to get as far away from Brenna as he could, to sail to the Far East and never see her again. He had only gotten as far as Birka before he was ready to turn back. He assumed Brenna would already be with her own people, and he came home simply to tell his father that he was going to bring her back, that he had finally concluded that he could not live without her, regardless of how she felt about him.

He was greeted with the news that she was still here, and the reason for it amazed him. Though he could not go to her then, for fear of upsetting her in her condition, each day he rode through the woods near her house, hoping to see her. And today, hearing her scream, then finding her unconscious—he was devastated with fear.

"A male child," Uda said, and held the infant in the air by its feet.

Garrick watched in awe, his eyes fastened on the tiny baby. Uda shook the child, then shook it again. Garrick held his breath, waiting for some sign of life.

"I am sorry," Uda said. "The baby is dead."

"Nay!" Garrick bellowed and came into the room. He took his son in his large hands and then stared helplessly at Uda. "He must not die. She will say I killed him!"

"The child cannot breathe. This happens to many babies. There is naught we can do."

Garrick looked down at the unmoving infant in his hands. "You must live! You must breathe!"

Heloise came to his side, tears in her eyes. "Garrick, please. You only torture yourself."

He did not hear his mother. He was torn apart inside, so aware of the air that moved his own chest yet did not move his son's. He stared at the tiny chest, willing it to fill with air. Without thinking, he blew his own breath into the baby's mouth.

"Aiee!" Uda shrieked. "What is he doing?" She ran from the room screaming. "He is mad!"

Nothing came of Garrick's desperate attempt to breathe

his own life into his son. But he was beyond rational thinking and tried again, this time covering the infant's mouth
and nose so the air would have no place to go but into his
son. The tiny chest filled and the arms thrashed, then the
infant gulped air by itself and emitted a cry so loud it
echoed through the house.

"Praise God for this miracle!" Linnet cried, and fell to
her knees to give thanks.

" 'Tis indeed a miracle, Garrick," Heloise said softly.
"But one that you brought about. You gave life to your
son."

He let her take the screaming baby from him. Miracle or
not, he was too relieved to speak. He felt such overwhelming pride, as if this was the greatest accomplishment of his
life, and nothing would ever come close to it again.

"I need not ask if you accept this child," Heloise said as
she wrapped the baby in a blanket and placed it at Garrick's feet for the ceremonial acts of birth.

He bent down and held the child on his knee, then
sprinkled water on it from a cup Heloise brought. He had
seen his father do this to his sister, and he knew the same
had been done to himself and Hugh.

"This child shall be called Selig, the Blessed."

"A good name, for he is surely blessed," Heloise remarked proudly, and took the baby once again. "Now go
below and tell your father he has another grandson. His
pride and joy will be as great as yours."

Garrick did not move toward the door; instead he walked
slowly to his bed. Brenna's eyes were closed. He looked
questioningly at Linnet.

"She fainted when the child was born," she told him as
she wiped moisture from Brenna's brow. "She does not
know you fought to save her son, but I will tell her."

But will she believe you? Garrick wondered. "I know she
lost much blood. Will she live?"

"The bleeding has stopped. She will be weak, as the child
is. We can only pray that they both gain strength quickly."

"Do not worry, Garrick," Heloise said from across the
room where she bathed Selig in warm water, against his
loud protests. "All that you did cannot be for naught. Both
child and mother will live."

Chapter 46

FOR the first week after the baby's birth, every time Brenna woke she was filled with fear, and she could not dispel her feelings of apprehension until she assured herself her baby was all right. Her aunt had told her a wild tale about Garrick having saved her son's life, but she could not bring herself to believe it. If it were true, if he cared for the child at all, he would have come to see it. Not once did he come.

Brenna recovered slowly from the birthing, but Selig gained weight rapidly. It was a grievous disappointment to Brenna that she was not responsible for his glowing health. She had so wanted to give her baby the nourishment he needed, to be the only one he would be dependent on. But for some reason, either because of her weak condition or the fact that she did not take better care of herself in the early months when she carried him, her milk lasted only a fortnight.

She was filled with self-recriminations when Heloise insisted on bringing in a woman who had ample milk to give, having just lost her own child at birth. But Brenna accepted the situation quickly, knowing it was the only way. She made up for her lack with extra love, spending every possible moment fussing over her son. Then she was scolded by her aunt for overdoing it. She began to feel as if everyone was trying to alienate her from her child, that she could do nothing right.

Fortunately, her resentment did not last long and she bowed to the wisdom of her elders. She began to relax in the presence of her tiny son, to stop smothering him with this new love that she felt so strongly. Finally she was at ease when she cared for him, dressed him and bathed him. She let their relationship develop slowly. When he first smiled at her, she knew he was aware of her love.

Brenna also knew it was time they went home. The only reason she had stayed this long in Garrick's house, nearly three months, was because she had not once seen Garrick in all that time. She did not know where he slept, or if he was even in the house. Nor could she bring herself to ask anyone about him, not even Janie or Maudya.

Her two old friends cooed over Selig every time they brought Brenna her meals, and they remarked many a time at how improved their lives were since he was born. Brenna did not question this either. She could only assume that Garrick was so loath to be near that he had gone to live elsewhere, no doubt at Morna's, while she occupied his house.

When Brenna told her aunt that she was ready to go home, Linnet did not voice any objections. "You will live with me, will you not?" Brenna asked hopefully.

"For a while more. But eventually I will return to Anselm's settlement."

"But you are a freewoman now," Brenna protested. "You need not go back there."

"I have many friends there."

Brenna sighed. "And you miss Heloise?"

"Yea."

"And Garrick's father?"

"I am not ashamed that I share his bed on occasion, Brenna," Linnet said defensively.

"I do not judge you, Aunt. If this is what you want, then who am I to tell you nay?"

"I know that Anselm's one true love is Heloise, but he does care for me. And I love Heloise also. She has been a true and worthy friend." Linnet laughed. "A strange relationship we have. Still, I am content with it."

"You should have better."

"Nay, Brenna, I am happy," Linnet said. "I know you hate Anselm, but—"

"I do not hate him anymore, Aunt." Brenna interrupted. "When Anselm first held my son in his arms, I remembered the day he attacked our manor, the hatred and bloodlust on his face. Yet when he held his grandson, there was such love in his expression. He has done much for me that I am grateful for. I still do not know if I can ever completely forgive what he did, but there is no longer hate in me."

"I am pleased," Linnet smiled. "I think you have finally grown up, Brenna."

Brenna returned to her little house the day before the first winter storm. When she trudged through the snow in search of game, she actually felt as if she had grown accustomed to this land and its harsh climate.

And so the time passed. Still Garrick did not come to see his son. After the winter solstice celebration, which Linnet attended without Brenna even though she had been invited too, Linnet returned to Anselm's settlement. Brenna missed her, but she did not lack for company. Leala, the woman Heloise had found for Selig, still lived with her, having taken Elaine's place. And Cordella came often to visit with little Athol.

Brenna returned home early from hunting, for she had quickly exhausted her supply of arrows. She was angry at herself for having missed one rabbit so many times before it finally got away. When she left the woods and saw the horse in her yard, Garrick's horse, she was first filled with mixed feelings, but then her anger grew. How dare he come now, seven months after the birth of his son?

She entered her house quickly, but stopped short at the sight that met her eyes. Selig was sitting on his father's lap by the fire, giggling and playing with the fastenings on Garrick's cloak. Garrick was surprised to see her, but Brenna did not notice. She saw only her son and how happy he was. Her anger came to the surface again, knowing that

Selig had been denied the pleasure of his father because of Garrick's hate for her.

"Do you approve of the name I gave him?" Garrick asked awkwardly.

"I accepted it, since it was all his father would ever give him."

Garrick put Selig down on the floor and both parents watched him crawl slowly across the rushes to a toy beneath the table. There he stopped to examine it with tiny fingers, unaware of the tension in the room.

Their eyes met for the first time. "I am sorry you found me here, Brenna. It will not happen again."

"Why did you come?"

"To see my son."

"Why now, after so long?" she demanded.

"Do you truly think I have not seen him before this? I have come here at least once a week since you returned, whenever you are off hunting. And when you stayed at my house, I saw him every day."

"How?"

"Once he was fed, he was mine to hold before he was returned to you."

Brenna's eyes were wide with fury. "Why was this kept from me?"

"You thought I would hurt the boy, so I saw him only in secret. I did not want to upset you."

Brenna turned to Leala, who was huddled in the corner away from the shouting voices she did not understand. "Why did you not tell me Selig's father has come to see him here?"

"He has the right, mistress. He should not have to hide his love for Selig."

Brenna paled to a sickly white as soon as she asked the question. She did not hear the answer. She had trusted her long-kept secret to Leala because she lived with her and they had to communicate for Selig's sake. And now, because of her anger, Garrick knew.

"I will go, Brenna."

She looked back at him, startled. He was going to let her blunder pass, but she could not.

"You heard me speak your tongue. Why do you not accuse me of keeping this from you?"

Garrick shrugged. "You have been here long enough to learn it, Brenna."

He was being too condoning and she could not stand it. "I was taught your language before I was brought here, Garrick. It was my one weapon against you that you could not take from me, even though I never made use of it."

"I know."

Her eyes widened. "You know?"

"Your aunt told me a long time ago. I sought to know more about you, and she told me much that was useful. You also spoke both tongues when you were sick with fever."

"Why did you never say anything?"

"I wanted you to tell me," he said levelly. "And so you have at last."

"Only it does not matter now."

"It matters."

Brenna was shaken by the softness of his voice. He came forward until he stood directly before her. She met his eyes and there was no anger or hatred there, just the soft blue-green of shallow waters.

And then his arms pulled her to him and she felt her heart skip a beat. He kissed her, and great longing passed between them. All these many months she had tried not to think of him, for they had had more than a year of separation. Yet she wanted him so badly, and had tried to pretend otherwise.

He held her close, unable to do more because of Leala's presence. Brenna wanted the moment to last forever, but there was a nagging devil in her mind that could not forget the past. What was happening was like a dream. It defied reality.

She gazed up at Garrick, her eyes a cloudy gray, seeking understanding. "What does this mean?"

"Spring is nearing, Brenna. My father has given his word that he will take you home." He hesitated, fighting his pride. "I do not want you to go."

Brenna saw a glimmer of hope. "What then do you want?"

"I want you for my wife. I want to forget the past and start anew."

His words were like music to her ears. To be his wife

341

was what she had wanted so badly before, yet she had been willing to forsake that because he had been so against it. Why had he changed?

"Is it me you want, Garrick, or do you say this because you know when I leave I will take Selig with me?"

"I love my son. I cannot deny this."

"And me?"

"I would not ask to wed you, Brenna, just to keep my son here. I want you more than any other woman." He held her closer. "I have regretted a thousand times my rash decision to give you up. I have been miserable without you."

"But do you love me?"

"After what I have said, how can you doubt it?"

At that moment, her joy knew no bounds. "Then you finally believe I told the truth, that I did not run away from you a second time?"

"I am willing to forget the past."

Brenna stiffened and drew back from him. "Willing to forget? Then you still do not believe me?"

"You swore you killed Cedric Borgsen, yet he lives, Brenna."

" 'Tis not possible!"

"I have seen him."

"But—but he fell on my dagger, the one you gave me! He did not move. How could he live after that?"

"Cease pretending, Brenna!" Garrick said sharply. "I have said I will let the past die."

"But you do not believe me!" she cried.

"I know why you left, Brenna, why you broke your word. 'Twas unforgivable the way I forced myself on you that last time. I took my anger out on you and I was wrong to do this. So you ran away, then returned, unwilling to admit the truth. But it does not matter anymore. I love you enough to forget it all."

"But not enough to trust me?"

He turned away, giving her his answer without speaking. Selig started crying and Leala rushed to him. Brenna stared dismally at her son, feeling once again that he would never know his father. Her hopes had been brought so high, and now fell so devastatingly.

She felt crushed when Garrick looked at her with yearning, despite all that was said. How could he do this to her? Did he think this bridge between them would not matter?

"Leave, Garrick." Her voice was shallow, her pain evident. "I cannot wed you when I know you will never trust me."

"Mayhaps in time—"

"Nay, there will always be this between us. I wish it were not so, for I will always love you, Garrick."

"At least stay here, Brenna." He looked at Selig, then at her again. "Do not take him so far away from me."

Brenna choked on her emotions. God, it hurt to see his pain! "You think me heartless and selfish, but I cannot live this close to you, Garrick. To be near you, loving you, yet knowing there is no hope for us, is too painful."

"You have time before you sail to change your mind, Brenna. You need only come to me."

He left and Brenna cried her heart out on Leala's shoulder. It did not help. Only putting a great distance between them would do so.

Chapter 47

SPRING came quickly and Brenna was told to prepare to leave in less than a fortnight. She heard this news with a heavy heart, yet she felt she had made the right decision. She could not stay near Garrick without having him, and she could not have him without his trust. If only it was not so important to her, that trust. But she knew with certainty that their love would not last without it.

She grieved most when she looked at her son, so unaware of the turmoil in their lives. She was denying him his father and his grandparents, being so utterly selfish. She considered leaving him here, but only for a brief moment. He was her life, and nothing on earth would ever separate them.

She could never forget the fear she had for him before he was born, even though she knew now how foolish she had been. And then she feared again when he was born so weak. Now he was strong and nothing could hurt him, save his mother's decision to take him away. Thankfully, he would not remember, though she would.

She had prayed for a little girl with her own coloring who would not remind her of Garrick in any way. Selig had raven curls and sharp gray eyes, but more and more he was the image of his father. She could never forget Garrick when she cherished his son. Even if Selig had never been conceived, she would not forget Garrick.

Leala, to Brenna's surprise, had agreed to sail with her. She had no family here, having lost her husband even before her newborn child. She claimed Selig was the only important one in her life, and she could not bear to part with him. Brenna's relief was great. Even though her son no longer needed his wet nurse, Brenna had grown attached to this stout Norwegian woman.

On the morrow, Brenna would sail home. Leala had gone to bid her few friends farewell, and Brenna prepared to take Selig to see his father one last time. It would be the final time she would see him also, and her heart ached with this knowledge.

"Come, my sweet," Brenna picked up Selig. "Your father does not know we are coming, but I am sure he will be pleased." At the child's inquisitive stare, she added, "Thank God you do not understand. For you, our journey across the sea will be an adventure. For me—"

She could not finish. Her pain was greater than it had ever been, but she still believed she had chosen the right course.

She started for the door, but it opened before she reached it. Garrick stood there, his face a mixture of sadness and yearning, yet there was also reluctance in his bearing. Brenna was sorry for that. She wished he would be forceful once more as he had been so often before. She wanted desperately to feel his arms around her one last time. But there was a wall between them. Brenna could not blame him for not believing her. After he told of seeing Cedric alive, she had begun to doubt herself.

"I should have sent word, Garrick. I was just leaving to bring Selig to you, so you could have this day with him."

"Set the boy down, Brenna."

His voice sounded strange. Was he bitter again? Brenna put Selig back in his little play area in the corner.

"You can stay here with him if you like," Brenna said, feeling very awkward. "Leala will not return until eventide, and I will still go to your house, to say farewell to Erin and the others. So you can be alone with Selig for a while."

He did not answer her, and for the first time she noticed the many weapons hanging from his belt, more than she had ever seen him wear at one time, and a rope he held in his hand.

"Why did you come here, Garrick. You look prepared for battle." She felt a coldness seep into her bones. "Will you use those weapons on me? If you love him so that you will kill me to keep him, then do it, for I cannot live without him."

He shook his head at the ridiculous conclusion she had come to. "No matter how much I love him and want him, Brenna, I could not kill his mother."

"Then why—"

"I could keep you here by force. I have thought of it many times. Last year when I sailed east, wanting to get far away from you, I realized that was not what I wanted at all. I wanted you with me, by my side for the rest of our lives. 'Twas late summer and I assumed my father had long since taken you back to your people. Since he had given you your freedom, he had the right to know I was going to take that freedom away again, so I came here to tell him that I was going to bring you back and keep you here whether you agreed or not."

"Is—is that what you intend now?"

Garrick shook his head. "You value your freedom too much—I know this. There is one other solution."

"I wish there was, but I cannot see it."

"The truth—the end of all doubt, that is the only solution, Brenna. I pray with all my heart that I was wrong to mistrust you. If you did lie, I will know it now. And then I can only hope that you will never feel the need to lie again."

"I do not understand, Garrick. You did not accept my word before, and I have no proof to offer you."

"I will believe in you, Brenna, from this day forward, because I must—I love you!" Garrick said earnestly. "But I still must know the truth."

He pulled on the rope he held in his hand, and even in her confusion, Brenna was appalled that he would bring his horse into her house. But what followed the rope was not his mighty steed, but Cedric Borgsen, bound at the wrists, with blood oozing from a gash on his head. Brenna turned

347

stark white as if she were seeing the living dead. Cedric also paled, but quickly got his surprise under control.

"Why did you bring me here, Haardrad?" Cedric demanded in a contemptuous manner. "You must know this outrage cannot go unanswered."

"Yea, but which outrage, Cedric?"

"You waited this long to settle an old score?" Cedric laughed, then all his humor disappeared and hate dripped from his words. "The past has been dead these many years. Your brother killed mine and that was enough for our fathers. Now you want more blood!"

"The past has naught to do with your being here. You have a more recent crime to answer for."

"Truly?"

Garrick came closer and pointed to Brenna. "You know this woman?"

Cedric looked at Brenna as if for the first time. His whole being relaxed and he grinned. "A pretty wench, but none that I have ever seen before."

Brenna felt her stomach turn. She looked at Garrick, who was watching them both, and his disappointment was clear to see. This could not be happening.

"He lies, Garrick!" Brenna spoke Norwegian for Cedric's benefit. There was pain and disbelief in her voice. "I swear to you he lies!"

"It does not matter, Brenna."

"But it does—it does!" She turned to Cedric frantically. "Tell him the truth. Tell him how you stole me away!"

Cedric shrugged, feigning bewilderment. "The wench is mad. I know not what she is raving about."

"Liar!" Brenna stormed, and blinding fury made her tremble. "I thought my blade had killed you, but I should have made certain." She drew the dagger that was always on her hip. "This time I *will* be sure!"

Garrick knocked the dagger from her hand before she took even one step. "He is bound and helpless, Brenna. We do not kill unarmed men."

Her frustration was so great that she screamed. It was her word against Cedric's, but her story, the trials she endured, were unbelievable. She knew it and could do nothing. Then she saw the answer, and hope finally entered her eyes.

"My blade pierced his chest, Garrick," she said quickly. "He may not have died from the wound, but there will be a scar—the proof you seek."

Garrick moved to Cedric, who was grinning from ear to ear. "I have many scars," he said confidently. "Which would you like to see?"

Garrick ripped open Cedric's tunic nonetheless, but indeed there were many scars. With slumped shoulders, he pushed Cedric toward the door.

"I will take you back to where I found you."

"Do not think I will let this insult pass," Cedric sneered. "Because of the ravings of a madwoman, you attacked me and dragged me here to be further insulted."

Garrick shrugged, too disillusioned to care. He had put all his hopes into this confrontation, shunning common sense and praying that Brenna's story was true. Now . . .

"Do you wish to challenge me, Cedric?"

"Nay, I am no fool!" he retorted. "But my father will know of this!"

"I am sure he will."

"Garrick, wait!" Brenna cried. She could not believe that Garrick had given up so easily. He would never believe her now, and even if he swore it did not matter, she knew it always would.

"Brenna, there is no point in prolonging this."

"He has another scar, Garrick, like no other! 'Tis long and jagged on the front of his hip. I saw it when he tried to force himself on me."

She watched the color leave Garrick's face before she finished. Cedric also blanched, but she saw this too late. He panicked and acted quickly, raising his bound fists to strike at Garrick from behind. Garrick fell forward against the table, hit his head, then slipped to the floor and was still.

Brenna stared in disbelief. It was as if she were reliving the scene in the woods when the bear attacked Garrick. He lay unconscious or dead, but the beast was still alive, still threatening. She looked for her dagger, but she was too late. Cedric had it and was trying to cut through the ropes that bound him. Brenna raced to him, but he pushed her away with a mighty shove. She fell, but scrambled to her feet and ran for her other weapons. Again she was too late.

Cedric was free and behind her before she reached her crossbow. He jerked her about, then slapped her to the floor.

"I want you to know what to expect, wench," he said in a frenzied voice. "I nearly died because of you, and would have if Arno had not come when he did to stop the bleeding. I could not follow you then, but I did when I was well enough. Only I learned from a slave that you had not returned and were thought dead. The slave lied, I see."

"Nay," Brenna said in a whisper. "I rounded the fjord, and this took many weeks."

He laughed. " 'Tis no wonder he did not believe you. If you could endure that, then you will last long for what I have planned for you."

"Do not be a fool," Brenna said, her blood chilling. "Garrick wanted only the truth; that is why he brought you here."

"And so he has it. It went well until you mentioned the scar that he gave me in our youth. Only he and I knew of it. 'Twas an accident, but one I have never forgotten—nor has he."

He looked at Garrick with loathing, and Brenna caught her breath. "If you go now, 'twill be the end of it. I will see that he never seeks you out again."

"Yea, I suppose you could do that. You have power in your beauty. But you will not be here to see to anything. You will come with me."

Cedric started for Garrick, pulling Brenna's dagger from his belt. Brenna gasped and jumped to her feet. She caught Cedric's arm and jerked him back to face her.

"You cannot do this! He saved you when I would have killed you. He *saved* you!"

"He must die, as you will also. But first you will suffer the agonies of your Christian Hell. Your fate was set when you tried to kill me!"

"If you kill him, then you will die too—if not by me, for I will surely try, then by his brother or father. They are not fools. They know my story and if they find Garrick dead and me gone, they will know you did it."

"Nay, wench, they will blame you," he laughed.

"I would not kill the father of my son, the man I love with all my heart."

He saw the truth in her words and hesitated. At last he noticed Selig in the corner, playing undisturbed with his wooden toys, thankfully unaware of the tragedy around him.

"If you are so intent on having revenge against me, then take me far away where Garrick cannot find us. But let him live, for your own sake."

He hesitated for a few agonizing seconds, then without another word, he took her hand and pulled her behind him. She wanted to beg him to let her take her son, but she would not jeopardize his life. He would be unattended until Garrick woke, and he might get into mischief, but he would not be in any real danger. And Garrick would live to care for him.

They mounted the two horses Garrick and Cedric had come on and rode toward Garrick's house. Now that Brenna did not have to fear for Garrick, she became terrified for herself. She had escaped this man once, and she would do it again, she assured herself. They rode only a short way before they were hailed by another rider, a woman. Brenna was surprised when Cedric halted.

When Yarmille saw Cedric and Brenna together, she became alarmed. The bungling oaf had taken too long to finish the task she paid him for. Why did he have to come now, when Brenna was to leave on the morrow, taking her son with her?

So many times she had tried to do away with the Celtic wench, who was one more obstacle in her way. When the girl had the fever, Yarmille had nursed her well. She had given her potions which made her body reject all nourishment. And she thought surely that leaving the balcony door open in Garrick's room for most of the day would have done the trick. But the girl lived.

It was too bad it was not Garrick who had become ill and she was summoned to tend him. Then she would not have had to worry about his future entanglements and the bastards he might sire. And breed he did, another heir to stand in her way. She had thought his son would never be when Brenna took her fall in the woods. Again her long-awaited goal was thwarted.

Yarmille had yet to devise a means to kill Garrick and his brother. But she would eventually—and their sons. At least if Cedric finally took Brenna away, there would be no more sons born to stand in her way.

Brenna felt hope when she recognized Yarmille, but that was quickly shattered when Yarmille reached them and Brenna saw the horse she rode, the horse that had run her down in the woods.

"You remember me, Borgsen? I am Adosinda."

Cedric laughed. "I did think you were younger, mistress."

"It has taken you long enough to finish what I paid you for," she said angrily, ignoring his remark.

"I thought her dead until Garrick brought me here to face her. She will not return again, mistress."

"Garrick brought you here! Where is he?" Yarmille asked excitedly. "Did you kill him?"

"Nay, I left him alive. I have no time for further questioning. He will not be unconscious long."

"Never fear, Borgsen," Yarmille laughed. "I will take care of Garrick *and* his son. He will not follow you."

"Nay, mistress. I will be blamed."

"Fool!" Yarmille shouted wildly. *"She* will be blamed! 'Tis well known she hates both father and son. Anselm Haardrad was taking her away on the morrow, away from his family before she kills them all!"

"She lies, Cedric!" Brenna gasped. "Her name is Yarmille. Her son is Anselm's bastard."

"Yea, and I hate them as she does. But my son, not hers, will be Anselm's heir!"

"Hugh is heir, and he has a son. Will you kill them also?"

"Hugh does not have a son, nor will he ever. When he was a child with the fever, it rendered him only half a man. Your sister lied and I told Anselm this, but he did not believe me. So yea, they will die also. All of Anselm's sons and their sons. All but mine!" Yarmille rode on toward Brenna's house.

"You must stop her!" Brenna cried.

"There is no time, wench."

"You will be hunted down for her deed."

"I let Garrick live, knowing he would follow. There is no difference. I will sail to Erin or Finland, far away."

"She is going to kill my son!" Brenna screamed, beside herself with fear. She tried to turn her horse around, but

Cedric grabbed the reins. However, Brenna could not be stopped now, not unless he killed her. She jumped off her horse and started running back to her son and Garrick. She had to stop Yarmille, she had to! Cedric rode up beside her and lifted her onto his horse. She fought like a cornered tiger, until a blow to her head brought blackness, and a terrifying end to her struggles.

Chapter 48

THE water of the fjord was choppy, the current swift. Brenna was aroused by the rocking of a small boat. Fear had not left her for a second and she awoke thrashing her arms, still fighting to be free. But she was not bound and Cedric's back was to her as he pushed the boat away from Garrick's landing.

Brenna's desperation defied reason. She thought only of getting back to the landing, of finding Yarmille before it was too late. Without taking into account her inability to swim, she jumped into the water before Cedric was aware that she was conscious. She went under instantly, but fought her way back to the surface. She could hear Cedric screaming at her before she sank again.

The current carried her along and she smashed into the boards under the landing. She pulled herself back to the surface, clinging to a wooden plank, and then she saw Cedric coming toward her in the boat. Why in God's name didn't he give up and go away?

Brenna tried reaching the bank where she could easily get to the path leading up the cliff. But Cedric was too close. He would be there before she crawled out of the water. She maneuvered her way under the landing, propelling herself from plank to plank, until she reached the other side. Cedric was forced to go around, which gave her more time. Here there was only jagged rock for many yards, blocking her way to the cliff path. She skirted around the rock, cutting her fingers as she clung to it. Finally she came to an area where she could crawl out of the water. It did not matter that she was already exhausted, for Cedric was fast approaching, rowing the little boat like a man possessed.

Brenna scaled the cliff as quickly as she could, grabbing branches, sharp rocks and anything else her fingers touched, to secure her hold. She edged her way back toward the landing, sure that Cedric could move no faster than she and so would have no advantage. But he had already left the boat and was gaining on her, screaming that he would kill her now. And then there was nothing left for her to grab hold of, only smooth rock. She could no longer move up or to the left. Cedric was directly below her.

When she felt his fingers touch her ankle, she screamed at the futility of her efforts. She kicked out at him to keep him away, but he kept trying to grab hold of her. Finally she hit his head with her foot and he fell a few feet, but quickly secured another hold and began to climb up again. How long could this go on? She was so close to the edge of the path, with no way to reach it.

She screamed again when Cedric's fingers stretched up at her. And then she heard her name called, though it seemed far away, muffled by the racing water and her own heavy breathing. At first she thought her mind was playing tricks on her, offering her hope when there was none. Then she heard the voice again, louder, and recognized it.

"Garrick! Hurry—Hurry!"

Cedric heard him too and no longer tried to reach Brenna. She watched as he scrambled down the cliff and in a panic, jumped into his boat. The impact of his body capsized the small vessel, and Cedric tumbled into the water. The current caught him and carried him with it. Brenna saw him fighting against the water, trying to swim. His head went under once, then again, and she saw him no more.

Garrick found her staring blankly at the black water of the fjord. He reached out to her, their hands only just meeting, and pulled her around a smooth boulder to the path. She fell into his arms and did not protest as he carried her to the top of the cliff and into his house.

Garrick put Brenna down by the fire in the hall and quickly brought her wine. "You must get out of those wet clothes, Brenna."

"Nay, let me rest first."

He did not argue, but sat down with her on the fur rug. His eyes were downcast, his anxiety great. Brenna knew why.

"Can you ever forgive me?"

She touched his cheek. "Hush. 'Tis over now."

"Nay. I caused you endless grief. I nearly cost you your life by bringing Cedric here to discover the truth when I should have believed in you."

"I do not blame you, Garrick. As long as you trust me now. Do you?"

"Yea, and I will always," he whispered, and kissed her tenderly. Will you wed me now?"

"If you still want me."

"Want you?" he shouted in amazement. "Woman, how can you doubt it?"

She laughed and snuggled in his arms. "We have so much to be thankful for, Garrick. You, me, Selig—we all could have died." She sat up. "Where is Selig?"

"He is safe."

She relaxed again. "I shudder to think what would have happened if you did not come when you did. Cedric was bent on revenge against me because I nearly killed him. When he heard you call, he tried to escape, but fell into the water and drowned." She trembled as she spoke of it.

" 'Tis fortunate your horse is indeed faster than mine. I reached here in only minutes."

"The wind must have carried you," she smiled. "But thank God you woke in time."

Garrick laughed. "That you can thank our son for. He roused me by pounding on my chest, no doubt thinking he had discovered a new toy to play with."

"Where did you leave him? With Erin?"

"Nay. Just as I left your house with him, Yarmille came, to bid you farewell, she said. I asked her to take him to my parents."

Brenna's blood turned to ice. "Garrick—nay! Say you jest!"

"What is wrong?"

Brenna jumped to her feet. "She is going to kill him! She went there to kill you both!"

Garrick did not stop to doubt her words. They both ran to the stable for fresh horses and rode with terrifying speed to Brenna's house. Behind her house, Garrick found the trail of Yarmille's horse leading into the woods, not to his parents' house.

They did not talk as they followed the trail. Brenna could hardly see through the wash of tears she shed. Still she managed to keep up, uttering hopeful prayers every step of the way. When Garrick lost the trail in underbrush, Brenna thought she would die of grief. What hope did her little son have against Yarmille? Too much time had passed.

Garrick tried to insist Brenna go for help, but she could not bear to leave the woods when Selig might be close. So they continued on blindly, looking for signs of Yarmille's trail. When Brenna saw her coming slowly toward them, she raced ahead of Garrick and reached Yarmille first. The older woman was alone.

"Where is he?" Brenna cried.

Yarmille shook her head, staring at her upturned hands. "I could not do it myself. I am a mother too. I could not."

Brenna slid off her horse and pulled Yarmille down from hers. She shook her roughly. "Where is he?"

Yarmille pointed further into the woods. "I just left him."

Garrick came up behind them, his voice disturbingly gentle. "Where, Yarmille?"

"Not far." She looked up, her eyes strangely lighted. "There, you can hear him crying. Fairfax always did cry the loudest. I must go to him."

Garrick rode on, and Brenna mounted her horse and followed him. She did not hate Yarmille for her treachery, for the woman was so very mad. But she could not pity her either.

They found Selig beneath a tall pine tree, whimpering because he could not crawl without pricking himself on pine needles. When Garrick handed him to Brenna, her tears were at last happy ones. But with the anxiety of a mother, she knew it would be a long time before she let this little boy out of her sight for even a short while. They passed the spot where they had spoken to Yarmille, who was gone.

"She planned it all, Garrick," Brenna said as they rode slowly toward home. "Yarmille was the one who paid Cedric to take me away. And I recognized her horse. She is the woman who tried to kill me in the woods."

"Why you, Brenna? This is what I cannot understand."

"She feared my child, not me. Selig was one more heir of Anselm's that she would have to be rid of before her son would be the only heir."

"She must have been mad for many years to think she could accomplish such a task."

"I should have realized she was the one responsible. I knew she hated your family, but because of my jealousy, I thought Morna was involved."

"Morna!"

"She wants you for herself. And—and you did turn to her when we were parted."

"So you did believe that," Garrick frowned. "Because of my anger, I wanted you to think so. But 'tis not true, Brenna. She and I would have wed years ago for reasons other than love. I wanted her for her beauty and she desired me only because I was a chieftain's son. I know that now."

"She means naught to you anymore?"

"Nay. She only reminds me what a fool I was to take her rejection so to heart. I was a fool in many ways. Can you forgive me for all the pain I have caused you?"

"Of course," she smiled. "You will only give me happiness from this day on."

Later, judgment was passed on Yarmille, and she was banished from the land. Her son Fairfax elected to go with her, since she could no longer care for herself. He had known nothing about her scheming and was as shocked as everyone else to learn the truth. Brenna thought the punishment harsh, but her own family came first, and with Yarmille gone, her fears were put to rest.

Chapter 49

IS Selig asleep?"

"Yea, my love," Brenna replied, and crawled into bed to snuggle close to Garrick. "He woke with belly pains, no doubt from all the sweets your father gave him earlier."

"He does spoil him overmuch."

"I cannot argue that point," she grinned.

"And why, wench, would you wish to argue any point with me?" he said in mock astonishment.

She leaned back, pretending anger. "Do not think that because we are wed, your will shall be my will, Viking."

He chuckled and pulled her close. "You are strong-minded and stubborn. This I know well. Did you not insist on the day we were wed that I set Janie free so Perrin could claim her as I claimed you? You did bend me easily to your will."

"You were as pleased as I to see their happiness," she scoffed at him.

"I suppose," he grinned. "I still wonder how I could have been so unaware of their plight. Why did Perrin not speak to me about her? We had our disagreements for a while, but that did not last after Selig was born."

"He wanted to buy Janie, but he was reluctant to ask

you for her, for fear you would refuse. You were never in an agreeable mood for very long."

"Yea. Even after Selig was born and I knew such pride and joy in him, I was still depressed because of you, wanting to go to you all those months, yet afraid you would reject me. I can see why Perrin would not have wanted to approach me on the matter."

"So you would put the blame on me, eh?"

"You *were* overly stubborn, wench!"

Brenna smiled and kissed him lightly, teasingly. "I suppose I will always be. But you love me anyway."

"Do I?"

"Garrick!"

He laughed and rolled on top of her. "Never doubt it, Brenna. Never. You are mine now, whether you admit it or not."

"Oh, I admit it—gladly."

The balcony doors were open to let in the light of the midnight sun. Its orange rays cast a soft glow on the couple entwined on the bed. They were wed four weeks now. The pagan ceremony had been beautiful, but Brenna still wanted God's blessing, and was determined to have a Christian ceremony one day.

Brenna no longer had thoughts of returning to the land of her youth. This was her home now, here with her husband and son. The boy she had once tried to be was dead. She was a woman now, complete.